TOM BROWN'S SCHOOL-DAYS

The group on the island slope.—Page 113.

TOM BROWN'S SCHOOL-DAYS

BY

AN OLD BOY

WITH ILLUSTRATIONS

BY

EDMUND J. SULLIVAN

LONDON: MACMILLAN AND CO., LIMITED
NEW YORK: THE MACMILLAN COMPANY
1903

First printed in Macmillan's Illustrated Pocket Classics, 1903.

TO

MRS. ARNOLD,

OF FOX HOWE,

THIS BOOK IS (WITHOUT HER PERMISSION)

Dedicated

BY THE AUTHOR,

WHO OWES MORE THAN HE CAN EVER ACKNOWLEDGE

OR FORGET TO HER AND HERS.

Thos. Arnold 1795 - 1842
(H.M. fm 1828)

PREFACE

TO THE SIXTH EDITION

I RECEIVED the following letter from an old friend soon after the last edition of this book was published, and resolved, if ever another edition were called for, to print it. For it is clear from this and other like comments, that something more should have been said expressly on the subject of bullying, and how it is to be met.

"MY DEAR ——,

"I blame myself for not having earlier suggested whether you could not, in another edition of Tom Brown or another story, denounce more decidedly the evils of *bullying* at schools. You have indeed done so, and in the best way, by making Flashman the bully the most contemptible character; but in that scene of the *tossing*, and similar passages, you hardly suggest that such things should be stopped—and do not suggest any means of putting an end to them.

"This subject has been on my mind for years. It fills me with grief and misery to think what weak and nervous children go through at school—how their health and character for life are destroyed by rough and brutal treatment.

"It was some comfort to be under the old delusion that fear and nervousness can be cured by violence, and that knocking about will turn a timid boy into a bold one. But now we know well enough that is not true. Gradually training a timid child to do bold acts would be most desirable; but *frightening* him and ill-treating him will not make him courageous. Every medical man knows the fatal effects of terror, or agitation, or excitement, to nerves that are over-sensitive. There are different kinds of courage, as you have shown in your character of Arthur.

"A boy may have moral courage, and a finely organised brain and nervous system. Such a boy is calculated, if judiciously educated, to be great, wise, and useful; but he may not possess *animal courage*; and one night's *tossing*, or bullying, may produce such an injury to his brain and nerves that his usefulness is spoiled for life. I verily believe that hundreds of noble organisations are thus destroyed every year. Horse-jockeys have learnt to be wiser; they know that a highly nervous horse is utterly destroyed by harshness. A groom who tried to cure a shying horse by roughness and violence would be discharged as a brute and a fool. A man who would regulate his watch with a crowbar would be considered an ass. But the person who thinks a child of delicate and nervous organisation can be made bold by bullying is no better.

"He can be made bold by *healthy exercise* and *games* and *sports*; but that is quite a different thing. And even these games and sports should bear some proportion to his strength and capacities.

"I very much doubt whether small children should play with big ones—the rush of a set of great fellows at football, or the speed of a cricket ball sent by a strong hitter, must be very alarming to a nervous child, to a child who might stand up boldly enough among children of his own size and height.

"Look at half-a-dozen small children playing cricket by themselves; how feeble are their blows, how slowly they bowl. You can measure in that way their capacity.

"Tom Brown and his eleven were bold enough in playing against the eleven of about their own calibre; but I suspect they would have been in a precious funk if they had played against eleven giants, whose bowling bore the same proportion to their strength that theirs does to the small children's above.

"To return to the *tossing*. I must say I think some means might be devised to enable schoolboys to go to bed in quietness and peace—and that some means ought to be devised and enforced. No good, moral or physical, to those who bully or those who are bullied, can ensue from such scenes as take place in the dormitories of schools. I suspect that British wisdom and ingenuity are sufficient to discover a remedy for this evil, if directed in the right direction.

"The fact is, that the position of a small boy at a large school is one of peculiar hardship and suffering. He is entirely at the mercy of proverbially the roughest things in the universe—great schoolboys; and he is deprived of the protection which the weak have in civilised society; for he may not complain; if he does, he is an outlaw—he has no protector but public opinion, and that a public opinion of the very lowest grade, the opinion of rude and ignorant boys.

"What do schoolboys know of those deep questions of moral and physical philosophy, of the anatomy of mind and body, by which the treatment of a child should be regulated?

"Why should the laws of civilisation be suspended for schools? Why should boys be left to herd together with no law but that of force or cunning? What would become of society if it were constituted on the same principles? It would be plunged into anarchy in a week.

"One of our judges, not long ago, refused to extend the protection of the law to a child who had been ill-treated at school. If a party of navvies had given *him* a licking, and he had brought the case before a magistrate, what would he have thought if the magistrate had refused to protect him, on the ground that if such cases were brought before him he might have fifty a day from one town only?

"Now I agree with you that a constant supervision of the master is not desirable or possible—and that telling tales, or constantly referring to the master for protection, would only produce ill-will and worse treatment.

"If I rightly understand your book, it is an effort to improve the condition of schools by improving the tone of morality and public opinion in them. But your book contains the most indubitable proofs that the condition of the younger boys at public schools, except under the rare dictatorship of an old Brooke, is one of great hardship and suffering.

"A timid and nervous boy is from morning till night in a state of bodily fear. He is constantly tormented when trying to learn his lessons. His play-hours are occupied in fagging, in a horrid funk of cricket-balls and footballs, and the violent sport of creatures who, to him, are giants. He goes to his bed in fear and trembling,—worse than the reality of the rough treatment to which he is perhaps subjected.

"I believe there is only one complete remedy. It is not in magisterial supervision; nor in telling tales; nor in raising the tone of public opinion among schoolboys—but in the *separation of boys of different ages into different schools*.

"There should be at least *three* different classes of schools,—the first for boys from nine to twelve; the second for boys from twelve to fifteen; the third for those above fifteen. And these schools should be in different localities.

"There ought to be a certain amount of supervision by the masters at those times when there are special occasions for bullying, *e.g.* in the long winter evenings, and when the boys are congregated together in the bedrooms. Surely it cannot be an impossibility to keep order and protect the weak at such times. Whatever evils might arise from supervision, they could hardly be greater than those produced by a system which divides boys into despots and slaves.

"Ever yours, very truly,

F. [illegible]"

The question of how to adapt English public school education to nervous and sensitive boys (often the highest and noblest subjects which this education has to deal with) ought to be looked at from a new point of view.* I here add a few extracts from the letter of an old friend and schoolfellow, than whom no man [illegible] is better able to speak on the subject.

"What's the use of sorting [illegible] boys [illegible] ages, unless you do so by strength; and who are often [illegible] bullies? The strong young [illegible] of fourteen, while the victim [illegible] years or two years older . . . . [illegible] the fact about the bad [illegible] is trouble at times, and always will be; but [illegible] there is [illegible] — [illegible] little girl, who looks like an angel, was bullying the smallest [illegible].

"Bullying must be fought [illegible] the ways,—by getting [illegible] the S[illegible] to put it down, [illegible] the [illegible] fellow to scorn it, and by [illegible] mercilessly the incorrigible; and [illegible] master who really cares for his boys is pretty sure to know instinctively who in his house are likely to be bullied, and knowing a fellow [illegible] tim[illegible]ed and har[illegible] I am sure that he can stop it if he [illegible] resolved. There are many kinds of annoyance—sometimes of real [illegible] persecution for righteousness' sake—that he can't stop [illegible] shed in the world [illegible] can do very much [illegible] to make the shafts of the wicked pointless.

* For those who believe [illegible] school education, the fact [illegible] in the following extract from a [illegible] will be hailed [illegible] especially now that our alliance with [illegible] (the most natural and healthy [illegible] alliance for Protestant England) is [illegible] so [illegible] stronger and deeper [illegible] for[illegible] Speaking of this book he says, [illegible] the author is mistaken in saying that public schools, in the English sense, are [illegible] England. Schul Pforte in the [illegible] province of Saxony is [illegible] institutions. I like [illegible] the more for having been [illegible] for [illegible]."

"But though, for quite other reasons, I don't like to see very young boys launched at a public school, and though I don't deny (I wish I could) the existence from time to time of bullying, I deny its being a constant condition of school life, and still more the possibility of meeting it by the means proposed. . . . .

"I don't wish to understate the amount of bullying that goes on, but my conviction is that it must be fought, like all school evils, but it more than any, by *dynamics* rather than *mechanics*, by getting the fellows to respect themselves and one another, rather than by sitting by them with a thick stick."

And now, having broken my resolution never to write a Preface, there are just two or three things which I should like to say a word about.

Several persons, for whose judgment I have the highest respect, while saying very kind things about this book, have added, that the great fault of it is "too much preaching;" but they hope I shall amend in this matter should I ever write again. Now this I most distinctly decline to do. Why, my whole object in writing at all was to get the chance of preaching! When a man comes to my time of life and has his bread to make, and very little time to spare, is it likely that he will spend almost the whole of his yearly vacation in writing a story just to amuse people? I think not. At any rate, I wouldn't do so myself.

The fact is, that I can scarcely ever call on one of my contemporaries now-a-days without running across a boy already at school, or just ready to go there, whose bright looks and supple limbs remind me of his father, and our first meeting in old times. I can scarcely keep the Latin Grammar out of my own house any longer: and the sight of sons, nephews, and godsons, playing trap-bat-and-ball and reading "Robinson Crusoe," makes one ask one's self whether there isn't something one would like to say to them before they as their first plunge into the stream of life, away from their own homes, or while they are yet shivering after the first plunge. My sole object in writing was to preach to boys; if ever I write again, it will be to preach to some other age. I can't see that a man has any business to write at all unless he has something which he thoroughly believes and wants to preach about. If he has this, and the chance of delivering himself of it, let him by all means put it in the shape in which it will be most likely to get a hearing; but let him never be so carried away as to forget that preaching is his object.

A black soldier in a West Indian regiment, tied up to receive a couple of dozen for drunkenness, cried out to his captain, who was exhorting him to sobriety in future, "Cap'n, if you preach, preach; or if you flog, flog; but no preachee and floggee too!" to which his captain might have replied, "No, Pompey, I must preach whenever I see a chance of being listened to, which I never did before: so now you must have it all together; and I hope you may remember some of it."

There is one point which has been made by several of the reviewers who have noticed this book, and it is one which, as I am writing a Preface, I cannot pass over. They have said that the Rugby undergraduates they remember at the Universities were "a solemn array," "boys turned into men before their time," "a semi-political, semi-sacerdotal fraternity," &c., giving the idea that Arnold turned out a set of young square-toes, who wore long-fingered black gloves and talked with a snuffle. I can only say that their acquaintance must have been limited and exceptional. For I can assure them that every man who has had anything like a wide or continuous knowledge of boys brought up at Rugby, from the times of which this book treats down to this day, will bear me out in saying, that the mark by which you may know them, is, their genial and hearty freshness and youthfulness of character. They lose nothing of the boy that is worth keeping, but build up the man upon it. This is their *differentia* as Rugby boys; and if they never had it, or have lost it, it must be, not because they were at Rugby, but in spite of their having been there; the stronger it is in them the more deeply you may be sure have they drunk of the spirit of their school.

But this boyishness in the highest sense is not incompatible with seriousness,—or earnestness, if you like the word better.* Quite the contrary. And I can well believe that casual observers, who have never been intimate with Rugby boys of the true stamp, but have met them only in the every-day society of the Universities, at wines, breakfast parties and the like, may have seen a good deal more of the serious or earnest side of their characters than of any other. For the more the boy was alive in them, the less will they have been able to conceal their thoughts, or their opinion of what was taking place under their noses; and if the greater part of that didn't square with their notions of what was right, very likely they showed pretty clearly that it did not, at whatever risk of being taken for young prigs. They may be open to the charge of having old heads on young shoulders; I think they are, and always were, as long as I can remember; but so long as they have young hearts to keep head and shoulders in order, I, for one, must think this only a gain.

And what gave Rugby boys this character, and has enabled the School, I believe, to keep it to this day? I say fearlessly,

* "To him (Arnold) and his admirers we owe the substitution of the word 'earnest' for its predecessor 'serious.'"—*Edinburgh Review*, No. 217, p. 183.

—Arnold's teaching and example—above all, that part of it which has been, I will not say sneered at, but certainly not approved—his unwearied zeal in creating "moral thoughtfulness" in every boy with whom he came into personal contact.

He certainly *did* teach us—thank God for it!—that we could not cut our life into slices and say, "In this slice your actions are indifferent, and you needn't trouble your heads about them one way or another; but in this slice mind what you are about, for they are important"—a pretty muddle we should have been in had he done so. He taught us that in this wonderful world no boy or man can tell which of his actions is indifferent and which not; that by a thoughtless word or look we may lead astray a brother for whom Christ died. He taught us that life is a whole, made up of actions and thoughts and longings, great and small, noble and ignoble; therefore the only true wisdom for boy or man is to bring the whole life into obedience to Him whose world we live in, and who has purchased us with His blood; and that whether we eat or drink, or whatsoever we do, we are to do all in His name and to His glory; in such teaching, faithfully, as it seems to me, following that of Paul of Tarsus, who was in the habit of meaning what he said, and who laid down this standard for every man and boy in his time. I think it lies with those who say that such teaching will not do for us now, to show why a teacher in the nineteenth century is to preach a lower standard than one in the first.

However, I won't say that the reviewers have not a certain plausible ground for their dread. For a short time after a boy has taken up such a life as Arnold would have urged upon him, he has a hard time of it. He finds his judgment often at fault, his body and intellect running away with him into all sorts of pitfalls, and himself coming down with a crash. The more seriously he buckles to his work the oftener these mischances seem to happen; and in the dust of his tumbles and struggles, unless he is a very extraordinary boy, he may often be too severe on his comrades, may think he sees evil in things innocent, may give offence when he never meant it. At this stage of his career, I take it, our Reviewer comes across him, and, not looking below the surface (as a Reviewer ought to do), at once sets the poor boy down for a prig and a Pharisee, when in all likelihood he is one of the humblest and truest and most child-like of the Reviewer's acquaintance.

But let our Reviewer come across him again in a year or two, when the "thoughtful life" has become habitual to him, and fits him as easily as his skin; and, if he be honest, I think he will see cause to reconsider his judgment. For he will find the boy grown into a man, enjoying every-day life, as no man can who has not found out whence comes the capacity for enjoyment, and Who is the Giver of the least of the good things of this world—humble, as no man can be who has not proved his own powerlessness to do right in the smallest act which he ever had to do—tolerant, as no man can be who does not live daily and hourly in the knowledge of how Perfect Love is for ever about his path, and bearing with and upholding him.

CONTENTS

PART I

PART II

LIST OF ILLUSTRATIONS

PART I

PART II

TOM BROWN'S SCHOOL-DAYS

BY AN OLD BOY

CHAPTER I

THE BROWN FAMILY

"I'm the Poet of White Horse Vale, Sir,
With liberal notions under my cap."
Ballad.

THE Browns have become illustrious by the pen of Thackeray and the pencil of Doyle, within the memory of the young gentlemen who are now matriculating at the Universities. Notwithstanding the well-merited but late fame which has now fallen upon them, any one at all acquainted with the family must feel, that much has yet to be written and said before the British nation will be properly sensible of how much of its greatness it owes to the Browns. For centuries, in their quiet, dogged, homespun way, they have been subduing the earth in most English counties, and leaving their mark in American forests and Australian uplands. Wherever the fleets and armies of England have won renown, there stalwart sons of the Browns have done yeomen's work. With the yew bow and cloth-yard shaft at Cressy and Agincourt—with the brown bill and pike under the brave Lord Willoughby—with culverin and demi-culverin against Spaniards and Dutchmen—with hand-grenade and sabre, and musket and bayonet, under Rodney and St. Vincent, Wolfe and Moore, Nelson and Wellington, they have carried their lives in their hands; getting hard knocks and hard work in plenty; which was, on the whole, what they looked for, and the best thing for them; and little praise or pudding, which indeed they, and most of us, are better without. Talbots and Stanleys, St. Maurs, and such-like folk, have led armies and made laws time out of mind; but those noble families would be somewhat astounded—if the accounts ever came to be fairly taken—to find how small their work for England has been by the side of that of the Browns.

These latter, indeed, have until the present generation rarely been sung by poet, or chronicled by sage. They have wanted their "sacer vates," having been too solid to rise to the top by themselves, and not having been largely gifted with the talent of catching hold of, and holding on tight to, whatever good thing happened to be going,—the foundation of the fortunes of so many noble families. But the world goes on its way, and the wheel turns, and the wrongs of the Browns, like other wrongs, seem in a fair way to get righted. And this present writer having for many years of his life been a devout Brown-worshipper, and moreover having the honour of being nearly connected with an eminently respectable branch of the great Brown family, is anxious, so far as in him lies, to help the wheel over, and throw his stone on to the pile.

However, gentle reader, or simple reader, whichever you may be, lest you should be led to waste your precious time upon these pages, I make so bold as at once to tell you the sort of folk you'll have to meet and put up with, if you and I are to jog on comfortably together. You shall hear at once what sort of folk the Browns are, at least my branch of them; and then, if you don't like the sort, why cut the concern at once, and let you and I cry quits before either of us can grumble at the other.

In the first place, the Browns are a fighting family. One may question their wisdom, or wit, or beauty, but about their fight there can be no question. Wherever hard knocks of any kind, visible or invisible, are going, there the Brown who is nearest must shove in his carcase. And these carcases for the most part answer very well to the characteristic propensity; they are a squareheaded and snake-necked generation, broad in the shoulder, deep in the chest, and thin in the flank, carrying no lumber. Then for clanship, they are as bad as Highlanders; it is amazing the belief they have in one another

With them there is nothing like the Browns, to the third and fourth generation. "Blood is thicker than water," is one

They can't be happy unless they are always meeting one another.

of their pet sayings. They can't be happy unless they are always meeting one another. Never were such people for family gatherings, which were you a stranger, or sensitive, you might think had better not have been gathered together. For during the whole time of their being together they luxuriate in telling one another their minds on whatever subject turns up; and their minds are wonderfully antagonistic, and all their opinions are downright beliefs. Till you've been among them some time and understand them, you can't think but that they are quarrelling. Not a bit of it. They love and respect one another ten times the more after a good set family arguing bout, and go back, one to his curacy, another to his chambers, and another to his regiment, freshened for work, and more than ever convinced that the Browns are the height of company.

This family training, too, combined with their turn for combativeness, makes them eminently quixotic. They can't let anything alone which they think going wrong. They must speak their mind about it, annoying all easy-going folk; and spend their time and money in having a tilt at it, however hopeless the job. It is an impossibility to a Brown to leave the most disreputable lame dog on the other side of a stile. Most other folk get tired of such work. The old Browns, with red faces, white whiskers, and bald heads, go on believing and fighting to a green old age. They have always a crotchet going, till the old man with the scythe reaps and garners them away for troublesome old boys as they are.

And the most provoking thing is, that no failures knock them up, or make them hold their hands, or think you, or me, or other sane people in the right. Failures slide off them like July rain off a duck's back feathers. Jem and his whole family turn out bad, and cheat them one week, and the next they are doing the same thing for Jack; and when he goes to the treadmill, and his wife and children to the workhouse, they will be on the look-out for Bill to take his place.

However, it is time for us to get from the general to the particular; so, leaving the great army of Browns, who are scattered over the whole empire on which the sun never sets, and whose general diffusion I take to be the chief cause of that empire's stability, let us at once fix our attention upon the small nest of Browns in which our hero was hatched, and which dwelt in that portion of the royal county of Berks which is called the Vale of White Horse.

Most of you have probably travelled down the Great Western Railway as far as Swindon. Those of you who did so with their eyes open, have been aware, soon after leaving the Didcot station, of a fine range of chalk hills running parallel with the railway on the left-hand side as you go down, and distant some two or three miles, more or less, from the line. The highest point in the range is the White Horse Hill, which you come in front of just before you stop at the Shrivenham station. If you love English scenery and have a few hours to spare, you can't do better, the next time you pass, than stop at the Farringdon-road or Shrivenham station, and make your way to that highest point. And those who care for the vague old stories that haunt country sides all about England, will not, if they are wise, be content with only a few hours' stay: for, glorious as the view is, the neighbourhood is yet more interesting for its relics of bygone times. I only know two English neighbourhoods thoroughly, and in each, within a circle of five miles, there is enough of interest and beauty to last any reasonable man his life. I believe this to be the case almost throughout the country, but each has a special attraction, and none can be richer than the one I am speaking of and going to introduce you to very particularly; for on this subject I must be prosy; so those that don't care for England in detail may skip the chapter.

Oh, young England! young England! You who are born into these racing railroad times, when there's a Great Exhibition, or some monster sight, every year; and you can get over a couple of thousand miles of ground for three pound ten, in a five weeks' holiday; why don't you know more of your own birthplaces? You're all in the ends of the earth, it seems to me, as soon as you get your necks out of the educational collar, for midsummer holidays, long vacations, or what not. Going round Ireland with a return ticket, in a fortnight! dropping your copies of Tennyson on the tops of Swiss mountains; or pulling down the Danube in Oxford racing-boats. And when you get home for a quiet fortnight, you turn the steam off, and lie on your backs in the paternal garden, surrounded by the last batch of books from Mudie's library, and half bored to death. Well, well! I know it has its good side. You all patter French more or less, and perhaps German; you have seen men and cities, no doubt, and have your opinions, such as they are ... schools of painting, high art, and all that; have seen the pictures at Dresden and the Louvre, and know the

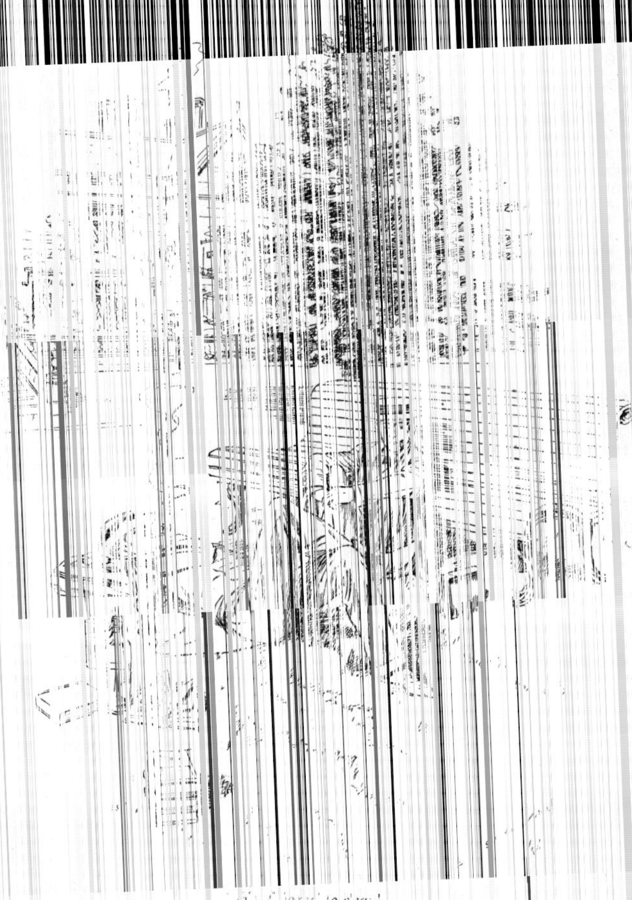

[illegible] to death.

taste of such things. All I say is, you don't know your own lanes and woods and fields. Though you may be chock full of science, not one in twenty of you knows where to find the wood-sorrel, or bee-orchis, which grow in the next wood, or on the down three miles off, or what the bog-bean and wood-sage are good for. And as for the country legends, the stories of the old gable-ended farmhouses, the place where the last skirmish was fought in the civil wars, where the parish butts stood, where the last highwayman turned to bay, where the last ghost was laid by the parson, they're gone out of date altogether.

Now, in my time, when we got home by the old coach, which put us down at the cross-roads with our boxes, the first day of the holidays, and had been driven off by the family coachman, singing "Dulce domum" at the top of our voices, there we were, fixtures, till black Monday came round. We had to cut out our own amusements within a walk or a ride of home. And so we got to know all the country folk, and their ways and songs and stories, by heart; and went over the fields, and woods, and hills, again and again, till we made friends of them all. We were Berkshire, or Gloucestershire, or Yorkshire boys; and you're young cosmopolites, belonging to all counties and no countries. No doubt it's all right, I dare say it is. This is the day of large views and glorious humanity, and all that; but I wish back-sword play hadn't gone out in the Vale of White Horse, and that that confounded Great Western hadn't carried away Alfred's Hill to make an embankment.

But to return to the said Vale of White Horse, the country in which the first scenes of this true and interesting story are laid. As I said, the Great Western now runs right through it, and it is a land of large rich pastures, bounded by ox-fences, and covered with fine hedgerow timber, with here and there a nice little gorse or spinney, where abideth poor Charley, having no other cover to which to betake himself for miles and miles, when pushed out some fine November morning by the Old Berkshire. Those who have been there, and well mounted, only know how he and the staunch little pack who dash after him—heads high and sterns low, with a breast-high scent—can consume the ground at such times. There being little plough-land, and few woods, the Vale is only an average sporting country, except for hunting. The villages are straggling, queer, old-fashioned places, the houses being dropped down without the least regularity, in nooks and out-of-the-way corners, by the sides of shadowy lanes and footpaths, each with its patch of garden. They are built chiefly of good grey stone and thatched, though I see that within the last year or two the red-brick cottages are multiplying, for the Vale is beginning to manufacture largely both brick and tiles. There are lots of waste ground by the side of the roads in every village, amounting often to village greens, where feed the pigs and ganders of the people; and these roads are old-fashioned homely roads, very dirty and badly made, and hardly endurable in winter, but still pleasant jog-trot roads running through the great pasture-lands, dotted here and there with little clumps of thorns, where the sleek kine are feeding, with no fence on either side of them, and a gate at the end of each field, which makes you get out of your gig (if you keep one), and gives you a chance of looking about you every quarter of a mile.

One of the moralists whom we sat under in our youth,—was it the great Richard Swiveller, or Mr. Stiggins?—says, "We are born in a vale, and must take the consequences of being found in such a situation." These consequences I for one am ready to meet. I pity people who weren't born in a vale. I don't mean a flat country, but a vale: that is, a flat country bounded by hills. The having your hill *always* in view if you choose to turn towards him, that's the essence of a vale. There he is for ever in the distance, your friend and companion; you never lose him as you do in hilly districts.

And then what a hill is the White Horse Hill! There it stands right up above all the rest, nine hundred feet above the sea, and the boldest, bravest shape for a chalk hill that you ever saw. Let us go up to the top of him, and see what is to be found there. Ay, you may well wonder, and think it odd you never heard of this before; but wonder or not, as you please, there are hundreds of such things lying about England, which wiser folk than you know nothing of, and care nothing for. Yes, it's a magnificent Roman camp, and no mistake, with gates and ditch and mounds, all as complete as it was twenty years after the strong old rogues left it. Here, right up on the highest point, from which they say you can see eleven counties, they trenched round all the table-land, some twelve or fourteen acres, as was their custom, for they couldn't bear anybody to overlook them, and made their eyrie. The ground falls away rapidly on all sides. Was there ever such turf in the whole world? You sink up to your ankles at every step, and yet the spring of it is delicious. There is always a breeze in the "camp," as it is called; and here it lies, just as the Romans left it, except that cairn on the east side, left by Her Majesty's corps of Sappers and Miners the other day, when they and the Engineer officer had finished their sojourn there, and their surveys for the Ordnance Map of Berkshire. It is altogether a place that you won't forget,—a place to open a man's soul and make him prophesy, as he looks down on that great Vale spread out as the garden of the Lord before him, and wave on wave of the mysterious downs behind; and to the right and left the chalk hills running away into the distance, along which he can trace for miles the old Roman road, "the Ridgeway" ("the Rudge" as the country folk call it), keeping straight along the highest back of the hills;—such a place as Balak brought Balaam to and told him to prophesy against the people in the valley beneath. And he could not, neither shall you, for they are a people of the Lord who abide there.

And now we leave the camp, and descend towards the west, and are on the Ash-down. We are treading on heroes. It is sacred ground for Englishmen, more sacred than all but one or two fields where their bones lie whitening. For this is the actual place where our Alfred won his great battle, the battle of Ashdown ("Æscendum" in the chroniclers), which broke the Danish power, and made England a Christian land. The Danes held the camp and the slope where we are standing—the whole crown of the hill in fact. "The heathen had beforehand seized the higher ground," as old Asser says, having wasted everything behind them from London, and being just ready to burst down on the fair vale, Alfred's own birthplace and heritage. And up the heights came the Saxons, as they did at the Alma. "The Christians led up their line from the lower ground. There stood also on that same spot a single thorn-tree, marvellous stumpy (which we ourselves with our very own eyes have seen)." Bless the old chronicler! does he think nobody ever saw the "single thorn-tree" but himself? Why, there it stands to this very day, just on the edge of the slope, and I saw it not three weeks since; an old single thorn-tree, "marvellous stumpy." At least if it isn't the same tree it ought to have been, for it's just in the place where the battle must have been won or lost—"around which, as I was saying, the two lines of heathen came together in battle with a huge shout. And in this place one of the two kings of the heathen and five of his earls fell down and died, and many thousands of the heathen side in the same place."[1] After which crowning mercy, the pious King, that there might never be wanting a sign and a memorial to the country-side, carved out on the northern side of the chalk hill, under the camp, where it is almost precipitous, the great Saxon white horse, which he who will may see from the railway, and which gives its name to the vale, over which it has looked these thousand years and more.

Right down below the White Horse is a curious deep and broad gully called "the Manger," into one side of which the hills fall with a series of the most lovely sweeping curves, known as "the Giant's Stairs;" they are not a bit like stairs, but I never saw anything like them anywhere else, with their short green turf, and tender bluebells, and gossamer and thistle-down gleaming in the sun, and the sheep-paths running along their sides like ruled lines.

The other side of the Manger is formed by the Dragon's Hill, a curious little round self-confident fellow, thrown forward from the range, utterly unlike everything round him. On this hill some deliverer of mankind, St. George, the country folk used to tell me, killed a dragon. Whether it were St. George, I cannot say; but surely a dragon was killed there, for you may see the marks yet where his blood ran down, and more by token the place where it ran down is the easiest way up the hill-side.

Passing along the Ridgeway to the west for about a mile, we come to a little clump of young beech and firs, with a growth of thorn and privet underwood. Here you may find nests of the strong down partridge and peewit, but take care that the keeper isn't down upon you; and in the middle of it is an old

[1] "Pagani editiorem locum præoccupaverant. Christiani ab inferiori loco aciem dirigebant. Erat quoque in eodem loco unica spinosa arbor, brevis admodum, quam nos ipsi nostris propriis oculis vidimus. Circa quam ergo hostiles inter se acies cum ingenti omnium clamore conveniunt. Quo in loco alter de duobus paganorum regibus et quinque comites occisi occubuerunt, et multa millia Paganæ partis in eodem loco. Cecidit illic ergo Bagsecg Rex, et Sidroc ille senex comes, et Sidroc junior comes, et Osbern comes," &c.—*Annales Rerum Gestarum Ælfredi Magni, Auctore Asserio. Recensuit Franciscus Wise.* Oxford, 1722, p. 23.

cromlech, a huge flat stone raised on seven or eight others, and led up to by a path, with large single stones set up on each side. This is Wayland Smith's cave, a place of classic fame now; but as Sir Walter has touched it, I may as well let it alone, and refer you to Kenilworth for the legend.

The thick deep wood which you see in the hollow, about a mile off, surrounds Ashdown Park, built by Inigo Jones. Four broad alleys are cut through the wood from circumference to centre, and each leads to one face of the house. The mystery of the downs hangs about house and wood, as they stand there alone, so unlike all around, with the green slopes studded with great stones just about this part, stretching away on all sides. It was a wise Lord Craven, I think, who pitched his tent there.

Passing along the Ridgeway to the east, we soon come to cultivated land. The downs, strictly so called, are no more; Lincolnshire farmers have been imported, and the long fresh slopes are sheep-walks no more, but grow famous turnips and barley. One of these improvers lives over there at the "Seven Barrows" farm, another mystery of the great downs. There are the Barrows still, solemn and silent, like ships in the calm sea, the sepulchres of some sons of men. But of whom? It is three miles from the White Horse, too far for the slain of Ashdown to be buried there—who shall say what heroes are waiting there? But we must get down into the vale again, and so away by the Great Western Railway to town, for time and the printer's devil press, and it is a terrible long and slippery descent, and a shocking bad road. At the bottom, however, there is a pleasant public, whereat we must really take a modest quencher, for the down air is provocative of thirst. So we pull up under an old oak which stands before the door.

"What is the name of your hill, landlord?"

"Blawing Stwun Hill, sir, to be sure."

[Reader. "*Sturm?*"

Author. "*Stone*, stupid: the Blowing *Stone*."]

"And of your house? I can't make out the sign."

"Blawing Stwun, sir," says the landlord, pouring out his old ale from a Toby Philpot jug, with a melodious crash, into the long-necked glass.

"What queer names!" say we, sighing at the end of our draught, and holding out the glass to be replenished.

"'Tain't queer at all, as I can see, sir," says mine host, handing back our glass, "seeing as this here is the 'Blawing Stwun' his self," putting his hand on a square lump of stone, some three feet and a half high, perforated with two or three queer holes, like petrified antediluvian rat-holes, which lies there close under the oak, under our very nose. We are more than ever puzzled, and drink our second glass of ale, wondering what will come next. "Like to hear un, sir?" says mine host, setting down Toby Philpot on the tray, and resting both hands on the "Stwun." We are ready for anything; and he, without waiting for a reply, applies his mouth to one of the rat-holes. Something must come of it, if he doesn't burst. Good heavens! I hope he has no apoplectic tendencies. Yes, here it comes, sure enough, a gruesome sound between a moan and a roar, and spreads itself away over the valley, and up the hill-side, and into the woods at the back of the house, a ghost-like awful voice. "Um do say, sir," says mine host, rising purple-faced, while the moan is still coming out of the Stwun, "as they used in old times to warn the country-side, by blawing the Stwun when the enemy was a-comin'—and as how folks could make un heered then for seven mile round; leastways, so I've heered Lawyer Smith say, and he knows a smart sight about them old times." We can hardly swallow Lawyer Smith's seven miles, but could the blowing of the stone have been a summons, a sort of sending the fiery cross round the neighbourhood in the old times? What old times? Who knows? We pay for our beer, and are thankful.

"And what's the name of the village just below, landlord?"

"Kingstone Lisle, sir."

"Fine plantations you've got here?"

"Yes, sir, the Squire's 'mazing fond of trees and such like."

"No wonder. He's got some real beauties to be fond of. Good day, landlord."

"Good day, sir, and a pleasant ride to 'e."

And now, my boys, you whom I want to get for readers, have you had enough? Will you give in at once, and say you're convinced, and let me begin my story, or will you have more of it? Remember, I've only been over a little bit of the hill-side yet, what you could ride round easily on your ponies in an hour. I'm only just come down into the vale, by Blowing Stone Hill; and if I once begin about the vale, what's

"*Blawing Stwun, sir,*" *says the landlord.*

to stop me, you'll have to hear all about Wantage, the birthplace of Alfred, and Farringdon, which held out so long for Charles the First (the vale was near Oxford, and dreadfully malignant—full of Throgmortons, Puseys, and Pyes, and such like; and their own wry-necked retainers). Did you ever read Thomas Ingoldsby's "Legend of Hamilton Tighe"? If you haven't, you ought to have. Well, Farringdon is where he lived, before he went to sea; his real name was Hamden Pye, and the Pyes were the great folk at Farringdon. Then there's Pusey. You've heard of the Pusey horn, which King Canute gave to the Puseys of that day, and which the gallant old squire, lately gone to his rest (whom Berkshire freeholders turned out of last Parliament, to their eternal disgrace, for voting according to his conscience), used to bring out on high days, holidays, and bonfire nights. And the splendid old cross church at Uffington, the Uffingas town;—how the whole countryside teems with Saxon names and memories! And the old moated grange at Compton, nestled close under the hillside, where twenty Marianas may have lived, with its bright water-lilies in the moat, and its yew walk, "the Cloister walk," and its peerless terrace gardens. There they all are, and twenty things beside, for those who care about them, and have eyes. And these are the sort of things you may find, I believe, every one of you in any common English country neighbourhood.

Will you look for them under your own noses, or will you not? Well, well; I've done what I can to make you, and if you will go gadding over half Europe now every holiday, I can't help it. I was born and bred a West-countryman, thank God! a Wessex man, a citizen of the noblest Saxon kingdom of Wessex, a regular "Angular Saxon," the very soul of me "adscriptus glebæ." There's nothing like the old countryside for me, and no music like the twang of the real old Saxon tongue, as one gets it fresh from the veritable chaw in the White Horse Vale: and I say with "Gaarge Ridler," the old West-country yeoman,

"Throo aall the waarld owld Gaarge would bwoast,
Commend me to merry owld England mwoast;
While vools gwoes prating vur and nigh,
We stwops at whum, my dog and I."

Here at any rate lived and stopped at home Squire Brown, J.P. for the county of Berks, in a village near the foot of the

Squire Brown, J.P. for the County of Bucks.

White Horse ranges. And here he dealt out justice and mercy in a rough way, and begat sons and daughters, and hunted the fox, and grumbled at the badness of the roads and the times. And his wife dealt out stockings, and calico shirts, and smock-frocks, and comforting drinks to the old folks with the "rheumatiz," and good counsel to all; and kept the coal and clothes clubs going for yule-tide, when the bands of mummers came round, dressed out in ribbons and coloured paper caps, and stamped round the Squire's kitchen, repeating in true sing-song vernacular the legend of St. George and his fight, and the ten-pound Doctor who plays his part at healing the Saint,—a relic, I believe, of the old Middle-age mysteries. It was the first dramatic representation which greeted the eyes of little Tom, who was brought down into the kitchen by his nurse to witness it, at the mature age of three years. Tom was the eldest child of his parents, and from his earliest babyhood exhibited the family characteristics in great strength. He was a hearty strong boy from the first, given to fighting with and escaping from his nurse, and fraternising with all the village boys, with whom he made expeditions all round the neighbourhood. And here in the quiet old-fashioned country village, under the shadow of the everlasting hills, Tom Brown was reared, and never left it till he went first to school when nearly eight years of age,—for in those days change of air twice a year was not thought absolutely necessary for the health of all her Majesty's lieges.

I have been credibly informed, and am inclined to believe, that the various Boards of Directors of Railway Companies, those gigantic jobbers and bribers, while quarrelling about everything else, agreed together some ten years back to buy up the learned profession of Medicine, body and soul. To this end they set apart several millions of money, which they continually distribute judiciously amongst the Doctors, stipulating only this one thing, that they shall prescribe change of air to every patient who can pay, or borrow money to pay, a railway fare, and see their prescription carried out. If it be not for this, why is it that none of us can be well at home for a year together? It wasn't so twenty years ago,—not a bit of it. The Browns didn't go out of the county once in five years. A visit to Reading or Abingdon twice a year, at Assizes or Quarter Sessions, which the Squire made on his horse with a pair of saddle-bags containing his wardrobe—a stay of a day or two at some country neighbour's—or an expedition to a county ball or the yeomanry review—made up the sum of the Brown locomotion in most years. A stray Brown from some distant county dropped in every now and then; or from Oxford, on grave nag, an old don, contemporary of the Squire; and were looked upon by the Brown household and the villagers with the same sort of feeling with which we now regard a man who has crossed the Rocky Mountains, or launched a boat on the Great Lake in Central Africa. The White Horse Vale, remember, was traversed by no great road: nothing but country parish roads, and these very bad. Only one coach ran there, and this one only from Wantage to London, so that the western part of the Vale was without regular means of moving on, and certainly didn't seem to want them. There was the canal, by the way, which supplied the countryside with coal, and up and down which continually went the long barges, with the big black men lounging by the side of the horses along the towing-path, and the women in bright-coloured handkerchiefs standing in the sterns steering. Standing I say, but you could never see whether they were standing or sitting, all but their heads and shoulders being out of sight in the cosy little cabins which occupied some eight feet of the stern, and which Tom Brown pictured to himself as the most desirable of residences. His nurse told him that those good-natured-looking women were in the constant habit of enticing children into the barges and taking them up to London and selling them, which Tom wouldn't believe, and which made him resolve as soon as possible to accept the oft-proffered invitation of these sirens to "young master," to come in and have a ride. But as yet the nurse was too much for Tom.

Yet why should I after all abuse the gadabout propensities of my countrymen? We are a vagabond nation now, that's certain, for better for worse. I am a vagabond; I have been away from home no less than five distinct times in the last year. The Queen sets us the example—we are moving on from top to bottom. Little dirty Jack, who abides in Clement's Inn gateway, and blacks my boots for a penny, takes his month's hop-picking every year as a matter of course. Why shouldn't he? I'm delighted at it. I love vagabonds, only I prefer poor to rich ones;—couriers and ladies' maids, impartials and travelling carriages, are an abomination unto me—I cannot away with them. But for us and every good fellow who, in the words of the capital French song, moves—

> Comme le limaçon,
> Portant tout son bagage,
> Ses meubles, sa maison,

on his own back, why, good luck to them, and many a merry roadside adventure, and steaming supper in the chimney corners of roadside inns, Swiss chalets, Hottentot kraals, or wherever else they like to go. So having succeeded in contradicting myself in my first chapter (which gives me great hopes that you will all go on, and think me a good fellow notwithstanding my crotchets), I shall here shut up for the present, and consider my ways; having resolved to "sar' it out," as we say in the Vale, "holus-bolus" just as it comes, and then you'll probably get the truth out of me.

CHAPTER II

THE VEAST

"And the King commandeth and forbiddeth, that from henceforth neither fairs nor markets be kept in Churchyards, for the honour of the Church."—STATUTES: 13 *Edw. I.* Stat. II. cap. vi.

As that venerable and learned poet (whose voluminous works we all think it the correct thing to admire and talk about, but don't read often) most truly says, "the child is father to the man;" *a fortiori*, therefore, he must be father to the boy. So, as we are going at any rate to see Tom Brown through his boyhood, supposing we never get any further (which, if you show a proper sense of the value of this history, there is no knowing but what we may), let us have a look at the life and environments of the child in the quiet country village to which we were introduced in the last chapter.

Tom, as has been already said, was a robust and combative urchin, and at the age of four began to struggle against the yoke and authority of his nurse. That functionary was a good-hearted, tearful, scatterbrained girl, lately taken by Tom's mother, Madam Brown, as she was called, from the village school to be trained as nurserymaid. Madam Brown was a rare trainer of servants, and spent herself freely in the profession; for profession it was, and gave her more trouble by half than many people take to earn a good income. Her servants were known and sought after for miles round. Almost all the girls who attained a certain place in the village school were taken by her, one or two at a time, as housemaids, laundrymaids, nurserymaids, or kitchen-maids, and after a year or two's drilling were started in life amongst the neighbouring families, with good principles and wardrobes. One of the results of this system was the perpetual despair of Mrs Brown's cook and own maid, who no sooner had a notable girl made to their hands than Missus was sure to find a good place for her and send her off, taking in fresh importations from the school. Another was, that the house was always full of young girls, with clean shining faces, who broke plates and scorched linen, but made an atmosphere of cheerful homely life about the place, good for every one who came within its influence. Mrs Brown loved young people, and in fact human creatures in general, above plates and linen. They were more like a lot of elder children than servants, and felt to her more as a mother or aunt than as a mistress.

Tom's nurse was one who took in her instruction very slowly,—she seemed to have two left hands and no head; and so Mrs. Brown kept her on longer than usual, that she might expend her awkwardness and forgetfulness upon those who would not judge and punish her too strictly for them.

Charity Lamb was her name. It had been the immemorial habit of the village to christen children either by Bible names, or by those of the cardinal and other virtues; so that one was for ever hearing in the village streets, or on the green, shrill sounds of "Prudence! Prudence! thee cum' out o' the gutter;" or "Mercy! d'rat the girl, what bist thee a doin' wi' little Faith?" and there were Ruths, Rachels, Keziahs, in every corner. The same with the boys; they were Benjamins, Jacobs, Noahs, Enochs. I suppose the custom has come down from Puritan times—there it is, at any rate, very strong still in the Vale.

Well, from early morn till dewy eve, when she had it out of him in the cold tub before putting him to bed, Charity and Tom were pitted against one another. Physical power was as yet on the side of Charity, but she hadn't a chance with him wherever headwork was wanted. This war of independence began every morning before breakfast, when Charity escorted her charge to a neighbouring farm-house which supplied the Browns, and where, by his mother's wish, Master Tom went to drink whey before breakfast. Tom had no sort of objection to whey, but he had a decided liking for curds, which were forbidden as unwholesome, and there was seldom a morning that he did not manage to secure a handful of hard curds, in defiance of Charity and of the farmer's wife.

The latter good soul was a gaunt, angular woman, who, with an old black bonnet on the top of her head, the strings dangling about her shoulders, and her gown tucked through her pocket-holes, went clattering about the dairy, cheese-room, and yard in high pattens. Charity was some sort of niece of the old lady's, and was consequently free of the farm-house and garden, into which she could not resist going for the purposes of gossip and flirtation with the heir-apparent, who was a dawdling fellow, never out at work as he ought to have been. The moment Charity had found her cousin, or any other occupation, Tom would slip away; and in a minute shrill cries would be heard from the dairy, "Charity, Charity, thee lazy huzzy, where bist?" and Tom would break cover, hands and mouth full of curds, and take refuge on the shaky surface of the great muck reservoir in the middle of the yard, disturbing the repose of the great pigs. Here he was in safety, as no grown person could follow without getting over their knees; and the luckless Charity, while her aunt scolded her from the dairy-door, for being "allus hankering about arter our Willum, instead of minding Master Tom," would descend from threats to coaxing to lure Tom out of the muck, which was rising over his shoes and would soon tell a tale on his stockings, for which she would be sure to catch it from Missus's maid.

Tom had two abettors in the shape of a couple of old boys, Noah and Benjamin by name, who defended him from Charity, and expended much time upon his education. They were both of them retired servants of former generations of the Browns. Noah Crooke was a keen, dry old man of almost ninety, but still able to totter about. He talked to Tom quite as if he were one of his own family, and indeed had long completely identified the Browns with himself. In some remote age he had been the attendant of a Miss Brown, and had conveyed her about the country on a pillion. He had a little round picture of the identical grey horse, caparisoned with the identical pillion, before which he used to do a sort of fetish worship, and abuse turnpike-roads and carriages. He wore an old full-bottomed wig, the gift of some dandy old Brown whom he had valeted in the middle of last century, which habiliment Master Tom looked upon with considerable respect, not to say fear; and indeed his whole feeling towards Noah was strongly tainted with awe; and when the old gentleman was gathered to his fathers, Tom's lamentation over him was not unaccompanied by a certain joy at having seen the last of the wig: "Poor old Noah dead and gone," said he, "Tom Brown so sorry. Put him in the coffin, wig and all."

But old Benjy was young Master's real delight and refuge. He was a youth by the side of Noah, scarce sixty years old. A cheery, humorous, kind-hearted old man, full of sixty years of Vale gossip, and of all sorts of helpful ways for young and old, but above all for children. It was he who bent the first pin with which Tom extracted his first stickleback out of "Pebbly Brook," the little stream which ran through the village. The first stickleback was a splendid fellow, with fabulous red and blue gills. Tom kept him in a small basin till the day of his death, and became a fisherman from that day. Within a month from the taking of the first stickleback, Benjy had carried off our hero to the canal, in defiance of Charity; and between them, after a whole afternoon's employment, they had caught three or four small coarse fish and a perch, averaging perhaps two and a half ounces each, which Tom bore home in rapture to his mother as a precious gift, and she received like a true mother with equal rapture, instructing the cook, nevertheless, in a private interview, not to prepare the same for the Squire's dinner. Charity had appealed against old Benjy in the meantime, representing the dangers of the canal banks; but Mrs. Brown, seeing the boy's inaptitude for female guidance, had decided in Benjy's favour, and from thenceforth the old man was Tom's dry nurse. And as they sat by the canal watching their little green and white float, Benjy would instruct him in the doings of the great Brown family. How his grandfather, in the early days of the great war, when there was much distress and crime in the Vale, and the magistrates had been threatened by the mob, had ridden in with a big stick in his hand and held the Petty Sessions by himself. How his great-uncle, the Rector, had encountered and laid the last ghost, who had frightened the old women, male and female, of the parish out of their senses, and who turned out to be the blacksmith's apprentice disguised in drink and a white sheet. It was Benjy too who saddled Tom's first pony, and instructed him in the mysteries of horsemanship, teaching him to throw his weight back and keep his hand low; and who stood chuckling outside the door of the girls' school, when

Old Benjy.

Tom rode his little Shetland into the cottage and round the table, where the old dame and her pupils were seated at their work.

Benjy himself was one of a family distinguished in the Vale for their prowess in all athletic games. Some half-dozen of his brothers and kinsmen had gone to the wars, of whom only one had survived to come home, with a small pension, and three bullets in different parts of his body; he had shared Benjy's cottage till his death, and had left him his old dragoon's sword and pistol, which hung over the mantel-piece, flanked by a pair of heavy single-sticks with which Benjy himself had won renown long ago as an old gamester, against the picked men of Wiltshire and Somersetshire, in many a good bout at the revels and pastimes of the country-side. For he had been a famous back-sword man in his young days, and a good wrestler at elbow and collar.

Back-swording and wrestling were the most serious holiday pursuits of the Vale—those by which men attained fame—and each village had its champion. I suppose that on the whole people were less worked then than they are now; at any rate, they seemed to have more time and energy for the old pastimes. The great times for back-swording came round once a year in each village, at the feast. The Vale "veasts" were not the common statute feasts, but much more ancient business. They are literally, so far as one can ascertain, feasts of the dedication, *i.e.* they were first established in the churchyard on the day on which the village church was opened for public worship, which was on the wake or festival of the patron Saint, and have been held on the same day in every year since that time.

There was no longer any remembrance of why the "veast" had been instituted, but nevertheless it had a pleasant and almost sacred character of its own. For it was then that all the children of the village, wherever they were scattered, tried to get home for a holiday to visit their fathers and mothers and friends, bringing with them their wages or some little gift from up the country for the old folk. Perhaps for a day or two before, but at any rate on "veast-day" and the day after, in our village, you might see strapping, healthy young men and women from all parts of the country going round from house to house in their best clothes, and finishing up with a call on

The laying of the last ghost.

Madam Brown, whom they would consult as to putting out their earnings to the best advantage, or how best to expend the same for the benefit of the old folk. Every household, however poor, managed to raise a "feast-cake" and a bottle of ginger or raisin wine, which stood on the cottage table ready for all comers, and not unlikely to make them remember feast time,—for feast-cake is very solid, and full of huge raisins. Moreover, feast-time was the day of reconciliation for the parish. If Job Higgins and Noah Freeman hadn't spoken for the last six months, their "old women" would be sure to get it patched up by that day. And though there was a good deal of drinking and low vice in the booths of an evening, it was pretty well confined to those who would have been doing the like, "veast or no veast," and on the whole, the effect was humanising and Christian. In fact, the only reason why this is not the case still, is that gentlefolk and farmers have taken to other amusements, and have, as usual, forgotten the poor. They don't attend the feasts themselves and call them disreputable, whereupon the steadiest of the poor leave them also, and they become what they are called. Class amusements, be they for dukes or plough-boys, always become nuisances and curses to a country. The true charm of cricket and hunting is, that they are still more or less sociable and universal; there's a place for every man who will come and take his part.

No one in the village enjoyed the approach of "veast day" more than Tom, in the year in which he was taken under old Benjy's tutelage. The feast was held in a large green field at the lower end of the village. The road to Farringdon ran along one side of it, and the brook by the side of the road; and above the brook was another large gentle sloping pasture-land, with a footpath running down it from the churchyard; and the old church, the originator of all the mirth, towered up with its grey walls and lancet windows, overlooking and sanctioning the whole, though its own share therein had been forgotten. At the point where the footpath crossed the brook and road, and entered on the field where the feast was held, was a long low roadside inn, and on the opposite side of the field was a large white thatched farm-house, where dwelt an old sporting farmer, a great promoter of the revels.

Past the old church, and down the footpath, pottered the old man and the child hand in hand early on the afternoon of the day before the feast, and wandered all round the ground, which was already being occupied by the "cheap Jacks," with their green covered carts and marvellous assortment of wares, and the booths of more legitimate small traders with their tempting arrays of fairings and eatables! and penny peep-shows and other shows, containing pink-eyed ladies, and dwarfs, and boa-constrictors, and wild Indians. But the object of most interest to Benjy, and of course to his pupil also, was the stage of rough planks some four feet high, which was being put up by the village carpenter for the back-swording and wrestling: and after surveying the whole tenderly, old Benjy led his charge away to the road-side inn, where he ordered a glass of ale and a long pipe for himself, and discussed these unwonted luxuries on the bench outside in the soft autumn evening with mine host, another old servant of the Browns, and speculated with him on the likelihood of a good show of old gamesters to contend for the morrow's prizes, and told tales of the gallant bouts of forty years back, to which Tom listened with all his ears and eyes.

But who shall tell the joy of the next morning, when the church bells were ringing a merry peal, and old Benjy appeared in the servants' hall, resplendent in a long blue coat and brass buttons, and a pair of old yellow buckskins and top-boots which he had cleaned for and inherited from Tom's grandfather, a stout thorn stick in his hand, and a nosegay of pinks and lavender in his button-hole, and led away Tom in his best clothes, and two new shillings in his breeches-pockets? Those two, at any rate, look like enjoying the day's revel.

They quicken their pace when they get into the church-yard, for already they see the field thronged with country-folk, the men in clean white smocks or velveteen or fustian coats, with rough plush waistcoats of many colours, and the women in the beautiful long scarlet cloak—the usual out-door dress of west-country women in those days, and which often descended in families from mother to daughter—or in new-fashioned stuff shawls, which, if they would but believe it, don't become them half so well. The air resounds with the pipe and tabor, and the drums and trumpets of the showmen shouting at the doors of their caravans, over which tremendous pictures of the wonders to be seen within hang temptingly;

while through all rises the shrill "too-too-too-too" of Mr Punch, and the unceasing pan-pipe of his satellite.

. . . . discussed these [illegible] outside.

"Lawk a' massey, Mr. Benjamin," cries a stout motherly woman in a red cloak, as they enter the field, "be that you

Well, I never! you do look purely. And how's the Squire, and Madam, and the family?"

Benjy graciously shakes hands with the speaker, who has left our village for some years, but has come over for Veast-day on a visit to an old gossip—and gently indicates the heir-apparent of the Browns.

"Bless his little heart! I must gi'un a kiss. Here, Susannah, Susannah!" cries she, raising herself from the embrace, "come and see Mr. Benjamin and young Master Tom. You minds our Sukey, Mr. Benjamin, she be growed a rare slip of a wench since you seen her, though her'll be sixteen come Martinmas. I do aim to take her to see Madam to get her a place."

And Sukey comes bouncing away from a knot of old school-fellows, and drops a curtsy to Mr. Benjamin. And elders come up from all parts to salute Benjy, and girls who have been Madam's pupils to kiss Master Tom. And they carry him off to load him with fairings; and he returns to Benjy, his hat and coat covered with ribands, and his pockets crammed with wonderful boxes which open upon ever new boxes, and popguns, and trumpets, and apples, and gilt gingerbread from the stall of Angel Heavens, sole vendor thereof, whose booth groans with kings and queens, and elephants and prancing steeds, all gleaming with gold. There was more gold on Angel's cakes than there is ginger in those of this degenerate age. Skilled diggers might yet make a fortune in the churchyards of the Vale, by carefully washing the dust of the consumers of Angel's gingerbread. Alas! he is with his namesakes, and his receipts have, I fear, died with him.

And then they inspect the penny peep-show, at least Tom does, while old Benjy stands outside and gossips, and walks up the steps, and enters the mysterious doors of the pink-eyed lady and the Irish Giant, who do not by any means come up to their pictures; and the boa will not swallow his rabbit, but there the rabbit is waiting to be swallowed—and what can you expect for tuppence? We are easily pleased in the Vale. Now there is a rush of the crowd, and a tinkling bell is heard, and shouts of laughter; and Master Tom mounts on Benjy's shoulders and beholds a jingling match in all its glory. The games are begun, and this is the opening of them. It is a quaint game, immensely amusing to look at, and as I don't know whether it is used in your counties, I had better describe it. A large roped ring is made, into which are put a dozen or so grinning boys and young men who mean to play; these are carefully blinded and turned loose into the ring, and then a man is introduced not blindfolded, with a bell hung round his neck, and his two hands tied behind him. Of course every time he moves the bell must ring, as he has no hand to hold it, and so the dozen blindfolded men have to catch him. This he cannot always manage if he is a lively fellow, but half of the blinded men always rush into the arms of the rest, or drive their heads together, or tumble over; and then the crowd laughs vehemently and invent nick-names for them on the spur of the moment, and they, if they be choleric, tear off the handkerchiefs which blind them, and not unfrequently pitch into one another, each thinking that the other must have run against him on purpose. It is great fun to look at a jingling match certainly, and Tom shouts and jumps on old Benjy's shoulders at the sight, until the old man feels weary and shifts him on to the strong young shoulders of the groom who has just got down to the fun.

And now, while they are climbing the pole in another part of the field, and muzzling in a flour-tub in another, the old farmer whose house, as has been said, overlooks the field, and who is master of the revels, gets up the steps on to the stage, and announces to the men that a half-sovereign in money will be forthcoming to the old gamester who breaks most heads; to which the Squire and he have added a new hat.

The amount of the prize is sufficient to stimulate the men of the immediate neighbourhood, but not enough to bring any very high talent from a distance; so, after a glance or two round, a tall fellow, who is a down shepherd, chucks his hat on to the stage and climbs up the steps, looking rather sheepish. The crowd of course first cheer, and then chaff as usual, as he picks up his hat and begins handling the sticks to see which will suit him.

"Wooy, Willum Smith, thee canst play wi' he arra daay," says his companion to the blacksmith's apprentice, a stout young fellow of nineteen or twenty. Willum's sweetheart is in the "veast" somewhere, and has strictly enjoined him not to get his head broke at back-swording, on pain of her highest displeasure; but as she is not to be seen (the women pretend

The mysterious doors of the pink-eyed lady and the Irish Giant.

[illegible] would like to see the backsword play, and keep away from the stage; and as his hat is the first on the stage, he chucks it into the stage, and follows it himself, hoping that he will only have to break other people's heads, and that after all Rachel won't really mind.

Then follows the greasy [illegible] of a half-gipsy, poaching, loafing fellow, who travels the Vale not for much good, I fancy:

'Full twenty times was Peter feared
For once that Peter was respected,'

in fact. And then three or four other hats, including the [illegible] castor of Joe Willis, the self-elected and would-be champion of the neighbourhood, a well-to-do young butcher of twenty-eight or thereabouts, and a great strapping fellow, with his full allowance of [illegible]. This is a capital show of gamesters, considering the amount of the prize; so while they are picking their sticks and drawing their lots, I think I must tell you, as shortly as I can, how the noble old game of back-sword is played; for it is sadly gone out of late, even in the Vale, and maybe you have never seen it.

The weapon is a good stout ash-stick with a large basket handle, heavier and somewhat shorter than a common single-stick. The players are called 'old gamesters'—why, I can't tell you,—and their object is simply to break one another's heads: for the moment that blood runs an inch anywhere above the eyebrow, the old gamester to whom it belongs is beaten, and has to stop. A very slight blow with the sticks will fetch blood, so that it is by no means a punishing pastime, if the men don't play on purpose, and savagely, at the body and arms of their adversaries. The old gamester going into action only takes off his hat and coat, and arms himself with a stick; he then loops the fingers of his left hand in a handkerchief or strap which he fastens round his left leg, measuring the length, so that when he draws it tight with his left elbow in the air, that elbow shall just reach as high as his crown. Thus you see, so long as he chooses to keep his left elbow up, regardless of cuts, he has a perfect guard for the left side of his head. Then he advances his right hand above and in front of his head, holding his stick across so that its point projects an inch or two over his left elbow, and thus his whole head is completely guarded, and he faces his man armed in like manner, and they stand some three feet apart, often nearer, and feint, and strike, and return at one another's heads until one cries "hold," or blood flows; in the first case they are allowed a minute's time, and go on again; in the latter, another pair of gamesters are called on. If good men are playing, the quickness of the return is marvellous; you hear the rattle like that a boy makes drawing his stick along palings, only heavier, and the closeness of the men in action to one another gives it a strange interest, and makes a spell at back-swording a very noble sight.

They are all suited now with sticks, and Joe Willis and the gipsy man have drawn the first lot. So the rest lean against the rails of the stage, and Joe and the dark man meet in the middle, the boards having been strewed with sawdust; Joe's white shirt and spotless drab breeches and boots contrasting with the gipsy's coarse blue shirt and dirty green velveteen breeches and leather gaiters. Joe is evidently turning up his nose at the other, and half insulted at having to break his head.

The gipsy is a tough, active fellow, but not very skilful with his weapon, so that Joe's weight and strength tell in a minute; he is too heavy metal for him: whack, whack, whack, come his blows, breaking down the gipsy's guard, and threatening to reach his head every moment. There it is at last—"Blood, blood!" shout the spectators, as a thin stream oozes out slowly from the roots of his hair, and the umpire calls to them to stop. The gipsy scowls at Joe under his brows in no pleasant manner, while Master Joe swaggers about, and makes attitudes, and thinks himself, and shows that he thinks himself, the greatest man in the field.

Then follow several stout sets-to between the other candidates for the new hat, and at last come the shepherd and Willum Smith. This is the crack set-to of the day. They are both in famous wind, and there is no crying "hold!" The shepherd is an old hand and up to all the dodges; he tries them one after another, and very nearly gets at Willum's head by coming in near, and playing over his guard at the half-stick, but somehow Willum blunders through, catching the stick on his shoulders, neck, sides, every now and then, anywhere but on his head, and his returns are heavy and straight, and he is the youngest gamester and a favourite in [illegible] and [illegible] gallant stand brings [illegible] shouts [illegible] think he'll win [illegible]

And [illegible] of [illegible]

[illegible] shoulder holds [illegible] and [illegible], and [illegible] excitement.

[illegible] his sweetheart [illegible] male

companionship has been hunting the booths to see where he can have got to, and now catches sight of him on the stage in full combat. She flushes and turns pale; her old aunt catches hold of her, saying, "Bless 'ee, child, doan't 'ee go a'nigst it;" but she breaks away and runs towards the stage calling his name. Willum keeps up his guard stoutly, but glances for a moment towards the voice. No guard will do it, Willum, without the eye. The shepherd steps round and strikes, and the point of his stick just grazes Willum's forehead, fetching off the skin, and the blood flows, and the umpire cries "Hold," and poor Willum's chance is up for the day. But he takes it very well, and puts on his old hat and coat, and goes down to be scolded by his sweetheart, and led away out of mischief. Tom hears him say coaxingly, as he walks off—

"Now doan't 'ee, Rachel! I wouldn't ha' done it, only I wanted summut to buy'ee a fairing wi', and I be as vlush o' money as a twod o' veathers."

"Thee mind what I tells 'ee," rejoins Rachel saucily, "and doan't 'ee kep blethering about fairings." Tom resolves in his heart to give Willum the remainder of his two shillings after the back-swording.

Joe Willis has all the luck to-day. His next bout ends in an easy victory, while the shepherd has a tough job to break his second head; and when Joe and the shepherd meet, and the whole circle expect and hope to see him get a broken crown, the shepherd slips in the first round and falls against the rails, hurting himself so that the old farmer will not let him go on, much as he wishes to try; and that impostor Joe (for he is certainly not the best man) struts and swaggers about the stage the conquering gamester, though he hasn't had five minutes' really trying play.

Joe takes the new hat in his hand, and puts the money into it, and then, as if a thought strikes him and he doesn't think his victory quite acknowledged down below, walks to each face of the stage, and looks down, shaking the money, and chaffing, as how he'll stake hat and money and another half-sovereign "agin any gamester as hasn't played already." Cunning Joe! he thus gets rid of Willum and the shepherd, who is quite fresh again.

No one seems to like the offer, and the umpire is just coming down, when a queer old hat, something like a doctor of Divinity's shovel, is chucked on to the stage, and an elderly quiet man steps out, who has been watching the play, saying he should like to cross a stick wi' the prodigalish young chap.

The crowd cheer and begin to chaff Joe, who turns up his [illegible] fingers across the [illegible] "Happen [illegible]sbird!" says he, "I'll break the [illegible] to the [illegible]."

The old boy is very bald, certainly, and the blood will show fast enough if you can touch him, Joe.

He takes off his long flapped coat, and stands up in a long-flapped waistcoat, which Sir Roger de Coverley might have worn when it was new, picks out a stick, and is ready for Master Joe, who loses no time, but begins making play, whack, whack, trying to break down the old man's guard by sheer strength. But it won't do—he catches every blow close by the basket, and though he is rather stiff in his returns, after a minute walks Joe about the stage, and is clearly a staunch old gamester. Joe now comes in, and making the most of his height, tries to get over the old man's guard at half-stick, by which he takes a smart blow in the shoulder, and nothing more. And now he loses wind and begins to puff, and the crowd laugh: "Cry 'old, Joe—thee'st met thy match!" Instead of taking good advice and getting his wind, Joe loses his temper, and strikes at the old man's body.

"Blood, blood!" shout the crowd, "Joe's head's broke!"

Who'd have thought it? How did it come? That body-blow left Joe's head unguarded for a moment, and with one turn of the wrist the old gentleman has picked a neat little bit of skin off the middle of his forehead, and though he won't believe it, and hammers on for three more blows despite of the shouts, is soon convinced by the blood trickling into his eye. Poor Joe is sadly crestfallen, and fumbles in his pocket for the other half-sovereign, but the old gamester won't have it. "Keep thy money, man, and gi's thy hand," says he, and they shake hands; but the old gamester gives the new hat to the shepherd, and, soon after, the half-sovereign to Willum, who thereupon decorates his sweetheart with ribbons to his heart's content.

"Who can a be?" "Wur do a cum from?" ask the crowd. And it soon flies about that the old West-country champion, who played a tie with Shaw the Life-guardsman at "Vizes" twenty years before, has broken Joe Willis's crown for him.

How my country fair is spinning out! I see I must skip the wrestling, and the boys jumping in sacks, and rolling wheel-barrows blindfolded; and the donkey-race, and the fight which arose thereout, marring the otherwise peaceful "veast"; and the frightened scurrying away of the female feast-goers, and descent of Squire Brown, summoned by the wife of one of the combatants to stop it; which he wouldn't start to do till he had got on his top-boots. Tom is carried away by old Benjy, dog-tired and surfeited with pleasure, as the evening comes on and the dancing begins in the booths; and though Willum, and Rachel in her new ribbons, and many another good lad and lass don't come away just yet, but have a good step out, and enjoy it, and get no harm thereby, yet we, being sober folk, will just stroll away up through the churchyard, and by the old yew-tree; and get a quiet dish of tea and a parley with our gossips, as the steady ones of our village do, and so to bed.

That's the fair true sketch, as far as it goes, of one of the larger village feasts in the Vale of Berks, when I was a little boy. They are much altered for the worse, I am told. I haven't been at one these twenty years, but I have been at the statute fairs in some west-country towns, where servants are hired, and greater abominations cannot be found. What village feasts have come to, I fear, in many cases, may be read in the pages of *Yeast* (though I never saw one so bad—thank God!).

Do you want to know why? It is because, as I said before, gentlefolk and farmers have left off joining or taking an interest in them. They don't either subscribe to the prizes, or go down and enjoy the fun.

Is this a good or a bad sign? I hardly know. Bad, sure enough, if it only arises from the further separation of classes consequent on twenty years of buying cheap and selling dear and its accompanying over-work; or because our sons and daughters have their hearts in London Club-life, or so-called Society, instead of in the old English home duties; because farmers' sons are apeing fine gentlemen, and farmers' daughters caring more to make bad foreign music than good English cheeses. Good, perhaps, if it be that the time for the old "veast" has gone by, that it is no longer the healthy, sound [illegible] country holiday-making [illegible] as [illegible] and are [illegible] feeling for [illegible] to find some better sub[illegible] [illegible] this to say [illegible] think that [illegible] boys and yo[illegible] however, wh[illegible] of the old [illegible] place of the [illegible] thing to try [illegible] their hearts [illegible] all the [illegible] is all left [illegible] Mechanics' Institutes [illegible] Christian Y[illegible] [illegible] [illegible] time. [illegible] skittles, or someth[illegible] better [illegible] part of every En[illegible] into the heads [illegible] you [illegible] swells who "[illegible] you who fre[illegible] always rea[illegible] old John, as [illegible] uncles), [illegible] pack-sadd[illegible] and [illegible] red-tape [illegible] [illegible] you yet--I [illegible] lecturing up and [illegible] busy with all [illegible] libraries [illegible] sides, and [illegible] you ar[illegible] your hearts, [illegible] ready you [illegible] [illegible] instead [illegible] old Parliam[illegible] of you (yo[illegible] line), a[illegible]

Which he wouldn't start to do till he had got on his top-boots.

of your friends, real friends, among us. You'll find a little trouble in getting at the rights of it, because all birds don't come kindly to your lure—but they will come. Take, say, two out of the professions, lawyer, parson, doctor—which you will; one out of trade, and three or four out of the working classes, tailors, engineers, carpenters, engravers—there's plenty of choice. Let them be men of your own ages, mind, and ask them to your homes; introduce them to your wives and sisters, and get introduced to theirs; give them good dinners and talk to them about what is really at the bottom of your hearts, and box and run, and row with them, when you have a chance. Do all this honestly as man to man, and by the time you come to ride old John Bull, you'll be able to do something more than sit on his back, and may feel his mouth with some stronger bridle than a red-tape one.

Ah, if you only would! But you have got too far out of the right rut, I fear. Too much over-civilisation, and the deceitfulness of riches. It is easier for a camel to go through the eye of a needle. More's the pity. I never came across but two of you who could value a man wholly and solely for what was in him; who thought themselves verily and indeed of the same flesh and blood as John Jones the attorney's clerk, and Bill Smith the costermonger, and could act as if they thought so.

CHAPTER III

SUNDRY WARS AND ALLIANCES

POOR old Benjy! The "rheumatiz" has much to answer for all through English country-sides, but it never played a scurvier trick than in laying thee by the heels, when thou wast yet in a green old age. The enemy, which had long been carrying on a sort of border warfare, and trying his strength against Benjy's on the battle-field of his hands and legs, now, mustering all his forces, began laying siege to the citadel, and overrunning the whole country. Benjy was seized in the back and loins; and though he made strong and brave fight, it was soon clear enough that all which could be beaten of poor old Benjy would have to give in before long.

It was as much as he could do now, with the help of his big stick and frequent stops, to hobble down to the canal with Master Tom, and bait his hook for him, and sit and watch his angling, telling him quaint old country stories, and, when Tom had no sport, and detecting a rat some hundred yards or so off along the bank, would rush off with Toby the turnspit terrier, his other faithful companion, in bootless pursuit, he might have tumbled in and been drowned twenty times over before Benjy could have got near him.

Cheery and unmindful of himself as Benjy was, this loss of locomotive power bothered him greatly. He had got a new object in his old age, and was just beginning to think himself useful again in the world. He feared much too lest Master Tom should fall back again into the hands of Charity and the women. So he tried everything he could think of to get set up. He even went an expedition to the dwelling of one of those queer mortals, who—say what we will, and reason how

[illegible]

Old Farmer Ives.

ks. And so the two [illegible] started behind old Dobbin [illegible] and jogged along the [illegible] pitch roads, which had not been mended after the [illegible]'s [illegible] towards the dwelling of the wizard. About [illegible] they passed the gate which opened [illegible] on to the large common [illegible] old Dobbin toiled slowly up the hill, while Benjy [illegible] the [illegible] single [illegible] out of which welled a [illegible] stream [illegible] they crept up the [illegible] the tops of a few [illegible] right, and [illegible] boughs; and then [illegible] curling up through the [illegible] enclosed ground [illegible] little white thatched [illegible] with the gay [illegible] Farmer Ives, [illegible] while [illegible] common rising behind [illegible] might travel for miles with traversing [illegible] left the main road and miles over the [illegible] common marked [illegible] and struck into a [illegible] down into the [illegible] with wheel and horse [illegible] and stopped at [illegible] farmer Ives. Here they found the farmer, an [illegible] with a bushy eyebrow [illegible] strong aquiline [illegible] of his vocations. He [illegible] a horse and [illegible] attending a sick [illegible] which had been sent [illegible] Benjy hailed him as an old friend, and [illegible] cordially [illegible] being however [illegible] Benjy and Tom to see whether there [illegible] easier than appeared at first sight. It was [illegible] difficulty and danger for Benjy to reach the [illegible] he managed to get without mishap [illegible] himself to unharness [illegible] Dobbin and turning [illegible] "a run" on the [illegible] of that [illegible] common. This done [illegible] extricated [illegible] from the cart, and they entered the farmer's [illegible] putting up the [illegible] which he was taking [illegible] the cow's back and [illegible] accompanied [illegible] courage. A big dog [illegible] got up slowly [illegible] stretching first one [illegible] leg and then the [illegible] Tom's caresses and the presence of [illegible] at a respectful distance with equal indifference.

"[illegible]'s be cum [illegible] been long [illegible] [illegible] for old sake's [illegible] I dwont get about [illegible] as I'd used [illegible] wi' th' rheumatics in [illegible] back." Benjy [illegible] drawing the farmer [illegible] once on the subject of his ailments without further direct application.

"Ah, I see as you bean't quite so lissom as you was," replied the farmer with a grim smile, as he lifted the latch of his door; "we bean't so young as we was, nother on us, wuss luck."

The farmer's cottage was very like those of the better class of peasantry in general. A snug chimney corner with two seats, and a small carpet on the hearth, an old flint gun and a pair of spurs over the fireplace, a dresser with shelves on which some bright pewter plates and crockeryware were arranged, an old walnut table, a few chairs and settles, some framed samplers, and an old print or two, and a bookcase with some dozen volumes on the walls, a rack with flitches of bacon, and other stores fastened to the ceiling, and you have the best part of the furniture No sign of occult art is to be seen, unless the bundles of dried herbs hanging to the rack and in the ingle and the row of labelled phials on one of the shelves betoken it.

Tom played about with some kittens who occupied the hearth, and with a goat who walked demurely in at the open door, while their host and Benjy spread the table for dinner—and was soon engaged in conflict with the cold meat, to which he did much honour. The two old men's talk was of old comrades and their deeds, mute inglorious Miltons of the Vale, and of the doings thirty years back—which didn't interest him much, except when they spoke of the making of the canal, and then indeed he began to listen with all his ears; and learned to his no small wonder that his dear and wonderful canal had not been there always—was not in fact so old as Benjy or Farmer Ives, which caused a strange commotion in his small brain.

After dinner Benjy called attention to a wart which Tom had on the knuckles of his hand, and which the family doctor had been trying his skill on without success, and begged the farmer to charm it away. Farmer Ives looked at it, muttered something or another over it, and cut some notches in a short stick, which he handed to Benjy, giving him instructions for cutting it down on certain days, and cautioning Tom not to meddle with the wart for a fortnight. And then they strolled out and sat on a bench in the sun with their pipes, and the pigs came up and grunted sociably and let Tom scratch them; and the farmer, seeing how he liked animals, stood up and held his arms in the air and gave a call, which brought a flock of pigeons wheeling and dashing through the birch-trees. They settled down in clusters on the farmer's arms and shoulders, making love to him and scrambling over one another's backs to get to his face; and then he threw them all off, and they fluttered about close by, and lighted on him again and again when he held up his arms. All the creatures about the place were clean and fearless, quite unlike their relations elsewhere; and Tom begged to be taught how to make all the pigs and cows and poultry in our village tame, at which the farmer only gave one of his grim chuckles.

It wasn't till they were just ready to go, and old Dobbin was harnessed, that Benjy broached the subject of his rheumatism again, detailing his symptoms one by one. Poor old boy! He hoped the farmer could charm it away as easily as he could Tom's wart, and was ready with equal faith to put another notched stick into his other pocket, for the cure of his own ailments. The physician shook his head, but nevertheless produced a bottle and handed it to Benjy with instructions for use. "Not as 't'll do 'ee much good—leastways I be afeared not," shading his eyes with his hand and looking up at them in the cart: "there's only one thing as I knows on as'll cure old folks like you and I o' th' rhumatis."

"Wot be that then, farmer?" inquired Benjy.

"Churchyard mould," said the old iron-grey man with another chuckle. And so they said their good-byes and went their ways home. Tom's wart was gone in a fortnight, but not so Benjy's rheumatism, which laid him by the heels more and more. And though Tom still spent many an hour with him, as he sat on a bench in the sunshine, or by the chimney corner when it was cold, he soon had to seek elsewhere for his regular companions.

Tom had been accustomed often to accompany his mother in her visits to the cottages, and had thereby made acquaintance with many of the village boys of his own age. There was Job Rudkin, son of widow Rudkin, the most bustling woman in the parish. How she could ever have had such a stolid boy as Job for a child must always remain a mystery. The first time Tom went to their cottage with his mother, Job

"Churchyard mould."

was not indoors, but he entered soon after, and stood with both hands in his pockets staring at Tom. Widow Rudkin, who would have had to cross Madam to get at young Hopeful—a breach of good manners of which she was wholly incapable—began a series of pantomime signs, which only puzzled him, and at last, unable to contain herself longer, burst out with "Job! Job! where's thy cap?"

"What! beant 'ee on my head, mother?" replied Job, slowly extricating one hand from a pocket and feeling for the article in question; which he found on his head sure enough, and left there, to his mother's horror and Tom's great delight.

Then there was poor Jacob Dodson, the half-witted boy, who ambled about cheerfully, undertaking messages and little helpful odds and ends for every one, which, however, poor Jacob managed always hopelessly to embrangle. Everything came to pieces in his hands, and nothing would stop in his head. They nicknamed him Jacob Doodle-calf.

But above all there was Harry Winburn, the quickest and best boy in the parish. He might be a year older than Tom, but was very little bigger, and he was the Crichton of our village boys. He could wrestle and climb and run better than all the rest, and learned all that the schoolmaster could teach him faster than that worthy at all liked. He was a boy to be proud of, with his curly brown hair, keen grey eye, straight active figure, and little ears and hands and feet, "as fine as a lord's," as Charity remarked to Tom one day, talking as usual great nonsense. Lords' hands and ears and feet are just as ugly as other folks' when they are children, as any one may convince himself if he likes to look. Tight boots and gloves, and doing nothing with them, I allow make a difference by the time they are twenty.

Now that Benjy was laid on the shelf, and his young brothers were still under petticoat government, Tom, in search of companions, began to cultivate the village boys generally more and more. Squire Brown, be it said, was a true blue Tory to the backbone, and believed honestly that the powers which be were ordained of God and that loyalty and steadfast obedience were men's first duties. Whether it were in consequence or in spite of his political creed I do not mean to give an opinion, though I have one; but certain it is, that he held therewith divers social principles not generally supposed to be true blue in colour. Foremost of these, and the one which the Squire loved to propound above all others, was the belief that a man is to be valued wholly and solely for that which he is in himself, for that which stands up in the four fleshly walls of him, apart from clothes, rank, fortune, and all externals whatsoever. Which belief I take to be a wholesome corrective of all political opinions, and, if held sincerely, to make all opinions equally harmless, whether they be blue, red, or green. As a necessary corollary to this belief, Squire Brown held further that it didn't matter a straw whether his son associated with lords' sons or ploughmen's sons, provided they were brave and honest. He himself had played football and gone birds'-nesting with the farmers whom he met at vestry and the labourers who tilled their fields, and so had his father and grandfather with their progenitors. So he encouraged Tom in his intimacy with the boys of the village, and forwarded it by all means in his power, and gave them the run of a close for a playground, and provided bats and balls and a football for their sports.

Our village was blessed amongst other things with a well-endowed school. The building stood by itself, apart from the master's house, on an angle of ground where three roads met; an old grey stone building with a steep roof and mullioned windows. On one of the opposite angles stood Squire Brown's stables and kennel, with their backs to the road, over which towered a great elm-tree; on the third stood the village carpenter and wheelwright's large open shop, and his house and the schoolmaster's, with long low eaves, under which the swallows built by scores.

The moment Tom's lessons were over, he would now get him down to this corner by the stables, and watch till the boys came out of school. He prevailed on the groom to cut notches for him in the bark of the elm, so that he could climb into the lower branches, and there he would sit watching the school door, and speculating on the possibility of turning the elm into a dwelling-place for himself and friends after the manner of the Swiss Family Robinson. But the school hours were long and Tom's patience short, so that soon he began to descend into the street, and go and peep in at the school door and the wheelwright's shop, and look out for something to while away the time. Now the wheelwright was a choleric n, and, one fine afternoon, returning from a short absence, found Tom occupied with one of his pet adzes, the edge of which was fast vanishing under our hero's care. A speedy flight saved Tom from all but one sound cuff on the ears, but he resented this unjustifiable interruption of his first essays at carpentering, and still more the further proceedings of the wheelwright, who cut a switch and hung it over the door of his workshop, threatening to use it upon Tom if he came within twenty yards of his gate. So Tom, to retaliate, commenced a war upon the swallows who dwelt under the wheelwright's eaves, whom he harassed with sticks and stones; and being fleeter of foot than his enemy, escaped all punishment, and kept him in perpetual anger. Moreover, his presence about the school door began to incense the master, as the boys in that neighbourhood neglected their lessons in consequence: and more than once he issued into the porch, rod in hand, just as Tom beat a hasty retreat. And he and the wheelwright, laying their heads together, resolved to acquaint the Squire with Tom's afternoon occupations; but in order to do it with effect, determined to take him captive and lead him away to judgment fresh from his evil doings. This they would have found some difficulty in doing, had Tom continued the war single-handed, or rather single-footed, for he would have taken to the deepest part of Holy Brook to escape them; but, like other active powers, he was ruined by his alliances. Poor Jacob Doodle-calf could not go to the school with the other boys, and one fine afternoon, about three o'clock (the school broke up at four), Tom found him ambling about the street, and pressed him into a visit to the school-porch. Jacob, always ready to do what he was asked, consented, and the two stole down to the school together. Tom first reconnoitred the wheelwright's shop, and seeing no signs of activity, thought all safe in that quarter, and ordered at once an advance of all his troops upon the school porch. The door of the school was ajar, and the boys seated on the nearest bench at once recognised and opened a correspondence with the invaders. Tom waxing bold kept putting his head into the school and making faces at the master when his back was turned. Poor Jacob, not in the least comprehending the situation, and in high glee at finding himself so near the school, which he had never been allowed to enter, suddenly, in a fit of enthusiasm, pushed by Tom, and ambling three steps into the school, stood there, looking round him and nodding with a self-approving smile. The master, who was stooping over a boy's slate, with his back to the door, became aware of something unusual, and turned quickly round. Tom rushed at Jacob, and began dragging him back by his smock-frock, and the master made at them, scattering forms and boys in his career. Even now they might have escaped, but that in the porch, barring retreat, appeared the crafty wheelwright, who had been watching all their proceedings. So they were seized, the school dismissed, and Tom and Jacob led away to Squire Brown as lawful prize, the boys following to the gate in groups, and speculating on the result.

The Squire was very angry at first, but the interview, by Tom's pleading, ended in a compromise. Tom was not to go near the school till three o'clock, and only then if he had done his own lessons well, in which case he was to be the bearer of a note to the master from Squire Brown, and the master agreed in such case to release ten or twelve of the best boys an hour before the time of breaking up, to go off and play in the close. The wheelwright's adzes and swallows were to be for ever respected; and that hero and the master withdrew to the servants' hall to drink the Squire's health, well satisfied with their day's work.

The second act of Tom's life may now be said to have begun. The war of independence had been over for some time: none of the women now, not even his mother's maid, dared offer to help him in dressing or washing. Between ourselves, he had often at first to run to Benjy in an unfinished state of toilet; Charity and the rest of them seemed to take a delight in putting impossible buttons and ties in the middle of his back; but he would have gone without nether integuments altogether, sooner than have had recourse to female valeting. He had a room to himself, and his father gave him sixpence a week pocket-money. All this he had achieved by Benjy's advice and assistance. But now he had conquered another step in life, the step which all real boys so long to make; he had got amongst his equals in age and strength, and could measure himself with other boys; he lived with those whose pursuits and wishes and ways were the same in kind as his own.

The little governess who had lately been installed in the house found her work grow wondrously easy, for Tom slaved at his lessons in order to make sure of his note to the schoolmaster. So there were very few days in the week in which Tom and the village boys were not playing in the close by three o'clock. Prisoner's base, rounders, high-cock-a-lorum, cricket, football, he was soon initiated into the delights of them all; and though most of the boys were older than himself, he managed to hold his own very well. He was naturally active and strong, and quick of eye and hand, and had the advantage of light shoes and well-fitting dress, so that in a short time he could run and jump and climb with any of them.

They generally finished their regular games half an hour or so before tea-time, and then began trials of skill and strength in many ways. Some of them would catch the Shetland pony who was turned out in the field, and get two or three together on his back, and the little rogue, enjoying the fun, would gallop off for fifty yards and then turn round, or stop short and shoot them on to the turf, and then graze quietly on till he felt another load; others played at peg-top or marbles, while a few of the bigger ones stood up for a bout at wrestling. Tom at first only looked on at this pastime, but it had peculiar attractions for him, and he could not long keep out of it. Elbow and collar wrestling, as practised in the western counties, was, next to back-swording, the way to fame for the youth of the Vale; and all the boys knew the rules of it, and were more or less expert. But Job Rudkin and Harry Winburn were the stars, the former stiff and sturdy, with legs like small towers, the latter pliant as india-rubber, and quick as lightning. Day after day they stood foot to foot, and offered first one hand and then the other, and grappled and closed and swayed and strained, till a well-aimed crook of the heel or thrust of the loin took effect, and a fair back-fall ended the matter. And Tom watched with all his eyes, and first challenged one of the least scientific, and threw him; and so one by one wrestled his way up to the leaders.

Then indeed for months he had a poor time of it; it was not long indeed before he could manage to keep his legs against Job, for that hero was slow of offence, and gained his victories chiefly by allowing others to throw themselves against his immovable legs and loins. But Harry Winburn was undeniably his master; from the first clutch of hands when they stood up, down to the last trip which sent him on to his back on the turf, he felt that Harry knew more and could do more than he. Luckily Harry's bright unconsciousness, and Tom's natural good temper, kept them from ever quarrelling; and so Tom worked on and on, and trod more and more nearly on Harry's heels, and at last mastered all the dodges and falls except one. This one was Harry's own particular invention and pet; he scarcely ever used it except when hard pressed, but then out it came, and as sure as it did, over went poor Tom. He thought about that fall at his meals, in his walks, when he lay awake in bed, in his dreams—but all to no purpose; until Harry one day in his open way suggested to him how he thought it should be met, and in a week from that time the boys were equal, save only the slight difference of strength in Harry's favour which some extra ten months of age gave. Tom had often afterwards reason to be thankful for that early drilling, and above all for having mastered Harry Winburn's fall.

Besides their home games, on Saturdays the boys would wander all over the neighbourhood; sometimes to the downs, or up to the camp where they cut their initials out in the springy turf, and watched the hawks soaring, and the "peert" bird, as Harry Winburn called the grey plover, gorgeous in his wedding feathers; and so home, racing down the Manger with many a roll among the thistles, or through Uffington-wood to watch the fox-cubs playing in the green rides; sometimes to Rosy Brook, to cut long whispering reeds which grew there, to make pan-pipes of; sometimes to Moor Mills, where was a piece of old forest land, with short browsed turf and tufted brambly thickets stretching under the oaks, amongst which rumour declared that a raven, last of his race, still lingered; or to the sand-hills, in vain quest of rabbits; and birds'-nesting, in the season, anywhere and everywhere.

The few neighbours of the Squire's own rank every now and then would shrug their shoulders as they drove or rode by a party of boys with Tom in the middle, carrying along bulrushes or whispering reeds, or great bundles of cowslip and meadow-sweet, or young starlings or magpies, or other spoil of wood, brook, or meadow: and Lawyer Red-tape might mutter to Squire Straightback at the Board that no good [illegible] the young Bro[illegible] wild [illegible] village boys, [illegible] sons

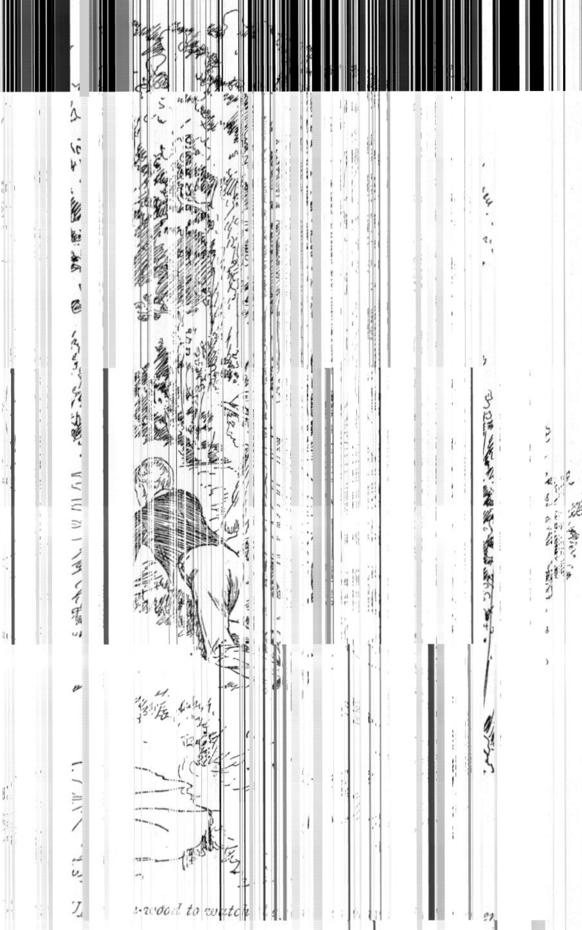

T[illegible]-wood to watch [illegible]

[illegible] play with. [illegible] with [illegible] that *his* sons [illegible] equals, and never went into the village without the governess or a footman. But, luckily, Squire Brown was full as stiff-backed as his neighbours, and so went on his own way; and Tom and his younger brothers, as they grew up, went on playing with the village boys, without the idea of equality or inequality (except in wrestling, running, and climbing) ever entering their heads, as it doesn't till it's put there by Jack Nastys or fine ladies' maids.

I don't mean to say it would be the case in all villages, but it certainly was so in this one; the village boys were full as manly and honest, and certainly purer, than those in a higher rank; and Tom got more harm from his equals in his first fortnight at a private school, where he went when he was nine years old, than he had from his village friends from the day he left Charity's apron-strings.

Great was the grief amongst the village schoolboys when Tom drove off with the Squire, one August morning, to meet the coach on his way to school. Each of them had given him some little present of the best that he had, and his small private box was full of peg-tops, white marbles (called "alley-taws" in the Vale), screws, birds'-eggs, whip-cord, jews-harps, and other miscellaneous boys' wealth. Poor Jacob Doodle-calf, in floods of tears, had pressed upon him with spluttering earnestness his lame pet hedgehog (he had always some poor broken-down beast or bird by him); but this Tom had been obliged to refuse by the Squire's order. He had given them all a great tea under the big elm in their playground, for which Madam Brown had supplied the biggest cake ever seen in our village; and Tom was really as sorry to leave them as they to lose him, but his sorrow was not unmixed with the pride and excitement of making a new step in life.

And this feeling carried him through his first parting with his mother better than could have been expected. Their love was as fair and whole as human love can be, perfect self-sacrifice on the one side meeting a young and true heart on the other. It is not within the scope of my book, however, to speak of family relations, or I should have much to say on the subject of English mothers,—aye, and of English fathers, and sisters, and brothers too.

Neither have I room to speak of our private schools:

hat I have to say ... s ... ls, those much abused
nd much belaude ... to England. So ...

... fr ... ears

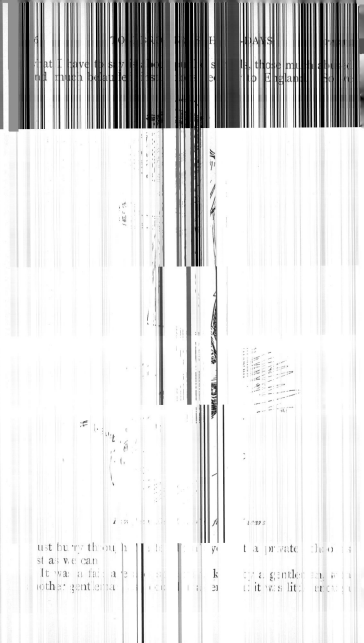

ust hurry through ... yo ... t a private ... as
st as we can.

It was a fair ... k ... y a gentleman, w ...
nother gentleman ... er ... it was little enough ...

of the real work they did—merely coming into school when lessons were prepared and all ready to be heard. The whole discipline of the school out of lesson hours was in the hands of the two ushers, one of whom was always with the boys in their playground, in the school, at meals—in fact, at all times and everywhere, till they were fairly in bed at night.

Now the theory of private schools is (or was) constant supervision out of school; therein differing fundamentally from that of public schools.

It may be right or wrong; but if right this supervision surely ought to be the especial work of the head-master, the responsible person. The object of all schools is not to ram Latin and Greek into boys, but to make them good English boys, good future citizens; and by far the most important part of that work must be done, or not done, out of school hours. To leave it, therefore, in the hands of inferior men, is just giving up the highest and hardest part of the work of education. Were I a private schoolmaster, I should say, let who will hear the boys their lessons, but let me live with them when they are at play and rest.

The two ushers at Tom's first school were not gentlemen, and very poorly educated, and were only driving their poor trade of usher to get such living as they could out of it. They were not bad men, but had little heart for their work, and of course were bent on making it as easy as possible. One of the methods by which they endeavoured to accomplish this was by encouraging tale-bearing, which had become a frightfully common vice in the school in consequence, and had sapped all the foundations of school morality. Another was, by favouring grossly the biggest boys, who alone could have given them much trouble; whereby those young gentlemen became most abominable tyrants, oppressing the little boys in all the small mean ways which prevail in private schools.

Poor little Tom was made dreadfully unhappy in his first week, by a catastrophe which happened to his first letter home. With huge labour he had, on the very evening of his arrival, managed to fill two sides of a sheet of letter-paper with assurances of his love for dear mamma, his happiness at school, and his resolves to do all she would wish. This missive, with the help of the boy who sat at the desk next him, also a new arrival, he managed to fold successfully; but this done, they were sadly put to it for means ... velopes were then ... they had no ... disturb the stil... evening ... the ... and going to ask ... for some ... being of an inge... of mind, suggested ... and the latter ... ingly stuck down ... and duly hand...

on his way to ... keeper to be post... not till four ... the good dame ... and produce ... and some wax, ... Master Brown, ... be ... but your ... sealed." ... residence and sealed ... with a huge ... coat during the p... then run away ... of the playground ... into an agony ... a of his mother ... after day for ... ised her at once, ... thinking him ... he had done all ... to make good ... bite a grief ... he had to ... long year. His ... was proper ... he was aware ... who stopped ... one of whom ... fellow pointed ... him "Young ... Whereupon ... going thus to ... shame and ... der of the nose, ... to bleed—wh... ... freely flowing to ... who reported ... and unprovoked ... battery ... is a felony pun... floggings, ... misdemeanour— ... not altogether ... Tom however e... penalty ... grus and having ... second letter ... closing some forg... which he ... half-holiday walk ... happy again ... by visiting a good ... new life.

These half-holid... the great events ... The whole fifty ... dinner with me ... for Hazeldown ... or some mile or ... school. Hazeldown ... some three miles ... in the neighbour... ... al woods full of ... of birds and ... usher walked slo... the down with ... to accompany him ... scattered in all ... only bound to ...

With huge labour.

when the usher [illegible] his round, and [illegible]
home. [illegible] however, to go [illegible]
on the down and [illegible] the village [illegible]
prohibited [illegible] and unctuous [illegible]
procured in [illegible] of the realm.

Various were [illegible] to which the boys [illegible]
themselves. [illegible] the down [illegible]
like [illegible] downs. This [illegible]
weekly [illegible] at a game called [illegible]
name of [illegible] boys who [illegible]
sides under [illegible] one side of [illegible]
Then, all [illegible] ed themselves [illegible]
of turf [illegible] -cheese knives [illegible]
remained at [illegible] eeded to [illegible]
advancing [illegible] cover of a [illegible]
and then [illegible] y with the [illegible]
was their [illegible] uld, even [illegible]
the summit, [illegible] urn became [illegible]
was a good [illegible] and of great [illegible]
acting the [illegible] s of the school [illegible]
of the boys [illegible] owns looking for the [illegible]
humble-bees [illegible] they dig up [illegible]
(I regret to say [illegible] ning the [illegible]
do not regret [illegible] well stung by [illegible]
Others went [illegible] nd birds' eggs [illegible]
and Tom found [illegible] for the first [illegible]
little blue [illegible] n spots on [illegible]
had never seen [illegible] vns, and dug [illegible]
martin's nest. [illegible] even ensued [illegible]
for the sand-m[illegible] high bank [illegible]
consequently [illegible] ut one of the [illegible]
school, who [illegible] ppy unless he was [illegible]
thing to which [illegible] asily persuaded [illegible]
bounds and [illegible] bank. From [illegible]
only a step to [illegible] what could [illegible]
than to go [illegible] their pockets [illegible]
certain [illegible] urn, a distribution [illegible]
having been [illegible] should shortly [illegible]
bidden [illegible] nd, [illegible] search [illegible]
the state of the [illegible] s of Tom and [illegible]
This [illegible] of [illegible] ed a desperate [illegible]

Getting well stung by the humble-bees.

[illegible]

morning at the breakfast-table, about a fortnight after Tom's return, he addressed his wife with—"My dear, I have arranged that Tom shall go to Rugby at once, for the last six weeks of this half-year, instead of wasting them, in riding and loitering about home. It is very kind of the Doctor to allow it. Will you see that his things are all ready by Friday, when I shall take him up to town, and send him down the next day by himself?"

Mrs. Brown was prepared for the announcement, and merely suggested a doubt whether Tom were yet old enough to travel by himself. However, finding both father and son against her on this point, she gave in, like a wise woman, and proceeded to prepare Tom's kit for his launch into a public school.

CHAPTER V

[illegible] COACH

[illegible] of the [illegible]

[illegible]

[illegible] if you please. [illegible] half an hour [illegible] of the Pe[illegible] morning [illegible] Tom at the [illegible] ting down a[illegible]

[illegible] ved in town [illegible] did not [illegible] at D[illegible] where [illegible] resolved that Tom [illegible] diverged fr[illegible]

[illegible] ndor, and [illegible] riage, where they [illegible] that he might [illegible] ious, gas-lit street[illegible] ing crowds [illegible] as soon as [illegible] him to R[illegible] he would [illegible]

And had fraternised with the Boots and Ostler.

[illegible] s melted [illegible] in [illegible]
[illegible] blic school-b[illegible] a [illegible]
[illegible] seeming [illegible]
[illegible]

[illegible] en had alight[illegible] t [illegible]
[illegible] and havi[illegible]
[illegible] t the bar, o[illegible]
[illegible] and seen [illegible]
[illegible] e room with [illegible]
[illegible] about him [illegible] a [illegible]
[illegible] n passing, a [illegible] it [illegible]
[illegible] whom he a[illegible]
[illegible] miles an h[illegible] e [illegible]
[illegible] e road set [illegible]
[illegible] su[illegible] red to sup[illegible] h [illegible]
[illegible] little bikes [illegible]
[illegible] k[illegible] nk mixed o[illegible] n [illegible]
[illegible] t[illegible] him—a [illegible]
[illegible] e story); [illegible] t [illegible]
[illegible] his father was [illegible] n [illegible]
[illegible] f[illegible] ring brandy [illegible]
[illegible] th[illegible] ed effects [illegible] e [illegible]
[illegible] t[illegible] ern, observing [illegible] e [illegible]
[illegible] s[illegible] ly nine o'clock [illegible]
[illegible] e fellow off [illegible]
[illegible] I'm having [illegible]
[illegible] h[illegible] sing should [illegible] t [illegible]
[illegible] g[illegible]

[illegible] T[illegible] my boy," s[illegible]
[illegible] t[illegible] own earnes[illegible]
[illegible] a young [illegible]
[illegible] an we shou[illegible]
[illegible] ey were in [illegible]
[illegible] things done [illegible]
[illegible] ou tell the [illegible] d [illegible]
[illegible] o or say [illegible] t [illegible]
[illegible] hear, and y[illegible]
[illegible] ve[illegible] on."

[illegible] o[illegible] other made [illegible] h [illegible]
[illegible] a[illegible] ed to have [illegible] ll [illegible]
[illegible] h[illegible] ent stipulati[illegible]

And a few parting words.

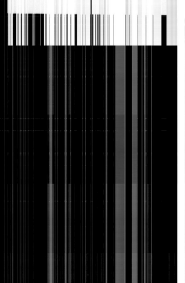

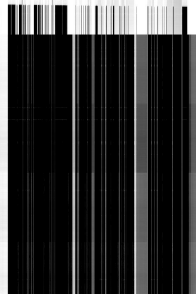

go. If he'll only turn out a brave, helpful, truth-telling Englishman, and a gentleman and a Christian, that's all I want," thought the Squire; and upon this view of the case he framed his last words of advice to Tom, which were well enough suited to his purpose.

For they were Tom's first thoughts as he tumbled out of bed at the summons of Boots, and proceeded rapidly to wash and dress himself. At ten minutes to three he was down in the coffee-room in his stockings, carrying his hat-box, coat, and comforter in his hand; and there he found his father nursing a bright fire, and a cup of hot coffee and a hard biscuit on the table.

"Now then, Tom, give us your things here, and drink this; there's nothing like starting warm, old fellow."

Tom addressed himself to the coffee, and prattled away while he worked himself into his shoes and his great coat, well warmed through; a Petersham coat with velvet collar, made tight after the abominable fashion of those days. And just as he is swallowing his last mouthful, winding his comforter round his throat, and tucking the ends into the breast of his coat, the horn sounds, Boots looks in and says, "Tally-ho, sir;" and they hear the ring and the rattle of the four fast trotters and the town-made drag, as it dashes up to the Peacock.

"Anything for us, Bob?" says the burly guard, dropping down from behind, and slapping himself across the chest.

"Young genl'm'n, Rugby; three parcels, Leicester; hamper o' game, Rugby," answers Ostler.

"Tell young gent to look alive," says Guard, opening the hind-boot and shooting in the parcels after examining them by the lamps. "Here, shove the portmanteau up a-top—I'll fasten him presently. Now then, sir, jump up behind."

"Good-bye, father—my love at home." A last shake of the hand. Up goes Tom, the guard catching his hat-box and holding on with one hand, while with the other he claps the horn to his mouth. Toot, toot, toot! the ostlers let go their heads, the four bays plunge at the collar, and away goes the Tally-ho into the darkness, forty-five seconds from the time they pulled up; Ostler, Boots, and the Squire stand looking after them under the Peacock lamp.

[illegible]

promises, and of his mother and sister, and his father's last words; and has made fifty good resolutions, and means to bear himself like a brave Brown as he is, though a young one. Then he has been forward into the mysterious boy-future, speculating as to what sort of a place Rugby is, and what they do there, and calling up all the stories of public schools which he has heard from big boys in the holidays. He is chock full of hope and life, notwithstanding the cold, and kicks his heels against the back-board, and would like to sing, only he doesn't know how his friend, the silent guard, might take it.

And now the dawn breaks at the end of the fourth stage, and the coach pulls up at a little road-side inn with huge stables behind. There is a bright fire gleaming through the red curtains of the bar window, and the door is open. The coachman catches his whip into a double thong, and throws it to the ostler; the steam of the horses rises straight up into the air. He has put them along over the last two miles, and is two minutes before his time; he rolls down from the box and into the inn. The guard rolls off behind. "Now, sir," says he to Tom, "you just jump down, and I'll give you a drop of something to keep the cold out."

Tom finds a difficulty in jumping, or indeed in finding the top of the wheel with his feet, which may be in the next world for all he feels; so the guard picks him off the coach-top, and sets him on his legs, and they stump off into the bar, and join the coachman and the other outside passengers.

Here a fresh-looking barmaid serves them each with a glass of early purl as they stand before the fire, coachman and guard exchanging business remarks. The purl warms the cockles of Tom's heart, and makes him cough.

"Rare tackle, that, sir, of a cold morning," says the coachman, smiling. "Time's up." They are out again and up; coachee the last, gathering the reins into his hands and talking to Jem the ostler about the mare's shoulder, and then swinging himself up on to the box—the horses dashing off in a canter before he falls into his seat. Toot-toot-tootle-too goes the horn, and away they are again, five-and-thirty miles on their road (nearly half-way to Rugby, thinks Tom), and the prospect of breakfast at the end of the stage.

And now they begin to see, and the early life of the country-side comes out; a market cart or two, men in smock-frocks

Our coachman, I perceive, who breakfasts with us, is a cold beef man.

p[illegible] looks [illegible] appro[illegible] ers [illegible] ditto [illegible]

[illegible] has eaten ki[illegible] coffee [illegible] skin i[illegible] has the pleasure of [illegible] his own purse [illegible] manne[illegible] and [illegible] to [illegible] ses [illegible] to. [illegible] is [illegible] high[illegible] by [illegible] enjoyed the [illegible] rried. Co[illegible] bill an[illegible] a [illegible] cigar w[illegible] th[illegible] Gu[illegible] from the t[illegible] whe[illegible] asting, lick[illegible] tough-looking [illegible] w[illegible] right ti[illegible] ur finger, a[illegible] thr[illegible] clock an[illegible] out o[illegible] time.

[illegible] pin[illegible] stand about [illegible] ing [illegible] a[illegible] to see us sta[illegible] up [illegible] do[illegible] ret [illegible] ate, on [illegible] know [illegible] and we [illegible] see h[illegible] and laughin[illegible]

[illegible], sir, please,' says the [illegible] the rest of the [illegible] are up; the guard [illegible] hind boot. "[illegible] run to [illegible]" s[illegible] to the pink[illegible] [illegible] the coachm[illegible] [illegible] Dick [illegible] drawing off the [illegible] their gl[illegible] through the [illegible] and dow[illegible] the [illegible] at the first [illegible], and [illegible] having [illegible] all the shop-b[illegible] the window [illegible] maids who are [illegible] look [illegible] as we rattle past, [illegible] the legit[illegible] amusement. [illegible] are w[illegible] the hedgerows [illegible] strikes eight. [illegible] almost [illegible] called all [illegible] loosened [illegible] couraged by [illegible] two of the guard's [illegible] of his own [illegible] and besides [illegible] ting [illegible] He is too [illegible] destination [illegible] and so ask[illegible] if he knows [illegible]

'[illegible] though it [illegible] twenty minutes [illegible] down—[illegible] clock [illegible]

'[illegible] sort of place, [illegible], please [illegible] T[illegible]

Guard looks at him with a comical expression. "Werry out-o'-the-way place, sir; no paving to streets, nor no lighting. 'Mazin' big horse and cattle fair in autumn—lasts a week—just over now. Takes town a week to get clean after it. Fairish hunting country. But slow place, sir, slow place: off the main road, you see—only three coaches a day, and one on 'em a two-oss wan, more like a hearse nor a coach—Regulator—comes from Oxford. Young genl'm'n at school calls her Pig and Whistle, and goes up to college by her (six miles an hour) when they goes to enter. Belong to school, sir?"

"Yes," says Tom, not unwilling for a moment that the guard should think him an old boy. But then having some qualms as to the truth of the assertion, and seeing that if he were to assume the character of an old boy he couldn't go on asking the questions he wanted, added—"that is to say, I'm on my way there. I'm a new boy."

The guard looked as if he knew this quite as well as Tom.

"You're werry late, sir," says the guard; "only six weeks to-day to the end of the half." Tom assented. "We takes up fine loads this day six weeks, and Monday and Tuesday arter. Hopes we shall have the pleasure of carrying you back."

Tom said he hoped they would; but he thought within himself that his fate would probably be the Pig and Whistle.

"It pays uncommon cert'nly," continues the guard. "Werry free with their cash is the young genl'm'n. But, Lor' bless you, we gets into such rows all 'long the road, what wi' their pea-shooters, and long whips, and hollering and upsetting every one as comes by; I'd a sight sooner carry one or two on 'em, sir, as I may be a carryin' of you now, than a coach-load."

"What do they do with the pea-shooters?" inquires Tom.

"Do wi' 'em! Why, peppers every one's faces as we comes near, 'cept the young gals, and breaks windows wi them too, some on 'em shoots so hard. Now 'twas just here last June, as we was a drivin' up the first-day boys, they was mendin' a quarter-mile of road, and there was a lot of Irish chaps, reg'lar roughs, a breaking stones. As we comes up, 'Now, boys,' says young gent on the box (smart young fellow and desper't reckless), 'here's fun! let the Pats have it about the ears.' 'God's sake, sir!' says Bob (that's my mate the coachman), 'don't go for to shoot at 'em, they'll knock us off the coach.'

[illegible] chee," says young [illegible] 'em have it." [illegible] shock[illegible] [illegible] come, [illegible] [illegible] and shakes [illegible] twenty [illegible] was [illegible] and [illegible] ha[illegible] [illegible] But, bless [illegible] way [illegible] that [illegible] line [illegible] line [illegible] pulls the [illegible] right [illegible] his [illegible] it is right [illegible] his [illegible] [illegible] gone; [illegible] wheres [illegible] for [illegible] I [illegible] up and [illegible] said Tom [illegible] his [illegible] he has [illegible]

Them Irishers last summer had all got stones ready for us, and was all but letting drive and we'd got two reverend gents aboard too. We pulled up at the beginning of the line, and pacified them, and we're never going to carry no more pea-shooters, unless they promises not to fire where there's a line of Irish chaps a stone-breaking." The guard stopped and pulled away at his cheroot, regarding Tom benignantly the while.

"Oh, don't stop! tell us somethin' more about the pea-shooting."

"Well, there'd like to have been a pretty piece of work over it at Bicester, a while back. We was six mile from the town, when we meets an old square-headed grey-haired yeoman chap, a jogging along quite quiet. He looks up at the coach, and just then a pea hits him on the nose, and some catches his cob behind and makes him dance up on his hind legs. I see'd the old boy's face flush and look plaguy awkward, and I thought we was in for somethin' nasty.

"He turns his cob's head, and rides quietly after us just out of shot. How that ere cob did step! we never shook him off not a dozen yards in the six miles. At first the young gents were werry lively on him; but afore we got in, seeing how steady the old chap come on, they was quite quiet, and laid their heads together what they should do. Some was for fighting, some for axing his pardon. He rides into the town close after us, comes up when we stops, and says the two as shot at him must come before a magistrate; and a great crowd comes round, and we couldn't get the 'osses to. But the young uns they all stand by one another, and says all or none must go, and as how they'd fight it out, and have to be carried. Just as 'twas gettin' serious, and the old boy and the mob was going to pull 'em off the coach, one little fellow jumps up and says, 'Here,—I'll stay—I'm only going three miles further. My father's name's Davis; he's known about here, and I'll go before the magistrate with this gentleman.' 'What! be thee parson Davis's son?' says the old boy. 'Yes,' says the young un. 'Well, I be mortal sorry to meet thee in such company, but for thy father's sake and thine (for thee bi'st a brave young chap) I'll say no more about it.' Didn't the boys cheer him, and the mob cheered the young chap—and then one of the biggest gets down, and begs his pardon werry gentle-

[illegible]

neared the milestone, the third from Rugby. By the stone two boys stood, their jackets buttoned tight, waiting for the coach.

"Look here, sir," says the guard, after giving a sharp toot-toot, "there's two on 'em, out and out runners they be. They comes out about twice or three times a week, and spirts a mile alongside of us."

And as they came up, sure enough, away went two boys along the footpath, keeping up with the horses; the first a light clean-made fellow going on springs, the other stout and round-shouldered, labouring in his pace, but going as dogged as a bull-terrier.

Old Blow-hard looked on admiringly. "See how beautiful that there un holds hisself together, and goes from his hips, sir," said he; "he's a 'mazin' fine runner. Now many coachmen as drives a first-rate team'd put it on, and try and pass 'em. But Bob, sir, bless you, he's tender-hearted; he'd sooner pull in a bit if he see'd 'em a gettin' beat. I do b'lieve too as that there un'd sooner break his heart than let us go by him afore next milestone."

At the second milestone the boys pulled up short, and waved their hats to the guard, who had his watch out and shouted "4.56," thereby indicating that the mile had been done in four seconds under the five minutes. They passed several more parties of boys, all of them objects of the deepest interest to Tom, and came in sight of the town at ten minutes before twelve. Tom fetched a long breath, and thought he had never spent a pleasanter day. Before he went to bed he had quite settled that it must be the greatest day he should ever spend, and didn't alter his opinion for many a long year—if he has yet.

[illegible]

[illegible]

[illegible]

round to Tom, and, after looking him over for a minute, began—

"I say, you fellow, is your name Brown?"

"*Here's Rugby, sir, at last.*"

"Yes," said Tom, in considerable astonishment, glad however to have lighted on some one already who seemed to know him.

ιway swaggers the young potentate, with his hands in his)ockets, and Tom at his side.

"All right, sir," says Cooey, touching his hat, with a leer ιnd a wink at his companions.

"Hullo tho'," says East, pulling up, and taking another ook at Tom, "this'll never do—haven't you got a hat?—ve never wear caps here. Only the louts wear caps. Bless 'ou, if you were to go into the quadrangle with that thing on,

The School Gates from High Street.

[——don't know what'd happen." The very idea was quite)eyond young Master East, and he looked unutterable things.

Tom thought his cap a very knowing affair, but confessed hat he had a hat in his hat-box; which was accordingly at)nce extracted from the hind boot, and Tom equipped in ıis go-to-meeting roof, as his new friend called it. But this lidn't quite suit his fastidious taste in another minute, being oo shiny; so, as they walk up the town, they dive into Nixon's he hatter's, and Tom is arrayed, to his utter astonishment, and

[illegible] ng [illegible] it, in a regulation [illegible] se[illegible] ud-
[illegible] x [illegible] erasing [illegible] u[illegible] the
[illegible] m S[illegible]ool-house, [illegible] half [illegible]
[illegible] a note [illegible] a [illegible]
[illegible] said Mentor [illegible]
[illegible] na [illegible] s des what [illegible]
[illegible] i [illegible] e began to be [illegible] ne [illegible] al
[illegible] d [illegible] it, and to lu[illegible]ate [illegible] d [illegible] on

The G[illegible]s

[illegible] school boy at la[illegible] e [illegible]
[illegible] nds ers in ha[illegible]
[illegible] e, [illegible] d his friend as [illegible]
[illegible] es [illegible] explanation of [illegible]
[illegible] ellow [illegible] ts up a[illegible]
[illegible] and answer [illegible] stra[illegible]
[illegible] e [illegible] Now, [illegible]
[illegible] a [illegible] I'm [illegible]
[illegible] s [illegible] father knows [illegible]

please the old lady. She gave me half-a-sov. this half, and perhaps'll double it next, if I keep in her good books."

There's nothing like candour for a lower-school boy, and East was a genuine specimen—frank, hearty, and good-natured, well satisfied with himself and his position, and chock full of life and spirits, and all the Rugby prejudices and traditions which he had been able to get together, in the long course

The Quadrangle.

of one half year during which he had been at the School-house.

And Tom, notwithstanding his bumptiousness, felt friends with him at once, and began sucking in all his ways and prejudices, as fast as he could understand them.

East was great in the character of cicerone; he carried Tom through the great gates, where were only two or three boys. These satisfied themselves with the stock questions,—"You fellow, what's your name? Where do you come from?

[illegible] you? Where do you [illegible] form [illegible]" and so they passed on [illegible] quadrangle [illegible] courtyard, upon which [illegible] of little [illegible] as his guide informed [illegible] of the [illegible] into the matron's [illegible] just in- [illegible] that dignitary [illegible] the key [illegible] that the matron might [illegible], and [illegible] of the hat and of his [illegible] mind: [illegible] where of the matron [illegible] him,

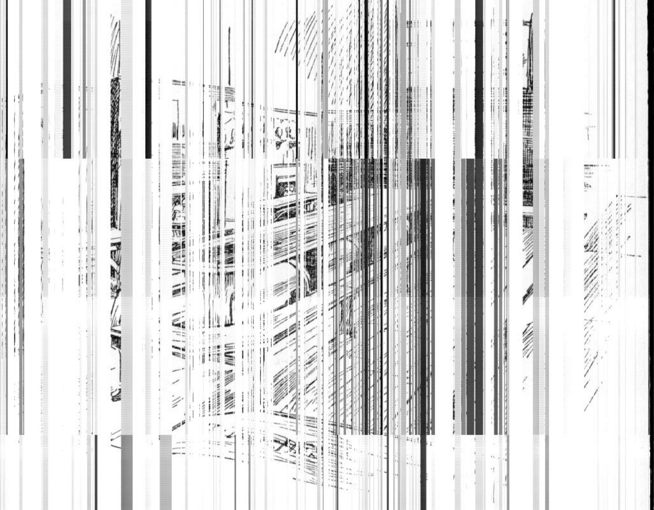

The Hall.

[illegible] new boy in the house [illegible] indignant [illegible] of newness [illegible] to the [illegible], and began showing him the [illegible] winning [illegible] literary attainments [illegible] was a [illegible] they would be in the same [illegible] would do [illegible] position.

[illegible] come in and see my study [illegible] just [illegible] and afterwards [illegible]; we'll [illegible]

Tom followed his guide through the School-house hall, which opens into the quadrangle. It is a great room thirty feet long and eighteen high, or thereabouts, with two great tables running

The Studies.

the whole length, and two large fireplaces at the side, with blazing fires in them, at one of which some dozen boys were standing and lounging, some of whom shouted to East to [illegible] shot through with his [illegible] and [illegible] him [illegible] dark passages, with a [illegible] at [illegible] end of [illegible] upon which the studies opened. [illegible] these, [illegible]

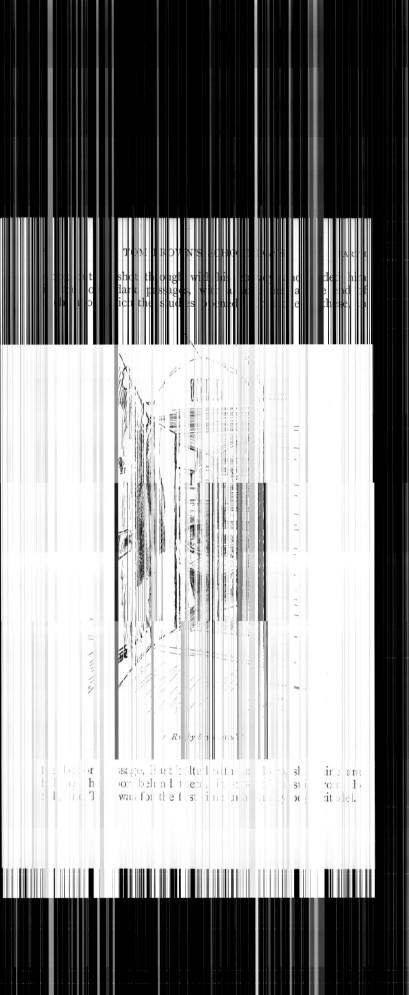

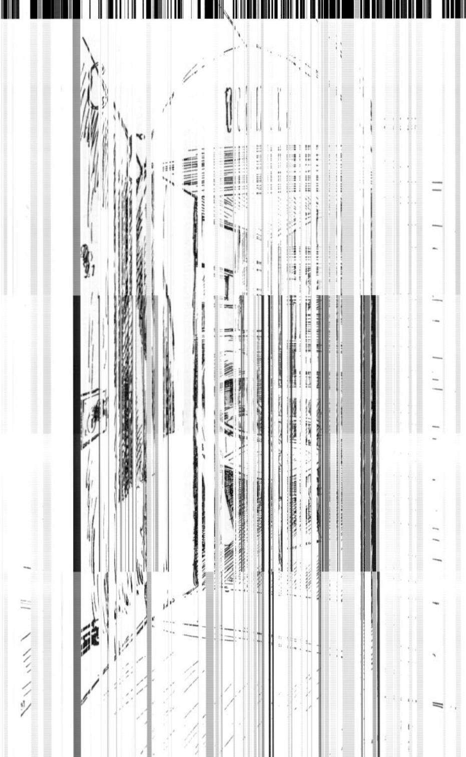

"A Rugby [illegible]"

[illegible] ssage, East bolted with [illegible] sl[illegible]ing and [illegible] the door behind them, in [illegible] from the [illegible] and Tom was for the first time in a [illegible] citadel.

He hadn't been prepared for separate studies, and was not a little astonished and delighted with the palace in question.

It wasn't very large certainly, being about six feet long by four broad. It couldn't be called light, as there were bars and a grating to the window; which little precautions were necessary in the studies on the ground-floor looking out into the close, to prevent the exit of small boys after locking-up, and the entrance of contraband articles. But it was uncommonly comfortable to look at, Tom thought. The space under the window at the further end was occupied by a square table covered with a reasonably clean and whole red-and-blue check tablecloth; a hard-seated sofa covered with red stuff occupied one side, running up to the end, and making a seat for one, or by sitting close, for two, at the table; and a good stout wooden chair afforded a seat to another boy, so that three could sit and work together. The walls were wainscoted half-way up, the wainscot being covered with green baize, the remainder with a bright-patterned paper, on which hung three or four prints of dogs' heads, Grimaldi winning the Aylesbury steeple-chase, Amy Robsart, the reigning Waverley beauty of the day, and Tom Crib in a posture of defence, which did no credit to the science of that hero, if truly represented. Over the door were a row of hat-pegs, and on each side book-cases with cupboards at the bottom; shelves and cupboards being filled indiscriminately with schoolbooks, a cup or two, a mousetrap and brass candle-sticks, leather straps, a fustian bag, and some curious-looking articles, which puzzled Tom not a little, until his friend explained that they were climbing-irons, and showed their use. A cricket bat and small fishing-rod stood up in one corner.

This was the residence of East and another boy in the same form, and had more interest for Tom than Windsor Castle, or any other residence in the British Isles. For was he not about to become the joint owner of a similar home, the first place which he could call his own? One's own—what a charm there is in the words! How long it takes boy and man to find out their worth! how fast most of us hold on to them! faster and more jealously, the nearer we are to that general home into which we can take nothing, but must go naked as we came into the world. When shall we learn that he who multiplieth possessions multiplieth troubles, and that the one [illegible] which [illegible] own is that they [illegible] of them [illegible]

"And shall I have [illegible]" said Tom.

"Yes, of course, [illegible] some fellow on Monday, and you can [illegible]"

"What [illegible] places [illegible]"

"They're [illegible] — that's [illegible] and I make [illegible] fire with [illegible] only that makes it so [illegible]"

"But there's [illegible]" said Tom.

"Precious little [illegible] that though," [illegible] East; "Jones the [illegible] the [illegible] he has rigged up [illegible] the passage [illegible] door open [illegible] of our studies after [illegible] However, he's taken to sit[illegible] bit of fire [illegible] only [illegible] that he don't catch [illegible] when he [illegible] down—that's all."

A quarter [illegible] bell began to ring for dinner, [illegible] took [illegible] places, Tom at the very [illegible] table, [illegible] præpostor ([illegible]) [illegible] a few paces higher [illegible] the first [illegible] his future schoolfellows [illegible] and ruddy [illegible] from hard reading [illegible] the fire at the pastrycook's [illegible] pickles and sauce [illegible] And a great big-bearded [illegible] Tom took [illegible] began calling over [illegible] rapidly carved on a [illegible] and the housekeeper [illegible] while he was all eyes [illegible] man who sat close to [illegible] a fine-looking [illegible] got up and walked [illegible] him, some [illegible] whispers to one another [illegible] shooting pellets, or digging their forks through the tablecloth. However, notwithstanding his curiosity, he managed to make a capital dinner by the time the big man called "Stand up!" and said grace.

As soon as dinner was over, and Tom had been questioned by such of his neighbours as were curious as to his birth, parentage, education, and other like matters, East, who evidently enjoyed his new dignity of patron and Mentor, proposed

The East gate of the Close.

having a look at the close, which Tom, athirst for knowledge, gladly assented to, and they went out through the quadrangle and past the big fives' court, into the great playground.

"That's the chapel, you see," said East, "and there just behind it is the place for fights; you see it's most out of the way of the masters, who all live on the other side and don't come by here after first lesson or callings-over. That's when the fights come off. And all this part where we are is the little-side ground, right up to the trees, and on the other side of

[illegible]

[illegible]

of the School at football. And we all wear white trousers, to show 'em we don't care for hacks. You're in luck to come to-day. You just will see a match; and Brooke's going to let me play in quarters. That's more than he'll do for any other lower-school boy, except James, and he's fourteen."

"Who's Brooke?"

"Why, that big fellow who called over at dinner, to be sure. He's cock of the school, and head of the School-house side, and the best kick and charger in Rugby."

The Island.

"Oh, but do show me where they play. And tell me about it. I love football so, and have played all my life. Won't Brooke let me play?"

"Not he," said East, with some indignation: "why, you don't know the rules—you'll be a month learning them. And then it's no joke playing-up in a match, I can tell you. Quite another thing from your private school games. Why, there's been two collar-bones broken this half, and a dozen fellows lamed. And last year a fellow had his leg broken."

Tom listened with the profoundest respect to this chapter of [illegible]dicants, [illegible] followed [illegible] o[illegible] le[illegible] level ground [illegible] came to a [illegible] ga[illegible] lows[illegible] two [illegible] poles [illegible] high, fixed [illegible] n[illegible] fourteen [illegible] apar[illegible] with a cross [illegible] one[illegible] ha[illegible] other at the height [illegible] ten feet or [illegible]

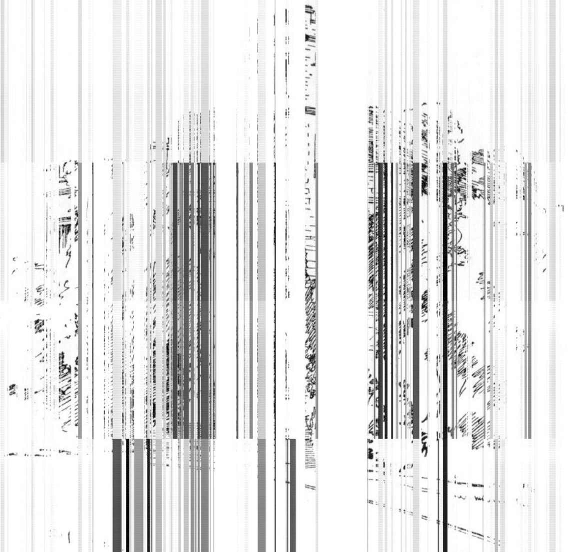

[illegible]

"This is [illegible] ai[illegible] and yo[illegible] other, across [illegible] ste[illegible] the Doc[illegible] wil[illegible] Well, the match [illegible] goals [illegible] which [illegible] kicks two goals [illegible] t [illegible] you see, just [illegible] the ball through these p[illegible] nu[illegible] over the cross ba[illegible] any height'll [illegible] be[illegible]en the posts. [illegible] have to stay in goal to touch the ball when it rolls behind the posts, because if the other side touch it they have a try at goal. Then we fellows in quarters, we play just about in front of goal here, and have to turn the ball and kick it back before the big fellows on the other side can follow it up. And in front of us all the big fellows play, and that's were the scrummages are mostly."

Tom's respect increased as he struggled to make out his friend's technicalities, and the other set to work to explain the mysteries of "off your side," "drop-kicks," "punts," "places," and the other intricacies of the great science of football.

"But how do you keep the ball between the goals?" said he; "I can't see why it mightn't go right down to the chapel."

"Why, that's out of play," answered East. "You see this gravel-walk running down all along this side of the playing-ground, and the line of elms opposite on the other? Well, they're the bounds. As soon as the ball gets past them, it's in touch, and out of play. And then whoever first touches it has to knock it straight out amongst the players-up, who make two lines with a space between them, every fellow going on his own side. Ain't there just fine scrummages then! and the three trees you see there which come out into the play, that's a tremendous place when the ball hangs there, for you get thrown against the trees, and that's worse than any hack."

Tom wondered within himself as they strolled back again towards the fives' court, whether the matches were really such break-neck affairs as East represented, and whether, if they were, he should ever get to like them and play-up well.

He hadn't long to wonder, however, for next minute East cried out, "Hurra! here's the punt-about,—come along and try your hand at a kick." The punt-about is the practice-ball, which is just brought out and kicked about anyhow from one boy to another before callings-over and dinner, and at other odd times. They joined the boys who had brought it out, all small School-house fellows, friends of East; and Tom had the pleasure of trying his skill, and performed very creditably, after first driving his foot three inches into the ground, and then nearly kicking his leg into the air, in vigorous efforts to accomplish a drop-kick after the manner of East.

Presently more boys and bigger came out, and boys from other houses on their way to calling-over, and more balls were

lower school boys employ the ten minutes which elapse before their names are called in pelting one another vigorously with acorns, which fly about in all directions. The small præpostors dash in every now and then, and generally chastise some quiet, timid boy who is equally afraid of acorns and canes, while the principal performers get dexterously out of the way; and so calling-over rolls on somehow, much like the big world, punishments lighting on wrong shoulders, and matters going generally in a queer cross-grained way, but the end coming somehow, which is after all the great point. And now the master of the week has finished, and locked up the big school; and the præpostors of the week come out, sweeping the last remnant of the school fags—who had been loafing about the corners by the fives' court, in hopes of a chance of bolting—before them into the close.

"Hold the punt-about!" "To the goals!" are the cries, and all stray balls are impounded by the authorities; and the whole mass of boys moves up towards the two goals, dividing as they go into three bodies. That little band on the left, consisting of from fifteen to twenty boys, Tom amongst them, who are making for the goal under the School-house wall, are the School-house boys who are not to play-up, and have to stay in goal. The larger body moving to the island goal, are the School boys in a like predicament. The great mass in the middle are the players-up, both sides mingled together; they are hanging their jackets, and all who mean real work, their hats, waistcoats, neck-handkerchiefs, and braces, on the railings round the small trees; and there they go by twos and threes up to their respective grounds. There is none of the colour and tastiness of get-up, you will perceive, which lends such a life to the present game at Rugby, making the dullest and worst fought match a pretty sight. Now each house has its own uniform of cap and jersey, of some lively colour: but at the time we are speaking of, plush caps have not yet come in, or uniforms of any sort except the School-house white trousers, which are abominably cold to-day: let us get to work, bare-headed, and girded with our plain leather straps—but we mean business, gentlemen.

And now that the two sides have fairly sundered, and each occupies its own ground, and we get a good look at them, what absurdity is this? You don't mean to say that those

fifty or sixty [illegible] it[illegible] users, many of them [illegible]
are going [illegible] s oppos[illegible] I[illegible]
gen[illegible] ng [illegible] any ra[illegible] and [illegible]
suc[illegible] it[illegible] words fo[illegible]
Bro[illegible] wit[illegible] halfpen[illegible] an[illegible]
of [illegible] you [illegible]
qui[illegible] n[illegible] towards t[illegible]
isla[illegible] goal [illegible] it will be [illegible] it[illegible]
Us[illegible] hit [illegible] m[illegible] how the Schoo[illegible]-h[illegible]
dri[illegible] You [illegible] part, that the six[illegible]
wh[illegible] the [illegible] spend his fore[illegible]
kee[illegible]s) so [illegible] while [illegible] th[illegible]
at distances [illegible] iv[illegible] apart; [illegible] safe a[illegible]
goa[illegible] the [illegible] f[illegible] play. Old Broo[illegible]
to [illegible] capt[illegible] t[illegible] and now he [illegible]es
ho[illegible] hit yo[illegible] re[illegible] his men the light b[illegible]
full[illegible] over the [illegible] a[illegible] between their own g[illegible]
bo[illegible] of thei[illegible] y[illegible] the heavy [illegible] ga[illegible]
aga[illegible] play [illegible] bo[illegible] There is young Broo[illegible]
bu[illegible]ngs—[illegible] w[illegible] they are the fighti[illegible]
the [illegible]-hand [illegible] leap-frog to keep [illegible]
wa[illegible] and [illegible] k[illegible] the another, and [illegible]
of [illegible] Brooke [illegible] ow[illegible] in the middle [illegible]
and [illegible] going [illegible] fi[illegible] separate wing[illegible]
up [illegible] with [illegible] o[illegible] ledged prowess to lo[illegible]
Wa[illegible] and [illegible] ge[illegible] over all is old Broo[illegible]
as [illegible] Br[illegible] se[illegible] ruling over [illegible]
wor[illegible]ping [illegible] tr[illegible] ball king. His fa[illegible]
and careful [illegible] s[illegible] over his tray [illegible]
plu[illegible] and ho[illegible] t[illegible] I hope to see in[illegible]
whe[illegible] I go o[illegible].

The Scho[illegible] gu[illegible]sed in the game [illegible]
goal-keepers [illegible] u[illegible] how and [illegible]-how[illegible]
dist[illegible]guish [illegible] p[illegible] and the boys [illegible]
and there is [illegible] le[illegible] but with such odds [illegible]
and [illegible]ght [illegible] e[illegible] that to hinder [illegible]
win[illegible]g [illegible] e[illegible] seem to think [illegible]or [illegible]
pla[illegible]-up [illegible] s[illegible]

[illegible] now [illegible] s[illegible] rows forward of [illegible]
hou[illegible]wing [illegible] you ready?" and [illegible]
tive [illegible]ply. [illegible] e[illegible] half-dozen quick [illegible]

away goes the ball spinning towards the School goal,—seventy yards before it touches ground, and at no point above twelve or fifteen feet high, a model kick-off; and the School-house cheer and rush on; the ball is returned, and they meet it and drive it back amongst the masses of the School already in motion. Then the two sides close, and you can see nothing for minutes but a swaying crowd of boys, at one point violently agitated. That is where the ball is, and there are the keen players to be met, and the glory and the hard knocks to be got: you hear the dull thud, thud of the ball, and the shouts of, "Off your side," "Down with him," "Put him over," "Bravo." This is what we call a scrummage, gentlemen, and the first scrummage in a School-house match was no joke in the consulship of Plancus.

But see! it has broken; the ball is driven out on the School-house side, and a rush of the School carries it past the School-house players-up. "Look out in quarters," Brooke's and twenty other voices ring out; no need to call though: the School-house captain of quarters has caught it on the bound, dodges the foremost School boys, who are heading the rush, and sends it back with a good drop-kick well into the enemy's country. And then follows rush upon rush, and scrummage upon scrummage, the ball now driven through into the School-house quarters, and now into the School goal; for the School-house have not lost the advantage which the kick-off and a slight wind gave them at the outset, and are slightly "penning" their adversaries. You say, you don't see much in it all; nothing but a struggling mass of boys and a leather ball which seems to excite them all to great fury, as a red rag does a bull. My dear sir, a battle would look much the same to you, except that the boys would be men, and the balls iron; but a battle would be worth your looking at for all that, and so is a football match. You can't be expected to appreciate the delicate strokes of play, the turns by which a game is lost and won,—it takes an old player to do that, but the broad philosophy of football you can understand if you will. Come along with me a little nearer, and let us consider it together.

The ball has just fallen again where the two sides are thickest, and they close rapidly around it in a scrummage; it must be driven through now by force or skill, till it flies out on one side of the [illegible] how differently [illegible] it! [illegible] outsiders [illegible] straight [illegible] the heart of the [illegible] bent on driving the ball [illegible] on the opposite side. [illegible] what they mean to [illegible] my sons! you [illegible] you [illegible] through the [illegible] and [illegible] own side, before you can [illegible] young Brooke, [illegible] head, and [illegible] ball, [illegible] a leaf [illegible] Speedicut, and [illegible] and great [illegible] after [illegible] wasn't that [illegible] But [illegible] drive that [illegible] the [illegible] what [illegible] sidney [illegible] mage [illegible] who keep out of [illegible] had rather [illegible]

Then the boys [illegible] side, [illegible] who [illegible] the chargers [illegible] they [illegible] coolness [illegible] so are [illegible] football.

Three-quarters of [illegible] and weight [illegible] School-house [illegible] ground. [illegible] shoulder [illegible] knack [illegible] penned in [illegible] under the [illegible] are the [illegible]

[illegible] further use. [illegible] himself [illegible] young chargers, [illegible] school-house bully [illegible] [illegible] by the [illegible] [illegible] don't [illegible] mage, changing all [illegible] to make [illegible] [illegible] and [illegible] players, [illegible] [illegible] first [illegible] Brooke [illegible] The School-house [illegible] the ball is behind [illegible] [illegible] anxious as [illegible] success of the School-house. We get a minute's breathing time before old Brooke kicks out, and he gives the word to play strongly for touch, by the three trees. Away goes the ball, and the bull-dogs after it, and in another minute there is shout of "In touch!" "Our ball!" Now's your time, old Brooke, while your men are still fresh. He stands with the ball in his hand, while the two sides form in deep lines opposite one another; he must strike it straight out between them. The lines are thickest close to him, but young Brooke and two or three of his men are shifting up further, where the opposite line is weak. Old Brooke strikes it out straight and strong, and it falls opposite his brother. Hurra! that rush has taken it right through the School line, and away past the three trees, far into their quarters, and young Brooke and the bull-dogs are close upon it. The School leaders rush back, shouting "Look out in goal," and strain every nerve to catch him, but they are after the fleetest foot in Rugby. There they go straight for the School goal-posts, quarters scattering before them. One after another the bull-dogs go down, but young Brooke holds on. "He is down." No! a long stagger, but the danger is past; that was the shock of Crew, the most dangerous of dodgers. And now he is close to the School goal, the ball not three yards before him. There is a hurried rush of the School fags to the spot, but no one throws himself on the ball, the only chance, and young Brooke has touched it right under the School goal-posts.

The School leaders come up furious, and administer toco to the wretched fags nearest at hand; they may well be angry, for it is all Lombard-street to a china orange that the School-house kick a goal with the ball touched in such a good place. Old Brooke of course will kick it out, but who shall catch and place it? Call Crab Jones. Here he comes, sauntering along with a straw in his mouth, the queerest, coolest fish in Rugby; if he were tumbled into the moon this minute, he would just pick himself up without taking his hands out of his pockets or turning a hair. But it is a moment when the boldest charger's heart beats quick. Old Brooke stands with the ball under his arm motioning the School back; he will not kick-out till they are all in goal, behind the posts; they are all edging forwards, inch by inch, to get nearer for the rush at Crab Jones, who stands there in front of old Brooke to catch the

East is hurled forward . . . and plunges on his shoulder.

a[illegible]ch in the si[illegible] and [illegible] play; that's what [illegible] of those bo[illegible].

[illegible]t now [illegible] the ball is placed [illegible] midway, and [illegible] to kick off. [illegible] rs have sent [illegible] and [illegible] rated the rest [illegible] ll, and one [illegible] red [illegible] ed players up are [illegible] bent on ret[illegible] ing [illegible] are to keep the [illegible] n front of the school [illegible] a[illegible] hen to drive [illegible] in [illegible] e[illegible] strength and weight [illegible] heavy play and no [illegible] ke, and so o[illegible] es that [illegible] one in [illegible] ers just before [illegible] re picked players, [illegible] ur[illegible] to keep the ball [illegible] here a try at goal, [illegible] a[illegible] ed, will b[illegible] es[illegible] dang[illegible] ont. He him[illegible] elf, [illegible] W[illegible] ner and [illegible] lge, who [illegible] mselves till now, [illegible] ead the charge.

[illegible] ar[illegible] you read[illegible] comes [illegible] he [illegible] [illegible] d high in the [illegible] e to rush or [illegible] [illegible] it fal[illegible]. And [illegible] mongst us. [illegible] [illegible] The English [illegible] boys, and charge [illegible] home. Now [illegible] the tim[illegible] mettle is in yo[illegible] [illegible] here shall be [illegible] warm [illegible] fire and honour, [illegible] ot of battle [illegible] does his duty in [illegible] ext half-hour. And [illegible] Again and again [illegible] [illegible] of the[illegible] our goal, and [illegible] s threatening [illegible] dge with young [illegible] te and the[illegible] through and carry [illegible] back; an[illegible] d like Jove's war- [illegible] the thickest [illegible] before his rush, [illegible] he waves before [illegible] heavy voice rings [illegible] the field, and [illegible] And if these miss [illegible] and it rolls [illegible] of our goal, [illegible] and his men [illegible] it away towards [illegible] d[illegible] with the [illegible] is worth living [illegible] the whole sum of [illegible] gathered up into [illegible] truggling, strug[illegible] worth a year of [illegible] on life.

[illegible] e quarter to [illegible] y slackers [illegible] a [illegible] e before go[illegible] the artful dodger [illegible] g the ball in [illegible] land side where [illegible] unters are [illegible] e to meet him? [illegible] look at little [illegible] equal distances between the two, and they rush together, the young man of seventeen and the boy of twelve, and kick it at the same moment. Crew passes on without a stagger; East is hurled forward by the shock, and plunges on his shoulder, as if he would bury himself in the ground; but the ball rises straight into the air, and falls behind Crew's back, while the "bravos" of the School-house attest the pluckiest charge of all that hard-fought day. Warner picks East up lame and half stunned,

School from the Close.

and he hobbles back into goal, conscious of having played the man.

And now the last minutes are come, and the School gather for their last rush, every boy of the hundred and twenty who has a run left in him. Reckless of the defence of their own goal, on they come across the level big-side ground, the ball well down amongst them, straight for our goal, like the column of the Old Guard up the slope at Waterloo. All former charges have been child's play to this. Warner and Hedge have met them, but still on they come. The bull-dogs rush in for the last time; they are hurled over or carried back, striving hand, foot, and eyelids. Old Brooke comes sweeping round [illegible] the play, and turning [illegible] ks out the [illegible] f the scrummage [illegible] avers for a [illegible] e has the ball [illegible] m, and his [illegible] out clear over the adv[illegible] e, look out in [illegible] b Jones catches [illegible]; before he [illegible] e rush [illegible] upon [illegible] m and he [illegible] lf up behind them with [illegible] s mouth, a [illegible] but as cool as ever.

[illegible] rolls slowly in behind [illegible] se goal not [illegible] in front of a dozen of the [illegible] players up. [illegible] ands the School-house [illegible] r, [illegible] st of goal- [illegible] l Tom Brown by his [illegible] earned his [illegible] s time. Now [illegible] e blood of [illegible] ns is up, and the [illegible] and throw [illegible] on the ball, under the [illegible] f advancing [illegible] e praepostor of [illegible] rching his [illegible] om all along [illegible] topple the [illegible] he rush shooting over [illegible] praepostor, [illegible] at on Tom, and knocking [illegible] out of his [illegible] e. 'Our ball' says the [illegible] r, [illegible] ng with his [illegible] get up there, there's [illegible] under you." [illegible] uled an [illegible] discovered a [illegible] ody.

[illegible] e picks him up. "[illegible] m air," he [illegible] hen feeling his limbs, [illegible] es broken. [illegible] feel, young un?"

[illegible]," gasps Tom, as his [illegible] k, "pretty [illegible] ou—all right."

[illegible] he?" says Brooke. "[illegible] he's a new [illegible]"

[illegible] him," says East, coming [illegible]

[illegible] is a plucky youngster, [illegible] a player,"

[illegible] 'clock strikes. [illegible] d the first [illegible] chool-house match is over.

CHAPTER VI

AFTER THE MATCH

"———Some food we had."—SHAKESPEARE.

ἦς πότος ἁδύς.—THEOCR. *Id.*

As the boys scattered away from the ground, and East, leaning on Tom's arm, and limping along, was beginning to consider what luxury they should go and buy for tea to celebrate that glorious victory, the two Brookes came striding by. Old Brooke caught sight of East, and stopped; put his hand kindly on his shoulder and said, "Bravo, youngster, you played famously; not much the matter, I hope?"

"No, nothing at all," said East, "only a little twist from that charge."

"Well, mind and get all right for next Saturday"; and the leader passed on, leaving East better for those few words than all the opodeldoc in England would have made him, and Tom ready to give one of his ears for as much notice. Ah! light words of those whom we love and honour, what a power ye are, and how carelessly wielded by those who can use you! Surely for these things also God will ask an account.

"Tea's directly after locking-up, you see," said East, hobbling along as fast as he could, "so you come along down to Sally Harrowell's; that's our School-house tuck-shop—she bakes such stunning murphies, we'll have a penn'orth each for tea; come along or they'll all be gone."

Tom's new purse and money burnt in his pocket; he wondered, as they toddled through the quadrangle and along the street, whether East would be insulted if he suggested further extravagance, as he had not sufficient faith in a pennyworth of potatoes. At last he blurted out,—

The hind carrier of a sedan-chair, the last of its race.

... get to grass. ... ike you ... &c., ... to ma ... d in the ... cleared off ... unning ... Sally" ... s," &c. ... he did, ...

... served ... as the ... ting the life ... Amongst his ... of a se ... ies still ... nessed a ... mischievous ... was too ... pursue ... when re ... r with.

... s of the School-house, ... lower- ... r or head- ... ead and ... l there was ... er luxu ... ething of ... could li ... great ... duced a ... he sausages, ... potatoes; ... d they'l ... toast ... four mo ... sausag ... atter cracked ... at they were ... festive cup ...

emptied, and Tom imparted of the sausages in small bits to many neighbours, and thought he had never tasted such good potatoes or seen such jolly boys. They on their part waived all ceremony, and pegged away at the sausages and potatoes, and remembering Tom's performance in goal, voted East's new crony a brick. After tea, and while the things were being cleared away, they gathered round the fire, and the talk on the match still went on; and those who had them to show

The Lower Fifth School.

pulled up their trousers and showed the hacks they had received in the good cause.

They were soon, however, all turned out of the school, and East conducted Tom up to his bedroom, that he might get on clean things and wash himself before singing.

"What's singing?" said Tom, taking his head out of his basin, where he had been plunging it in cold water.

"Well, you are jolly green," answered his friend from a neighbouring basin. "Why, the last six Saturdays of every half [illegible] this is the first [illegible] lesson [illegible] lie in bed to-mo[illegible]

"[illegible]

"[illegible] urse; you'll se[illegible] begin [illegible] and sing till be[illegible] goo[illegible] he summer ha[illegible] in th[illegible] under the library [illegible] ta[illegible] big boys sit ro[illegible] do[illegible] rday nights; [illegible] qu[illegible] gs, and it look[illegible] in [illegible] come and pou[illegible] a[illegible] n, and shout at [illegible] h[illegible] l. Come alo[illegible]

Th[illegible] nent in the study [illegible] East's [illegible] he drawers and [illegible] table [illegible] the bottom [illegible] was in [illegible] inging.

Su[illegible] rse at seven o'clock, [illegible] of bread [illegible], which was al[illegible] ing; [illegible] the fags went to work [illegible] the h[illegible] e hall, as has bee[illegible] long [illegible] rge fires on one si[illegible] iron-[illegible] ing down the mid[illegible] along [illegible] fire-places. Arou[illegible] the f[illegible] in the form of [illegible] upon [illegible] Saturday nigh[illegible] Then [illegible] drop in and take th[illegible] with [illegible] song-books; [illegible] knew [illegible] was the thing to h[illegible] script [illegible] some departed h[illegible] were [illegible] t.

The [illegible] d not yet appear[illegible] the g[illegible] time-honoured [illegible] throu[illegible] as placed on the [illegible] made [illegible] the penalty of [illegible] mug [illegible] esisted or broke [illegible] the n[illegible] nightingales [illegible] water [illegible] Tom, as his [illegible] old w[illegible] The Leather Bott[illegible] able [illegible] half-hour do[illegible] and f[illegible] e their places at [illegible] are filled up by the next biggest boys, the rest, for whom there is no room at the table, standing round outside.

The glasses and mugs are filled, and then the fugleman strikes up the old sea song—

> "A wet sheet and a flowing sea,
> And a wind that follows fast," &c.

which is the invariable first song in the School-house, and all the seventy voices join in, not mindful of harmony, but bent on noise, which they attain decidedly, but the general effect isn't bad. And then follow "The British Grenadiers," "Billy Taylor," "The Siege of Seringapatam," "Three Jolly Post-boys," and other vociferous songs in rapid succession, including "The Chesapeake and Shannon," a song lately introduced in honour of old Brooke; and when they come to the words—

> "Brave Broke he waved his sword, crying, Now my lads, aboard,
> And we'll stop their playing Yankee-doodle-dandy oh!"

you expect the roof to come down. The sixth and fifth know that "brave Broke" of the Shannon was no sort of relation to our old Brooke. The fourth form are uncertain in their belief, but for the most part hold that old Brooke *was* a midshipman then on board his uncle's ship. And the lower school never doubt for a moment that it was our old Brooke who led the boarders, in what capacity they care not a straw. During the pauses the bottled-beer corks fly rapidly, and the talk is fast and merry, and the big boys, at least all of them who have a fellow-feeling for dry throats, hand their mugs over their shoulders to be emptied by the small ones who stand round behind.

Then Warner, the head of the house, gets up and wants to speak, but he can't, for every boy knows what's coming; and the big boys who sit at the tables pound them and cheer; and the small boys who stand behind pound one another, and cheer, and rush about the hall cheering. Then silence being made, Warner reminds them of the old School-house custom of drinking the healths, on the first night of singing, of those who are going to leave at the end of the half. "He sees that they know what he is going to say already—(loud cheers)—and so won't keep them, but only ask them to treat the toast as it deserves. It is the head

of the [illegible] of big-side football [illegible]
on this [illegible]—[illegible]er Brooke!"

And [illegible]ding and cheering [illegible]
deafening [illegible] [illegible]ke gets on his legs [illegible]
having [illegible] a gallon or so of [illegible]
and [illegible]y, silence ensues, [illegible]
speaks, [illegible] on the table, and [illegible]
forwards [illegible] tricks of oratory [illegible]
and [illegible]

"Gentle[illegible] [illegible]chool-house! I am [illegible]
the way [illegible] [illegible]ve received my [illegible]
I could [illegible] [illegible]e in return. But I [illegible]
However, [illegible] I can to say what [illegible]
ought to [illegible] [illegible]ow who's just going [illegible]
who has [illegible] of his life here. [illegible]
and eight [illegible] I can never hope [illegible]
So now [illegible] [illegible]isten to me—(loud [illegible]
we will [illegible] to talk seriously [illegible]
to listen [illegible]'s the use of call[illegible]
and all [illegible] mind what I say [illegible]
going to [illegible]cause I feel so. [illegible]
too, getting [illegible]the half, and a goa[illegible]
first day [illegible]lause)—after one of [illegible]
fiercest [illegible] remember in eight [illegible]
shouting[illegible] [illegible]played splendidly, [illegible]
and kep[illegible] That last charge [illegible]
have [illegible] I never thought [illegible]
again [illegible] [illegible]xcept little pieces, [illegible]
tumbled [illegible]aughter and shouting, [illegible]
slipping [illegible] Jones by the boys [illegible]
Well [illegible] [illegible]cheers). Ay, but [illegible]
'em [illegible]—(shouts of 'your [illegible]
sense [illegible] and kick-off either [illegible]
do [illegible] we've half-a-dozen [illegible]
players in [illegible] have. I wouldn't [illegible]
and Hedge[illegible] [illegible]d the young un[illegible]
their side [illegible]s). But half-a-doz[illegible]
keep [illegible] against two hundred. [illegible]
then? [illegible] I think. It's because [illegible]
reliance [illegible]ore of a house feeling [illegible]
ship tha[illegible] [illegible]ol [illegible] have. Each of us [illegible]

depend on his next-hand man better—that's why we beat 'em to-day. We've union, they've division—there's the secret—(cheers). But how's this to be kept up? How's it to be improved? That's the question. For I take it we're all in earnest about beating the School, whatever else we care about. I know I'd sooner win two School-house matches running than get the Balliol scholarship any day—(frantic cheers).

"Now, I'm as proud of the house as any one. I believe it's the best house in the school, out-and-out—(cheers). But it's a long way from what I want to see it. First, there's a deal of bullying going on. I know it well. I don't pry about and interfere, that only makes it more underhand, and encourages the small boys to come to us with their fingers in their eyes telling tales, and so we should be worse off than ever. It's very little kindness for the sixth to meddle generally—you youngsters, mind that. You'll be all the better football players for learning to stand it, and to take your own parts, and fight it through. But depend on it, there's nothing breaks up a house like bullying. Bullies are cowards, and one coward makes many; so good-bye to the School-house match if bullying gets ahead here. (Loud applause from the small boys, who look meaningly at Flashman and other boys at the tables.) Then there's fuddling about in the public-house, and drinking bad spirits, and punch, and such rot-gut stuff. That won't make good drop-kicks or chargers of you, take my word for it. You get plenty of good beer here, and that's enough for you; and drinking isn't fine or manly, whatever some of you may think of it.

"One other thing I must have a word about. A lot of you think and say, for I've heard you, 'There's this new Doctor hasn't been here so long as some of us, and he's changing all the old customs. Rugby, and the School-house especially, are going to the dogs. Stand up for the good old ways, and down with the Doctor!' Now I'm as fond of old Rugby customs and ways as any of you, and I've been here longer than any of you, and I'll give you a word of advice in time, for I shouldn't like to see any of you getting sacked. 'Down with the Doctor's' easier said than done. You'll find him pretty tight on his perch, I take it, and an awkwar[illegible] to handle in tha[illegible] Be[illegible]s, now, what[illegible] to [illegible] as [illegible] put down? There [illegible] old custom [illegible] the linchpins out [illegible] far[illegible]s' and bagmen[illegible] the fairs, and a coward[illegible] custom it wa[illegible] w what came of it [illegible] w[illegible]er the Doctor obj[illegible]t. But come n[illegible] of [illegible]u, name a cu[illegible] as put down."

"The h[illegible]ds," [illegible] a fifth-form boy [illegible] cutaway wi[illegible] and cord trouse[illegible] of the sporting [illegible] puted a great rider [illegible] generally.

"Well, [illegible] even mangy harri[illegible] b[illegible]es belonging [illegible] 'll allow, and ha[illegible] years and [illegible] put them down. [illegible] ever came [illegible] nly rows with al[illegible] ten miles [illegible] side Hare and [illegible] fun [illegible] else?"

No ans[illegible]

"Well, [illegible] Think it ove[illegible] you'll find, [illegible] he don't medd[illegible] that's worth [illegible] d mind now, I sa[illegible] for squalls [illegible] your own way, [illegible] the Doctor [illegible] to grief. You [illegible] not he [illegible] aster through [illegible] I I saw hi[illegible] ball, or cricket [illegible] sparring, [illegible] s any fellow to [illegible] But he [illegible] rages them; di[illegible] out to-day fo[illegible] our watching [illegible] for the D[illegible] a strong, true [illegible] one too, [illegible] hool man too [illegible] let's stick [illegible] no more ro[illegible] as the he[illegible] e—(loud cheers). [illegible] done blow[illegible] y glad I am to [illegible] it's a solem[illegible] inking of leaving [illegible] has lived [illegible] r eight years; and [illegible] word for [illegible] old house at su[illegible] should be [illegible] bitter or sweet. I [illegible] proud of [illegible] u—ay, no one kn[illegible] I shouldn't [illegible] up. And now [illegible] But before [illegible] st give you a toast [illegible] three-times [illegible] the honours. It's [illegible] hope every one of us, wherever he may go hereafter, will never fail to drink when he thinks of the brave bright days of his boyhood. It's a toast which should bind us all together, and to those who've gone before and who'll come after us here. It is the dear old School-house—the best house of the best school in England!"

My dear boys, old and young, you who have belonged, or do belong, to other schools and other houses, don't

The Doctor's House.

begin throwing my poor little book about the room, and abusing me and it, and vowing you'll read no more when you get to this point. I allow you've provocation for it. But come now—would you, any of you, give a fig for a fellow who didn't believe in, and stand up for, his own house and his own school? You know you wouldn't. Then don't object to my cracking up the old School-house, Rugby. Haven't I a right to do it, when I'm taking all the trouble of

...for all of your ...
...te the history of your ...
...ay all you know of your ...
...ue, and I'll read ...

...e audience in...
...ther enthusias...
..."the best house of ...
...h for them al...
...erests off their...
...pped) resolut...
...ke's words: ...
...appear hereaf...
...Brooke's popularity...
...cially that re...
...oted holders...
...ver so foolis...
...as the school...
...every boy who...
...verence when he...
...his way to or...
...e boy who ...
...expounded wh...
...nough stuff to...

...trumpery little...
...e School as ...
...ians, and rega...
...rt of sacrileg...
...had a stronger...
...and sensible...
...most decided...
...one nor the ...
...e came into co...
...g for them b...
...hat he said ha...
...was beginning...
...that there w...
...ings his own ...
...e and loving ...
...nce had not h...

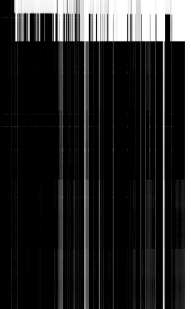

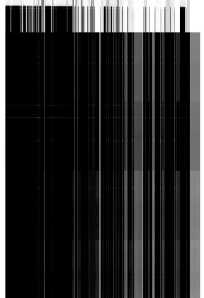

felt, except by a very few of the bigger boys with whom he came more directly into contact; and he was looked upon with great fear and dislike by the great majority even of his own house. For he had found School, and School-house, in a state of monstrous licence and misrule, and was still employed in the necessary but unpopular work of setting up order with a strong hand.

However, as has been said, old Brooke triumphed, and the boys cheered him and then the Doctor. And then more songs came, and the healths of the other boys about to leave, who each made a speech, one flowery, another maudlin, a third prosy, and so on, which are not necessary to be here recorded.

Half-past nine struck in the middle of the performance of "Auld Lang Syne," a most obstreperous proceeding; during which there was an immense amount of standing with one foot on the table, knocking mugs together and shaking hands, without which accompaniments it seems impossible for the youth of Britain to take part in that famous old song. The under-porter of the School-house entered during the performance, bearing five or six long wooden candle-sticks, with lighted dips in them, which he proceeded to stick into their holes in such part of the great tables as he could get at; and then stood outside the ring till the end of the song, when he was hailed with shouts.

"Bill, you old muff, the half-hour hasn't struck." "Here, Bill, drink some cocktail." "Sing us a song, old boy." "Don't you wish you may get the table?" Bill drank the proffered cocktail not unwillingly, and putting down the empty glass, remonstrated, "Now, gentlemen, there's only ten minutes to prayers, and we must get the hall straight."

Shouts of "No, no!" and a violent effort to strike up "Billy Taylor" for the third time. Bill looked appealingly to old Brooke, who got up and stopped the noise. "Now then, lend a hand, you youngsters, and get the tables back, clear away the jugs and glasses. Bill's right. Open the windows, Warner." The boy addressed, who sat by the long ropes, proceeded to pull up the great windows, and let in a clear fresh rush of night air, which made the candles flicker and gutter and the fires roar. The circle broke up, each collaring his own jug, glass, and song-book; Bill pounced on the big table,

and [illegible] e [illegible] way to its p [illegible]
doo [illegible] -p [illegible] e boys carri [illegible]
[illegible] er [illegible] while above [illegible]
[illegible] c [illegible] ating [illegible] ons [illegible]
[illegible] ng [illegible] performance [illegible] ng
[illegible] g [illegible] liam IV [illegible] s,
[illegible] ly [illegible] pular amongs [illegible] d t
[illegible] h [illegible] as chiefly kn [illegible] n
of [illegible] f [illegible] tly vulgar, so [illegible]
delighted [illegible]

> [illegible] n [illegible] ours all both g [illegible]
> [illegible] m [illegible] duties here [illegible]
> [illegible] ng 'Live Billy [illegible],'
> [illegible] ti [illegible] tax upon beer.

Others [illegible] e [illegible] ed in songs a [illegible]
[illegible], [illegible] I take to have been [illegible]
[illegible] v [illegible] gotten all but [illegible]

> "God [illegible] l [illegible] William, be his [illegible]
> [illegible] a [illegible] people, and the [illegible],

In [illegible] l [illegible] subjects in [illegible]
way. [illegible] o [illegible] ccessors mak [illegible]
Majesty, [illegible] in [illegible] gard to the g [illegible]
[illegible] d [illegible] ritten other [illegible]
more [illegible] e [illegible] our.

[illegible] er [illegible] ten struck, a [illegible]
The [illegible] th [illegible] m boys rang [illegible]
school [illegible]; [illegible] wall, on eithe [illegible]
the [illegible] d [illegible] per-school bo [illegible]
in the [illegible] t [illegible] all, and the [illegible]
the upper [illegible] h [illegible] ond long tab [illegible]
side [illegible] u [illegible] from the f [illegible]
himself [illegible] o [illegible] all, in a state [illegible]
at a [illegible], [illegible] thought an [illegible]
himself [illegible] c [illegible] n't, for the lif [illegible]
rap [illegible] h [illegible] ruses of som [illegible]
a [illegible] o [illegible] wondering a [illegible]
wai [illegible] e [illegible] ing what so [illegible]
The [illegible] e [illegible] orter are hea [illegible]
lig [illegible] h [illegible] or. "Hush [illegible]
boys [illegible] h [illegible] and then in [illegible]

on head, book in one hand, and gathering up his gown in the other. He walks up the middle, and takes his post by Warner, who begins calling over the names. The Doctor takes no notice of anything, but quietly turns over his book and finds the place, and then stands, cap in hand and finger in book, looking straight before his nose. He knows better than any one when to look, and when to see nothing; to-night is singing night, and there's been lots of noise and no harm done; nothing but beer drunk, and nobody the worse for it; though some of them do look hot and excited. So the Doctor sees nothing, but fascinates Tom in a horrible manner as he stands there, and reads out the Psalm, in that deep, ringing, searching voice of his. Prayers are over, and Tom still stares open-mouthed after the Doctor's retiring figure, when he feels a pull at his sleeve, and turning round, sees East.

"I say, were you ever tossed in a blanket?"

"No," said Tom; "why?"

"'Cause there'll be tossing to-night, most likely, before the sixth come up to bed. So if you funk, you just come along and hide, or else they'll catch you and toss you."

"Were you ever tossed? Does it hurt?" inquired Tom.

"Oh yes, bless you, a dozen times," said East, as he hobbled along by Tom's side up stairs. "It don't hurt unless you fall on the floor. But most fellows don't like it."

They stopped at the fireplace in the top passage, where were a crowd of small boys whispering together, and evidently unwilling to go up into the bedrooms. In a minute, however, a study door opened, a sixth-form boy came out, and off they all scuttled up the stairs, and then noiselessly dispersed to their different rooms. Tom's heart beat rather quick as he and East reached their room, but he had made up his mind. "I sha'n't hide, East," said he.

"Very well, old fellow," replied East, evidently pleased; "no more shall I—they'll be here for us directly."

The room was a great big one with a dozen beds in it, but not a boy that Tom could see, except East and himself. East pulled off his coat and waistcoat, and then sat on the bottom of his bed whistling and pulling off his boots; Tom followed his example.

A noise and steps are heard in the passage, the door opens, and in rush four or five great fifth-form boys, headed by Flashman in his glory.

[illegible] has [illegible]pt in the f[illegible]n, [illegible] se[illegible]t first.

[illegible] eh?" roared [illegible] the [illegible] er the beds [illegible] one nearest h[illegible] leg of a sma[illegible]

[illegible] d sung out [illegible] d, one of yo[illegible] e. Hold y[illegible]

[illegible] man, please, [illegible] ything only [illegible] said Flashma[illegible] you, —— yo[illegible]

[illegible] sung out ano[illegible] t old Pater [illegible] y one agains[illegible]

[illegible] oath and a[illegible] er his bed [illegible] d crept along[illegible] of the sixt[illegible]

[illegible] f youngsters [illegible] e's Scud E[illegible] Scud was Ea[illegible] his fleetnes[illegible] if you like, [illegible] er who didn[illegible] ?"

[illegible] wn, you don'[illegible] etting his fee[illegible] , boys," sung [illegible] g Tom and [illegible] all boys, wh[illegible]

[illegible] Scud is," sai[illegible]

[illegible] , too; he mu[illegible]

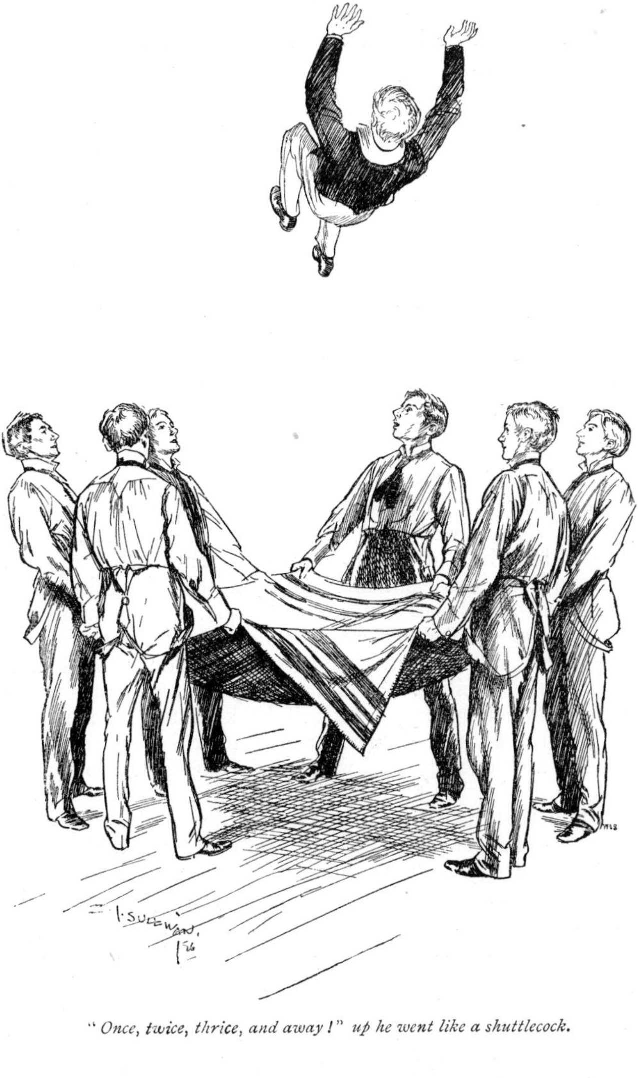

"*Once, twice, thrice, and away!*" *up he went like a shuttlecock.*

hardship of which is, that it's too much for human nature to lie still then and share troubles; and so the wretched pair of small boys struggle in the air which shall fall a-top in the descent, to the no small risk of both falling out of the blanket, and the huge delight of brutes like Flashman.

But now there's a cry that the præpostor of the room is coming; so the tossing stops, and all scatter to their different rooms; and Tom is left to turn in, with the first day's experience of a public school to meditate upon.

[illegible]

C[illegible]PTER [illegible]

[illegible]

[illegible] is m[illegible] I must [illegible] the first [illegible] —*B*[illegible]

Eve[illegible] [illegible] the dream [illegible] half awake, [illegible] begin[illegible] and night [illegible] following upon [illegible] experience[illegible]. There are few [illegible] life. The[illegible] they last [illegible] nurse [illegible] lying [illegible] more than five [illegible] them [illegible] stupid [illegible] which [illegible] our [illegible] back again [illegible] of [illegible]

It was in this state that Master Tom lay at half-past seven on the morning following the day of his arrival, and from his clean little white bed watched the movements of Bogle (the generic name by which the successive shoeblacks of the School-house were known), as he marched round from bed to bed, collecting the dirty shoes and boots, and depositing clean ones in their places.

There he lay, half doubtful as to where exactly in the universe he was, but conscious that he had made a step in life which he had been anxious to make. It was only just light as he looked lazily out of the wide windows, and saw the tops of the great elms, and the rooks circling about, and cawing remonstrances to the lazy ones of their commonwealth before starting in a body for the neighbouring ploughed fields. The noise of the room-door closing behind Bogle, as he made his exit with the shoe-basket under his arm, roused him thoroughly, and he sat up in bed and looked round the room. What in the world could be the matter with his shoulders and loins? He felt as if he had been severely beaten all down his back, the natural results of his performance at his first match. He drew up his knees and rested his chin on them, and went over all the events of yesterday, rejoicing in his new life, what he had seen of it, and all that was to come.

Presently one or two of the other boys roused themselves, and began to sit up and talk to one another in low tones. Then East, after a roll or two, came to an anchor also, and, nodding to Tom, began examining his ankle.

"What a pull," said he, "that it's lie-in-bed, for I shall be as lame as a tree, I think."

It was Sunday morning, and Sunday lectures had not yet been established; so that nothing but breakfast intervened between bed and eleven o'clock chapel—a gap by no means easy to fill up: in fact, though received with the correct amount of grumbling, the first lecture instituted by the Doctor shortly afterwards was a great boon to the School. It was lie-in-bed and no one was in a hurry to get up, especially in rooms where the sixth-form boy was a good-tempered fellow, as was the case in Tom's room, and allowed the small boys to talk and laugh and do pretty much what they pleased, so long as they didn't disturb him. His bed was a bigger one than the rest, standing in the corner by the fireplace, with a washing-stand and

[illegible] where he lay [illegible]
[illegible] form a [illegible]
[illegible] Tom, wh[illegible] sle[illegible]
[illegible] ouse himself [illegible]
[illegible] gin read[illegible]
[illegible] ck to the ro[illegible]
[illegible] arose, and m[illegible]
[illegible] oys, of [illegible]
[illegible] way his [illegible]
[illegible] een and [illegible]
[illegible] black [illegible]
[illegible] loor, a[illegible] were [illegible]
[illegible] ally en[illegible]
[illegible]; and [illegible]w, [illegible]
[illegible] were, [illegible]ch [illegible]
[illegible] he hand, [illegible]nd [illegible]
[illegible] whatever po[illegible]
[illegible]ch.

[illegible] the cor[illegible]r," [illegible]
[illegible] g round [illegible]is [illegible]
[illegible] nk down [illegible]nto [illegible]
[illegible] watch, [illegible]led "[illegible]
[illegible]"

[illegible] as partic[illegible]ar i[illegible]
[illegible] nd in [illegible] to [illegible]
[illegible] n; and [illegible]ter [illegible]
[illegible] ent d[illegible]
[illegible])

[illegible]" answere[illegible] th[illegible]

[illegible] "I'm [illegible]d [illegible]
[illegible] of yo[illegible] ha[illegible]
[illegible] bed, a[illegible]
[illegible] ssage [illegible]ch [illegible]
[illegible] his S[illegible]y [illegible]

[illegible]id Tom [illegible]
[illegible] a goo[illegible] ell[illegible]
[illegible] g and [illegible]e. [illegible]

[illegible] Tadpol[illegible]

started off down stairs, and through "Thos's hole," as the little buttery, where candles and beer and bread and cheese were served out at night, was called, across the School-house court, down a long passage, and into the kitchen; where, after some parley with the stalwart, handsome cook, who declared that she had filled a dozen jugs already, they got their hot water, and returned with all speed and great caution. As it was, they narrowly escaped capture by some privateers from the fifth-form rooms, who were on the look-out for the hot-water convoys, and pursued them up to the very door of their room, making them spill half their load in the passage. "Better than going down again though," as Tadpole remarked, "as we should have had to do if those beggars had caught us."

By the time that the calling-over bell rang, Tom and his new comrades were all down, dressed in their best clothes, and he had the satisfaction of answering "here" to his name for the first time, the præpostor of the week having put it in at the bottom of his list. And then came breakfast, and a saunter about the close and town with East, whose lameness only became severe when any fagging had to be done. And so they whiled away the time until morning chapel.

It was a fine November morning, and the close soon became alive with boys of all ages, who sauntered about on the grass, or walked round the gravel walk, in parties of two or three. East, still doing the cicerone, pointed out all the remarkable characters to Tom as they passed: Osbert, who could throw a cricket-ball from the little-side ground over the rook trees to the Doctor's wall; Gray, who had got the Balliol scholarship, and, what East evidently thought of much more importance, a half-holiday for the School by his success; Thorne, who had run ten miles in two minutes over the hour; Black, who had held his own against the cock of the town in the last row with the louts; and many more heroes, who then and there walked about and were worshipped, all trace of whom has long since vanished from the scene of their fame; and the fourth-form boy who reads their names rudely cut out on the old hall tables, or painted upon the big side-cupboard (if hall tables and big side-cupboards still exist), wonders what manner of boys they were. It will be the same with you who wonder, my sons, whatever your prowess may be in cricket, or scholarship, [illegible] years, more [illegible] wave will pas[illegible] Neverthele[illegible] see only th[illegible] take care of itself.

[illegible] during at a quarter [illegible] his place in [illegible] come in and take their [illegible] construe the Greek [illegible] the slightest [illegible] sisters, who walked [illegible] exalted boxes [illegible] the closing of the [illegible] the service, which [illegible] feeling of wor[illegible] on one side [illegible] filling in front, [illegible] name was, and whether [illegible] the other side [illegible] on the white [illegible] school were serious [illegible] by no means [illegible] again, he didn't [illegible] church.

[illegible] it was quite a [illegible] writing hom[illegible] morning; and [illegible] more th[illegible] young, and [illegible] ing to feel that [illegible] and that great [illegible] that day—the first ser[illegible]

[illegible] mine have [illegible] out by itself [illegible] kindling eye, [illegible] new clear and [illegible] him who stood [illegible] pleading for his [illegible] glory, with [illegible] he spoke. [illegible] faces, rising tier above tier down the whole length of the chapel, from the little boy's who had just left his mother to the young man's who was going out next week into the great world rejoicing in his strength. It was a great and solemn sight, and never more so than at this time of year, when the only lights in the chapel were in the pulpit and at the seats of the præpostors of the week, and the soft twilight stole over the rest of the chapel, deepening into darkness in the high gallery behind the organ.

But what was it after all which seized and held these three hundred boys, dragging them out of themselves, willing or unwilling, for twenty minutes, on Sunday afternoons? True, there always were boys scattered up and down the School, who in heart and head were worthy to hear and able to carry away the deepest and wisest words there spoken. But these were a minority always, generally a very small one, often so small a one as to be countable on the fingers of your hand. What was it that moved and held us, the rest of the three hundred reckless, childish boys, who feared the Doctor with all our hearts, and very little besides in heaven or earth; who thought more of our sets in the School than of the Church of Christ, and put the traditions of Rugby and the public opinion of boys in our daily life above the laws of God? We couldn't enter into half that we heard; we hadn't the knowledge of our own hearts or the knowledge of one another; and little enough of the faith, hope, and love needed to that end. But we listened, as all boys in their better moods will listen (ay, and men too for the matter of that), to a man whom we felt to be, with all his heart and soul and strength, striving against whatever was mean and unmanly and unrighteous in our little world. It was not the cold clear voice of one giving advice and warning from serene heights to those who were struggling and sinning below, but the warm living voice of one who was fighting for us and by our sides, and calling on us to help him and ourselves, and one another. And so, wearily and little by little, but surely and steadily on the whole, was brought home to the young boy, for the first time, the meaning of his life: that it was no fool's or sluggard's paradise, into which he had wandered by chance, but a battlefield ordained from of old, where there are no spectators, but the youngest must take his side, and the stakes are life and death. And he who

was drawing near, which kept everybody in a good humour, and the house was ruled well and strongly by Warner and Brooke. True, the general system was rough and hard, and there was bullying in nooks and corners, bad signs for the future; but it never got further, or dared show itself openly stalking about the passages and hall and bedrooms and making the life of the small boys a continual fear.

Tom, as a new boy, was of right excused fagging for the first month, but in his enthusiasm for his new life this privilege hardly pleased him; and East and others of his young friends discovering this, kindly allowed him to indulge his fancy, and take their turns at night fagging and cleaning studies. These were the principal duties of the fags in the house. From supper until nine o'clock three fags taken in order stood in the passages, and answered any præpostor who called "Fag," racing to the door, the last comer having to do the work. This consisted generally of going to the buttery for beer and bread and cheese (for the great men did not sup with the rest, but had each his own allowance in his study or the fifth-form room), cleaning candlesticks and putting in new candles, toasting cheese, bottling beer, and carrying messages about the house; and Tom, in the first blush of his hero-worship, felt it a high privilege to receive orders from, and be the bearer of the supper of old Brooke. And besides this night-work, each præpostor had three or four fags specially allotted to him, of whom he was supposed to be the guide, philosopher, and friend, and who in return for these good offices had to clean out his study every morning by turns, directly after first lesson, and before he returned from breakfast. And the pleasure of seeing the great men's studies, and looking at their pictures, and peeping into their books, made Tom a ready substitute for any boy who was too lazy to do his own work. And so he soon gained the character of a good-natured, willing fellow, who was ready to do a turn for any one.

In all the games too he joined with all his heart, and soon became well versed in all the mysteries of football, by continued practice at the School-house little-side, which played daily.

The only incident worth recording here, however, was his first run at hare-and-hounds. On the last Tuesday but one

Then the hounds clustered round Thorne, who explained shortly, "They're to have six minutes' law. We run into the Cock, and every one who comes in within a quarter of an hour of the hares 'll be counted, if he has been round Barby church." Then came a minute's pause or so, and then the watches are pocketed, and the pack is led through the gateway into the field which the hares had first crossed. Here they break into a trot, scattering over the field to find the first traces of the scent which the hares throw out as they go along. The old hounds make straight for the likely points, and in a minute a cry of "forward" comes from one of them, and the whole pack quickening their pace make for the spot, while the boy who hit the scent first, and the two or three nearest to him, are over the first fence, and making play along the hedgerow in the long grass-field beyond. The rest of the pack rush at the gap already made, and scramble through, jostling one another. "Forward" again, before they are half through; the pace quickens into a sharp run, the tail hounds all straining to get up with the lucky leaders. They are gallant hares, and the scent lies thick right across another meadow and into a ploughed field, where the pace begins to tell; then over a good wattle with a ditch on the other side, and down a large pasture studded with old thorns, which slopes down to the first brook; the great Leicestershire sheep charge away across the field as the pack comes racing down the slope. The brook is a small one, and the scent lies right ahead up the opposite slope, and as thick as ever; not a turn or a check to favour the tail hounds, who strain on, now trailing in a long line, many a youngster beginning to drag his legs heavily, and feel his heart beat like a hammer, and the bad-plucked ones thinking that after all it isn't worth while to keep it up.

Tom, East, and the Tadpole had a good start, and are well up for such young hands, and after rising the slope and crossing the next field, find themselves up with the leading hounds, who have over-run the scent and are trying back; they have come a mile and a half in about eleven minutes, a pace which shows that it is the last day. About twenty-five of the original starters only show here, the rest having already given in; the leaders are busy making casts into the fields on the left and right, and the others get their second winds.

Then comes the cry of "forward" again, from young

[illegible]

cross a lane after next field, keep down it, and you'll hit the Dunchurch road below the Cock," and then steams away for the run in, in which he's sure to be first, as if he were just starting. They struggle on across the next field, the "forwards" getting fainter and fainter, and then ceasing. The whole hunt is out of ear-shot, and all hope of coming in is over.

"Hang it all!" broke out East, as soon as he had got wind enough, pulling off his hat and mopping at his face, all spattered with dirt and lined with sweat from which went up a thick steam into the still, cold air. "I told you how it would be. What a thick I was to come! Here we are, dead beat, and yet I know we're close to the run in, if we knew the country."

"Well," said Tom, mopping away, and gulping down his disappointment, "it can't be helped. We did our best, anyhow. Hadn't we better find this lane and go down it, as young Brooke told us?"

"I suppose so—nothing else for it," grunted East. "If ever I go out last day again," growl—growl—growl.

So they tried back slowly and sorrowfully and found the lane, and went limping down it, plashing in the cold puddly ruts, and beginning to feel how the run had taken it out of them. The evening closed in fast, and clouded over, dark, cold and dreary.

"I say, it must be locking-up, I should think," remarked East, breaking the silence; "it's so dark."

"What if we're late?" said Tom.

"No tea, and sent up to the Doctor," answered East.

The thought didn't add to their cheerfulness. Presently a faint halloo was heard from an adjoining field. They answered it and stopped, hoping for some competent rustic to guide them, when over a gate some twenty yards ahead crawled the wretched Tadpole, in a state of collapse; he had lost a shoe in the brook, and been groping after it up to his elbows, in the stiff wet clay, and a more miserable creature in the shape of boy seldom has been seen.

The sight of him, notwithstanding, cheered them, for he was some degrees more wretched than they. They also cheered him, as he was no longer under the dread of passing his night alone in the fields. And so, in better heart, the three plashed painfully [illegible] the [illegible] At last it [illegible] as utter darkness [illegible] came out on a [illegible] and there [illegible] they had lost [illegible] and knew [illegible] right or left.

Luckily [illegible] decide, for lum[illegible] the road, [illegible] two spavined [illegible] shafts, came [illegible] after a moment [illegible] they recog[illegible], the redoubtable [illegible] Whistle.

It lumbe[illegible] slo[illegible] y [illegible] mustering [illegible] last [illegible] caught it [illegible] clambering up [illegible] which exp[illegible] g and fell flat [illegible] along the [illegible] the old [illegible] coachman [illegible] to take the [illegible] shilling; [illegible] back seat, [illegible] their heel[illegible] with cold, [illegible] into Rugby [illegible] locking-up.

Five [illegible] small, limping [illegible] figures stea[illegible] tor's garden, a[illegible] house by [illegible] the other gate [illegible] closed long [illegible] they [illegible] passage is [illegible] long [illegible] and keys i[illegible]

He stops [illegible] condition with a [illegible] "Ah! East [illegible] for locking-up [illegible] up to the D[illegible]

"Well [illegible] was first [illegible] put down [illegible]"

"Doctor's [illegible] one in—that's [illegible] replied [illegible] across the stairs a[illegible] the passage [illegible] Doctor's house [illegible] boys turned [illegible] by the [illegible] muttered [illegible] boys le in [illegible] referred to [illegible] but they [illegible] indicating [illegible] Upon the [illegible] of stairs the[illegible]

"Who'll [illegible]

"You—[illegible] East.

"Catch [illegible]" rejoined [illegible] ing the arm [illegible] behind you [illegible]."

"Well, [illegible] indicating [illegible]

Tom, with the others behina him, sidled into the room.

... [illegible] ... ; I'm wo[illegible] ... two to o[illegible] ... [illegible]ags o[illegible] my trou[illegible]."

"Tha[illegible] ... , [illegible] you can ke[illegible] ... behind t[illegible] ...

"Her[illegible] ... [illegible]-fi[illegible]re—you [illegible] ...

"But [illegible] ... y [illegible] ... I [illegible].

"Oh, [illegible] ... [illegible] that matter; [illegible] ... we're on [illegible] ... [illegible]ing here."

"Well, [illegible] ... [illegible]ther," said To[illegible] ... begin [illegible] to [illegible] ... [illegible] from [illegible] ... jackets [illegible] ... [illegible] and the [illegible] ... [illegible]; s[illegible] ... [illegible] through the sw[illegible] ... [illegible] o[illegible] ... [illegible]es in the [illegible] ...

"Tha[illegible] ..." [illegible] ... wh[illegible] ... Tom [illegible] ... [illegible] voices [illegible] ... came [illegible] ... [illegible] the [illegible] ... answered. [illegible] ... [illegible]r's voic[illegible] ... in," and [illegible] ... [illegible]e, and he wi[illegible] ... behind [illegible] ... [illegible].

The D[illegible] ... [illegible] talk; he was [illegible] ... with a g[illegible] ... [illegible] boy's sa[illegible] ... [illegible] of [illegible] ... fa[illegible]ing on [illegible] ... one of N[illegible] ... [illegible] three [illegible] ... [illegible] the [illegible] ... a large table [illegible] ... end, cov[illegible] ... [illegible], and a great [illegible] ... [illegible] gl[illegible] ... [illegible]. All loo[illegible] ... [illegible] ... [illegible]e, [illegible] boys too[illegible] ... moment, [illegible] ... the [illegible] ... [illegible] sofa [illegible] ... the c[illegible]ren, [illegible] ... casting [illegible] ... [illegible] the three [illegible] ... [illegible]ow.

"Well, [illegible] ... the Doctor, [illegible] ... up with [illegible] ... [illegible] one [illegible] ... coat-ai[illegible] ... [illegible] twinking [illegible] ... then ove[illegible] ... [illegible]?"

"[illegible]leas[illegible] ... [illegible]-s[illegible] [illegible]-an[illegible] ... lost our w[illegible] ...

"Hal[illegible] ... [illegible] suppose?"

"Well, [illegible] ... [illegible] and not [illegible] ... Doctor sh[illegible] ... [illegible] powers. "[illegible] ... [illegible] Ha[illegible] ..."

"Why, what a state you're in, my boy!" interrupted the Doctor, as the pitiful condition of East's garments was fully revealed to him.

"That's the fall I got, sir, in the road," said East looking down at himself; "the Old Pig came by——"

"The what?" said the Doctor.

"The Oxford coach, sir," explained Hall.

"Hah! yes, the Regulator," said the Doctor.

"And I tumbled on my face, trying to get up behind," went on East.

"You're not hurt, I hope?" said the Doctor.

"Oh, no, sir."

"Well now, run up stairs, all three of you, and get clean things on, and then tell the housekeeper to give you some tea. You're too young to try such long runs. Let Warner know I've seen you. Good night."

"Good night, sir." And away scuttled the three boys in high glee.

"What a brick, not to give us even twenty lines to learn!" said the Tadpole, as they reached their bedroom; and in half-an-hour afterwards they were sitting by the fire in the housekeeper's room at a sumptuous tea, with cold meat, "twice as good a grub as we should have got in the hall," as the Tadpole remarked with a grin, his mouth full of buttered toast. All their grievances were forgotten, and they were resolving to go out the first Big-side next half, and thinking Hare-and-hounds the most delightful of games.

A day or two afterwards the great passage outside the bedrooms was cleared of the boxes and portmanteaus, which went down to be packed by the matron, and great games of chariot-racing, and cock-fighting, and bolstering, went on in the vacant space, the sure sign of a closing half-year.

Then came the making up of parties for the journey home, and Tom joined a party who were to hire a coach, and post with four horses to Oxford.

Then the last Saturday on which the Doctor came round to each form to give out the prizes, and hear the masters' last reports of how they and their charges had been conducting themselves; and Tom, to his huge delight, was praised, and got his remove into the lower-fourth, in which all his School-house friends were.

On [illegible] ex[illegible] o'clock [illegible]
going [illegible] n [illegible] s a[illegible] matrons [illegible]
wrapped [illegible] muffins were [illegible]
mouth[illegible] ing over [illegible]
question[illegible] outside [illegible]
were [illegible] is [illegible] r-ho[illegible]
Tom's [illegible] poss[illegible] boys in th[illegible]
and b[illegible] hired f[illegible]
blowing [illegible] a clou[illegible]
all p[illegible] the High [illegible]
Every [illegible] bub[illegible]
staggered [illegible] the c[illegible]
louder [illegible] with a gr[illegible]
his side [illegible] ing [illegible] ney-m[illegible]
compari[illegible] ary [illegible] the din[illegible]
list in [illegible] the Doctor's is [illegible]
of his [illegible] side [illegible] is mouth [illegible]
his spe[illegible] . [illegible] had pru[illegible]
door, [illegible] ons [illegible] lely throu[illegible]
of he [illegible] d lost al[illegible]

"T[illegible] never ca[illegible]
a Du[illegible]ch.

"T[illegible], G[illegible]."

"H[illegible] T[illegible], [illegible] said. I was to [illegible]
ten; yo[illegible] r[illegible]."—(I[illegible]
Green [illegible] tr[illegible] y to truth [illegible]
his he[illegible] ne[illegible], and [illegible]
dirty [illegible] G[illegible] which the win[illegible]

"H[illegible] T[illegible], [illegible] l [illegible] nes [illegible]
"And [illegible] in [illegible] sh[illegible] d others [illegible]

One [illegible] ho[illegible] y [illegible] which. T[illegible]
got [illegible] pa[illegible] a [illegible] sa[illegible] out to [illegible]
carno[illegible] D[illegible] s of Bra[illegible]
proba[illegible] o [illegible] ns [illegible] which t[illegible]
postbo[illegible] ulging [illegible] ll [illegible]
fully s[illegible] h [illegible] ach and in the [illegible]
boots, [illegible] as [illegible] ble outs[illegible]
small [illegible] and the corno[illegible]
up be[illegible] boy [illegible] mostly [illegible]
pleasure [illegible] gen[illegible]
this is [illegible] method of noti[illegible] th[illegible]

Great games of chariot-racing, cock-fighting, and bolstering went on in the vacant space.

CHAPTER VIII

THE WAR OF INDEPENDENCE

"They are slaves who will not choose
Hatred, scoffing, and abuse,
Rather than in silence shrink
From the truth they needs must think:
They are slaves who dare not be
In the right with two or three."

LOWELL, *Stanzas on Freedom*.

THE lower-fourth form, in which Tom found himself at the beginning of the next half-year, was the largest form in the Lower school, and numbered upwards of forty boys. Young gentlemen of all ages from nine to fifteen were to be found there, who expended such part of their energies as was devoted to Latin and Greek upon a book of Livy, the Bucolics of Virgil, and the Hecuba of Euripides, which were ground out in small daily portions. The driving of this unlucky lower-fourth must have been grievous work to the unfortunate master, for it was the most unhappily constituted of any in the school. Here stuck the great stupid boys, who for the life of them could never master the accidence; the objects alternately of mirth and terror to the youngsters, who were daily taking them up and laughing at them in lesson, and getting kicked by them for so doing in play-hours. There were no less than three unhappy fellows in tail coats, with incipient down on their chins, whom the Doctor and the master of the form were always endeavouring to hoist into the Upper school, but whose parsing and construing resisted the most well-meant shoves. Then came the mass of the form, boys of eleven and twelve, the most mischievous and reckless age of British youth, of whom East and Tom Brown

Caned over the hand there and then.

coming out, and his eye beginning to burn, and his gown getting gathered up more and more tightly in his left hand. The suspense was agonising, and Tom knew that he was sure on such occasions to make an example of the School-house boys. "If he would only begin," thought Tom, "I shouldn't mind."

At last the whispering ceased, and the name which was called out was not Brown. He looked up for a moment, but the Doctor's face was too awful; Tom wouldn't have met his eye for all he was worth, and buried himself in his book again.

The boy who was called up first was a clever, merry School-house boy, one of their set: he was some connection of the Doctor's, and a great favourite, and ran in and out of his house as he liked, and so was selected for the first victim.

"Triste lupus stabulis," began the luckless youngster, and stammered through some eight or ten lines.

"There, that will do," said the Doctor; "now construe."

On common occasions, the boy could have construed the passage well enough probably, but now his head was gone.

"Triste lupus, the sorrowful wolf," he began.

A shudder ran through the whole form, and the Doctor's wrath fairly boiled over; he made three steps up to the construer, and gave him a good box on the ear. The blow was not a hard one, but the boy was so taken by surprise that he started back; the form caught the back of his knees, and over he went on to the floor behind. There was a dead silence over the whole school; never before and never again while Tom was at school did the Doctor strike a boy in lesson. The provocation must have been great. However, the victim had saved his form for that occasion, for the Doctor turned to the top bench, and put on the best boys for the rest of the hour; and though, at the end of the lesson, he gave them all such a rating as they did not forget, this terrible field-day passed over without any severe visitations in the shape of punishments or floggings. Forty young scapegraces expressed their thanks to the "sorrowful wolf" in their different ways before second lesson.

But a character for steadiness once gone is not easily recovered, as Tom found, and for years afterwards he went up the school without it, and the masters' hands were against

" *Triste lupus, the sorrowful wolf,*" he began.

While matters were in this state, East and Tom were one evening sitting in their study. They had done their work for first lesson, and Tom was in a brown study, brooding, like a young William Tell, upon the wrongs of fags in general, and his own in particular.

"I say, Scud," said he at last, rousing himself to snuff the candle, "what right have the fifth-form boys to fag us as they do?"

"No more right than you have to fag them," answered East, without looking up from an early number of Pickwick, which was just coming out, and which he was luxuriously devouring, stretched on his back on the sofa.

Tom relapsed into his brown study, and East went on reading and chuckling. The contrast of the boys' faces would have given infinite amusement to a looker-on, the one so solemn and big with mighty purpose, the other radiant and bubbling over with fun.

"Do you know, old fellow, I've been thinking it over a good deal," began Tom again.

"Oh, yes, I know, fagging you are thinking of. Hang it all,—but listen here, Tom—here's fun. Mr. Winkle's horse—"

"And I've made up my mind," broke in Tom, "that I won't fag except for the sixth."

"Quite right too, my boy," cried East, putting his finger on the place and looking up; "but a pretty peck of troubles you'll get into, if you're going to play that game. However, I'm all for a strike myself, if we can get others to join—it's getting too bad."

"Can't we get some sixth-form fellow to take it up?" asked Tom.

"Well, perhaps we might; Morgan would interfere, I think. Only," added East, after a moment's pause, "you see, we should have to tell him about it, and that's against School principles. Don't you remember what old Brooke said about learning to take our own parts?"

"Ah, I wish old Brooke were back again—it was all right in his time."

"Why, yes; you see, then the strongest and best fellows were in the sixth, and the fifth-form fellows were afraid of them, and they kept good order; but now our sixth-form fellows are too small, and the fifth don't care for them, and do what they like in the house."

n safe enough—don't you see how the door holds at top and ottom? so the bolts must be drawn. We should have forced he lock long ago." East gave Tom a nudge, to call attention o this scientific remark.

Then came attacks on particular panels, one of which at ast gave way to the repeated kicks; but it broke inwards, nd the broken piece got jammed across, the door being ined with green baize, and couldn't easily be removed from utside; and the besieged, scorning further concealment, trengthened their defences by pressing the end of their ofa against the door. So, after one or two more ineffectual fforts, Flashman & Co. retired, vowing vengeance in no nild terms.

The first danger over, it only remained for the besieged o effect a safe retreat, as it was now near bed-time. They istened intently and heard the supper-party resettle themelves, and then gently drew back first one bolt and then he other. Presently the convivial noises began again steadily. "Now then, stand by for a run," said East throwing the door vide open and rushing into the passage, closely followed by Tom. They were too quick to be caught, but Flashman was n the look-out, and sent an empty pickle-jar whizzing after hem, which narrowly missed Tom's head, and broke into wenty pieces at the end of the passage. "He wouldn't mind illing one, if he wasn't caught," said East, as they turned the orner.

There was no pursuit, so the two turned into the hall, vhere they found a knot of small boys round the fire. Their tory was told—the war of independence had broken out— vho would join the revolutionary forces? Several others resent bound themselves not to fag for the fifth form at nce. One or two only edged off and left the rebels. What else could they do? "I've a good mind to go to the Doctor straight," said Tom.

"That'll never do—don't you remember the levy of the school ast half?" put in another.

In fact, that solemn assembly, a levy of the school, had been held, at which the captain of the school had got up, and, after remising that several instances had occurred of matters having een reported to the masters; that this was against public norality and School tradition; that a levy of the sixth had

and he had a talent for destroying clothes and making himself look shabby. He wasn't on terms with Flashman's set, who sneered at his dress and ways behind his back, which he knew, and revenged himself by asking Flashman the most disagreeable questions, and treating him familiarly whenever a crowd of boys were round them. Neither was he intimate with any of the other bigger boys, who were warned off by his oddnesses, for he was a very queer fellow; besides, amongst other failings, he had that of impecuniosity in a remarkable degree. He brought as much money as other boys to school but got rid of it in no time, no one knew how. And then, being also reckless, borrowed from any one, and when his debts accumulated and creditors pressed, would have an auction in the Hall of everything he possessed in the world, selling even his school-books, candlestick and study table. For weeks after one of these auctions, having rendered his study uninhabitable, he would live about in the fifth-form room and Hall, doing his verses on old letter-backs and odd scraps of paper, and learning his lessons no one knew how. He never meddled with any little boys, and was popular with them, though they all looked on him with a sort of compassion, and called him "poor Diggs," not being able to resist appearances, or to disregard wholly even the sneers of their enemy Flashman. However, he seemed equally indifferent to the sneers of big boys and the pity of small ones, and lived his own queer life with much apparent enjoyment to himself. It is necessary to introduce Diggs thus particularly, as he not only did Tom and East good service in their present warfare, as is about to be told, but soon afterwards, when he got into the sixth, chose them for his fags, and excused them from study-fagging, thereby earning unto himself eternal gratitude from them, and from all who are interested in their history.

And seldom had small boys more need of a friend, for the morning after the siege the storm burst upon the rebels in all its violence. Flashman laid wait, and caught Tom before second lesson, and, receiving a point blank "No" when told to fetch his hat, seized him and twisted his arm, and went through the other methods of torture in use: "He couldn't make me cry though," as Tom said triumphantly to the rest of the rebels, "and I kicked his shins well, I know." And soon it crept out that a lot of the fags were in league, and

Flashman caught Tom, and seized him and twisted his arm.

heads together, and resolved to devote their ready cash (some four shillings sterling) to redeem such articles as that sum

A valuable assortment of old metals.

would cover. Accordingly, they duly attended to bid, and Tom became the owner of two lots of Diggs's things ;—lot 1, price

grumbling,—so many fewer tartlets and apples were eaten and fives'-balls bought on that Saturday; and after locking up, when the money would otherwise have been spent, consolation was carried to many a small boy by the sound of the night-fags shouting along the passages, "Gentlemen sportsmen of the School-house, the lottery's going to be drawn in the Hall." It was pleasant to be called a gentleman sportsman—also to have a chance of drawing a favourite horse.

The Hall was full of boys, and at the head of one of the long tables stood the sporting interest, with a hat before them, in which were the tickets folded up. One of them then began calling out the list of the house; each boy as his name was called drew a ticket from the hat and opened it; and most of the bigger boys, after drawing, left the Hall directly to go back to their studies or the fifth-form room. The sporting interest had all drawn blanks, and they were sulky accordingly; neither of the favourites had yet been drawn, and it had come down to the upper-fourth. So now, as each small boy came up and drew his ticket, it was seized and opened by Flashman, or some other of the standers-by. But no great favourite is drawn until it comes to the Tadpole's turn, and he shuffles up and draws, and tries to make off, but is caught, and his ticket is opened like the rest.

"Here you are! Wanderer! the third favourite," shouts the opener.

"I say, just give me my ticket, please," remonstrates Tadpole.

"Hullo, don't be in a hurry," breaks in Flashman; "what'll you sell Wanderer for now?"

"I don't want to sell," rejoins Tadpole.

"Oh, don't you! Now listen, you young fool—you don't know anything about it; the horse is no use to you. He won't win, but I want him as a hedge. Now, I'll give you half-a-crown for him." Tadpole holds out, but between threats and cajoleries at length sells half for one-shilling-and-sixpence, about a fifth of its fair market value; however, he is glad to realise anything, and as he wisely remarks, "Wanderer mayn't win, and the tizzy is safe anyhow."

East presently comes up and draws a blank. Soon after comes Tom's turn; his ticket, like the others, is seized and opened. "Here you are then," shouts the opener, holding it up, "Harkaway! By Jove, Flashey, your young friend's in luck."

except the sporting set of five or six, who stay to compare books, make bets, and so on, Tom, who doesn't choose to move while Flashman is at the door, and East, who stays by his friend anticipating trouble.

The sporting set now gathered round Tom. Public opinion wouldn't allow them actually to rob him of his ticket, but any humbug or intimidation by which he could be driven to sell the whole or part at an under-value was lawful.

"Now, young Brown, come, what'll you sell me Harkaway for? I hear he isn't going to start. I'll give you five shillings for him," begins the boy who had opened the ticket. Tom, remembering his good deed, and moreover in his forlorn state wishing to make a friend, is about to accept the offer, when another cries out, "I'll give you seven shillings." Tom hesitated, and looked from one to the other.

"No, no!" said Flashman, pushing in, "leave me to deal with him; we'll draw lots for it afterwards. Now, sir, you know me—you'll sell Harkaway to us for five shillings, or you'll repent it."

"I won't sell a bit of him," answered Tom, shortly.

"You hear that now!" said Flashman, turning to the others. "He's the coxiest young blackguard in the house—I always told you so. We're to have all the trouble and risk of getting up the lotteries for the benefit of such fellows as he."

Flashman forgets to explain what risk they ran, but he speaks to willing ears. Gambling makes boys selfish and cruel as well as men.

"That's true,—we always draw blanks," cried one. "Now, sir, you shall sell half, at any rate."

"I won't," said Tom, flushing up to his hair, and lumping them all in his mind with his sworn enemy.

"Very well then, let's roast him," cried Flashman, and catches hold of Tom by the collar: one or two boys hesitate, but the rest join in. East seizes Tom's arm and tries to pull him away, but is knocked back by one of the boys, and Tom is dragged along struggling. His shoulders are pushed against the mantelpiece, and he is held by main force before the fire, Flashman drawing his trousers tight by way of extra torture. Poor East, in more pain even than Tom, suddenly thinks of Diggs, and darts off to find him. "Will you sell now for ten shillings?" says one boy who is relenting.

Poor Tom is done already.

CHAPTER IX

A CHAPTER OF ACCIDENTS

"Wherein I [speak] of most disastrous chances,
Of moving accidents by flood and field,
Of hairbreadth 'scapes."—*Shakespeare.*

/HEN Tom came back into school after a couple of days in ie sick-room, he found matters much changed for the better, s East had led him to expect. Flashman's brutality had isgusted most even of his intimate friends, and his cowardice ad once more been made plain to the house; for Diggs had ncountered him on the morning after the lottery, and after igh words on both sides had struck him, and the blow as not returned. However, Flashy was not unused to this ort of thing, and had lived through as awkward affairs before, nd, as Diggs had said, fed and toadied himself back into .vour again. Two or three of the boys who had helped to oast Tom came up and begged his pardon, and thanked him or not telling anything. Morgan sent for him, and was iclined to take the matter up warmly, but Tom begged him ot to do it; to which he agreed, on Tom's promising to come o him at once in future—a promise which I regret to say he idn't keep. Tom kept Harkaway all to himself, and won the econd prize in the lottery, some thirty shillings, which he and ast contrived to spend in about three days in the purchase of ictures for their study, two new bats and a cricket-ball, all ie best that could be got, and a supper of sausages, kidneys, nd beef-steak pies to all the rebels. Light come, light go; iey wouldn't have been comfortable with money in their ockets in the middle of the half.

The embers of Flashman's wrath, however, were still nouldering, and burst out every now and then in sly blows

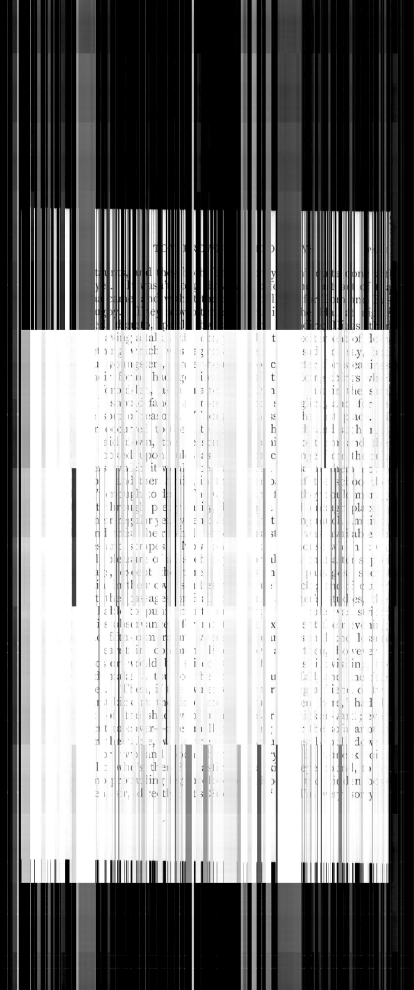

idn't know it was you, Snooks;" and then with well-feigned eal the door would be opened, young hopeful praying that iat beast Snooks mightn't have heard the scuffle caused by

The Library.

is coming. If a study was empty, Snooks proceeded to draw he passages and Hall to find the truants.

Well, one evening, in forbidden hours, Tom and East were

[illegible] The [illegible] he [illegible] s [illegible] re he [illegible] door, while [illegible] before [illegible] was bus[illegible] rs [illegible] and [illegible] together [illegible] of the [illegible] a [illegible] hich [illegible] a step [illegible] passage; [illegible] a moment [illegible] that it was [illegible] and the [illegible] open, and [illegible] didn't see [illegible] thought it a [illegible] boys didn't [illegible] of them, to [illegible] of his way.

"What's that for?" [illegible]

"Because I choose. [illegible] here; go to [illegible]"

"You can't send [illegible]"

"Can't I? Then [illegible] y," [illegible] Flashman [illegible] gely.

"I say, you two," [illegible] end of the [illegible] now, "you'll [illegible] in this lot [illegible] — I [illegible] fair [illegible]

[illegible] ashman was [illegible] two steps. [illegible] "Yes," said [illegible] So the [illegible] with clenched [illegible] up to his shoulder [illegible] and [illegible] his mon[illegible] toward us [illegible] as [illegible] fork, and so [illegible] "[illegible] guards!" [illegible] reach. [illegible] of his blows [illegible] goods, though [illegible] went [illegible] didn't [illegible] up there," [illegible] we [illegible]

"What the —— is it to you?" faltered Flashman, who began to lose heart.

"I'm going to see fair, I tell you," said Diggs with a grin, and snapping his great red fingers; "'tain't fair for you to be fighting one of them at a time. Are you ready, Brown? Time's up."

The small boys rushed in again. Closing they saw was their best chance, and Flashman was wilder and more flurried than ever: he caught East by the throat, and tried to force him back on the iron-bound table; Tom grasped his waist, and, remembering the old throw he had learned in the Vale from Harry Winburn, crooked his leg inside Flashman's, and threw his whole weight forward. The three tottered for a moment, and then over they went on to the floor, Flashman striking his head against a form in the Hall.

The two youngsters sprang to their legs, but he lay there still. They began to be frightened. Tom stooped down, and then cried out, scared out of his wits, "He's bleeding awfully; come here, East! Diggs,—he's dying!"

"Not he," said Diggs, getting leisurely off the table; "it's all sham—he's only afraid to fight it out."

East was as frightened as Tom. Diggs lifted Flashman's head, and he groaned.

"What's the matter?" shouted Diggs.

"My skull's fractured," sobbed Flashman.

"Oh, let me run for the housekeeper," cried Tom. "What shall we do?"

"Fiddlesticks! it's nothing but the skin broken," said the relentless Diggs, feeling his head. "Cold water and a bit of rag's all he'll want."

"Let me go," said Flashman, surlily, sitting up; "I don't want your help."

"We're really very sorry," began East.

"Hang your sorrow," answered Flashman, holding his handkerchief to the place; "you shall pay for this, I can tell you, both of you." And he walked out of the Hall.

"He can't be very bad," said Tom with a deep sigh, much relieved to see his enemy march so well.

"Not he," said Diggs, "and you'll see you won't be troubled with him any more. But, I say, your head's broken too—your collar is covered with blood."

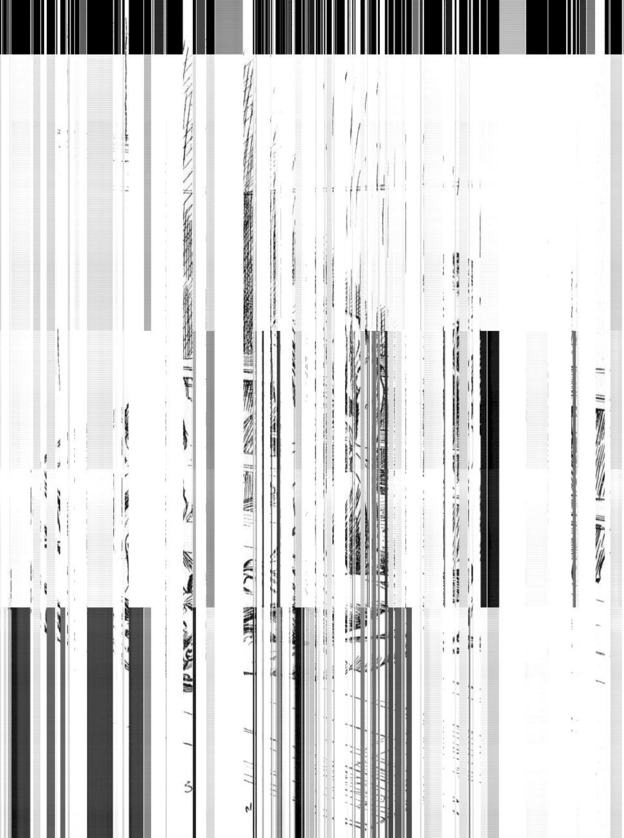

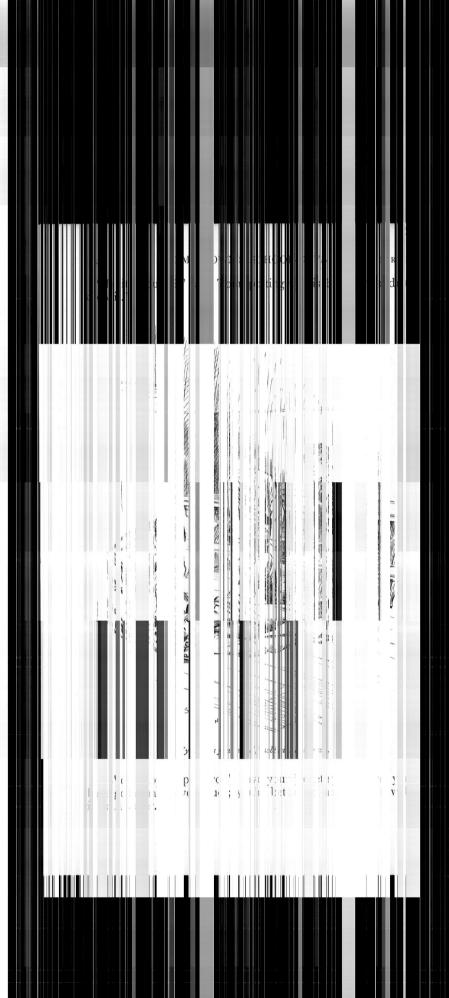

"Cheap enough too, if we've done with our old friend lashey," said East, as they made off upstairs to bathe their ounds.

They had done with Flashman in one sense, for he never laid nger on either of them again; but whatever harm a spiteful eart and venomous tongue could do them, he took care should e done. Only throw dirt enough, and some of it is sure to ick; and so it was with the fifth form and the bigger boys in eneral, with whom he associated more or less, and they not at l. Flashman managed to get Tom and East into disfavour, hich did not wear off for some time after the author of it had isappeared from the School world. This event, much prayed r by the small fry in general, took place a few months after e above encounter. One fine summer evening Flashman had een regaling himself on gin-punch, at Brownsover; and aving exceeded his usual limits, started home uproarious. e fell in with a friend or two coming back from bathing, roposed a glass of beer, to which they assented, the weather eing hot, and they thirsty souls, and unaware of the quantity f drink which Flashman had already on board. The short esult was, that Flashey became beastly drunk: they tried to et him along, but couldn't; so they chartered a hurdle and vo men to carry him. One of the masters came upon them, nd they naturally enough fled. The flight of the rest raised ie master's suspicions, and the good angel of the fags incited im to examine the freight, and, after examination, to convoy ie hurdle himself up to the School-house; and the Doctor, ho had long had his eye on Flashman, arranged for his ithdrawal next morning.

The evil that men, and boys too, do, lives after them: lashman was gone, but our boys, as hinted above, still felt ie effects of his hate. Besides, they had been the movers f the strike against unlawful fagging. The cause was righteous -the result had been triumphant to a great extent; but the est of the fifth, even those who had never fagged the small oys, or had given up the practice cheerfully, couldn't help eeling a small grudge against the first rebels. After all, their orm had been defied—on just grounds, no doubt; so just, indeed, that they had at once acknowledged the wrong, and emained passive in the strife; had they sided with Flashman nd his set, the rebels must have given way at once. They

for sons of heroes like old Brooke, but was quite another to do the like for Snooks and Green, who had never faced a good scrummage at football, and couldn't keep the passages in order at night. So they only slurred through their fagging ust well enough to escape a licking, and not always that, and got the character of sulky, unwilling fags. In the fifth-form room, after supper, when such matters were often discussed and arranged, their names were for ever coming up.

"I say, Green," Snooks began one night, "isn't that new boy, Harrison, your fag?"

"Yes; why?"

"Oh, I know something of him at home, and should like to excuse him. Will you swop?"

"Who will you give me?"

"Well, let's see, there's Willis, Johnson—No, that won't do. Yes, I have it—there's young East, I'll give you him."

"Don't you wish you may get it?" replied Green. "I'll ell you what I'll do—I'll give you two for Willis, if you ike."

"Who then?" asks Snooks.

"Hall and Brown."

"Wouldn't have 'em at a gift."

"Better than East, though; for they ain't quite so sharp," aid Green, getting up and leaning his back against the mantelpiece—he wasn't a bad fellow, and couldn't help not being able to put down the unruly fifth-form. His eye twinkled s he went on, "Did I ever tell you how the young vagabond old me last half?"

"No—how?"

"Well, he never half cleaned my study out, only just stuck he candlesticks in the cupboard, and swept the crumbs on to he floor. So at last I was mortal angry, and had him up, nade him go through the whole performance under my eyes: he dust the young scamp made nearly choked me, and showed hat he hadn't swept the carpet before. Well, when it was all nished, 'Now, young gentleman,' says I, 'mind, I expect this o be done every morning, floor swept, table-cloth taken off nd shaken, and everything dusted.' 'Very well,' grunts he. Not a bit of it though—I was quite sure in a day or two that e never took the table-cloth off even. So I laid a trap for im: I tore up some paper and put half-a-dozen bits on my

them store of good advice, by which they never in the least profited.

And even after the house mended, and law and order had been restored, which soon happened after young Brooke and Diggs got into the sixth, they couldn't easily or at once return into the paths of steadiness, and many of the old wild out-of-bounds habits stuck to them as firmly as ever. While they had been quite little boys, the scrapes they got into in the school hadn't much mattered to any one; but now they were in the upper school, all wrong-doers from which were sent up straight to the Doctor at once: so they began to come under his notice; and as they were a sort of leaders in a small way amongst their own contemporaries, his eye, which was everywhere, was upon them.

It was a toss-up whether they turned out well or ill, and so they were just the boys who caused most anxiety to such a master. You have been told of the first occasion on which they were sent up to the Doctor, and the remembrance of it was so pleasant that they had much less fear of him than most boys of their standing had. "It's all his look," Tom used to say to East, "that frightens fellows: don't you remember, he never said anything to us my first half-year, for being an hour late for locking up?"

The next time that Tom came before him, however, the interview was of a very different kind. It happened just about the time at which we have now arrived, and was the first of a series of scrapes into which our hero managed now to tumble.

The river Avon at Rugby is a slow and not very clear stream, in which chub, dace, roach, and other coarse fish are (or were) plentiful enough, together with a fair sprinkling of small jack, but no fish worth sixpence either for sport or food. It is, however, a capital river for bathing, as it has many nice small pools and several good reaches for swimming, all within about a mile of one another, and at an easy twenty minutes' walk from the school. This mile of water is rented, or used to be rented, for bathing purposes, by the Trustees of the School, for the boys. The footpath to Brownsover crosses the river by "the Planks," a curious old single-plank bridge, running for fifty or sixty yards into the flat meadows on each side of the river,—for in the winter there are frequent floods. Above the Planks were the bathing-places for the smaller boys;

gates as he rode past, and when he charged his horse at the mob of boys, and tried to thrash them with his whip, was driven back by cricket-bats and wickets, and pursued with pebbles and fives'-balls; while the wretched keepers' lives were a burthen to them, from having to watch the waters so closely.

The School-house boys of Tom's standing, one and all, as a protest against this tyranny and cutting short of their lawful amusements, took to fishing in all ways, and especially by means of night-lines. The little tackle-maker at the bottom of the town would soon have made his fortune had the rage lasted, and several of the barbers began to lay in fishing-tackle. The boys had this great advantage over their enemies, that they spent a large portion of the day in nature's garb by the river side, and so, when tired of swimming, would get out on the other side and fish, or set night-lines, till the keeper hove in sight, and then plunge in and swim back and mix with the other bathers, and the keepers were too wise to follow across the stream.

While things were in this state, one day, Tom and three or four others were bathing at Wratislaw's, and had, as a matter of course, been taking up and resetting night-lines. They had all left the water, and were sitting or standing about at their toilets, in all costumes from a shirt upwards, when they were aware of a man in a velveteen shooting-coat approaching from the other side. He was a new keeper, so they didn't recognise or notice him, till he pulled up right opposite, and began:—

"I see'd some of you young gentlemen over this side a fishing just now."

"Hullo, who are you? what business is that of yours, old Velveteens?"

"I'm the new under-keeper, and master's told me to keep a sharp look-out on all o' you young chaps. And I tells 'ee I means business, and you'd better keep on your own side, or we shall fall out."

"Well, that's right, Velveteens—speak out, and let's know your mind at once."

"Look here, old boy," cried East, holding up a miserable coarse fish or two and a small jack, "would you like to smell 'em and see which bank they lived under?"

"I'll give you a bit of advice, keeper," shouted Tom, who was sitting in his shirt paddling with his feet in the river;

It isn't often that great chub, or any other coarse fish, are in earnest about anything, but just then they were thoroughly bent on feeding, and in half-an-hour Master Tom had deposited three thumping fellows at the foot of the giant willow. As he was baiting for a fourth pounder, and just going to throw in again, he became aware of a man coming up the bank not one hundred yards off. Another look told him that it was the under-keeper. Could he reach the shallow before him? No, not carrying his rod. Nothing for it but the tree; so Tom laid his bones to it, shinning up as fast as he could, and dragging up his rod after him. He had just time to reach and crouch along upon a huge branch some ten feet up, which stretched out over the river, when the keeper arrived at the clump. Tom's heart beat fast as he came under the tree; two steps more and he would have passed, when, as ill-luck would have it, the gleam on the scales of the dead fish caught his eye, and he made a dead point at the foot of the tree. He picked up the fish one by one; his eye and touch told him that they had been alive and feeding within the hour. Tom crouched lower along the branch, and heard the keeper beating the clump. "If I could only get the rod hidden," thought he, and began gently shifting it to get it alongside him; "willow-trees don't throw out straight hickory shoots twelve feet long, with no leaves, worse luck." Alas! the keeper catches the rustle, and then a sight of the rod, and then of Tom's hand and arm.

"Oh, be up ther', be 'ee?" says he, running under the tree. "Now you come down this minute."

"Tree'd at last," thinks Tom, making no answer, and keeping as close as possible, but working away at the rod, which he takes to pieces: "I'm in for it, unless I can starve him out." And then he begins to meditate getting along the branch for a plunge, and a scramble to the other side; but the small branches are so thick, and the opposite bank so difficult, that the keeper will have lots of time to get round by the ford before he can get out, so he gives that up. And now he hears the keeper beginning to scramble up the trunk. That will never do; so he scrambles himself back to where his branch joins the trunk, and stands with lifted rod.

"Hullo, Velveteens, mind your fingers if you come any higher."

"Oh, be up ther', be 'ee?" says he. "Now you come down this minute.'

three minutes to the hour. They all pulled up, and took their time. When the hour struck, doors were closed, and half the school late. Thomas being set to make inquiry,

. . . *bought some big nails, and after one or two attempts, scaled the Schools.*

discovers their names on the minute-hand, and reports accordingly; and they are sent for, a knot of their friends making derisive and pantomimic allusions to what their fate will be as they walk off.

. . . *finished up with inscribing H. East, T. Brown, on the minute-hand.*

want to speak to you about two boys in your form, East and Brown ; I have just been speaking to them. What do you think of them ? "

" Well, they are not hard workers, and very thoughtless and ull of spirits—but I can't help liking them. I think they are sound good fellows at the bottom."

" I'm glad of it. I think so too. But they make me very uneasy. They are taking the lead a good deal amongst the ags in my house, for they are very active, bold fellows. I should be sorry to lose them, but I sha'n't let them stay if I don't see them gaining character and manliness. In another year they may do great harm to all the younger boys."

" Oh, I hope you won't send them away," pleaded their master.

" Not if I can help it. But now I never feel sure, after any half-holiday, that I sha'n't have to flog one of them next morning, for some foolish, thoughtless scrape. I quite dread seeing either of them."

They were both silent for a minute. Presently the Doctor began again :—

" They don't feel that they have any duty or work to do in he school, and how is one to make them feel it ? "

" I think if either of them had some little boy to take care of, it would steady them. Brown is the most reckless of the wo, I should say ; East wouldn't get into so many scrapes without him."

" Well," said the Doctor, with something like a sigh, " I'll hink of it." And they went on to talk of other subjects.

TOM BROWN'S SCHOOL-DAYS

PART II

CHAPTER I

HOW THE TIDE TURNED

"Once to every man and nation, comes the moment to decide,
In the strife of Truth with Falsehood, for the good or evil side:
*   *   *   *   *
Then it is the brave man chooses, while the coward stands aside,
Doubting in his abject spirit, till his Lord is crucified."

LOWELL.

THE turning-point in our hero's school career had now come, and the manner of it was as follows. On the evening of the first day of the next half-year, Tom, East, and another School-house boy, who had just been dropped at the Spread Eagle by the old Regulator, rushed into the matron's room in high spirits, such as all real boys are in when they first get back, however fond they may be of home.

"Well, Mrs. Wixie," shouted one, seizing on the methodical, active little dark-eyed woman who was busy stowing away the linen of the boys who had already arrived into their several pigeon-holes, "here we are again, you see, as jolly as ever. Let us help you put the things away."

"And, Mary," cried another (she was called indifferently by either name), "who's come back? Has the Doctor made old Jones leave? How many new boys are there?"

"Am I and East to have Gray's study? You know you promised to get it for us if you could," shouted Tom.

"And am I to sleep in No. 4?" roared East.

"How's old Sam, and Bogle, and Sally?"

"Bless the boys!" cries Mary, at last getting in a word, "why, you'll shake me to death. There, now do go away up to the housekeeper's room and get your suppers; you know

"*Bless the boys!*" *cries Mary* . . . "*why, you'll shake me to death.*"

The young ones got on fast and well.

young Brooke shake hands, and look one another in the face; and he didn't fail to remark that Brooke was nearly as tall and quite as broad as the Doctor. And his cup was full, when in another moment his master turned to him with another warm shake of the hand, and, seemingly oblivious of all the late scrapes which he had been getting into, said, "Ah, Brown, you here! I hope you left your father and all well at home?"

Bilton Grange.

"Yes, sir, quite well."

"And this is the little fellow who is to share your study. Well, he doesn't look as we should like to see him. He wants some Rugby air, and cricket. And you must take him some good long walks, to Bilton Grange, and Caldecott's Spinney, and show him what a little pretty country we have about here."

Tom wondered if the Doctor knew that his visits to Bilton Grange were for the purpose of taking rooks' nests (a proceeding strongly discountenanced by the owner thereof),

. . . like young bears with all their troubles to come.

not more than about sixteen years old, they were all bound to be up and in bed by ten; the sixth-form boys came to bed from ten to a quarter-past (at which time the old verger came round to put the candles out), except when they sat up to read.

Within a few minutes therefore of their entry, all the other boys who slept in Number 4 had come up. The little fellows went quietly to their own beds, and began undressing and talking to each other in whispers; while the elder, amongst whom was Tom, sat chatting about on one another's beds, with their jackets and waistcoats off. Poor little Arthur was overwhelmed with the novelty of his position. The idea of sleeping in the room with strange boys had clearly never crossed his mind before, and was as painful as it was strange to him. He could hardly bear to take his jacket off; however, presently, with an effort, off it came, and then he paused and looked at Tom, who was sitting at the bottom of his bed talking and laughing.

"Please, Brown," he whispered, "may I wash my face and hands?"

"Of course, if you like," said Tom, staring; "that's your washhand-stand, under the window, second from your bed. You'll have to go down for more water in the morning if you use it all." And on he went with his talk, while Arthur stole timidly from between the beds out to his washhand-stand, and began his ablutions, thereby drawing for a moment on himself the attention of the room.

On went the talk and laughter. Arthur finished his washing and undressing, and put on his nightgown. He then looked round more nervously than ever. Two or three of the little boys were already in bed, sitting up with their chins on their knees. The light burned clear, the noise went on. It was a trying moment for the poor little lonely boy; however, this time he didn't ask Tom what he might or might not do, but dropped on his knees by his bedside, as he had done every day from his childhood, to open his heart to Him who heareth the cry and beareth the sorrows of the tender child, and the strong man in agony.

Tom was sitting at the bottom of his bed unlacing his boots, so that his back was towards Arthur, and he didn't see what had happened, and looked up in wonder at the

candle was out, and then stole out and said his prayers, in fear lest some one should find him out. So did many another poor little fellow. Then he began to think that he might just as well say his prayers in bed, and then that it didn't matter whether he was kneeling, or sitting, or lying down. And so it had come to pass with Tom, as with all who will not confess their Lord before men; and for the last year he had probably not said his prayers in earnest a dozen times.

Poor Tom! the first and bitterest feeling which was like to break his heart was the sense of his own cowardice. The vice of all others which he loathed was brought in and burned in on his own soul. He had lied to his mother, to his conscience, to his God. How could he bear it? And then the poor little weak boy, whom he had pitied and almost scorned for his weakness, had done that which he, braggart as he was, dared not do. The first dawn of comfort came to him in swearing to himself that he would stand by that boy through thick and thin, and cheer him, and help him, and bear his burdens, for the good deed done that night. Then he resolved to write home next day and tell his mother all, and what a coward her son had been. And then peace came to him as he resolved, lastly, to bear his testimony next morning. The morning would be harder than the night to begin with, but he felt that he could not afford to let one chance slip. Several times he faltered, for the devil showed him first all his old friends calling him "Saint" and "Square-toes," and a dozen hard names, and whispered to him that his motives would be misunderstood, and he would only be left alone with the new boy; whereas it was his duty to keep all means of influence, that he might do good to the largest number. And then came the more subtle temptation, "Shall I not be showing myself braver than others by doing this? Have I any right to begin it now? Ought I not rather to pray in my own study, letting other boys know that I do so, and trying to lead them to it, while in public at least I should go on as I have done?" However, his good angel was too strong that night, and he turned on his side and slept, tired of trying to reason, but resolved to follow the impulse which had been so strong, and in which he had found peace.

Next morning he was up and washed and dressed, all but his jacket and waistcoat, just as the ten minutes' bell began to

ing, and then in the face of the whole room knelt down to ray. Not five words could he say—the bell mocked him; he vas listening for every whisper in the room—what were they ll thinking of him? He was ashamed to go on kneeling, shamed to rise from his knees. At last, as it were from his nmost heart, a still small voice seemed to breathe forth the vords of the publican, "God be merciful to me a sinner!" Ie repeated them over and over, clinging to them as for his ife, and rose from his knees comforted and humbled, and eady to face the whole world. It was not needed: two other oys besides Arthur had already followed his example, and he vent down to the great School with a glimmering of another esson in his heart—the lesson that he who has conquered is own coward spirit has conquered the whole outward world; nd that other one which the old prophet learnt in the cave n Mount Horeb, when he hid his face, and the still small oice asked, "What doest thou here, Elijah?" that however ve may fancy ourselves alone on the side of good, the King nd Lord of men is nowhere without his witnesses; for in very society, however seemingly corrupt and godless, there re those who have not bowed the knee to Baal.

He found too how greatly he had exaggerated the effect to e produced by his act. For a few nights there was a sneer r a laugh when he knelt down, but this passed off soon, and ne by one all the other boys but three or four followed the ead. I fear that this was in some measure owing to the ct that Tom could probably have thrashed any boy in the oom except the præpostor; at any rate, every boy knew at he would try upon very slight provocation, and didn't hoose to run the risk of a hard fight because Tom Brown ad taken a fancy to say his prayers. Some of the small oys of Number 4 communicated the new state of things to eir chums, and in several other rooms the poor little fellows ied it on; in one instance or so, where the præpostor heard f it and interfered very decidedly, with partial success; but the rest, after a short struggle, the confessors were bullied r laughed down, and the old state of things went on for some me longer. Before either Tom Brown or Arthur left the chool-house, there was no room in which it had not become e regular custom. I trust it is so still, and that the old eathen state of things has gone out for ever.

night only frighten Arthur, and the remembrance of the esson he had learnt from him on his first night at Number 4. Then he would resolve to sit still, and not say a word till Arthur began; but he was always beat at that game, and had presently o begin talking in despair, fearing lest Arthur might think ne was vexed at something if he didn't, and dog tired of sitting ongue-tied.

It was hard work! But Tom had taken it up, and meant to stick to it, and go through with it so as to satisfy himself; in which resolution he was much assisted by the chaffing of East and his other old friends, who began to call him "dry-nurse," and otherwise to break their small wit on him. But when they ook other ground, as they did every now and then, Tom was sorely puzzled.

"Tell you what, Tommy," East would say, "you'll spoil young Hopeful with too much coddling. Why can't you let him go about by himself and find his own level? He'll never be worth a button, if you go on keeping him under your skirts."

"Well, but he ain't fit to fight his own way yet; I'm trying o get him to it every day—but he's very odd. Poor little beggar! I can't make him out a bit. He ain't a bit like anything I've ever seen or heard of—he seems all over nerves; anything you say seems to hurt him like a cut or a blow."

"That sort of boy's no use here," said East; "he'll only spoil. Now I'll tell you what to do, Tommy. Go and get a nice arge band-box made, and put him in with plenty of cotton-wool, and a pap-bottle, labelled 'With care—this side up,' and end him back to mamma."

"I think I shall make a hand of him though," said Tom, miling, "say what you will. There's something about him, every now and then, which shows me he's got pluck somewhere n him. That's the only thing after all that'll wash, ain't it, ld Scud? But how to get at it and bring it out?"

Tom took one hand out of his breeches-pocket and stuck : in his back hair for a scratch, giving his hat a tilt over his ose, his one method of invoking wisdom. He stared at the round with a ludicrously puzzled look, and presently looked p and met East's eyes. That young gentleman slapped him n the back, and then put his arm round his shoulder, as they trolled through the quadrangle together. "Tom," said he,

"Pretty little dear," said East, patting the top of his hat; "hark how he swears, Tom. Nicely brought-up young man, ain't he, I don't think."

"Let me alone, —— you," roared the boy, foaming with rage, and kicking at East, who quietly tripped him up, and deposited him on the floor in a place of safety.

"Gently, young fellow," said he; "'tain't improving for little whippersnappers like you to be indulging in blasphemy; so you stop that, or you'll get something you won't like."

"I'll have you both licked when I get out, that I will," rejoined the boy, beginning to snivel.

"Two can play at that game, mind you," said Tom, who had finished his examination of the list. "Now you just listen here. We've just come across the fives'-court, and Jones has four fags there already, two more than he wants. If he'd wanted us to change, he'd have stopped us himself. And here, you little blackguard, you've got seven names down on your list besides ours, and five of them School-house." Tom walked up to him, and jerked him on to his legs; he was by this time whining like a whipped puppy.

"Now just listen to me. We ain't going to fag for Jones. If you tell him you've sent us, we'll each of us give you such a thrashing as you'll remember." And Tom tore up the list and threw the pieces into the fire.

"And mind you, too," said East, "don't let me catch you again sneaking about the School-house, and picking up our fags. You haven't got the sort of hide to take a sound licking kindly"; and he opened the door and sent the young gentleman flying into the quadrangle with a parting kick.

"Nice boy, Tommy," said East, shoving his hands in his pockets and strolling to the fire.

"Worst sort we breed," responded Tom, following his example. "Thank goodness, no big fellow ever took to petting me."

"You'd never have been like that," said East. "I should like to have put him in a museum:—Christian young gentleman, nineteenth century, highly educated. Stir him up with a long pole, Jack, and hear him swear like a drunken sailor! He'd make a respectable public open its eyes, I think."

"Think he'll tell Jones?" said Tom.

"No," said East. "Don't care if he does."

"Why don't you call me Tom? lots of boys do that I don't like half so much as you. What are you reading, then? Hang it, you must come about with me, and not mope yourself," and Tom cast down his eyes on the book, and saw it

"Why, young un! what's the matter?" said he, kindly; "you ain't unhappy, are you?"

was the Bible. He was silent for a minute, and thought to himself, "Lesson Number 2, Tom Brown;" and then said gently—

the name; you English boys for whom this book is meant (God bless your bright faces and kind hearts!) will learn it all soon enough.

Into such a parish and state of society Arthur's father had been thrown at the age of twenty-five, a young married parson, full of faith, hope, and love. He had battled with it like a man, and had lots of fine Utopian ideas about the perfectibility of mankind, glorious humanity and such-like, knocked out of his head; and a real wholesome Christian love for the poor struggling, sinning men, of whom he felt himself one, and with and for whom he spent fortune, and strength, and life, driven into his heart. He had battled like a man, and gotten a man's reward. No silver teapots or salvers, with flowery inscriptions setting forth his virtues and the appreciation of a genteel parish; no fat living or stall, for which he never looked, and didn't care; no sighs and praises of comfortable dowagers and well got-up young women, who worked him slippers, sugared his tea, and adored him as "a devoted man;" but a manly respect, wrung from the unwilling souls of men who fancied his order their natural enemies; the fear and hatred of every one who was false or unjust in the district, were he master or man; and the blessed sight of women and children daily becoming more human and more homely, a comfort to themselves and to their husbands and fathers.

These things of course took time, and had to be fought for with toil and sweat of brain and heart, and with the life-blood poured out. All that, Arthur had laid his account to give, and took as a matter of course; neither pitying himself, nor looking on himself as a martyr, when he felt the wear and tear making him feel old before his time, and the stifling air of fever-dens telling on his health. His wife seconded him in everything. She had been rather fond of society, and much admired and run after before her marriage: and the London world to which she had belonged pitied poor Fanny Evelyn when she married the young clergyman, and went to settle in that smoky hole Turley, a very nest of Chartism and Atheism in a part of the country which all the decent families had had to leave for years. However, somehow or other she didn't seem to care. If her husband's living had been amongst green fields and near pleasant neighbours

by the request of the Committee of a Freethinking Club, established in the town by some of the factory hands (which he had striven against with might and main, and nearly suppressed), that some of their number might be allowed to help bear the coffin, than by anything else. Two of them were chosen, who with six other labouring men, his own fellow-workmen and friends, bore him to his grave—a man who had fought the Lord's fight even unto the death. The shops were closed and the factories shut that day in the parish, yet no master stopped the day's wages; but for many a year afterwards the townsfolk felt the want of that brave, hopeful, loving parson and his wife, who had lived to teach them mutual forbearance and helpfulness, and had *almost* at last given them a glimpse of what this old world would be if people would live for God and each other instead of for themselves.

What has all this to do with our story? Well, my dear boys, let a fellow go on his own way, or you won't get anything out of him worth having. I must show you what sort of a man it was who had begotten and trained little Arthur, or else you won't believe in him, which I am resolved you shall do; and you won't see how he, the timid weak boy, had points in him from which the bravest and strongest recoiled, and made his presence and example felt from the first on all sides, unconsciously to himself, and without the least attempt at proselytising. The spirit of his father was in him, and the Friend to whom his father had left him did not neglect the trust.

After supper that night, and almost nightly for years afterwards, Tom and Arthur, and by degrees East occasionally, and sometimes one, sometimes another, of their friends, read a chapter of the Bible together, and talked it over afterwards. Tom was at first utterly astonished, and almost shocked, at the sort of way in which Arthur read the book and talked about the men and women whose lives were there told. The first night they happened to fall on the chapters about the famine in Egypt, and Arthur began talking about Joseph as if he were a living statesman; just as he might have talked about Lord Grey and the Reform Bill; only that they were much more living realities to him. The book was to him, Tom saw, the most vivid and delightful history of real people, who might do right or wrong, just like any one who was

out what it's right to do the best you can, though it mayn't be the best absolutely. Every man isn't born to be a martyr."

"Of course, of course," said East; "but he's on one of his pet hobbies. How often have I told you, Tom, that you must drive a nail where it'll go?"

"And how often have I told you," rejoined Tom, "that it'll always go where you want, if you only stick to it and hit hard enough? I hate half-measures and compromises."

"Yes, he's a whole-hog man, is Tom. Must have the whole animal, hair and teeth, claws and tail," laughed East. "Sooner have no bread any day than half the loaf."

"I don't know," said Arthur, "it's rather puzzling; but ain't most right things got by proper compromises, I mean where the principle isn't given up?"

"That's just the point," said Tom; "I don't object to a compromise, where you don't give up your principle."

"Not you," said East laughingly. "I know him of old, Arthur, and you'll find him out some day. There isn't such a reasonable fellow in the world, to hear him talk. He never wants anything but what's right and fair; only when you come to settle what's right and fair, it's everything that he wants, and nothing that you want. And that's his idea of a compromise. Give me the Brown compromise when I'm on his side."

"Now, Harry," said Tom, "no more chaff—I'm serious. Look here—this is what makes my blood tingle"; and he turned over the pages of his Bible and read, "Shadrach, Meshach, and Abednego answered and said to the king, 'O Nebuchadnezzar, we are not careful to answer thee in this matter. If it *be* so, our God whom we serve is able to deliver us from the burning fiery furnace, and He will deliver us out of thine hand, O king. But *if not*, be it known unto thee, O king, that we will *not* serve thy gods, nor worship the golden image which thou hast set up.'" He read the last verse twice, emphasising the nots, and dwelling on them as if they gave him actual pleasure and were hard to part with.

They were silent a minute, and then Arthur said, "Yes, that's a glorious story, but it don't prove your point, Tom, I think. There are times when there is only one way, and that the highest, and then the men are found to stand in the breach."

CHAPTER III

ARTHUR MAKES A FRIEND

"Let Nature be your teacher:
Sweet is the lore which Nature brings;
Our meddling intellect
Mis-shapes the beauteous forms of things.
We murder to dissect—
Enough of Science and of Art;
Close up those barren leaves;
Come forth, and bring with you a heart
That watches and receives."—WORDSWORTH.

ABOUT six weeks after the beginning of the half, as Tom and Arthur were sitting one night before supper beginning their verses, Arthur suddenly stopped, and looked up, and said, "Tom, do you know anything of Martin?"

"Yes," said Tom, taking his hand out of his back hair, and delighted to throw his Gradus ad Parnassum on to the sofa; "I know him pretty well. He's a very good fellow, but as mad as a hatter. He's called Madman, you know. And never was such a fellow for getting all sorts of rum things about him. He tamed two snakes last half, and used to carry them about in his pocket, and I'll be bound he's got some hedgehogs and rats in his cupboard now, and no one knows what besides."

"I should like very much to know him," said Arthur; "he was next to me in the form to-day, and he'd lost his book and looked over mine, and he seemed so kind and gentle, that I liked him very much."

"Ah, poor old Madman, he's always losing his books," said Tom, "and getting called up and floored because he hasn't got them."

magpie fluttered down into the court, swearing, and the Madman danced out, howling, with his fingers in his mouth. The Doctor caught hold of him, and called to us to fetch some water. 'There, you silly fellow,' said he, quite pleased though to find he wasn't much hurt, 'you see you don't know the least what you're doing with all these things; and now, mind, you must give up practising chemistry by yourself.' Then he took hold of his arm and looked at it, and I saw he had to bite his lip, and his eyes twinkled; but he said, quite grave, 'Here, you see, you've been making all these foolish marks on yourself, which you can never get out, and you'll be very sorry for it in a year or two: now come down to the housekeeper's room, and let us see if you are hurt.' And away went the two, and we all stayed and had a regular turn-out of the den, till Martin came back with his hand bandaged and turned us out. However, I'll go and see what he's after, and tell him to come in after prayers to supper." And away went Tom to find the boy in question, who dwelt in a little study by himself, in New Row.

The aforesaid Martin, whom Arthur had taken such a fancy for, was one of those unfortunates who were at that time of day (and are, I fear, still) quite out of their places at a public school. If we knew how to use our boys, Martin would have been seized upon and educated as a natural philosopher. He had a passion for birds, beasts, and insects, and knew more of them and their habits than any one in Rugby; except perhaps the Doctor, who knew everything. He was also an experimental chemist on a small scale, and had made unto himself an electric machine, from which it was his greatest pleasure and glory to administer small shocks to any small boys who were rash enough to venture into his study. And this was by no means an adventure free from excitement; for, besides the probability of a snake dropping on to your head or twining lovingly up your leg, or a rat getting into your breeches-pocket in search of food, there was the animal and chemical odour to be faced, which always hung about the den, and the chance of being blown up in some of the many experiments which Martin was always trying, with the most wondrous results in the shape of explosions and smells that mortal boy ever heard of.

fed the young birds with his other hand; his attention was divided, and his shots flew wild, while every one of theirs told on his face and hands, and drove him into howlings and imprecations. He had been driven to ensconce the nest in a corner of his already too well-filled den.

His door was barricaded by a set of ingenious bolts of his own invention, for the sieges were frequent by the neighbours when any unusually ambrosial odour spread itself from the den to the neighbouring studies. The door panels were in a normal state of smash, but the frame of the door resisted all besiegers, and behind it the owner carried on his varied pursuits; much in the same state of mind, I should fancy, as a border farmer lived in, in the days of the old moss-troopers, when his hold might be summoned or his cattle carried off at any minute of night or day.

"Open, Martin, old boy—it's only I, only Tom Brown."

"Oh, very well, stop a moment." One bolt went back. "You're sure East isn't there?"

"No, no; hang it, open." Tom gave a kick, the other bolt creaked, and he entered the den.

Den indeed it was, about five feet six inches long by five wide, and seven feet high. About six tattered school-books, and a few chemical books, Taxidermy, Stanley on Birds, and an odd volume of Bewick, the latter in much better preservation, occupied the top shelves. The other shelves, where they had not been cut away and used by the owner for other purposes, were fitted up for the abiding places of birds, beasts, and reptiles. There was no attempt at carpet or curtain. The table was entirely occupied by the great work of Martin, the electric machine, which was covered carefully with the remains of his table-cloth. The jackdaw cage occupied one wall; the other was adorned by a small hatchet, a pair of climbing irons, and his tin candle-box, in which he was for the time being endeavouring to raise a hopeful young family of field-mice. As nothing should be let to lie useless, it was well that the candle-box was thus occupied, for candles Martin never had. A pound was issued to him weekly, as to the other boys, but as candles were available capital, and easily exchangeable for birds'-eggs or young birds, Martin's pound invariably found its way in a few hours to Howlett's the bird-fancier's, in the Bilton Road, who would give a hawk's or

fact, was the centre and turning-point of his school-life, that which was to make him or mar him; his appointed work and trial for the time being. And Tom was becoming a new boy, though with frequent tumbles in the dirt and perpetual hard battle with himself, and was daily growing in manfulness and thoughtfulness, as every high-couraged and well-principled boy must, when he finds himself for the first time consciously at grips with self and the devil. Already he could turn almost without a sigh from the school-gates, from which had just scampered off East and three or four others of his own particular set, bound for some jolly lark not quite according to law, and involving probably a row with louts, keepers, or farm-labourers, the skipping dinner or calling-over, some of Phœbe Jennings's beer, and a very possible flogging at the end of all as a relish. He had quite got over the stage in which he would grumble to himself, "Well, hang it, it's very hard of the Doctor to have saddled me with Arthur. Why couldn't he have chummed him with Fogey, or Thomkin, or any of the fellows who never do anything but walk round the close, and finish their copies the first day they're set?" But although all this was past, he often longed, and felt that he was right in longing, for more time for the legitimate pastimes of cricket, fives, bathing, and fishing within bounds, in which Arthur could not yet be his companion; and he felt that when the young un (as he now generally called him) had found a pursuit and some other friend for himself, he should be able to give more time to the education of his own body with a clear conscience.

And now what he so wished for had come to pass; he almost hailed it as a special providence (as indeed it was, but not for the reasons he gave for it—what providences are?) that Arthur should have singled out Martin of all fellows for a friend. "The old Madman is the very fellow," thought he; "he will take him scrambling over half the country after birds' eggs and flowers, make him run and swim and climb like an Indian, and not teach him a word of anything bad, or keep him from his lessons. What luck!" And so, with more than his usual heartiness, he dived into his cupboard, and hauled out an old knuckle-bone of ham, and two or three bottles of beer, together with the solemn pewter only used on state occasions; while Arthur, equally elated at the easy accomplishment of his first

get Martin and Arthur together alone at first had overcome his scruples, he was now heartily glad to open the door, broach another bottle of beer, and hand over the old ham-knuckle to the searching of his old friend's pocket-knife.

"Ah, you greedy vagabonds," said East, with his mouth full, "I knew there was something going on when I saw you cut off out of Hall so quick with your suppers. What a stunning tap, Tom! You are a wunner for bottling the swipes."

"I've had practice enough for the sixth in my time, and it's hard if I haven't picked up a wrinkle or two for my own benefit."

"Well, old Madman, and how goes the birds'-nesting campaign? How's Howlett? I expect the young rooks 'll be out in another fortnight, and then my turn comes."

"There'll be no young rooks fit for pies for a month yet; shows how much you know about it," rejoined Martin, who, though very good friends with East, regarded him with considerable suspicion for his propensity to practical jokes.

"Scud knows nothing and cares for nothing but grub and mischief," said Tom; "but young rook pie, especially when you've had to climb for them, is very pretty eating. However, I say, Scud, we're all going after a hawk's nest to-morrow, in Caldecott's Spinney; and if you'll come and behave yourself, we'll have a stunning climb."

"And a bathe in Aganippe. Hooray! I'm your man."

"No, no; no bathing in Aganippe; that's where our betters go."

"Well, well, never mind. I'm for the hawk's nest and anything that turns up."

And the bottled-beer being finished, and his hunger appeased, East departed to his study, "that sneak Jones," as he informed them, who had just got into the sixth and occupied the next study, having instituted a nightly visitation upon East and his chum, to their no small discomfort.

When he was gone, Martin rose to follow, but Tom stopped him. "No one goes near New Row," said he, "so you may just as well stop here and do your verses, and then we'll have some more talk. We'll be no end quiet; besides, no præpostor comes here now,—we haven't been visited once this half."

So the table was cleared, the cloth restored, and the three fell to work with Gradus and dictionary upon the morning's vulgus.

They were three very fair examples of the way in which

hands bequeathed vulgus-books have accumulated, are prepared with three or four vulguses on any subject in heaven or earth, or in "more worlds than one," which an unfortunate master can pitch upon. At any rate, such lucky fellows had generally one for themselves and one for a friend in my time. The only objection to the traditionary method of doing your vulguses was, the risk that the successions might have become confused, and so that you and another follower of traditions should show up the same identical vulgus some fine morning; in which case, when it happened, considerable grief was the result—but when did such risk hinder boys or men from short cuts and pleasant paths?

Now in the study that night, Tom was the upholder of the traditionary method of vulgus doing. He carefully produced two large vulgus-books, and began diving into them, and picking out a line here, and an ending there (tags as they were vulgarly called), till he had gotten all that he thought he could make fit. He then proceeded to patch his tags together with the help of his Gradus, producing an incongruous and feeble result of eight elegiac lines, the minimum quantity for his form, and finishing up with two highly moral lines extra, making ten in all, which he cribbed entire from one of his books, beginning "O genus humanum," and which he himself must have used a dozen times before, whenever an unfortunate or wicked hero, of whatever nation or language under the sun, was the subject. Indeed he began to have great doubts whether the master wouldn't remember them, and so only threw them in as extra lines, because in any case they would call off attention from the other tags, and if detected, being extra lines, he wouldn't be sent back to do two more in their place, while if they passed muster again he would get marks for them.

The second method, pursued by Martin, may be called the dogged, or prosaic method. He, no more than Tom, took any pleasure in the task, but having no old vulgus-books of his own, or any one's else, could not follow the traditionary method, for which too, as Tom remarked, he hadn't the genius. Martin then proceeded to write down eight lines in English, of the most matter-of-fact kind, the first that came into his head; and to convert these, line by line, by main force of Gradus and dictionary, into Latin that would scan. This was

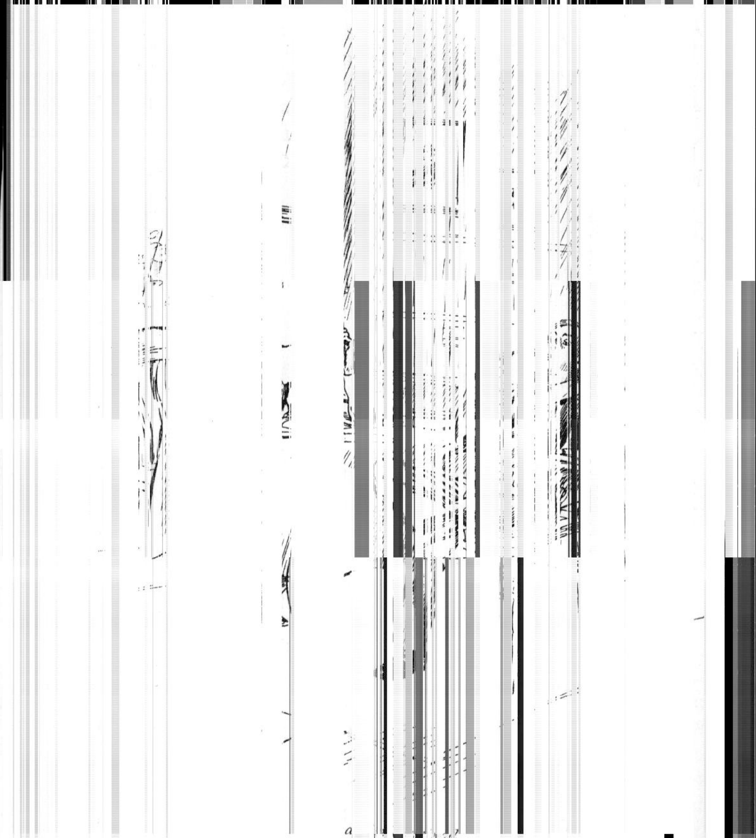

idered first what point in the character or event which was ne subject could most neatly be brought out within the limits f a vulgus, trying always to get his idea into the eight lines, ut not binding himself to ten or even twelve lines if he ouldn't do this. He then set to work, as much as possible vithout Gradus or other help, to clothe his idea in appropriate atin or Greek, and would not be satisfied till he had polished well up with the aptest and most poetic words and phrases e could get at.

A fourth method indeed was used in the school, but of oo simple a kind to require a comment. It may be called he vicarious method, obtained amongst big boys of lazy r bullying habits, and consisted simply in making clever boys vhom they could thrash do their whole vulgus for them, and onstrue it to them afterwards; which latter is a method not o be encouraged, and which I strongly advise you all not o practise. Of the others, you will find the traditionary nost troublesome, unless you can steal your vulguses whole *experto crede*), and that the artistic method pays the best oth in marks and other ways.

The vulguses being finished by nine o'clock, and Martin aving rejoiced above measure in the abundance of light, nd of Gradus and dictionary, and other conveniences lmost unknown to him for getting through the work, and aving been pressed by Arthur to come and do his verses here whenever he liked, the three boys went down to Martin's en, and Arthur was initiated into the lore of birds'-eggs, to is great delight. The exquisite colouring and forms stonished and charmed him, who had scarcely ever seen any ut a hen's egg or an ostrich's, and by the time he was igged away to bed he had learned the names of at ast twenty sorts, and dreamt of the glorious perils of ee-climbing, and that he had found a roc's egg in the island s big as Sinbad's, and clouded like a tit-lark's, in blowing hich Martin and he had nearly been drowned in the yolk.

"Why, young un," said he, "what have you been after? ou don't mean to say you've been wading?"

The tone of reproach made poor little Arthur shrink p in a moment and look piteous, and Tom with a shrug of s shoulders turned his anger on Martin.

"Well, I didn't think, Madman, that you'd have been ıch a muff as to let him be getting wet through at this time f day. You might have done the wading yourself."

"So I did, of course, only he would come in too, to see the est. We left six eggs in; they'll be hatched in a day or vo."

"Hang the eggs!" said Tom; "a fellow can't turn his back or a moment but all his work's undone. He'll be laid up or a week for this precious lark, I'll be bound."

"Indeed, Tom, now," pleaded Arthur, "my feet ain't et, for Martin made me take off my shoes and stockings and ousers."

"But they are wet, and dirty too—can't I see?" answered 'om; "and you'll be called up and floored when the master es what a state you're in. You haven't looked at second sson, you know." Oh Tom, you old humbug! you to be pbraiding any one with not learning their lessons. If you adn't been floored yourself now at first lesson, do you mean say you wouldn't have been with them? And you've taken vay all poor little Arthur's joy and pride in his first birds' eggs, nd he goes and puts them down in the study, and takes own his books with a sigh, thinking he has done something orribly wrong, whereas he has learnt on in advance much ore than will be done at second lesson.

But the old Madman hasn't, and gets called up and makes ome frightful shots, losing about ten places, and all but etting floored. This somewhat appeases Tom's wrath, and y the end of the lesson he has regained his temper. And terwards in their study he begins to get right again, as e watches Arthur's intense joy at seeing Martin blowing the ggs and glueing them carefully on to bits of cardboard, and otes the anxious, loving looks which the little fellow casts delong at him. And then he thinks, "What an ill-tempered east I am! Here's just what I was wishing for last night ome about, and I'm spoiling it all," and in another five inutes has swallowed the last mouthful of his bile, and is

"There, don't you see?" said East pointing to a lump of nistletoe in the next tree, which was a beech: he saw that Martin and Tom were busy with the climbing-irons, and ouldn't resist the temptation of hoaxing. Arthur stared nd wondered more than ever.

"Well, how curious! it doesn't look a bit like what I ex-ected," said he.

"Very odd birds, kestrels," said East, looking waggishly t his victim, who was still star-gazing.

"But I thought it was in a fir-tree?" objected Arthur.

"Ah, don't you know that's a new sort of fir which old Caldecott brought from the Himalayas?"

"Really!" said Arthur; "I'm glad I know that—how nlike our firs they are! They do very well too here, don't hey? the Spinney's full of them."

"What's that humbug he's telling you?" cried Tom, ooking up, having caught the word Himalayas, and suspect-ng what East was after.

"Only about this fir," said Arthur, putting his hand on the tem of the beech.

"Fir!" shouted Tom, "why, you don't mean to say, oung un, you don't know a beech when you see one?"

Poor little Arthur looked terribly ashamed, and East xploded in laughter which made the wood ring. "I've ardly ever seen any trees," faltered Arthur.

"What a shame to hoax him, Scud!" cried Martin. "Never mind, Arthur, you shall know more about trees han he does in a week or two."

"And isn't that the kestrel's nest then?" asked Arthur.

"That! why, that's a piece of mistletoe. There's the est, that lump of sticks up this fir."

"Don't believe him, Arthur," struck in the incorrigible East; "I just saw an old magpie go out of it."

Martin did not deign to reply to this sally, except by a runt, as he buckled the last buckle of his climbing-irons; nd Arthur looked reproachfully at East without speaking.

But now came the tug of war. It was a very difficult ree to climb until the branches were reached, the first of which was some fourteen feet up, for the trunk was too large t the bottom to be swarmed; in fact, neither of the boys ould reach more than half round it with their arms. Martin

"All right—four eggs!" shouted he.

he would wait till they came close to him and then fly on for forty yards or so, and, with an impudent flicker of his tail, dart into the depths of the quickset), came beating down a high double hedge, two on each side.

"Ugh, ugh! something to drink—ugh! it was addled," spluttered he.

"There he is again," "Head him," "Let drive," "I had him there," "Take care where you're throwing, Madman," the shouts might have been heard a quarter of a mile off. They were heard some two hundred yards off by a farmer and

subject, and bent on making an example of the first boys he could catch. So he and his shepherds crouched behind the hurdles, and watched the party, who were approaching all unconscious.

Why should that old guinea-fowl be lying out in the hedge just at this particular moment of all the year? Who can say? Guinea-fowls always are—so are all other things, animals, and persons, requisite for getting one into scrapes, always ready when any mischief can come of them. At any rate, just under East's nose popped out the old guinea-hen, scuttling along and shrieking "Come back, come back," at the top of her voice. Either of the other three might perhaps have withstood the temptation, but East first lets drive the stone he has in his hand at her, and then rushes to turn her into the hedge again. He succeeds, and then they are all at it for dear life, up and down the hedge in full cry, the "Come back, come back," getting shriller and fainter every minute.

Meantime, the farmer and his men steal over the hurdles and creep down the hedge towards the scene of action. They are almost within a stone's throw of Martin, who is pressing the unlucky chase hard, when Tom catches sight of them, and sings out, "Louts, 'ware louts, your side! Madman, look ahead!" and then catching hold of Arthur, hurries him away across the field towards Rugby as hard as they can tear. Had he been by himself, he would have stayed to see it out with the others, but now his heart sinks and all his pluck goes. The idea of being led up to the Doctor with Arthur for bagging fowls quite unmans and takes half the run out of him.

However, no boys are more able to take care of themselves than East and Martin; they dodge the pursuers, slip through a gap, and come pelting after Tom and Arthur, whom they catch up in no time; the farmer and his men are making good running about a field behind. Tom wishes to himself that they had made off in any other direction, but now they are all in for it together, and must see it out.

"You won't leave the young un, will you?" says he, as they haul poor little Arthur, already losing wind from the fright, through the next hedge. "Not we," is the answer from both. The next hedge is a stiff one; the pursuers gain horribly on them, and they only just pull Arthur through, with two great rents in his trousers, as the foremost shepherd comes up on the

I tells 'ee," shouted he, as Holmes stands between Martin and Willum, "and have druv a matter of a dozen young pullets pretty nigh to death."

"Oh, there's a whacker!" cried East; "we haven't been within a hundred yards of his barn; we haven't been up here above ten minutes, and we've seen nothing but a tough old guinea-hen, who ran like a greyhound."

"Indeed, that's all true, Holmes, upon my honour," added Tom; "we weren't after his fowls; guinea-hen ran out of the hedge under our feet, and we've seen nothing else."

"Drat their talk. Thee catch hold o' t'other, Willum, and come along wi' 'un."

"Farmer Thompson," said Holmes, warning off Willum and the prong with his stick, while Diggs faced the other shepherd, cracking his fingers like pistol shots, "now listen to reason—the boys haven't been after your fowls, that's plain."

"Tells 'ee I see'd 'em. Who be you, I should like to know?"

"Never you mind, Farmer," answered Holmes. "And now I'll just tell you what it is—you ought to be ashamed of yourself for leaving all that poultry about, with no one to watch it, so near the School. You deserve to have it all stolen. So if you choose to come up to the Doctor with them, I shall go with you, and tell him what I think of it."

The farmer began to take Holmes for a master; besides, he wanted to get back to his flock. Corporal punishment was out of the question, the odds were too great; so he began to hint at paying for the damage. Arthur jumped at this, offering to pay anything, and the farmer immediately valued the guinea-hen at half-a-sovereign.

"Half-a-sovereign!" cried East, now released from the farmer's grip; "well, that is a good one! the old hen ain't hurt a bit, and she's seven years old, I know, and as tough as whipcord; she couldn't lay another egg to save her life."

It was at last settled that they should pay the farmer two shillings, and his man one shilling, and so the matter ended, to the unspeakable relief of Tom, who hadn't been able to say a word, being sick at heart at the idea of what the Doctor would think of him: and now the whole party of boys marched off down the footpath towards Rugby. Holmes, who was one of the best boys in the School, began to im-

which decoration, however, he carefully concealed from Tom. Before the end of the half-year he had trained into a bold climber and good runner, and, as Martin had foretold, knew twice as much about trees, birds, flowers, and many other things, as our good-hearted and facetious young friend Harry East.

every boy who was ever likely to fight at all knew all his neighbours' prowess perfectly well, and could tell to a nicety what chance he would have in a stand-up fight with any other boy in the house. But of course no such experience could be gotten as regarded boys in other houses; and as most of the other houses were more or less jealous of the School-house, collisions were frequent.

After all, what would life be without fighting, I should like to know? From the cradle to the grave, fighting, rightly understood, is the business, the real, highest, honestest business of every son of man. Every one who is worth his salt has his enemies, who must be beaten, be they evil thoughts and habits in himself or spiritual wickednesses in high places, or Russians, or Border-ruffians, or Bill, Tom, or Harry, who will not let him live his life in quiet till he has thrashed them.

It is no good for Quakers, or any other body of men, to uplift their voices against fighting. Human nature is too strong for them, and they don't follow their own precepts. Every soul of them is doing his own piece of fighting, somehow and somewhere. The world might be a better world without fighting, for anything I know, but it wouldn't be our world; and therefore I am dead against crying peace when there is no peace, and isn't meant to be. I am as sorry as any man to see folk fighting the wrong people and the wrong things, but I'd a deal sooner see them doing that, than that they should have no fight in them. So having recorded, and being about to record, my hero's fights of all sorts, with all sorts of enemies, I shall now proceed to give an account of his passage-at-arms with the only one of his school-fellows whom he ever had to encounter in this manner.

It was drawing towards the close of Arthur's first half-year, and the May evenings were lengthening out. Locking-up was not till eight o'clock, and everybody was beginning to talk about what he would do in the holidays. The shell, in which form all our *dramatis personæ* now are, were reading amongst other things the last book of Homer's Iliad, and had worked through it as far as the speeches of the women over Hector's body. It is a whole school-day, and four or five of the School-house boys (amongst whom are Arthur, Tom, and East) are preparing third lesson together. They have finished the regulation forty lines, and are for the most part getting very tired,

ἀλλὰ σὺ τόν γ' ἐπέεσσι παραιφάμενος κατέρυκες,
Σῇ τ' ἀγανοφροσύνῃ καὶ σοῖς ἀγανοῖς ἐπέεσσιν.

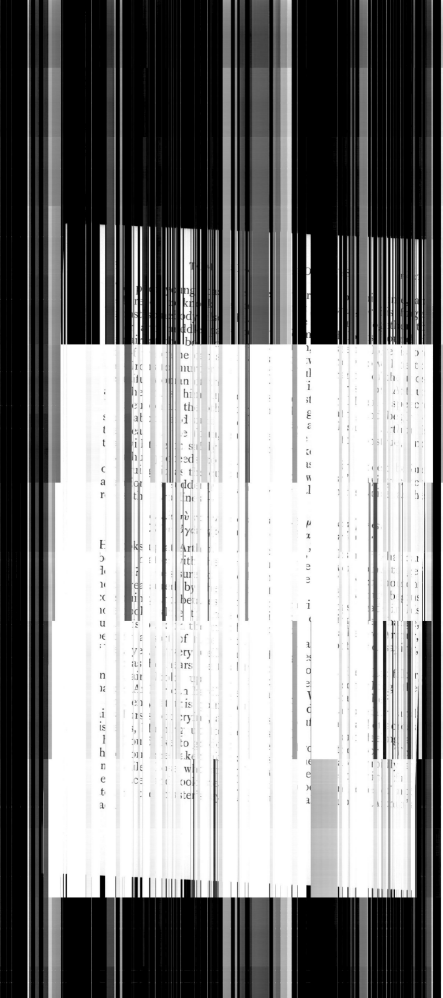

The master looks puzzled for a moment, and then seeing, as the fact is, that the boy is really affected to tears by the most touching thing in Homer, perhaps in all profane poetry put together, steps up to him and lays his hand kindly on his shoulder, saying, "Never mind, my little man, you've construed very well. Stop a minute, there's no hurry."

Now, as luck would have it, there sat next above Tom on that day, in the middle bench of the form, a big boy, by name Williams, generally supposed to be the cock of the shell, therefore of all the school below the fifths. The small boys, who are great speculators on the prowess of their elders, used to hold forth to one another about Williams's great strength, and to discuss whether East or Brown would take a licking from him. He was called Slogger Williams, from the force with which it was supposed he could hit. In the main, he was a rough, good-natured fellow enough, but very much alive to his own dignity. He reckoned himself the king of the form, and kept up his position with the strong hand, especially in the matter of forcing boys not to construe more than the legitimate forty lines. He had already grunted and grumbled to himself, when Arthur went on reading beyond the forty lines. But now that he had broken down just in the middle of all the long words, the Slogger's wrath was fairly roused.

"Sneaking little brute," muttered he, regardless of prudence, "clapping on the waterworks just in the hardest place; see if I don't punch his head after fourth lesson."

"Whose?" said Tom, to whom the remark seemed to be addressed.

"Why, that little sneak, Arthur's," replied Williams.

"No, you sha'n't," said Tom.

"Hullo!" exclaimed Williams, looking at Tom with great surprise for a moment, and then giving him a sudden dig in the ribs with his elbow, which sent Tom's books flying on to the floor, and called the attention of the master, who turned suddenly round, and seeing the state of things, said—

"Williams, go down three places, and then go on."

The Slogger found his legs very slowly, and proceeded to go below Tom and two other boys with great disgust, and then, turning round and facing the master, said, "I haven't learnt any more, sir; our lesson is only forty lines."

"Huzza, there's going to be a fight between Slogger Williams and Tom Brown!"

The news ran like wild-fire about, and many boys who were on their way to tea at their several houses turned back, and sought the back of the chapel, where the fights come off.

"Just run and tell East to come and back me," said Tom to a small School-house boy, who was off like a rocket to Harrowell's, just stopping for a moment to poke his head into the School-house hall, where the lower boys were already at tea, and sing out, "Fight! Tom Brown and Slogger Williams."

Up start half the boys at once, leaving bread, eggs, butter, sprats, and all the rest to take care of themselves. The greater part of the remainder follow in a minute, after swallowing their tea, carrying their food in their hands to consume as they go. Three or four only remain, who steal the butter of the more impetuous, and make to themselves an unctuous feast.

In another minute East and Martin tear through the quadrangle, carrying a sponge, and arrive at the scene of action just as the combatants are beginning to strip. Tom felt he had got his work cut out for him, as he stripped off his jacket, waistcoat, and braces. East tied his handkerchief round his waist, and rolled up his shirt-sleeves for him: "Now, old boy, don't open your mouth to say a word, or try to help yourself a bit, we'll do all that; you keep all your breath and strength for the Slogger." Martin meanwhile folded the clothes, and put them under the chapel rails; and now Tom, with East to handle him and Martin to give him a knee, steps out on the turf, and is ready for all that may come: and here is the Slogger too, all stripped, and thirsting for the fray.

It doesn't look a fair match at first glance: Williams is nearly two inches taller, and probably a long year older than his opponent, and he is very strongly made about the arms and shoulders; "peels well," as the little knot of big fifth-form boys, the amateurs, say; who stand outside the ring of little boys, looking complacently on, but taking no active part in the proceedings. But down below he is not so good by any means; no spring from the loins, and feeblish, not to say shipwrecky, about the knees. Tom, on the contrary, though

Making play with both hands.

Tom's face begins to look very one-sided—there are little queer bumps on his forehead, and his mouth is bleeding; but East keeps the wet sponge going so scientifically, that he comes up looking as fresh and bright as ever. Williams is only slightly marked in the face, but by the nervous movement of his elbows you can see that Tom's body-blows are telling. In fact, half the vice of the Slogger's hitting is neutralised, for he daren't lunge out freely for fear of exposing his sides. It is too interesting by this time for much shouting, and the whole ring is very quiet.

"All right, Tommy," whispers East; "hold on's the horse that's to win. We've got the last. Keep your head, old boy."

But where is Arthur all this time? Words cannot paint the poor little fellow's distress. He couldn't muster courage to come up to the ring, but wandered up and down from the great fives'-court to the corner of the chapel rails. Now trying to make up his mind to throw himself between them and try to stop them; then thinking of running in and telling his friend Mary, who he knew would instantly report to the Doctor. The stories he had heard of men being killed in prize-fights rose up horribly before him.

Once only, when the shouts of "Well done, Brown!" "Huzza for the School-house!" rose higher than ever, he ventured up to the ring, thinking the victory was won. Catching sight of Tom's face in the state I have described, all fear of consequences vanishing out of his mind, he rushed straight off to the matron's room, beseeching her to get the fight stopped, or he should die.

But it's time for us to get back to the close. What is this fierce tumult and confusion? The ring is broken, and high and angry words are being bandied about: "It's all fair,"—"It isn't,"—"No hugging!" the fight is stopped. The combatants, however, sit there quietly, tended by their seconds, while their adherents wrangle in the middle. East can't help shouting challenges to two or three of the other side, though he never leaves Tom for a moment, and plies the sponges as fast as ever.

The fact is, that at the end of the last round, Tom, seeing a good opening, had closed with his opponent, and after a moment's struggle had thrown him heavily, by help of

"You'd better stop, gentlemen," he says; "the Doctor knows that Brown's fighting—he'll be out in a minute."

"You go to Bath, Bill," is all that that excellent servitor gets by his advice. And being a man of his hands, and a staunch upholder of the School-house, can't help stopping to look on for a bit, and see Tom Brown, their pet craftsman, fight a round.

It is grim earnest now, and no mistake. Both boys feel this, and summon every power of head, hand, and eye to their aid. A piece of luck on either side, a foot slipping, a blow getting well home, or another fall, may decide it. Tom works slowly round for an opening; he has all the legs, and can choose his own time; the Slogger waits for the attack, and hopes to finish it by some heavy right-handed blow. As they quarter slowly over the ground, the evening sun comes out from behind a cloud and falls full on Williams's face. Tom darts in; the heavy right-hand is delivered, but only grazes his head. A short rally at close quarters, and they close; in another moment the Slogger is thrown again heavily for the third time.

"I'll give you three to two on the little one in half-crowns," said Groove to Rattle.

"No, thank'ee," answers the other, diving his hands further into his coat-tails.

Just at this stage of the proceedings, the door of the turret which leads to the Doctor's library suddenly opens, and he steps into the close, and makes straight for the ring, in which Brown and the Slogger are both seated on their seconds' knees for the last time.

"The Doctor! the Doctor!" shouts some small boy who catches sight of him, and the ring melts away in a few seconds, the small boys tearing off, Tom collaring his jacket and waistcoat, and slipping through the little gate by the chapel, and round the corner to Harrowell's with his backers, as lively as need be; Williams and his backers making off not quite so fast across the close; Groove, Rattle, and the other bigger fellows trying to combine dignity and prudence in a comical manner, and walking off fast enough, they hope, not to be recognised, and not fast enough to look like running away.

Young Brooke alone remains on the ground by the time the

"Now remember," added the Doctor, as he stopped at the turret-door, "this fight is not to go on."

"Down in the country when I was a boy."

Tom and the Slogger shook hands with great satisfaction and mutual respect.

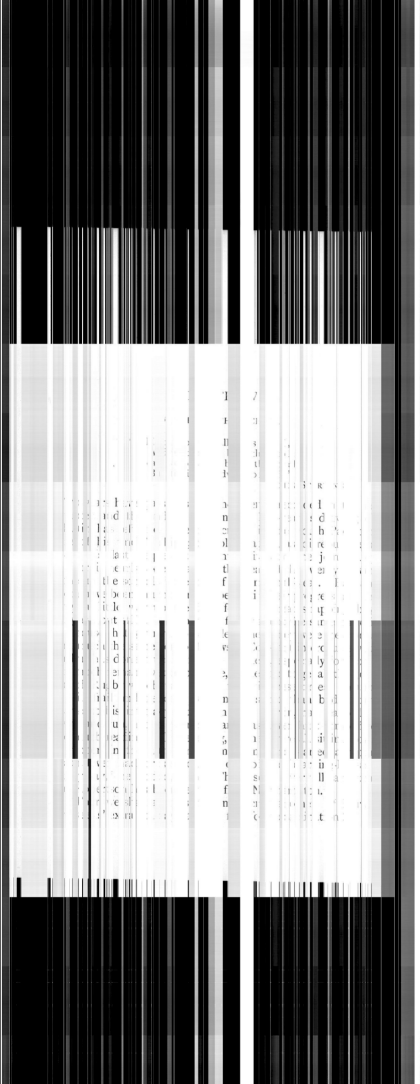

"I hope not," said Tom; "there'll be no Marylebone match then at the end of the half."

Some thought one thing, some another, many didn't believe the report; but the next day, Tuesday, Dr. Robertson arrived, and stayed all day, and had long conferences with the Doctor.

On Wednesday morning, after prayers, the Doctor addressed the whole School. There were several cases of fever in different houses, he said; but Dr. Robertson, after the most careful examination, had assured him that it was not infectious, and that if proper care were taken, there could be no reason for stopping the school work at present. The examinations were just coming on, and it would be very unadvisable to break-up now. However, any boys who chose to do so were at liberty to write home, and, if their parents wished it, to leave at once. He should send the whole School home if the fever spread.

The next day Arthur sickened, but there was no other case. Before the end of the week thirty or forty boys had gone, but the rest stayed on. There was a general wish to please the Doctor, and a feeling that it was cowardly to run away.

On the Saturday Thompson died, in the bright afternoon, while the cricket-match was going on as usual on the big-side ground: the Doctor coming from his death-bed, passed along the gravel-walk at the side of the close, but no one knew what had happened till the next day. At morning lecture it began to be rumoured, and by afternoon chapel was known generally; and a feeling of seriousness and awe at the actual presence of death among them came over the whole school. In all the long years of his ministry the Doctor perhaps never spoke words which sank deeper than some of those in that day's sermon. "When I came yesterday from visiting all but the very death-bed of him who has been taken from us, and looked around upon all the familiar objects and scenes within our own ground, where your common amusements were going on with your common cheerfulness and activity, I felt there was nothing painful in witnessing that; it did not seem in any way shocking or out of tune with those feelings which the sight of a dying Christian must be supposed to awaken. The unsuitableness in point of natural feeling between scenes of mourning and scenes of liveliness did not at all present itself.

Arthur was lying on the sofa by the open window.

"Oh, I know, Tom; Mary has told me every day about you, and how she was obliged to make the Doctor speak to you to keep you away. I'm very glad you didn't get up, for you might have caught it; and you couldn't stand being ill, with all the matches going on. And you're in the eleven, too, I hear—I'm so glad."

"Yes, ain't it jolly?" said Tom proudly; "I'm ninth too. I made forty at the last pie-match, and caught three fellows out. So I was put in above Jones and Tucker. Tucker's so savage, for he was head of the twenty-two."

"Well, I think you ought to be higher yet," said Arthur, who was as jealous for the renown of Tom in games, as Tom was for his as a scholar.

"Never mind, I don't care about cricket or anything now you're getting well, Geordie; and I shouldn't have hurt, I know, if they'd have let me come up,—nothing hurts me. But you'll get about now directly, won't you? You won't believe how clean I've kept the study. All your things are just as you left them; and I feed the old magpie just when you used, though I have to come in from big-side for him, the old rip. He won't look pleased all I can do, and sticks his head first on one side and then on the other, and blinks at me before he'll begin to eat, till I'm half inclined to box his ears. And whenever East comes in, you should see him hop off to the window, dot and go one, though Harry wouldn't touch a feather of him now."

Arthur laughed. "Old Gravey has a good memory, he can't forget the sieges of poor Martin's den in old times." He paused a moment, and then went on: "You can't think how often I've been thinking of old Martin since I've been ill; I suppose one's mind gets restless, and likes to wander off to strange unknown places. I wonder what queer new pets the old boy has got; how he must be revelling in the thousand new birds, beasts, and fishes!"

Tom felt a pang of jealousy, but kicked it out in a moment. "Fancy him on a South-Sea Island, with the Cherokees or Patagonians, or some such wild niggers!" (Tom's ethnology and geography were faulty, but sufficient for his needs); "they'll make the old Madman cock medicine-man and tattoo him all over. Perhaps he's cutting about now all blue, and has a squaw and a wigwam. He'll improve their boomerangs,

now, if you don't mind. I've asked Mary to tell the Doctor that you are with me, so you needn't go down to calling-over; and I mayn't have another chance, for I shall most likely have to go home for change of air to get well, and mayn't come back this half."

"Oh, do you think you must go away before the end of the half? I'm so sorry. It's more than five weeks yet to the holidays, and all the fifth-form examination and half the cricket-matches to come yet. And what shall I do all that time alone in our study? Why, Arthur, it will be more than twelve weeks before I see you again. Oh, hang it, I can't stand that! Besides, who's to keep me up to working at the examination books? I shall come out bottom of the form, as sure as eggs is eggs."

Tom was rattling on, half in joke, half in earnest, for he wanted to get Arthur out of his serious vein, thinking it would do him harm; but Arthur broke in—

"Oh, please Tom, stop, or you'll drive all I had to say out of my head. And I'm already horribly afraid I'm going to make you angry."

"Don't gammon, young un," rejoined Tom (the use of the old name, dear to him from old recollections, made Arthur start and smile, and feel quite happy); "you know you ain't afraid, and you've never made me angry since the first month we chummed together. Now I'm going to be quite sober for a quarter of an hour, which is more than I am once in a year; so make the most of it; heave ahead, and pitch into me right and left"

"Dear Tom, I ain't going to pitch into you," said Arthur, piteously; "and it seems so cocky in me to be advising you, who've been my backbone ever since I've been at Rugby, and have made the school a paradise to me. Ah, I see I shall never do it, unless I go head-over-heels at once, as you said when you taught me to swim. Tom, I want you to give up using vulgus-books and cribs."

Arthur sank back on his pillow with a sigh, as if the effort had been great; but the worst was now over, and he looked straight at Tom, who was evidently taken aback. He leant his elbows on his knees, and stuck his hands into his hair, whistled a verse of "Billy Taylor," and then was quite silent for another minute. Not a shade crossed his face, but he

Arthur saw that he had got his point; he knew his friend well, and was wise in silence as in speech. He only said, "I would sooner have the Doctor's good opinion of me as I really am, than any man's in the world."

After another minute, Tom began again: "Look here, young un, how on earth am I to get time to play the matches this half, if I give up cribs? We're in the middle of that long crabbed chorus in the Agamemnon; I can only just make head or tail of it with the crib. Then there's Pericles's speech coming on in Thucydides, and 'The Birds' to get up for the examination, besides the Tacitus." Tom groaned at the thought of his accumulated labours. "I say, young un, there's only five weeks or so left to holidays; mayn't I go on as usual for this half? I'll tell the Doctor about it some day, or you may."

Arthur looked out of the window; the twilight had come on, and all was silent. He repeated in a low voice, "In this thing the Lord pardon thy servant, that when my master goeth into the house of Rimmon to worship there, and he leaneth on my hand, and I bow down myself in the house of Rimmon, when I bow down myself in the house of Rimmon, the Lord pardon thy servant in this thing."

Not a word more was said on the subject, and the boys were again silent—one of those blessed, short silences in which the resolves which colour a life are so often taken.

Tom was the first to break it. "You've been very ill indeed, haven't you, Geordie?" said he, with a mixture of awe and curiosity, feeling as if his friend had been in some strange place or scene, of which he could form no idea, and full of the memory of his own thoughts during the last week.

"Yes, very. I'm sure the Doctor thought I was going to die. He gave me the Sacrament last Sunday, and you can't think what he is when one is ill. He said such brave, and tender, and gentle things to me, I felt quite light and strong after it, and never had any more fear. My mother brought our old medical man, who attended me when I was a poor sickly child; he said my constitution was quite changed, and that I'm fit for anything now. If it hadn't, I couldn't have stood three days of this illness. That's all thanks to you, and the games you've made me fond of."

frightened. I thought I should die, and I could not face it for a moment. I don't think it was sheer cowardice at first, but I thought how hard it was to be taken away from my mother and sisters, and you all, just as I was beginning to see my way to many things, and to feel that I might be a man and do a man's work. To die without having fought, and worked, and given one's life away, was too hard to bear. I got terribly impatient, and accused God of injustice, and strove to justify myself; and the harder I strove, the deeper I sank. Then the image of my dear father often came across me, but I turned from it. Whenever it came, a heavy numbing throb seemed to take hold of my heart, and say, 'Dead—dead—dead.' And I cried out, 'The living, the living shall praise Thee, O God; the dead cannot praise Thee. There is no work in the grave; in the night no man can work. But I can work. I can do great things. I *will* do great things. Why wilt Thou slay me?' And so I struggled and plunged, deeper and deeper, and went down into a living black tomb. I was alone there, with no power to stir or think; alone with myself; beyond the reach of all human fellowship; beyond Christ's reach, I thought, in my nightmare. You, who are brave and bright and strong, can have no idea of that agony. Pray to God you never may. Pray as for your life."

Arthur stopped—from exhaustion, Tom thought; but what between his fear lest Arthur should hurt himself, his awe, and longing for him to go on, he couldn't ask, or stir to help him.

Presently he went on, but quite calm and slow. "I don't know how long I was in that state. For more than a day, I know; for I was quite conscious, and lived my outer life all the time, and took my medicines, and spoke to my mother, and heard what they said. But I didn't take much note of time; I thought time was over for me, and that that tomb was what was beyond. Well, on last Sunday morning, as I seemed to lie in that tomb, alone, as I thought, for ever and ever, the black dead wall was cleft in two, and I was caught up and borne through into the light by some great power, some living mighty Spirit. Tom, do you remember the living creatures and the wheels in Ezekiel? It was just like that: 'when they went I heard the noise of

shall surely come, it shall not tarry.' It was early morning I know, then, it was so quiet and cool, and my mother was fast

"Yes, indeed, I've known him for years," and she held out her hand to Tom.

asleep in the chair by my bedside; but it wasn't only a dream of mine. I know it wasn't a dream. Then I fell into a deep sleep, and only woke after afternoon chapel; and the Doctor

The old gentleman loved to bowl slow twisters to him.

and then for the first time was aware of a beautiful new fishing-rod, with old Eton's mark on it, and a splendidly bound Bible, which lay on his table, on the title page of which was written—"TOM BROWN, from his affectionate and grateful friends, Frances Jane Arthur; George Arthur."

I leave you all to guess how he slept, and what he dreamt of.

"I don't know about ruin," answered Tom; "I know that you and I would have had the sack long ago, if it hadn't been for him. And you know it as well as I."

"Well, we were in a baddish way before he came, I own; but this new crotchet of his is past a joke."

"Let's give it a trial, Harry; come—you know how often he has been right and we wrong."

"Now, don't you two be jawing away about young Squaretoes," struck in Gower. "He's no end of a sucking wiseacre, I dare say; but we've no time to lose, and I've got the fives'-court at half-past nine."

"I say, Gower," said Tom, appealingly, "be a good fellow, and let's try if we can't get on without the crib."

"What! in this chorus? Why, we sha'n't get through ten lines."

"I say, Tom," cried East, having hit on a new idea, "don't you remember, when we were in the upper fourth, and old Momus caught me construing off the leaf of a crib which I'd torn out and put in my book, and which would float out on to the floor, he sent me up to be flogged for it?"

"Yes, I remember it very well."

"Well, the Doctor, after he'd flogged me, told me himself that he didn't flog me for using a translation, but for taking it into lesson, and using it there when I hadn't learnt a word before I came in. He said there was no harm in using a translation to get a clue to hard passages, if you tried all you could first to make them out without."

"Did he, though?" said Tom; "then Arthur must be wrong."

"Of course he is," said Gower, "the little prig. We'll only use the crib when we can't construe without it. Go ahead, East."

And on this agreement they started: Tom, satisfied with having made his confession, and not sorry to have a *locus pœnitentiæ*, and not to be deprived altogether of the use of his old and faithful friend.

The boys went on as usual, each taking a sentence in turn, and the crib being handed to the one whose turn it was to construe. Of course Tom couldn't object to this, as, was it not simply lying there to be appealed to in case the sentence should prove too hard altogether for the construer? But it

using a crib? Hang it, Tom, if you're going to deprive all our school-fellows of the chance of exercising Christian benevolence and being good Samaritans, I shall cut the concern."

"I wish you wouldn't joke about it, Harry; it's hard enough to see one's way, a precious sight harder than I thought last night. But I suppose there's a use and an abuse of both, and one'll get straight enough somehow. But you can't make out anyhow that one has a right to use old vulgus-books and copy-books."

"Hullo, more heresy! How fast a fellow goes down hill when he once gets his head before his legs. Listen to me, Tom. Not use old vulgus-books?—why, you Goth! ain't we to take the benefit of the wisdom, and admire and use the work of past generations? Not use old copy-books! Why you might as well say we ought to pull down Westminster Abbey, and put up a go-to-meeting-shop with churchwarden windows; or never read Shakspere, but only Sheridan Knowles. Think of all the work and labour that our predecessors have bestowed on these very books; and are we to make their work of no value?"

"I say, Harry, please don't chaff; I'm really serious."

"And then, is it not our duty to consult the pleasure of others rather than our own, and above all that of our masters? Fancy then the difference to them in looking over a vulgus which has been carefully touched and retouched by themselves and others, and which must bring them a sort of dreamy pleasure, as if they'd met the thought or expression of it somewhere or another—before they were born, perhaps; and that of cutting up, and making picture-frames round all your and my false quantities, and other monstrosities. Why, Tom, you wouldn't be so cruel as never to let old Momus hum over the 'O genus humanum' again, and then look up doubtingly through his spectacles, and end by smiling and giving three extra marks for it: just for old sake's sake, I suppose."

"Well," said Tom, getting up in something as like a huff as he was capable of, "it's deuced hard that when a fellow's really trying to do what he ought his best friends 'll do nothing but chaff him and try to put him down." And he stuck his books under his arm and his hat on his head, preparatory to rushing out into the quadrangle, to testify with his own soul of the faithlessness of friendships.

Tom looked at him pleased, and a little puzzled. He had never heard East speak his mind seriously before, and couldn't help feeling how completely he had hit his own theory and practice up to that time.

"Thank you, old fellow," said he. "You're a good old brick to be serious, and not put out with me. I said more than I meant, I dare say, only you see I know I'm right: whatever you and Gower and the rest do, I shall hold on—I must. And as it's all new and an uphill game, you see, one must hit hard and hold on tight at first."

"Very good," said East; "hold on and hit away, only don't hit under the line."

"But I must bring you over, Harry, or I sha'n't be comfortable. Now, I allow all you've said. We've always been honourable enemies with the masters. We found a state of war when we came, and went into it of course. Only don't you think things are altered a good deal? I don't feel as I used to the masters. They seem to me to treat one quite differently."

"Yes, perhaps they do," said East; "there's a new set you see, mostly, who don't feel sure of themselves yet. They don't want to fight till they know the ground."

"I don't think it's only that," said Tom. "And then the Doctor, he does treat one so openly, and like a gentleman, and as if one was working with him."

"Well, so he does," said East; "he's a splendid fellow, and when I get into the sixth I shall act accordingly. Only, you know, he has nothing to do with our lessons now, except examining us. I say, though," looking at his watch, "it's just the quarter. Come along."

As they walked out they got a message, to say that Arthur was just starting, and would like to say good-bye; so they went down to the private entrance of the School-house, and found an open carriage, with Arthur propped up with pillows in it, looking already better, Tom thought.

They jumped up on to the steps to shake hands with him, and Tom mumbled thanks for the presents he had found in his study, and looked round anxiously for Arthur's mother.

East, who had fallen back into his usual humour, looked quaintly at Arthur, and said—

"So you've been at it again, through that hot-headed

But he turns you and me round his little finger, old boy—there's no mistake about that." And East nodded at Tom sagaciously.

"Now or never!" thought Tom; so, shutting his eyes and hardening his heart, he went straight at it, repeating all that Arthur had said, as near as he could remember it, in the very words, and all he had himself thought. The life seemed to ooze out of it as he went on, and several times he felt inclined to stop, give it all up, and change the subject. But somehow he was borne on, he had a necessity upon him to speak it all out, and did so. At the end he looked at East with some anxiety, and was delighted to see that that young gentleman was thoughtful and attentive. The fact is, that in the stage of his inner life at which Tom had lately arrived, his intimacy with and friendship for East could not have lasted if he had not made him aware of, and a sharer in, the thoughts that were beginning to exercise him. Nor indeed could the friendship have lasted if East had shown no sympathy with these thoughts; so that it was a great relief to have unbosomed himself, and to have found that his friend could listen.

Tom had always had a sort of instinct that East's levity was only skin-deep; and this instinct was a true one. East had no want of reverence for anything he felt to be real; but his was one of those natures that burst into what is generally called recklessness and impiety the moment they feel that anything is being poured upon them for their good which does not come home to their inborn sense of right, or which appeals to anything like self-interest in them. Daring and honest by nature, and outspoken to an extent which alarmed all respectabilities, with a constant fund of animal health and spirits which he did not feel bound to curb in any way, he had gained for himself with the steady part of the school (including as well those who wished to appear steady as those who really were so) the character of a boy with whom it would be dangerous to be intimate; while his own hatred of everything cruel, or underhand, or false, and his hearty respect for what he could see to be good and true, kept off the rest.

Tom, besides being very like East in many points of character, had largely developed in his composition the capacity for taking the weakest side. This is not putting it strongly enough;

and leant his head on one hand, taking up a pencil with the other, and working little holes with it in the table-cover. After a bit he looked up, stopped the pencil, and said, "Thank you very much, old fellow; there's no other boy in the house would have done it for me but you or Arthur. I can see well enough," he went on after a pause, "all the best big fellows look on me with suspicion; they think I'm a devil-may-care, reckless young scamp. So I am—eleven hours out of twelve, but not the twelfth. Then all of our contemporaries worth knowing follow suit, of course; we're very good friends at games and all that, but not a soul of them but you and Arthur ever tried to break through the crust, and see whether there was anything at the bottom of me; and then, the bad ones I won't stand, and they know that."

"Don't you think that's half fancy, Harry?"

"Not a bit of it," said East bitterly, pegging away with his pencil. "I see it all plain enough. Bless you, you think everybody's as straightforward and kindhearted as you are."

"Well, but what's the reason of it? There must be a reason. You can play all the games as well as any one, and sing the best song, and are the best company in the house. You fancy you're not liked, Harry. It's all fancy."

"I only wish it was, Tom. I know I could be popular enough with all the bad ones, but that I won't have, and the good ones won't have me."

"Why not?" persisted Tom; "you don't drink or swear, or get out at night; you never bully, or cheat at lessons. If you only showed you liked it, you'd have all the best fellows in the house running after you."

"Not I," said East. Then with an effort he went on, "I'll tell you what it is. I never stop the Sacrament. I can see from the Doctor downwards, how that tells against me."

"Yes, I've seen that," said Tom, "and I've been very sorry for it, and Arthur and I have talked about it. I've often thought of speaking to you, but it's so hard to begin on such subjects. I'm very glad you've opened it. Now, why don't you?"

"I've never been confirmed," said East.

"Not been confirmed!" said Tom in astonishment. "I never thought of that. Why weren't you confirmed with the

"Ah!" groaned East, "but there again, that's just another of my difficulties whenever I think about the matter. I don't want to be one of your saints, one of your elect, whatever the right phrase is, my sympathies are all the other way; with the many, the poor devils who run about the streets and don't go to church. Don't stare, Tom; mind, I'm telling you all that's in my heart—as far as I know it—but it's all a muddle. You must be gentle with me if you want to land me. Now I've seen a deal of this sort of religion, I was bred up in it, and I can't stand it. If nineteen-twentieths of the world are to be left to uncovenanted mercies, and that sort of thing, which means in plain English to go to hell, and the other twentieth are to rejoice at it all, why—"

"Oh! but, Harry, they ain't, they don't," broke in Tom, really shocked. "Oh, how I wish Arthur hadn't gone! I'm such a fool about these things. But it's all you want too, East; it is indeed. It cuts both ways somehow, being confirmed and taking the Sacrament. It makes you feel on the side of all the good and all the bad too, of everybody in the world. Only there's some great dark strong power, which is crushing you and everybody else. That's what Christ conquered, and we've got to fight. What a fool I am! I can't explain. If Arthur were only here!"

"I begin to get a glimmering of what you mean," said East.

"I say now," said Tom eagerly, "do you remember how we both hated Flashman?"

"Of course I do," said East; "I hate him still. What then?"

"Well, when I came to take the Sacrament, I had a great struggle about that. I tried to put him out of my head; and when I couldn't do that, I tried to think of him as evil, as something that the Lord who was loving me hated, and which I might hate too. But it wouldn't do. I broke down: I believe Christ himself broke me down; and when the Doctor gave me the bread and wine, and leant over me praying, I prayed for poor Flashman, as if it had been you or Arthur."

East buried his face in his hands on the table. Tom could feel the table tremble. At last he looked up, "Thank you again, Tom," said he; "you don't know what you may have done for me to-night. I think I see now how the right sort of sympathy with poor devils is got at."

"I burst out crying, and he sat down by me and stroked my head."

occasion; so he proceeded to expound Arthur's theory about not being sorry for his friend's death, which he had hitherto kept in the background, and by which he was much exercised; for he didn't feel it honest to take what pleased him and throw over the rest, and was trying vigorously to persuade himself that he should like all his best friends to die off-hand.

But East's powers of remaining serious were limited, and in five minutes he was saying the most ridiculous things he could think of, till Tom was almost getting angry again.

Despite of himself, however, he couldn't help laughing and giving it up, when East appealed to him, "Well, Tom, you ain't going to punch my head, I hope, because I insist upon being sorry when you got to Jericho."

And so their talk finished for that time, and they tried to learn first lesson; with very poor success, as appeared the next morning, when they were called up and narrowly escaped being floored, which ill-luck, however, did not sit heavily on either of their souls.

CHAPTER VIII

TOM BROWN'S LAST MATCH

"Heaven grant the manlier heart, that timely, ere
Youth fly, with life's real tempest would be coping;
The fruit of dreamy hoping
Is, waking, blank despair."

CLOUGH, *Ambarvalia.*

THE curtain now rises upon the last act of our little drama —for hard-hearted publishers warn me that a single volume must of necessity have an end. Well, well! the pleasantest things must come to an end. I little thought last long vacation, when I began these pages to help while away some spare time at a watering-place, how vividly many an old scene, which had lain hid away for years in some dusty old corner of my brain, would come back again, and stand before me as clear and bright as if it had happened yesterday. The book has been a most grateful task to me, and I only hope that all you, my dear young friends, who read it (friends assuredly you must be, if you get as far as this) will be half as sorry to come to the last stage as I am.

Not but what there has been a solemn and a sad side to it. As the old scenes became living, and the actors in them became living too, many a grave in the Crimea and distant India, as well as in the quiet churchyards of our dear old country, seemed to open and send forth their dead, and their voices and looks and ways were again in one's ears and eyes, as in the old school-days. But this was not sad; how should it be, if we believe as our Lord has taught us? How should it be, when one more turn of the wheel, and we shall be by their sides again, learning from them again, perhaps, as we did when we were new boys?

of the world, the flesh, and the devil; for self alone, and not for their fellow-men, their country, or their God, that we must mourn and pray without sure hope and without light; trusting only that He, in Whose hands they as well as we are, Who has died for them as well as for us, Who sees all His creatures

"With larger other eyes than ours,
To make allowance for us all,"

will, in His own way and at His own time, lead them also home.

* * * * *

Another two years have passed, and it is again the end of the summer half-year at Rugby; in fact, the School has broken up. The fifth-form examinations were over last week, and upon them have followed the Speeches, and the sixth-form examinations for exhibitions; and they too are over now. The boys have gone to all the winds of heaven, except the town boys and the eleven, and the few enthusiasts besides who have asked leave to stay in their houses to see the result of the cricket matches. For this year the Wellesburn return match and the Marylebone match are played at Rugby, to the great delight of the town and neighbourhood, and the sorrow of those aspiring young cricketers who have been reckoning for the last three months on showing off at Lord's ground.

The Doctor started for the Lakes yesterday morning, after an interview with the Captain of the eleven, in the presence of Thomas, at which he arranged in what School the cricket dinners were to be, and all other matters necessary for the satisfactory carrying out of the festivities; and warned them as to keeping all spirituous liquors out of the close, and having the gates closed by nine o'clock.

The Wellesburn match was played out with great success yesterday, the School winning by three wickets; and to-day the great event of the cricketing year, the Marylebone match, is being played. What a match it has been! The London eleven came down by an afternoon train yesterday, in time to see the end of the Wellesburn match; and as soon as it was over, their leading men and umpire inspected the ground, criticising it rather unmercifully. The Captain of the School

But when a quarter to nine struck, and he saw old Thomas beginning to fidget about with the keys in his hand, he thought of the Doctor's parting monition, and stopped the cornopean at once, notwithstanding the loud-voiced remonstrances from all sides; and the crowd scattered away from the close, the eleven all going into the School-house, where supper and beds were provided for them by the Doctor's orders.

Deep had been the consultations at supper as to the order of going in, who should bowl the first over, whether it would be best to play steady or freely; and the youngest hands declared that they shouldn't be a bit nervous, and praised their opponents as the jolliest fellows in the world, except perhaps their old friends the Wellesburn men. How far a little good-nature from their elders will go with the right sort of boys!

The morning had dawned bright and warm, to the intense relief of many an anxious youngster, up betimes to mark the signs of the weather. The eleven went down in a body before breakfast, for a plunge in the cold bath in the corner of the close. The ground was in splendid order, and soon after ten o'clock, before the spectators had arrived, all was ready, and two of the Lord's men took their places at the wickets; the School, with the usual liberality of young hands, having put their adversaries in first. Old Bailey stepped up to the wicket, and called play, and the match has begun.

* * * * *

"Oh, well bowled! well bowled, Johnson!" cries the Captain, catching up the ball and sending it high above the rook trees, while the third Marylebone man walks away from the wicket, and old Bailey gravely sets up the middle stump again and puts the bails on.

"How many runs?" Away scamper three boys to the scoring-table, and are back again in a minute amongst the rest of the eleven, who are collected together in a knot between wicket. "Only eighteen runs, and three wickets down!" "Huzza for old Rugby!" sings out Jack Raggles, the long-stop, toughest and burliest of boys, commonly called 'Swiper Jack'; and forthwith stands on his head, and brandishes his legs in the air in triumph, till the next

The captain of the eleven scored twenty-five in beautiful style.

one may judge from the thoughtfulness of his face, which is somewhat paler too than one could wish; but his figure, though slight, is well knit and active, and all his old timidity has disappeared, and is replaced by silent quaint fun, with which his face twinkles all over, as he listens to the broken talk between the other two, in which he joins every now and then.

All three are watching the game eagerly, and joining in the cheering which follows every good hit. It is pleasing to see the easy friendly footing which the pupils are on with their master, perfectly respectful, yet with no reserve and nothing forced in their intercourse. Tom has clearly abandoned the old theory of "natural enemies" in this case at any rate.

But it is time to listen to what they are saying, and see what we can gather out of it.

"I don't object to your theory," says the master, "and I allow you have made a fair case for yourself. But now, in such books as Aristophanes, for instance, you've been reading a play this half with the Doctor, haven't you?"

"Yes, the Knights," answered Tom.

"Well, I'm sure you would have enjoyed the wonderful humour of it twice as much if you had taken more pains with your scholarship."

"Well, sir, I don't believe any boy in the form enjoyed the sets-to between Cleon and the Sausage-seller more than I did—eh, Arthur?" said Tom, giving him a stir with his foot.

"Yes, I must say he did," said Arthur. "I think, sir, you've hit upon the wrong book there."

"Not a bit of it," said the master. "Why, in those very passages of arms, how can you thoroughly appreciate them unless you are master of the weapons? and the weapons are the language, which you, Brown, have never half worked at; and so, as I say, you must have lost all the delicate shades of meaning which make the best part of the fun."

"Oh! well played—bravo, Johnson!" shouted Arthur, dropping his bat and clapping furiously, and Tom joined in with a "bravo, Johnson!" which might have been heard at the chapel.

"Eh, what was it? I didn't see," inquired the master; "they only got one run, I thought?"

"No, but such a ball, three-quarters length and coming straight for his leg bail. Nothing but that turn of the wrist

chance, sir, of seeing a hard hit or two," adds he, smiling, and turning to the master.

"Come, none of your irony, Brown," answers the master. "I'm beginning to understand the game scientifically. What a noble game it is, too!"

"Isn't it? But it's more than a game. It's an institution," said Tom.

"Yes," said Arthur, "the birthright of British boys old and young, as *habeas corpus* and trial by jury are of British men."

"The discipline and reliance on one another which it teaches is so valuable, I think," went on the master, "it ought to be such an unselfish game. It merges the individual in the eleven; he doesn't play that he may win, but that his side may."

"That's very true," said Tom, "and that's why football and cricket, now one comes to think of it, are much better games than fives, or hare-and-hounds, or any others where the object is to come in first or to win for one's self, and not that one's side may win."

"And then the Captain of the eleven!" said the master, "what a post is his in our School-world! almost as hard as the Doctor's; requiring skill and gentleness and firmness, and I know not what other rare qualities."

"Which don't he may wish he may get!" said Tom, laughing; "at any rate he hasn't got them yet, or he wouldn't have been such a flat to-night as to let Jack Raggles go in out of his turn."

"Ah! the Doctor never would have done that," said Arthur, demurely. "Tom, you've a great deal to learn yet in the art of ruling."

"Well, I wish you'd tell the Doctor so then, and get him to let me stop till I'm twenty. I don't want to leave, I'm sure."

"What a sight it is," broke in the master, "the Doctor as a ruler! Perhaps ours is the only little corner of the British Empire which is thoroughly, wisely, and strongly ruled just now. I'm more and more thankful every day of my life that I came here to be under him."

"So am I, I'm sure," said Tom; "and more and more sorry that I've got to leave."

"Every place and thing one sees here reminds one of some

ball is a very swift one, and rises fast, catching Jack on the outside of the thigh, and bounding away as if from india-rubber, while they ran two for a leg-bye amidst great applause, and shouts from Jack's many admirers. The next ball is a beautifully pitched ball for the outer stump, which the reckless and unfeeling Jack catches hold of, and hits right round to leg for five, while the applause becomes deafening: only seventeen runs to get with four wickets—the game is all but ours!

It is over now, and Jack walks swaggering about his wicket, with the bat over his shoulder, while Mr. Aislabie holds a short parley with his men. Then the cover-point hitter, that cunning man, goes on to bowl slow twisters. Jack waves his hand triumphantly towards the tent, as much as to say, "See if I don't finish it all off now in three hits."

Alas, my son Jack! the enemy is too old for thee. The first ball of the over Jack steps out and meets, swiping with all his force. If he had only allowed for the twist! but he hasn't, and so the ball goes spinning up straight into the air, as if it would never come down again. Away runs Jack, shouting and trusting to the chapter of accidents, but the bowler runs steadily under it, judging every spin, and calling out "I have it," catches it, and playfully pitches it on to the back of the stalwart Jack, who is departing with a rueful countenance.

"I knew how it would be," says Tom, rising. "Come along, the game's getting very serious."

So they leave the island and go to the tent, and after deep consultation Arthur is sent in, and goes off to the wicket with a last exhortation from Tom to play steady and keep his bat straight. To the suggestions that Winter is the best bat left, Tom only replies, "Arthur is the steadiest, and Johnson will make the runs if the wicket is only kept up."

"I am surprised to see Arthur in the eleven," said the master, as they stood together in front of the dense crowd, which was now closing in round the ground.

"Well, I'm not quite sure that he ought to be in for his play," said Tom, "but I couldn't help putting him in. It will do him so much good, and you can't think what I owe him."

The master smiled. The clock strikes eight, and the whole field becomes fevered with excitement. Arthur, after two

the man in charge of the tent, and walked quietly away to the gate where the master was waiting, and the two took their way together up the Hillmorton road.

Of course they found the master's house locked up, and all the servants away in the close, about this time, no doubt footing it away on the grass with extreme delight to themselves, and in utter oblivion of the unfortunate bachelor their master, whose one enjoyment in the shape of meals was his "dish of tea" (as our grandmothers called it) in the evening; and the phrase was apt in his case, for he always poured his out into the saucer before drinking. Great was the good man's horror at finding himself shut out of his own house. Had he been alone, he would have treated it as a matter of course, and would have strolled contentedly up and down his gravel-walk until some one came home; but he was hurt at the stain on his character of host, especially as the guest was a pupil. However, the guest seemed to think it a great joke, and presently, as they poked about round the house, mounted a wall, from which he could reach a passage window: the window, as it turned out, was not bolted, so in another minute Tom was in the house and down at the front door, which he opened from inside. The master chuckled grimly at his burglarious entry, and insisted on leaving the hall-door and two of the front windows open, to frighten the truants on their return, and then the two set about foraging for tea, in which operation the master was much at fault, having the faintest possible idea of where to find anything, and being, moreover, wondrously short-sighted; but Tom by a sort of instinct knew the right cupboards in the kitchen and pantry, and soon managed to place on the snuggery table better materials for a meal than had appeared there probably during the reign of his tutor, who was then and there initiated, amongst other things, into the excellence of that mysterious condiment, a dripping-cake. The cake was newly baked, and all rich and flaky; Tom had found it reposing in the cook's private cupboard, awaiting her return; and as a warning to her, they finished it to the last crumb. The kettle sang away merrily on the hob of the snuggery, for, notwithstanding the time of year, they lighted a fire, throwing both the windows wide open at the same time; the heap of books and papers were pushed away to the other end of the table, and the great solitary engraving of King's College Chapel over the

will have really to do, and make one's living by. I want to be doing some real good, feeling that I am not only at play in

"What do you mean by 'at work in the world'?" said the master.

the world," answered Tom, rather puzzled to find out himself what he really did mean.

"You are mixing up two very different things in your head,

the end of one half-year, when you were in the shell, and had been getting into all sorts of scrapes?"

"Yes, well enough," said Tom; "it was the half-year before Arthur came."

"Exactly so," answered the master. "Now, I was with him a few minutes afterwards, and he was in great distress about you two. And, after some talk, we both agreed that you in particular wanted some object in the School beyond games and mischief; for it was quite clear that you never would make the regular school work your first object. And so the Doctor, at the beginning of the next half-year, looked out the best of the new boys, and separated you and East, and put the young boy into your study, in the hope that when you had somebody to lean on you, you would begin to stand a little steadier yourself, and get manliness and thoughtfulness. And I can assure you he has watched the experiment ever since with great satisfaction. Ah! not one of you boys will ever know the anxiety you have given him, or the care with which he has watched over every step in your school lives."

Up to this time, Tom had never wholly given in to or understood the Doctor. At first he had thoroughly feared him. For some years, as I have tried to show, he had learnt to regard him with love and respect, and to think him a very great and wise and good man. But, as regarded his own position in the School, of which he was not a little proud, Tom had no idea of giving any one credit for it but himself; and, truth to tell, was a very self-conceited young gentleman on the subject. He was wont to boast that he had fought his own way fairly up the School, and had never made up to, or been taken up by any big fellow or master, and that it was now quite a different place from what it was when he first came. And, indeed, though he didn't actually boast of it, yet in his secret soul he did to a great extent believe that the great reform in the School had been owing quite as much to himself as to any one else. Arthur, he acknowledged, had done him good, and taught him a good deal, so had other boys in different ways, but they had not had the same means of influence on the School in general; and as for the Doctor, why, he was a splendid master, but every one knew that masters could do very little out of school hours. In short, he felt on terms of equality with his chief, so far as the social

"*For he's a jolly good fellow.*"

CHAPTER IX

FINIS

> "Strange friend, past, present, and to be;
> Loved deeplier, darklier understood;
> Behold, I dream a dream of good,
> And mingle all the world with thee."—TENNYSON.

IN the summer of 1842, our hero stopped once again at the well-known station; and, leaving his bag and fishing-rod with a porter, walked slowly and sadly up towards the town. It was now July. He had rushed away from Oxford the moment that term was over, for a fishing ramble in Scotland with two college friends, and had been for three weeks living on oatcake, mutton hams, and whiskey, in the wildest parts of Skye. They had descended one sultry evening on the little inn at Kyle Rhea ferry; and while Tom and another of the party put their tackle together and began exploring the stream for a sea-trout for supper, the third strolled into the house to arrange for their entertainment. Presently he came out in a loose blouse and slippers, a short pipe in his mouth, and an old newspaper in his hand, and threw himself on the heathery scrub which met the shingle, within easy hail of the fishermen. There he lay, the picture of free-and-easy, loafing, hand-to-mouth young England, "improving his mind," as he shouted to them, by the perusal of the fortnight-old weekly paper, soiled with the marks of toddy-glasses and tobacco-ashes, the legacy of the last traveller, which he had hunted out from the kitchen of the little hostelry, and, being a youth of a communicative turn of mind, began imparting the contents to the fishermen as he went on.

"What a bother they are making about these wretched Corn-laws; here's three or four columns full of nothing but sliding-scales and fixed duties.—Hang this tobacco, it's always

"*Hullo, Brown! here's something for you. Arnold of Rugby is dead.*"

Away he strode over the moor.

He felt shy and afraid of being seen, and took the back streets.

[illegible]

[illegible]

[illegible]

the shutters came down, it would be to welcome a stranger. All that was left on earth of him whom he had honoured, was lying cold and still under the chapel floor. He would go in and see the place once more, and then leave it once for all. New men and new methods might do for other people;

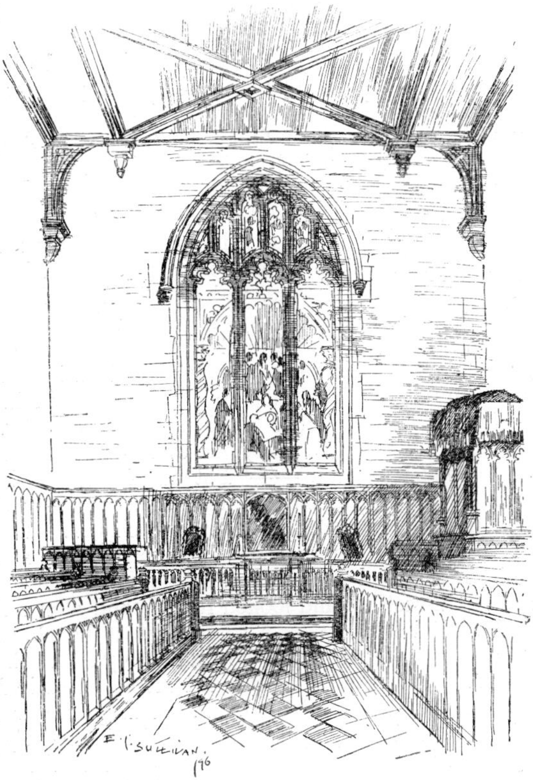

The School Chapel, looking East.

let those who would, worship the rising star: he at least would be faithful to the sun which had set. And so he got up, and walked to the chapel-door and unlocked it, fancying

Knelt down humbly and hopefully.

YOU'D THINK THE end of the world would be exciting, but this apocalypse is about as much fun as dental surgery.

Take the current situation. Sitting at a dead stop in traffic, as lively as a stone angel over a tomb. Not one car has moved in ten minutes. It's bumper to bumper on Sunset Boulevard, which is nothing new, but this kind of traffic is 24/7 these days, as it seems like half the city is hightailing it out of Dodge all at once. And the rain. It's been coming down nonstop for two weeks. It's like L.A. lost a bet with God and the old bastard is pissing his Happy Hour whiskey all over the city. Which, when you get down to it, isn't far from the truth. This isn't how I figured I'd ring in the apocalypse.

"Any time now, Jeff Gordon," says Candy from the passenger seat. "I thought this was supposed to be a car chase."

"By current L.A. standards, this *is* a car chase."

"Current L.A. seriously blows. And I think my boots are starting to grow gills."

We're in an Escalade I stole in Westwood. I hate these showboats, but it can handle the flooded streets and gets me high enough over the other cars that I can keep an eye on a cherry black '69 Charger up ahead. There's a guy inside that U.S. Marshal Wells, grand high shitbird boss of the Golden Vigil, wants to talk to.

"I should go up there, rip the fucker's door off, and stuff him in the back of the van."

"And you could take a brass band so no one misses the show. Your boss would love that."

"He wants discreet, but he knows I'm not good at discreet. I swear he did this to me on purpose."

I reach for the Maledictions in my coat pocket. Drop them and the lighter on the floor on Candy's side. She picks them up and taps out a cigarette.

"Marshal Wells is a man of God," says Candy, grinning. "He only has your best interests at heart."

"Abraham was a man of God and he almost did a Jack the Ripper on his kid to prove it."

"See? You get off light. Your father figure just sends you out in the rain to drown."

Candy flicks the lighter and sparks a cigarette. Hands it to me and rolls down her window to let out the smoke.

I say, "Wells is a father figure like I'm one of Santa's elves."

"There you go. You're getting into the Christmas spirit. I'll have to get you a pointy hat with a bell so you feel like a real elf."

"You already gave me the Colt. I thought that was my present. And I gave you the guitar."

"That was different. Those were 'We might die tonight' presents. And it was November, so they don't count."

"This is just you angling to get another present."

"It's the end of the world, sweetheart. Crack open the piggy bank."

"We spent the piggy bank on Max Overdrive."

She shrugs.

"That's your problem. I already have something picked out for you, so don't try to weasel out of this. I want a real damned present on real damned Christmas morning."

I puff the Malediction. Brake lights go dark in the distance.

"Yes, ma'am. Anything else? Eight maids a-milking maybe?"

"Are they hot maids? 'Cause I never had a nine-way before, so, yeah."

Somewhere far away a car moves. More brake lights go off ahead of us. In the distance, I actually see a truck inch forward.

"It's a Christmas miracle," shouts Candy. "God bless us every one."

Like some great wheezing machine no one has fired up since D-Day, cars around us begin to creep tentatively forward. I take my foot off the brake and let the Escalade roll.

At that moment the sky opens up. I hit the windshield wipers, but a second after the glass goes clear, it's drenched again. I roll down my window and stick my head out. The Malediction is instantly soggy. I spit it out. The sky has gone dark gray, dulling the colors on all the cars. In the downpour I lose sight of the Charger.

"Do you see it?"

Candy has her head out her window.

"It's about a block ahead," she says. Then, "Wait. It's got its signal on. I think it's turning. Yeah, there it goes."

Traffic lurches to a stop. Horns honk. People shout at each other.

"Wait. He's gone?"

"Yeah, around the first corner."

It's a sea of brake lights again. No one is going anywhere.

"Know what?"

"What?" says Candy.

"I'm about to call in that brass band. Get your head back inside the car."

"Now you're talking."

Traffic is ass to nose again. I put the Escalade in reverse and ram the car behind me. Put it in drive and ram the car ahead. Reverse again, then drive the van up onto the sidewalk. I hit the horn and floor it.

Angelinos are used to desert heat and chocolate-colored smog skies. Rain is kryptonite to these people, so there's hardly anyone outside. The few rain birds hear me coming and jump out of the way. The only casualty of my sidewalk Le Mans is a sign outside a café and a bench outside a Chinese restaurant. No one's used the damned thing in weeks and no one will until the world ends, which means it shouldn't even be there, so fuck it.

I turn hard at the corner. The rear end of the van fishtails and hits a mailbox. Letters explode like New Year's confetti over the stalled cars.

"Jerk," says Candy. "Now people's Christmas cards are getting wet."

"Will you shut up about Christmas and help me look for the car?"

Traffic is a little lighter on the side street, so the Charger could still be ahead. Or have pulled off into a parking lot or another side street.

"Shit. Shit. Shit."

On the next block is a row of warehouses. Distribution points. The kind of places that get goods from big warehouses and parcel them out to regular stores.

"There," says Candy. "By the open loading dock."

I look to where she's pointing and spot the Charger. It's sideways to the dock and the driver-side door is open; not parked, but abandoned. I stop the Escalade and get out. Instantly, I'm soaked. My frock coat, motorcycle pants, and boots weren't made for this Noah's ark bullshit. It feels like I've gained twenty pounds before I take a step.

Candy comes around the van. I start across the street.

"You got your gun?"

She holds up her Swiss folding pistol. Unopened, it looks kind of like a skinny lunch box. She's covered it with stickers from some of her favorite animes. *FLCL. Ghost in the Shell. Blood. Appleseed.* She pushes a button and the lunch box unfolds like a matte-black Transformer into an extended 9mm pistol with a shoulder stock. She grins. She always grins when she gets to use her gun because she thinks she's Modesty Blaise and who am I to tell her she's not?

"I'm going in the front. Go around the side and see if there's a back way in. If you can't get through it, make sure no one gets out."

As she starts away she says, "Be careful."

"I'm always careful."

"Right. That's how you got all those scars. From being careful."

I wait for her to disappear around the side of the building before I go in. I jump up onto the Charger's hood and from there onto the dock platform.

It's at least twenty degrees colder inside the warehouse. I spot maybe fifteen people working. Carrying boxes and driving forklifts. It's a meat-packing plant, prepping orders to take to butcher shops. I can see my breath in front of my face.

Wells gave me a photo of the man I'm supposed to follow but I don't see him among the faces up front. I head into the back of the plant to the big freezer. The entrance is covered with a thick plastic curtain with slits every couple of feet so forklifts can pass in and out. I grab a clipboard off a nail on the wall and stroll past a forklift coming the other way.

Inside the freezer the real cold hits me. This isn't muggy L.A. showers weather. This is penguin country. I swear my wet clothes start freezing to my body.

They must be doing good business at the warehouse. The freezer stretches away in both directions, full of sides of beef on nasty-looking meat hooks. I don't want to go in unarmed, but I might as well try the discretion thing as long as I can. I take out the na'at instead of my gun. The na'at is a weapon I picked up in the arena in Hell. It collapses to no longer than a cop's riot baton, but can extend like a spear or a whip. It isn't always a quiet weapon because of all the screaming, but it's more subtle than a Colt pistol.

I snap open the na'at into a spear shape and move through the meat forest as quietly as I can. This might be a mistake. Maybe I should have checked the office first. But Wells didn't say anything about the guy working here and most people when they're scared head as far from the front door as possible. That's back here. Still, after staring at row after row of dead cow, I'm getting bored and hungry. Then I spot a different kind of light a few rows ahead. It's softer and more diffuse than in the rest of the freezer, and tinged in pink. I head for it and find Mr. Charger. He's not alone.

Thirteen of them stand in a circle in an open area in the back of the freezer. By open area, I mean there aren't any sides of beef hanging back here, but there's a hell of a lot of meat. They've made a whole cathedral of the stuff. Arches made from ribs, livers, hearts, and leg bones all frozen together. A vaulted ceiling from muscle trimmed from sides of beef hanging on high hooks. Their flesh church even has nave windows made of stitched-together sheets of pig caul. The light back here is a milky crimson.

All thirteen of them, six men and seven women, smile at me. Big and toothy.

"It took you long enough to find us," says Mr. Charger.

"Sorry. I took a wrong turn at the pork chops."

"No worries. You're here. That's all that matters."

I know I should watch the crazies, but I can't take my eyes off the meat Notre-Dame.

"I love what you've done with the place. Ed Gein chic."

"Thank you. It took some time to get it just right."

"Who's your decorator? We're finishing my new place and there's all this leftover chorizo. Maybe we could use it for a rumpus room."

Mr. Charger doesn't say anything because he's watching me as I see it.

Not all the meat in the church is animal. There's a human body cut into six pieces—arms, legs, torso, and head—hanging like nightmare piñatas over the smiling circle of freaks.

Mr. Charger says, "Do you understand why you're here?"

"If you think I'm going to be the next one hanging from those hooks, you're extremely mistaken."

Normally, I could probably handle a flock of unarmed fruit bats. Hell, the freezer is big enough that I could just run away if I broke a nail. But these particular fruit bats are all armed. Each holds a wicked-looking motorized meat saw, like an oversize electric knife. Outwardly they all look calm, but they're sweating, even in this cold. They smell of fear and adrenaline. The sweat steams from their bodies and collects at the ceiling like incense in their mad church.

Mr. Charger shakes his head.

"We're not here to hurt you. You're here to help us."

"How did you know I was coming?"

Mr. Charger looks around at his friends

"God told us."

I shake my head.

"I'm kind of acquainted with God and I don't think he told you dick."

A thin redhead from the back says, "We mean the true God."

"Oh hell. You're Angra worshipers, aren't you? Is that what this is all about? I don't mean to cramp your little chautauqua, but my boss wants a word with you. How about you put down the saws and you can come and be crazy where it's warm?"

A chuckle goes around the circle.

"I'm not going with you because I'm not here for you. You're here for us," says Mr. Charger.

"If you're selling candy bars to go to summer camp, I'm tapped out right now."

Mr. Charger raises his meat saw. I move my weight onto my back leg, ready to move when he tells them to rush me.

"We don't want anything from you except to be our witness."

"To what?"

"The sacrifice."

Without another word or a signal, all thirteen of them raise their meat saws to their throats.

Mr. Charger is the first to shove the buzzing saw into his neck. He screams, but just for a second before the blade rips through his larynx and his throat fills with blood. He goes down twitching as the others fire up their own saws, following their leader's example. It's the same for all of them. A small scream as the blade tears into them. A gurgling as their voice box goes, the blood fills their throat and jets from their severed arteries. It only takes a few seconds and all thirteen are on the floor, their blood steaming on the cold metal. Their saws rattle and buzz where they dropped them.

I've seen some cold moves in my time, I've fought and killed in Hell and on earth, but I've never seen anything quite like this before.

Over the sound of the saws I hear voices. All the screaming got someone's attention. That's all I need. A warehouse of hysterical meat packers with big knives and cell phones. Imagine explaining this to a 911 operator. It might take awhile to get a patrol car. But still, it's the principle of the thing. I'm not in the mood to deal with another crazed mob right now.

They're getting near me now and I let them. When the first few tough guys emerge from the rows of beef and see me in the meat cathedral surrounded by freezing corpses, they stop. Good. They're not going to rush me but they're still between me and the door. I pull the Colt and shoot three rounds into the floor by their feet. That alters their mood and sends them scurrying like sensible rats out of there.

Only one person is still coming in my direction. Candy shoulders her way between the beef rows, her gun up, sweeping the room. But when she sees me, even she stops. For a second I can see it in her eyes. She wonders if I did this. Then she sees the meat saws and relaxes. She lowers her gun and comes over to me.

"Oh man," she says. "I mean. Oh man."

I go from saw to saw and turn them off. The sound is giving me a headache.

"Yeah."

"What were they . . . ?"

"It was a sacrifice to one of their idiot Angra gods."

"Couldn't they have just had a bake sale?"

I walk over and put my hand on her gun, lowering it to her side. I put my arm around her. I haven't seen her this freaked out before. She presses against me.

I say, "Wells is going to be pissed."

She nods.

"He can't blame you for this insanity."

"Wells blames me for tooth decay. He can sure blame me for this. But maybe there's something I can do. Help me find a cooler and some dry ice."

There's a stack of Styrofoam coolers just outside the freezer. I grab one and Candy gets plastic packets of dry ice. We go back into the cooler. I have to work fast. Someone's called the cops by now. For all I know, one of the workers has a pistol in the back of their truck. There's a lot of that going around these days. When we get back to the suicide circle, I tell Candy to go back and guard the door.

"You just don't want me to see you do it," she says.

"You're right. But I also want you to guard the door."

"Okay."

She runs back to the freezer entrance. I turn on one of the meat saws and get to work. It doesn't take long. Mr. Charger did the hard part himself. All I have to do is get through some gristle and the spinal cord so I can twist his head all the way off.

When I do, I put it in the cooler and pack ice around it.

Candy shakes her head when she sees me with the container.

"I've dated some messed-up people in my time."

"Write 'Dear Abby.' Let's get out of here."

"Let's."

There's a nice dark shadow by a stack of boxes on the loading dock. I start to pull Candy through and stop.

"What you said before. Eight maids and you. That's a nine-way. Where am I in all this?"

"That's your present. You get to watch."

"I can see it for free on the Web."

"I'm better than the Web."

"I'll give you that. But you're still coming out ahead on this deal. Better get me that pointy hat so I won't feel cheated."

She takes my hand.

"You got it, Jingles."

We step into a shadow and come out in the Golden Vigil's

new L.A. headquarters right off the eight hole of the Wilshire Golf Club. They eminent-domained the place right out from under the blue bloods, paying cents on the dollar for what it's worth. It's the first time I ever really respected the Vigil. Marshals and Vigil-rich doctors still dress up in pricy sports clothes and play round after round of existential golf on the grounds. No one keeps score, but someone has to be out on the greens keeping up the appearance that the club is still just a place for rich morons to blow an afternoon. I like it. Maybe none of the locals noticed the surplus Iraq War ASVs, enough lab gear to restart the Manhattan Project, and about a hundred blacked-out bulletproof vans sneaking into the club.

A man is waiting for me inside the clubhouse. He's wearing a black suit and skinny tie, with a flag pin on the lapel. He looks like a mortician's idea of a high school principal.

U.S. Marshal Larson Wells is God's own Pinkerton on Earth. The Golden Vigil is Homeland Security's dirty little secret—an investigation and law enforcement operation for supernatural activity. Which is a nice way of saying they're dedicated to harassing people like me and pretty much everyone I know. They're thorough and obsessive. From what I've heard, they still have Lucifer on a terrorist watch list with a price on his head.

Wells is a charming piece of work. A Nevada Holy Roller marshal who hates working with me as much as I hate working for him. But we both have a vested interest in stopping the old gods, the Angra Om Ya, from returning and eating the world. Wells has a habit of calling all Sub Rosa and Lurkers "pixies," which isn't so bad on its own. It's just that he says it the way a backwoods redneck says "faggot." He used to run the Vigil with an angel named Aelita. She's dead. I didn't do it, but I would have been happy to.

I've been back on the Vigil payroll for a couple of weeks and things are going swell.

"Where is he?" says Wells when he sees me and Candy.

"There was a problem," I say.

"What kind of problem?"

I hold out the ice chest. Wells's eyes narrow and he opens the lid an inch before dropping it down again.

"What in all of God's creation is wrong with you? I sent you on a simple snatch-and-grab. I wanted to question this man. Where's the rest of him?"

"In a meat locker near Sunset and Echo Park, along with a dozen other dead Angra fans. They built a Sistine Chapel out of body parts in one of the freezers. You might want to send a team over before the cops haul away all the evidence. You can get the GPS off my phone."

"Don't move," says Wells. He pulls out his BlackBerry and thumbs in a text like he wants to punch the keys in the face. When he's done he sighs and peeks in the cooler again.

"Why did you even bring that thing here? I'm not paying you by the scalp."

"He didn't do it," says Candy. "Well, not all of it. Just the last part to get his head off. The guy did the rest himself."

Wells turns to Candy. It's the first time he's acknowledged her presence.

"It's truly a comfort knowing that your paramour only partly cut off the head on a key witness in our investigation."

"Just 'cause he's dead doesn't mean we can't still question him. That's why he's on ice," I say.

"Go on."

"There's this ritual I know. It's messy [illegible] right, I can catch his soul before he goes into [illegible] afterlife."

"And how, pray tell, does the ritual work?"

"First I have to die a little."

Wells puts up his hands and [illegible].

"Well, isn't that peachy? Another death today. And a suicide. Right here in Vigil headquarters. [illegible] Washington [illegible] that at all. Please go ahead [illegible]"

"It isn't technically suicide because I'm only partway dead and only for a little while."

"Good, because suicide is a sin, this is consecrated ground, and I've already broken enough commandments just letting you in here."

I hand [illegible] the folder and go up to Wells.

"You came to me for help, remember? You don't know what I do and how I work. Anytime you don't want me around I'm gone. But when I leave, the Mag[illegible] comes with me."

"So you can lose the weapon again. How about you clean this mess before you go calling [illegible]."

"Fine. Get me a room where I can do the ritual. Preferably new, quiet and private. There's going to be some blood."

"More good news," he says. "Come with me. I wanted you to see this anyway. It's one of [illegible]. We've turned [illegible] into a kind of [illegible] magic [illegible] whatever without contaminating or [illegible] us out of the new agents."

"They sound a little too sensitive to be cops."

"Don't bad-mouth my people. None of them [illegible] ever come back with a head in a box."

"Maybe you didn't ask nice enough."

Wells leads us through the place. The building is swarming with agents. Some in dark suits like Wells's. Some in lab coats.

The building doesn't resemble much of a country club anymore. They've knocked down walls and torn out floors and ceilings to bring in their special tech. I never had much use for the stuff, but I guess it suits whatever most of them do. The tech is a mix of hush-hush black budget science-fiction toys crossed with angelic hoodoo they used to get from Aelita. I don't know what they're doing for it now. Maybe they have another angel on the payroll. They sure can't ask me for help. I'm a nephilim. Half human, half angel. And I worked hard to get the angel part of me under control. The little prick is a boy scout and a bore. I'm not bringing him out again just to sup up some laptops and ray guns.

Wells leads us into what used to be one of the business offices. Now the windows have been blacked out and it's been turned into an occult space. A place where disreputable pixies like me can perform forbidden rites and magical high jinks.

Candy sets the cooler down on a worktable piled high with old books and manuscripts.

"What do you think? Looks like you finally got your hoodoo man-cave."

"I've seen the Vigil do worse. At least they're admitting that they need something more than angelic halo polishers on their side."

Candy flips through the old books, looking for wood prints of medieval monsters, one of her favorite things. I look around.

There are lab coats, [illegible]ors, [illegible], and eye protection by the door. [illegible] books [illegible] ound[illegible] ing one wall, covered in English [illegible] ept. A fe[illegible] to [illegible] what loo[illegible] like a[illegible] ald[illegible] s[illegible] in the c[illegible]r [illegible] est [illegible] tubes, bu[illegible] er[illegible] ale[illegible] n[illegible] en[illegible] h[illegible]bs, [illegible]rs, and pow-ders to b[illegible] c[illegible] he[illegible] g[illegible] ma[illegible]. [illegible] books [illegible]s [illegible] sta[illegible]d a silver ma[illegible]ic circle [illegible] the [illegible] r. [illegible] s [illegible] cru[illegible] to the back [illegible] the d[illegible]r. [illegible]b's [illegible] desi[illegible] to [illegible] unholy m[illegible]gic fro[illegible] cont[illegible]in[illegible]ating [illegible] V[illegible] quarters [illegible] sa[illegible]e as alwa[illegible]. They [illegible] his hoo[illegible] c[illegible] they nev[illegible] le[illegible] us forget [illegible] at w[illegible] t[illegible] in the b[illegible]k [illegible] the [illegible]us

"Wha[illegible] s t[illegible]at?" say[illegible] [illegible]dy.

Back [illegible] y the p[illegible]ants [illegible] d a[illegible] a b[illegible]k[illegible]-down Japa-nese sh[illegible]r[illegible]e, [illegible] st [illegible] ig[illegible] [illegible] to h[illegible] [illegible] izere[illegible] ol[illegible] [illegible]d. The coffin-si[illegible]e s[illegible]ine [illegible] hundred[illegible] of [illegible] ea[illegible]s old. The bo[illegible] sit[illegible] cr[illegible]ss-leg[illegible]ed in a [illegible] ation p[illegible]e. It's [illegible] in gold [illegible] re[illegible] on[illegible] ro[illegible] a[illegible]d [illegible] that so[illegible] one is lo[illegible]king a[illegible] it [illegible] p[illegible]r-th[illegible] [illegible] stretch[illegible]s [illegible] bones. [illegible] a[illegible] [illegible] he[illegible]d. [illegible] body [illegible] at all, [illegible]t a stat[illegible] [illegible] fro[illegible] [illegible] w[illegible]od. The[illegible] offering[illegible] o[illegible] [illegible], an[illegible] [illegible]ges, a[illegible] i[illegible] ense a[illegible] the [illegible] of [illegible] shrine.

I go [illegible] ver and touch [illegible] e [illegible] k[illegible], [illegible] -ea[illegible] n [illegible] on the [illegible] of the [illegible] r[illegible].

"Do[illegible] t [illegible] o[illegible] [illegible] s[illegible] k [illegible] Bat[illegible]s [illegible] p[illegible]."

We[illegible] co[illegible] es [illegible] and [illegible] e.

"Do[illegible] 't [illegible] uc[illegible] [illegible] ba[illegible]k[illegible]

"W[illegible] 's the d[illegible]al [illegible] h sk[illegible] e?"

Wi[illegible] a [illegible] ea[illegible], he [illegible] m[illegible] [illegible] head.

"[illegible] the d[illegible]al with [illegible] [illegible] yi[illegible]"

Slowly, the mummy monk unfolds its arms and legs. It's so slow and delicate, it looks like a giant stick insect waking up.

I take a few steps back. Candy comes around the table and stands beside me, holding on to my arm. Not out of fright but in a "Holy shit can you believe this shit?" way.

Finally, the mummy is standing. The golden robes hang off him like a layer of extra flesh. He stands up straight, puts out his arms, and stretches.

"Nice nap," he says, then looks back at me. "You're the one I've heard so much about. You been running around shooting more people, fatso?"

Dead man or not, Candy steps up.

"Don't call him names, you bony bastard. He's skinny as a rail."

The mummy waves a dismissive hand at her.

"You need glasses."

"That's a holy man, young lady," says Wells. "You do not speak to him like that."

"Then he shouldn't call people names," she says.

"Stark, let me introduce you to Ishiro Shonin."

Before Candy can start arguing with Wells, I go over to the mummy, hoping this is all some kind of hazing ritual.

"What's your story, dead man? I hear you speaking English, but your mouth is doing something else."

He shuffles to the table with the herbs and lab equipment. Drinks something green from an Erlenmeyer flask.

"Ah," he says when he's done. "You have good eyes for a fool. I speak how I like and you hear how you like. Same thing for me. I hear you, so you make sense. Not that someone like you makes much sense."

[illegible] talent [illegible]. Do [illegible] [illegible]"

"[illegible] too [illegible] much [illegible] some [illegible] [illegible] the [illegible]? [illegible] here to [illegible] [illegible] with the [illegible].

"[illegible] the [illegible], why don't you get [illegible] eye? [illegible] dead [illegible] before he's [illegible]. You [illegible] around here."

[illegible] glass [illegible] chest. I [illegible] [illegible]

"[illegible] called [illegible]

"[illegible] nal. [illegible] effective. It's the [illegible] Cube [illegible]

[illegible]

[illegible] you [illegible] with [illegible] your [illegible]. Lots of [illegible] and [illegible] you'd choose this one."

"[illegible] be [illegible] good [illegible] [illegible]."

"[illegible] blas[illegible]," says [illegible].

"[illegible] because you're in love with [illegible]" says the [illegible]. "You die a li[illegible] and come back. [illegible] again and over like [illegible]." He [illegible] Carl. "Is [illegible] bad [illegible] friend?"

"[illegible] great."

"[illegible] shouldn't let [illegible] stupid."

"[illegible] that [illegible]?"

The [illegible] [illegible] with [illegible] fingers. [illegible] small [illegible] probably [illegible].

"[illegible] spirit [illegible] that kind of thing [illegible] true."

"Me? I believe in everything. How does it work?"

"You make a tea. You meditate. You enter the spirit realm and find your man before he drifts away. That okay with you, fatty?"

"Great. Brew some up. I'll try it."

"You know how to meditate?"

"Everyone in L.A. knows how to meditate."

The Shonin looks as doubtful as a skeleton can. He puts water on a small flame to boil. Drops the twig into the pot.

"I should do it. I have more experience," says the Shonin.

"And I have trust issues. I'll do it."

"If you get lost and can't come back, don't blame me."

"If I get stuck because of your hoodoo juice, my ghost is going to come back and shit in your skull."

The Shonin shakes his head. It sounds like twigs cracking.

"No reasoning with some people."

"Amen to that," says Wells.

Candy says, "You're really going to drink that stuff?"

I take off my wet coat and throw it over the back of a chair.

"If I don't have to slice and dice myself, I'm willing to try it. Wells won't let him kill me, will you, Wells? I'm the only one with experience handling the 8 Ball."

"So far," says Wells. "But there's always tomorrow."

"Maybe not too many," says Candy. "You might want to remember that."

The Shonin takes the tea off the burner and pours a brown mess into a small ceramic cup.

"The girl . . ."

"Candy," she says.

The Shonin looks at her.

"Okay," the Shonin says. "Now you meditate. You need a *zafu* to sit on? What kind of meditation do you do?"

I pull a flask from my back pocket.

"The liquid kind," I say, unscrewing the top and downing a long drink of Aqua Regia, the number one booze in Hell. It goes down like gasoline and hot pepper and washes the taste of baboon out of my mouth.

The Shonin says, "Drink all you want, dummy. You won't find God in a bottle."

"I already found God," I say. "That's why I drink."

I hand Candy the flask and she takes a quick gulp before putting it in her pocket. I'm used to Aqua Regia's kick, but down enough at once and it's going to turn anyone's cerebral cortex into chocolate pudding. I let it and the tea do their work. They fight it out in my stomach. The Hellion hoodoo wrestling whatever kind of magic Mr. Bones uses. My stomach cramps and for a few seconds I want to throw up. But I hold on and the feeling passes. The room gets thin, like it's made of black gauze. I put the crow feather between my teeth just as I fall out of myself.

I'm standing on an alkali plain stretching out flat and cracked in all directions. In the far distance is a shaft of light, but it never moves. The sky is dim, like just before sunrise or after sunset. Flip a coin to decide. The air is thick and hard to breathe. I wouldn't want to have to run a marathon here.

The dead man wanders around shivering. Probably from being on ice for so long. I'm glad it worked and I didn't have to come halfway to Hell for nothing.

The dead man stumbles back a couple of steps when he sees me. A second later he recognizes me and starts over, a little cautious.

"You were the witness to our sacrifice. An ordinary, mortal man shattered by such a holy rite was our way to paradise."

"And yet here you are. Downtown Nowheresville. Like the view?"

Hobaica comes at me.

"You did this."

He tries to grab me. I sidestep, give him a little shove to throw him off balance, and stomp on the back of his knee. He goes down on his face, hurt but in one piece.

"You got that out of your system and now you're going to be smart, right? Good. First off, who told you I was following you?"

Hobaica nurses his hurt knee, but manages a smile.

"A little birdie. *Der Zorn Götter* has friends in many places."

I've heard of them. An upper-crust Angra sect. They have connections in money and politics all over the Sub Rosa and civilian world. Could they have connections to the Vigil?

"You made a mistake asking me to be your witness, genius. First, I'm not exactly mortal, and second, I spent eleven years in Hell. You think a bunch of nitwits sawing their own heads off is going to shatter me? In Hell we called that 'Wednesday.' "

I go over and pull Hobaica to his feet.

"This is a trick," he says.

"Show me what's in your head. I want to see what you expected when you died. Show me the Flayed Heart."

"Never."

"Listen, man. I know you don't mind a little pain, but you're dead now. You don't need to have to do that anymore. Show me what I want or it's going to hurt."

each other. A few piles of limbs have pulled together enough pieces to form a complete body. These climb up the sides of the tooth lotus, pushing back bodies that miss the Flayed Heart's mouth and try to get away. Others swim through the fire into caverns at the base of the lotus.

Since he's dead, I can't gauge Hobaica's mood by the smell of his sweat or the sound of his heartbeat, but being in his head, I can feel his excitement. This is what Hobaica hoped for when he cut his head off. To be one of those bodies falling into Zhuyigdanatha's mouth, feeding his master.

The old Angra moves as it chews its lunch, twisting this way and that to catch the choicest bodies. If you see it from different angles, Zhuyigdanatha changes. It becomes a slimy lizard, snaring falling bodies with a prehensile tongue a thousand miles long. A baobab tree, with razor foliage and a trunk made of rheumy eyes. A crawling fungal mass plucking bloating corpses from a sea of sewage. At least I know this really is an Angra I'm seeing. Zhuyigdanatha isn't really changing. It's a transdimensional being. We ordinary slobs can only see one dimensional aspect of the God at once, so it seems to change as it moves and dreams.

From inside Hobaica's head, I can feel the man wilt as it finally comes to him that he'll never be saved by his God. His sacrifice was a joke. The Angras are in another dimension. The other God, the God of this dimension, isn't wild about people deity shopping. It starts to dawn on Hobaica that he's not only lost his personal Jesus, but killing himself as a sacrifice to the Flayed Heart means he's pissed off the other God. With his frequent asshole miles he's earned himself a window seat on the big coal cart to Hell. He's not even scared. He's beyond fear or [illegible] he knows he's lost. [illegible] he [illegible] someone else's blood [illegible]

[illegible] in [illegible] ge [illegible]

[illegible] and [illegible] struggle [illegible] they

[illegible] these [illegible]

[illegible]."

[illegible] appears in the [illegible] light

[illegible] plain.

[illegible] isn't [illegible] I'm [illegible]

[illegible] ad. [illegible] eats [illegible]."

[illegible] is [illegible] over his face [illegible] the

[illegible]

[illegible] wrong ho[illegible] first

[illegible] you [illegible] up [illegible]

[illegible] for the su[illegible] had

[illegible] But Hoba[illegible]

[illegible]. The [illegible]

[illegible] he isn't already doing.

He says, "What do I do now?"

"[illegible] when you [illegible] which

[illegible] things are going [illegible]

[illegible] side."

"[illegible]"

"Yes."

"So, [illegible] somewhere [illegible]

[illegible]'s [illegible] choice [illegible] know?"

[illegible] He [illegible] clothes are [illegible] blood

[illegible] like what [illegible]

[illegible]er, [illegible] pathetic.

"Which would you choose?" he says.

"I didn't get to make a choice when I went. But if I were you, I'd choose to be someplace. All they can do in Hell is hurt you. Out here with nothing but yourself to talk to, you're going to destroy your mind. Being alone is worse than being somewhere bad."

He nods. Even manages the faintest smile in human history.

"Thank you," he says, and starts for the mountains.

"Vaya con Dios."

He stops.

"Is that a joke?"

"Yeah. Not one of my best."

"A bad joke isn't much of a send-off before an eternity in Hell."

"I could tell you the one about the one-eyed priest and the bowlegged nun."

"I'll be going now."

He walks to the mountain and goes into the tunnel without looking back. It closes behind him. Alone on the alkali plain, I sit down with my legs crossed. I wipe the blood off my face with my hand and the alkali burns the cut in my forehead. The drunken feeling comes over me again. My shoulders sag. My head falls forward and my mouth opens. Something light drifts out and settles on my leg.

I wake up in the circle across from the severed head. There's a puddle underneath it where it's starting to defrost. Candy takes my arm and helps me up. I run my fingers over my forehead. No blood. Score one for the bag of bones. I didn't have to bleed in real life after all.

"Zhuyigdanatha likes underground places," says Shonin to Wells. "If there's a larger Angra group, you might find them there."

Wells shifts his weight from one foot to the other.

"What caves are we talking about? Carlsbad Caverns? A salt mine in Louisiana? Lascaux?"

The Shonin pours out the muck he gave me. Puts water and green tea into the pot and places it back on the burner.

"These were California boys, so it will be a California cave that connects, at least on a spirit level, with the Flayed Heart's dwelling place."

I start to say something, but don't. I know some caves nearby, but if the Vigil doesn't know about them I'm not going to tell them yet. I need to check with someone first.

Candy is slumped on a metal stool on the other of the room, away from everyone. She's pale and fidgety. I go over to her.

"You all right?"

"I'm fine," she says. "Just let me sit here."

"I can take you home if you want."

"I'm fine. Okay?"

I nod.

"Okay."

"Stark," says Wells. "You know lowlifes. Any of your pixie friends like to spend their time underground?"

"What makes you think the Sub Rosa or Lurkers have anything to do with this? Angra worshipers are mostly lily-white civilians."

"You didn't answer my question."

I look at the Shonin.

"Watch the profanity," says Wells.

I go over to him.

"Exactly what is Mr. Bones doing here?"

"He was a *yamabushi* back in Japan. A lone mountain monk in Sennizawa. They called them Swamp Wizards. He has a deep background in the mystical arts. He's going to figure out how to make the Qomrama Om Ya work."

"I'm supposed to be lab partners with this guy?"

The Vigil has the 8 Ball locked up in a secure clean room all by itself, suspended in a magnetic field. It floats in the air and changes shape as you walk around it.

"Not supposed to," says Wells. "You are. It's done and settled. He'll figure out the Qomrama and you'll use it."

"Why don't you clue me in on these things from time to time so I know what to expect?"

Wells pushes the cooler against the wall with the toe of his highly polished shoe.

"Fine. Here's your clue for today. I want you to write down everything that happened before the man you brought in died and everything you saw and heard when you went inside his head. Make sure Ishiro Shonin gets a copy and so do I."

"Now I'm your secretary."

"For the kind of money we're paying you, you're whatever I need. Today you weren't much of anything at all."

"Speaking of money, I still don't have my first check."

Wells squares his shoulders.

"I wanted a man to question and you bring me back a horror show. This isn't a good time to complain to management about your salary."

I look over at Candy. She's leaning her elbows on the table.

I say, "I'll see you at home."

Candy doesn't say anything. Just walks away.

I remember that she still has my gun and I almost go after her. But I don't. Maybe some space is what she needs right now. Anyway, whatever's wrong, Allegra's clinic will fix her up.

I find a good shadow by the lab door and go through, coming out at home. Maximum Overdrive. The video store I run with a not-quite-dead man named Kasabian.

MAX OVERDRIVE IS located on Las Palmas, right off Hollywood Boulevard. It sits midway between Donut Universe and Bamboo House of Dolls, the only junk-food place and bar that matters in L.A.

Kasabian used to run the store. When I came back from Hell I cut off his head. I might have been a little hasty, but he'd just shot me and I wasn't feeling entirely reasonable at the time.

The trick with the black blade I used on him is that if you hold it just right it cuts, but it doesn't kill. And that's what I did to Kasabian. He's spent most of the last year as a disembodied head and he hasn't shut up about it.

Lately I started feeling sorry for him, so I had a Tick Tock Man called Manimal Mike attach Kas to a mechanical hellhound. Now he sort of has a body, even if it's a little wobbly and whirs like a toy train when he moves.

Some Lurkers are in the store. A young Lyph whose denim jacket looks like it was mugged by a Bedazzler. All rhinestones and shiny bits on the back. Jim Morrison's face in flames. Underneath it says LIGHT MY FIRE. Lyph have horns

What we rent mostly now are lost movies. Movies cut to pieces by the studios or lost in fires or time. Movies that literally don't or shouldn't exist anymore in this dimension of reality.

"*London After Midnight* is fun. It's a murder mystery. Lon Chaney plays a creepy guy with a giant set of fangs and a weird beaver hat, who might be a vampire."

Eye Patch leans back, frowning.

"Silent movies? Those are as scary as a damp sponge."

"That means you wouldn't like *Metropolis.* I have the only totally complete copy in the world with the original score, you know."

He shakes his head.

"Not interested."

This isn't the first time this has happened. We only have one rack of special discs. We're still building up inventory. You think it's easy conjuring video and film from other dimensions? It's not. And the young *curandera* I contracted with to get them charges a fortune for each one.

"What is it you want?"

"Action. Guns. Explosions."

"Go home, crack open a light beer, turn on your TV, and find some Michael Bay shit."

"Come on, man. You have any Clint Eastwood?"

"No special ones. You like his spaghetti westerns?"

The shorter vampire comes over when I mention westerns.

"Who doesn't?" he says.

I point to an old poster on the wall.

"You know that gangster flicks are the natural descendants of those Italian westerns, right? Action. Crime. Law-

"The discs are hexed. They know when they're being copied and melt down like a nuke plant, killing themselves and whatever machine they're in. We have an alarm rigged up that goes off when it happens. Store policy is that you kill my disc, well, you know."

"You kill them?"

"Don't be stupid. I can't kill off my customer base. No, I just cut off their fingers and feed them to Kasabian."

From the back room Kasabian yells, "I heard that. Fuck you."

"See? A barely controlled beast."

"Take it easy, Stark," says Eye Patch. "How long do we have the movie?"

"Three days. After that, it's a hundred-dollar-a-day late fee."

The short vampire gets their umbrellas from the bin up front.

"You're a fucking thief, you know that?" he says.

"Wrong. I'm P. T. Barnum. You want to see the Fiji mermaid, I'm the only one in town who has one and no one gets in free."

"This movie better be fucking great."

"If you don't like it, come back and you can exchange it for one of these."

I hold up my middle finger.

Eye Patch laughs. When his friend takes a step toward me, he puts a hand on his shoulder and he backs down. Yeah, the short one is new to the bloodsucker game. Anxious to show off his power. Good thing he's got Eye Patch looking out for him. He might actually make it to New Year's.

"Which ones?"

"In the early sixties they used to erase a lot of TV to save on videotape. They lost old *Doctor Whos*. *The Avengers*. Cool shows like that. I have friends who'd kill for those."

"Tell you what, make me a list of what you want and I'll see what I can do."

From the back, Kasabian yells, "That's TV. We don't do TV."

I shake my head.

"Ignore him. He's a snob. Bring me the list and your next rental is free."

"Awesome," she says. She gets her umbrella, does her old lady trick, and heads out. Stopping by the door she says, "Merry Christmas."

"Same to you, Mrs. Cratchit."

She opens the door and a blast of wind blows rain inside. It's coming down hard enough that the street out front is flooding again. I lock the door behind her.

"Cute girl," says Kasabian, coming out of the back. His mechanical legs click with each step. He wears a loose knock-off Nike tracksuit. It makes him look like the movie version of a Russian mobster, if Russian mobsters were robots.

"Nice salesmanship with her," he says. "Not so much with the guys you threatened."

"The little guy annoyed me. Anyway, we need signs or warning labels or something on the discs. I don't want to keep having that conversation."

"If it'll calm you down I'll print out something."

"Yeah, it would."

Kasabian has lost more hair in the year since I've been

"What are these?"

"Requests from potential clients."

Kasabian started a little side business a few weeks back and it's taken off like a bottle rocket out of a carny's ass. He can't go to Hell like I can, but he can see into the place. He set himself up as an online seer. For a fee, he'll tell you how the dearly departed are getting on in the Abyss. Seeing as how most people seem to end up down there, he doesn't lack for clients.

Kasabian riffles the pages with his pointy hellhound claws.

"All these people have family or friends Downtown. And all want more than I can give them. Paying clients don't want to hear about sweet Aunt Suzy up to her eyeballs in a river of shit."

"And this concerns me how?"

"Most of these people want to, you know, talk to the departed. Hear a story about redemption, maybe. Mostly, they want to know where they hid the good silver or did they really love them. You know. Normal family bullshit."

"And you want me to go Downtown and play twenty questions with damned souls because they don't have enough problems."

"Yes. That's what I always want. Come on, man. Look at the streets. This city is going to be empty soon. Empty and underwater. It's no-shit Ragnarök. People want to know what to expect on the other side."

I shake my head. Push the papers back across the counter.

"Not my problem. And I told you. Mr. Muninn is still pissed at me for stealing Father Traven's soul. He doesn't want me back in his petting zoo playing with the animals."

"I just would."

"Okay, Cassandra, there's something else. Did it rain much when you were down there?"

"No. I don't remember it raining at all."

"Well, it is now. Raining cats and dogs and little imps with pitchforks. I mean, there's doomed. There's screwed. And there's monsoons-in-Hell fucked. And we're at fucked o'clock."

Suddenly I want a cigarette. I take out the Maledictions. I go to the back door and open it, blowing the smoke outside. Candy doesn't like me stinking the place up with cigarettes that smell like a tire fire.

"I don't get it. Could the Angra be doing it?"

"Who cares? It's happening and whoever's in charge down there can't stop it. What makes you think I can?"

"You were the Devil," says Kasabian.

It's true. I got stuck with Lucifer's job for three miserable months. And what do you know? I wasn't good at being a bureaucrat or a diplomat. I fucked Hell up worse than it was when I got there, and barely made it out with my hide intact.

"You know God," Kasabian says. "Get him off his backside. Or better yet, hide us in your magic room. You've always said that nothing can get in there. It's the perfect fallout shelter."

I puff the Malediction, cupping it in my hand so the rain doesn't put it out.

"So your solution to the end of the universe is to hide for the next billion years in the Room of Thirteen Doors? A room with nothing in it and nowhere to go."

"Okay. It doesn't sound great when you say it like that.

dishwasher. I would have been happy eating off paper plates with plastic forks for the rest of my life, but Candy said I should stop pretending that the world is a squat and that I'm just passing through. I've stuck around for almost a year, so maybe she's right. After losing room service and our cushy life at the Chateau Marmont, there was nowhere else for us to go but Max Overdrive. I don't think Candy ever lived anywhere very long before Doc Kinski took her in. She doesn't talk about her life before that. If playing *Ozzie and Harriet* makes her happy, then it's all right with me. But I'm still not folding fucking pillowcases. Good thing for everyone there's a laundry down the block.

Why has she been moody and off her feed lately? Today wasn't the first time she's been mad enough to snap. What if she feels like she got in too deep with the domestic bliss stuff? She dumped me once before, back when I disappeared for three months in Hell. Wouldn't it be a hoot if after getting sheets and plates and all kinds of kitchen trinkets, she decides she can't handle it? It wouldn't exactly surprise me. Most of my luck revolves around breaking things. If every day was car chases and sawing people's heads off, I'd be the Pope of Lucky Town.

CANDY COMES HOME about an hour later. I have *Spirited Away* going on the big screen. Her favorite movie when she's feeling down. She sticks her head around the door and raps on it with her knuckles.

"Knock, knock," she says. "I brought a peace offering. Burritos from Bamboo House of Dolls."

"Then you may enter."

"What do other domestic ladies do? You could take up needlepoint or do crossword puzzles. Maybe get into Valium and martinis."

"I like the sound of the last part. But seriously, Allegra has all the help she needs at the clinic and I like being Robin to your Batman. That and my Duo-Sonic are about the only things I give a shit about right now."

I gave Candy a cherry-red electric guitar a few weeks back. She got herself a little used Roland CUBE amp and bashes away every moment she can. She only knows about three chords, but she plays them with great conviction. Sometimes Fairuza, a Ludere who works with Allegra at the clinic, jams with her on drums. They're talking about starting a band, calling it the Bad Touch Sugar Cookies because it sounds like one of the *idoru* bands they like. Supposedly, Fairuza's old band once opened for Shonen Knife at the Whiskey. I think Candy about dumped me for her when she heard that, but I have a better movie collection, so she stayed.

I take a blanket off the back of the couch and wrap it around Candy and we watch the rest of the movie. After that, I write the report I promised Wells, and e-mail it to him. I still can't figure out what the mess in Hobaica's demented head meant. Tooth flowers. Seas of fire. Hacked-up bodies. It's like a Texas Chain Saw wet dream. Maybe it doesn't mean anything at all. Maybe I just left him on ice too long and Hobaica's soul was all screwed up from his brain getting frozen and oxygen deprived. Anyway, it's not my job to figure out. That's for the bag of Shonin bones.

Later, Candy reheats the burritos and we eat them while watching *Hausu,* a funny Japanese haunted-house flick.

From up here, through the air that's been washed clean by the rain, the city is beautiful. L.A. always looks best in the dark, when it's just lights and the ugly hulks of the buildings have been softened to vague night shapes. Even from up here, I can see the traffic snarling the main streets and spilling out onto the Hollywood Freeway. People are leaving town and they don't even know why. They're running just to run. Some animal part of their brain knows something bad is coming and they want to get as far from it as possible. Who can blame them? But if the Angra come stomping back to the world, there won't be anywhere too remote to hide. In the meantime, they run like lemmings.

Idiot that I am, I didn't bring a shovel, so I have to dig with my hands. I put the bones in the ground between the H and the O in HOLLYWOOD. I don't know if being in soil will help those ghosts rest easier, but I'll sleep better knowing I'm not just another liar in a city built on slick pitchmen who'd sell you their mother's kidneys if it got them salesman of the month.

It's dark up here and there isn't a shadow in sight. I turn on the LED flashlight and bury one end in the ground. I get in front of the beam and step into my own shadow, soaked and cold, heading home.

Later, Candy comes upstairs. Her T-shirt is soaked through with sweat.

"Having a little drink?"

"I went out. I'm trying to get the chill out of my bones."

She takes off her shirt and tosses it on the back of a chair. She comes over and straddles me on the couch, presses her warm body into mine.

a hollow husk. After all I've been through, here I am, dying at the hands of a freak in the basement of a goddamn department store. I cramp again. This time I'm sure it's real.

The dream changes. I'm back in Vigil headquarters. Their first one, down south of L.A. Aelita is there. She's an angel. One of God's most hard-core. Pure Old Testament rage. She runs the Vigil with Wells. Only she's crazy, or maybe I make her crazy. The knowledge of my existence does. I'm Abomination. Nephilim. I shouldn't exist and yet God lets me live. She does Ferox's trick. Pig-sticks me with a flaming angelic sword. Kills me good. My first death. But I got over it and stabbed her right back. Still, I can feel her sticking me more than I can feel any satisfaction in getting revenge.

My stomach burns like it's filled with fire and metal.

All these scars. The road map of my life. My armor. Sometimes being hard to kill isn't exactly a blessing. Maybe that's the point. Maybe it's my punishment for being born a freak. I don't think even God knows at this point. He's broken up enough these days I don't know if I'd trust any answers he gave me.

Aelita declared war on God before she died. Wanted nothing more than to murder him. Here I am with her former friends trying to do the same thing to the Angra Om Ya. Who's right and who's wrong doesn't matter anymore. Maybe God did trick the old gods out of this universe and steal it for himself. But here's the scary question: which God is worse? The Angra, who might be competent, but want to wipe us out, or our God, who isn't good at his job, but if not benign, is at least indifferent to us? Parental neglect is starting to look pretty good right now, isn't it?

"It's not a big deal. There's a council in charge of things like how many of us there are in the world and when we need more. Don't worry about it. They're not going to ask me to pop out little Jadelets."

"How do you know?"

"Because I'm fucking a monster. The biggest monster on Earth. You've polluted my precious bodily fluids."

She says it like it's a big joke, but she's never talked much about Jade life before.

"Tell me the truth," I say. "Did I fuck up some big deal for you? Get you on the outs with the other Jades?"

She sits up and puts her hand on my arm.

"You didn't fuck up anything. I chose to be here with you, remember? If any of the Jade Ommahs have a problem with that, they can take away my cookies and my merit badges and I won't care."

"Thanks. If that ever changes you better tell me."

She gives me a push.

"Shut up and go to work, drama queen."

I lean against the bedroom door and pull on my boots.

"I have to spend the day with cops and you get to hang out in bed."

"Sucks to be you," she says.

"Maybe I should call in sick."

"Maybe you should go and get us some money and find out more about what was going on in that meat locker. Don't you sort of wonder about that?"

"Not really."

"Well, I do. Don't come back without some answers and ice cream."

been sawn off, revealing the gray brain matter. Each brain sports three incense sticks jammed right into the head meat.

I look at Wells.

"You give me a hard time and this guy's one step away from turning these people into bongs."

"Very funny. This man has been doing real work while you've been lying around at home."

I walk between the tables, checking out the bodies. It's like a weird corpse maze. Each head has a sigil painted with a brush a little below the hairline. Over their third eye. My guess is that the Shonin has been poking around in some of these dead people's memories.

I say, "How did you get the bodies? You scoop them up before the cops get there?"

"No such luck. Local law enforcement arrived just as we were removing the physical evidence."

"Dead people, you mean."

"Among other pieces of evidence, yes. I'm afraid there was an ugly scene. I don't enjoy territorial clashes, but I suppose with a crime this large local authorities are bound to be . . ."

"Emotional?"

"Clingy. However, when I explained the gravity of the situation to the commanding officer, he was happy to allow us to assist in the investigation."

"You pulled rank, didn't you? Got all federal. Maybe threatened to bring in Homeland Security."

"I didn't have to. As I said, the commander was a reasonable man."

"LAPD is a lot of things, but I don't remember reasonable."

[illegible] he chief of [illegible] Rosa, so he understands how import[illegible] [illegible] vestigation [illegible]

"[illegible] aving fun, [illegible] y?" says [illegible] the [illegible]. "Does he alw[illegible] [illegible] time like this?"

"He's a child," says Wells. "A mischievous child. [illegible] I'm so reluctant to give him this."

[illegible] Shetnik laughs a grumbling laugh. Like rocks [illegible] [illegible] er. I hope I don't hear him do it again.

"We're getting [illegible] Christmas gifts? [illegible] [illegible] me."

Wells reaches into his jacket pocket and takes out a [illegible] of leather. [illegible] it to me. Inside is a card with [illegible] portrait and the [illegible] Vigil insignia.

"This is official Vigil I.D. If a situation develops with law enforcement, show it to them. [illegible] won't work in [illegible] k town, but [illegible] will in L.A. [illegible] you're [illegible] going [illegible] anytime soon, are you?"

"Not with the [illegible] Out of Jail Free card, I'm not."

"Don't even [illegible] think about [illegible] using the autho[illegible] [illegible] ted to you by this identification."

"[illegible] wouldn't dream of it. But LAPD [illegible] knows [illegible] [illegible] ies, so the thing might actually come in handy."

Wells takes back the ID.

"Speaking of your previous criminal activities, understand [illegible] this identification is only good while you work for [illegible] [illegible] zation. My organization. You get [illegible] of the [illegible] and I'll throw you to the wolves. Do you understand me?"

"I'm a team player, sir. I won't let you down."

"See that you don't," he says, and [illegible] back the [illegible] in my pocket before Wells can [illegible] it away again.

The Shonin crooks his finger at me and says, "Come over here and see what real mystical forensics looks like."

I go over. He waits on the other side of a table holding Hobaica's body.

"The man's name is Joseph Hobaica. He's thirty-eight years old, and by the cross around his neck, a good Catholic boy."

"Wow. You and your mystical powers found his driver's license and a first communion present. You're goddamn Kreskin."

"Language. He runs the distribution company where you witnessed the ceremony," says Wells.

"Was that even a ceremony? It just looked like some kind of elaborate suicide pact to me."

"You know damned well it was an Angra offering ritual. Stop being a smartass."

"What I'm saying is, the all-beef church aside, the whole thing looked kind of thrown together. There weren't any ritual objects. They didn't have time to do an invocation before I got there. They didn't even have decent suicide instruments. What kind of Gods want a life offering made with something you can get at a hardware store?"

"Do you have any brilliant theories?"

"I think they were freaked out and desperate. I could smell it on them. Maybe they were offering themselves to their freaky God, but they were also splitting town. Just like all the other suckers clogging the freeways."

Wells nods.

"You might actually have a point there."

"But you're wrong about there being no ritual objects. Did you see the amputated limbs hanging among the circle?"

"They were a little hard to miss."

The Shonin goes to a table nearby and throws back a [illegible] sheet revealing arms, legs, h[illegible], a whole buffet of parts.

"These are what Marshal Wells's men brought back from the scene. Four arms. Four legs. Four [illegible]ds. Four feet. [illegible] the idea."

"Yeah, they butchered two poor [illegible] or two of [illegible] [illegible]tted suicide before and let themselves be cut up."

The Shonin shakes his head.

"You were closer to right on your first guess. The [illegible] and his men saw this collection of [illegible] human[illegible] and [illegible]ically assumed that with this particular inventory of parts, there were the remains of two bodies."

"But there's more, aren't there?"

Wells goes to the table and pulls the sheet back over the [illegible].

The Shonin expressed some doubts after examining the [illegible], so we ran DNA from each limb. There are parts of twelve [illegible] here. I seriously doubt they butchered twelve of their own members just so that thirteen more could commit suicide."

"So, what are you saying? They're part of some kind of crazy [illegible] Manson gang?"

"You'd like it to be that simple, wouldn't you, [illegible]?" says the Shonin.

Wells picks up a manila envelope from a nearby desk.

"This isn't the first time we've seen this kind of [illegible] desecration. Limbs severed and mixed together."

"I saw something like that in [illegible]'s head. Body parts [illegible] the fire."

Wells opens the manila envelope. Looks at a couple of pages.

He says, "Have you heard of a killer called Saint Nick?"

"I think maybe I saw something when Kasabian was channel-surfing. A killer running around in the rain. So what? L.A. cranks out more serial killers than shitty sitcoms. He sounds like cop business to me."

"To me too until yesterday," says Wells. "Do you know why they call him Saint Nick?"

"Because it's close to Christmas?"

"Half right," the Shonin says. "He's Saint Nick because he likes to give his victims a little cut." He laughs.

"You mean he chops them up?"

Wells nods.

"And removes some of the parts. Different combinations of limbs and organs with each killing."

"Why?

"We don't have a motive yet," says Wells. He tosses the manila envelope back on the desk. "But we found some notes and coded e-mails that lead us to think that this Angra bunch wanted to die by his hand. They thought they'd draw him out by imitating him."

"That explains all the mystery bodies."

"Right."

"But he never showed up," says the Shonin. "Hobaica was afraid that they'd been rejected by their God."

"So, this Saint Nick guy is an Angra worshiper?"

"Who knows?" says Wells. "But this bunch thought he was, and when they felt rejected they did the only thing that made sense to them."

four hundred years ago," says the Shonin. "Happy hunting for that."

Wells looks at me like he's thinking of taking the ID back.

"Get out of here for now," he says. "But keep your phone on. I might need you later. I want to sort this Saint Nick thing out fast."

"What about the 8 Ball?" I say. "Shouldn't the bag of bones be working on that instead of playing medical examiner?"

"Unlike some people, I can multitask," says the Shonin. "So fuck you, round boy."

"Please," says Wells. "The profanity. You're a holy man."

"Your nephilim is right about himself. He's a bad influence. Go home and infect your friends."

"Don't leave yet," says Wells. "I need you to go and see Marshal Sola."

"Julie Sola is back in the Vigil?"

"Marshal Sola is with us again. And she has some papers to go over with you."

"What kind of papers?"

Wells smiles.

"Part one of your psych evaluation."

"Excuse me?"

"Everybody goes through it. I did it. Marshal Sola—"

"How about Aelita?"

That stops him cold.

He says, "You will go to Marshal Sola, do her paperwork, and pass the evaluation or you don't get paid."

"This is bullshit."

"Watch your language. And this is nonnegotiable."

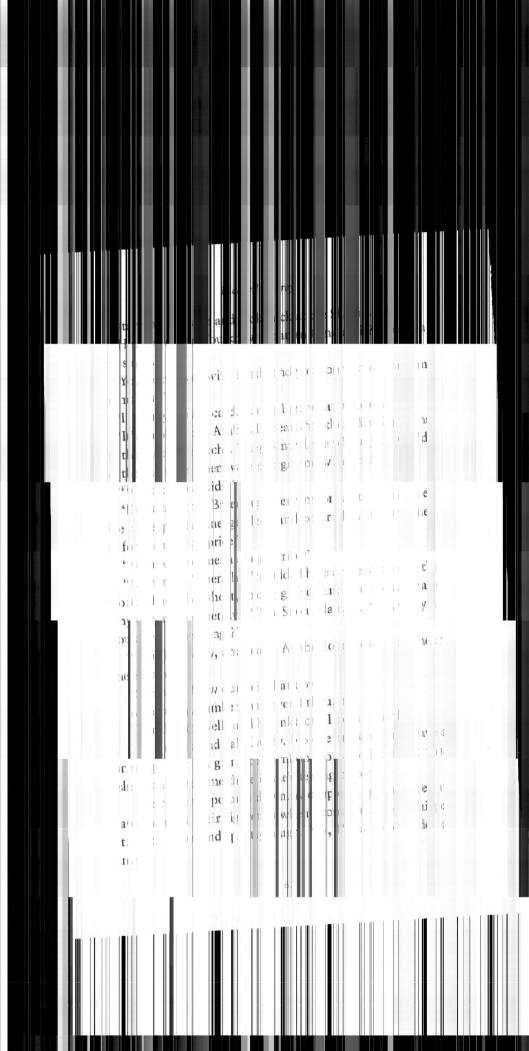

Six Vigil agents in expensive golf clothes play a round under oversize umbrellas. Disguised spooks playing a fake round of a brain-dead game in a billionaire's playpen in a monsoon while around them, the city reaches population zero. If the Angra have a sense of humor they won't be able to invade. They'll laugh themselves stupid and wait for us to die off pretending that nothing is wrong.

I STEP THROUGH a shadow and come out in front of Bamboo House of Dolls. It's my Sistine Chapel. My home away from home. The best bar in L.A. The first bar I walked into after escaping from Hell. It's a punk tiki joint. Old Germs, Circle Jerks, Iggy and the Stooges posters on the wall. Plastic palm trees and hula girls around the liquor bottles. And there's Carlos, the bartender, mixing drinks in a Hawaiian shirt. On the jukebox, Martin Denny is playing an exotic palm-tree version of "Winter Wonderland."

It's a small, damp afternoon crowd in the place. Smaller than usual. Few civilians. Mostly Lurkers. Three gloomy necromancers play bridge with a Hand of Glory filling the fourth seat. A couple of blue-skinned schoolgirl Luderes play their favorite scorpion-and-cup game. A table of excited Goth kids throw D&D dice and cop discreet glances at the crowd from the back of the room. Games for everyone. A necessary distraction when the sky is falling. Still, it's Christmas and the mood isn't bad. *It's a Wonderful Life* crossed with *Night of the Living Dead.*

Carlos serves drinks wearing a Santa hat.

"The salaryman returns," he says when I sit down at the bar. "How's life behind a desk?"

"What was that?"

Carlos says, "Exactly what it looked like. Protection. But for real. Do you know how many cops are left in the city? They're splitting town just like everybody else. The cops that are left, they need a little extra motivation to answer the phone if there's trouble."

"A nice racket."

Carlos shakes his head and throws back his drink.

"The price of doing business in L.A."

He pours us both another round and holds up his glass for a toast.

"Merry Christmas."

We clink glasses and drink. I shake my head.

"I can't believe it's Christmas again. How do you people stand having the same holidays over and over? In Hell they only have holidays when Lucifer feels like it, so it's always a surprise and all the little goblins are giddy as kindergartners."

"You going back to the old country for the holidays?"

"Yeah, I'm Hell's Secret Santa, bringing all the good little imps coal and fruitcake."

"How do you tell the difference?" says someone behind me.

I turn and find Eugène Vidocq, besides Candy probably my best friend on this stupid planet. He doesn't like talking about his age and swears he isn't a day over a hundred and fifty, but I know he's well over two hundred. He's also immortal. And a thief. And after being in the States for more than a hundred years, he still has a French accent thick enough to slice Brie, a last remnant of his home that he won't ever let go of.

ber?" says Carlos. "I didn't know about any of you Sub Rosas or Lurkers back then. If those fuckers came in here these days, I'd give them a faceful of this."

He holds up a potion from behind the bar.

I look at Vidocq.

"One of yours?"

"You're not the only one who barters for drinks," he says.

"Rumor has it you're doing some freelance work for the Vigil these days too. How does it feel to be back?"

Vidocq shakes his head. Regards his drink.

"Strange. As strange as I bet it is for you."

"I'm still not sure it's the right thing to be doing, but if I wasn't working for them I don't know if I'd be doing anything at all."

"Confusion. Strange alliances. God's new deluge. These are the things the world has been reduced to. Apocalypse. *Le merdier.* So let's drink to the void."

Brigitte sighs and picks up her wine.

"You boys are too grim for me. I'm going to find more congenial company."

I say, "Sorry. I didn't mean to be a drag."

"You're never a drag, Jimmy, but I see a studio friend I met when I first came here. A girl must maintain her connections, mustn't she? Maybe I can be in the last movie before the world ends."

"Now who's the drag?"

She shrugs extravagantly.

"Knock 'em dead," I tell her.

I turn back to the bar and pick up my drink. I haven't had a cigarette in hours. My lungs are aching for abuse.

of his survival gear on the table. Lengths of paracord. Sapper gloves. A multicaliber pistol. Condoms in Bubble Wrap. A multitool with more moving parts than a Stealth bomber. Watching her smile, I wonder if Brigitte is pulling out of her depression or if she's just an actress playing at being all right.

"There were suicides and riots. Fury and ecstatic joy, and all for the same reason. The world would end or be transformed, and unlike now, in this age of science and desperate rationality, there was nothing we could do about it. So each of us did what made sense. Drink. Pray. Stay with loved ones or sail off to the ends of the earth."

"And here you are."

"And here I am. Alive and not quite yet mad."

He finishes his drink and holds up the empty glass for another.

"The point is that I believe we will survive. Or enough of us will to make the world worth fighting for."

"It better be. I'm not kickboxing monsters so the Vigil and Homeland Security can turn L.A. into one big It's a Small World ride."

One of the Luderes gives a little shriek. She's been stung by one of the scorpions. The shrieker gives the room a little wave.

"Sorry. Everyone's fine. Carry on."

She and her friend crack up.

I turn back to Vidocq, but there's someone in the way. One of the Goth boys from the table in the back has joined us. He's dressed in a long high-collared coat and has wild Robert Smith hair. He looks vaguely like a mad scientist disguised as a priest. There's something funny about his eyes. I glance over at his friends. They look as surprised as I am.

We go out into the rain. Smokers huddle under the awning. A few of the regulars nod and wave. I don't wave back.

The kid walks all the way to the curb. I stay a couple of steps behind him. We stand there in the rain like a couple of assholes. He steps into the street between two cars, looking around like he's waiting for a cab.

"You saw a golden woman in the water. There," he says, pointing west to the Pacific.

"I remember."

When Kill City collapsed into the ocean a few weeks ago, I was in it. Something that looked like a woman covered in gold swam up from the wreckage and tried to pull me down.

"She served the Hand. She was beautiful."

"Except for the part where half her face was missing."

He nods. His long hair is plastered to his head, covering one eye.

"She was incomplete. That won't happen again."

"You couldn't tell me this inside, where it's dry?"

He holds his hands out wide.

"You don't understand what's happening and even if you did you can't stop it. The old ones are coming. They will bless us with annihilation."

A delivery truck speeds up the street. It swerves toward the curb. Hits the cars the kid is standing between. The impact drives both cars up onto the sidewalk. The kid is still between them, but now he's in two pieces. A girl screams and keeps on screaming.

The kid's friends must have followed us outside. A couple of the other Goth kids run to the curb like maybe they can put their friend back together again. I climb over the trunk of one

The line static clears up.

"Deumos?"

She's another fallen angel. She ran another underground, radical church in Hell. Except it was all a con job. She was working with Merihim to bring the Angra back. I guess you can't trust Hellions or preachers. Who would have guessed?

"The who doesn't matter. The what matters. Return the Qomrama Om Ya. That's the only way the killing will end."

"So you can summon the Angra? I know how you want things to end."

"Admit it. You're as exhausted by existence as we are. Help us end it."

"Hello? Say that again. It's hard to hear you over the bullshit."

There's a pause. I start to think that the line has gone dead.

"Hello?"

"You'll find each other sooner or later, and when you do, you'll see how pointless your cowboy antics really are."

I hear a click and the call is over. I drop the kid's phone in my pocket and take out my own. I hit redial and call Candy.

It rings twice and she picks up.

"You all right?" I say.

"Yeah. Why wouldn't I be?"

"No reason. You weren't feeling well earlier."

"Where are you?"

"Bamboo House."

"I'll be there soon."

"Don't bother. Cops are on the way."

"Are you okay?"

I switch the phone to my left hand. There must have been blood on the kid's phone. I wipe my right hand on my coat.

really wanted to get in they could. Still, I'd like to know who I'm dealing with. I flip on the outside light and go behind the counter. We installed a surveillance camera over the door when Kasabian and I had the place fixed up. Except tonight all I can see is the outline of a body outside and heavy rain. More pounding on the door.

"Stark. I know you're in there. Open up, dammit."

It's a woman's voice.

I take a chance and look around the shade that covers the door and recognize Marshal Julie Sola. I stuff the Colt in my waistband and unlock the door. She brushes past me to get out of the rain. She's in a long slicker raincoat with the hood pulled up over her head. Still, she's drenched and making a puddle on the floor. I point to the peg on the wall where people can hang their raincoats. She gives a soft "Ah," takes off her coat, and hangs it up.

Her hair is long and dark, pulled up high and pinned in place. It was, at least. Now it's a wet rat's nest. She's dressed in light, loose-fitting sportswear, a kind of idiot camouflage the Vigil makes many agents wear to try and blend in with their country-club location. She looks vaguely embarrassed, but quickly shakes it off.

"Thanks," she says. "I thought I'd find you here."

"You're half drowned. Why didn't you wait till I came in tomorrow?"

"Would you have really come to see me?"

"Maybe not first thing, but sure. I like you fine."

"That isn't what I mean," she says. "This is what I mean."

She hands me the manila envelope she's been holding. She had it under the jacket, but the front is still damp.

"I met him once. Creepy guy. He called me 'tubby.' I don't look fat to you, do I?"

"I don't know. He called me 'lardass' last time I saw him."

Candy comes down the stairs.

"Is this where the party is?"

"Candy, this is Julie Sola. Marshal Sola these days. Julie, this is Candy."

Candy comes down and they shake hands. She has powdered sugar on her fingers and it rubs off on Julie.

"Sorry," she says, and holds out the bag she's holding. "Want a donut?"

"No thanks. I was just dropping off some paperwork."

Candy says, "You're the private eye he talked about. You got him onto the zombie case."

Julie nods.

"Yeah. We thought it was a simple demon possession at the time. He saved us."

"Yeah, he does that."

"I've seen you around Vigil headquarters."

"Don't bring me any paperwork. I'm just this one's unofficial assistant."

"Don't worry. If you're not on the payroll you don't have to take the psych evaluation."

Candy looks at me and laughs.

"You're supposed to pass a government psych evaluation? Oh man, I hope you like the smell of a rubber room because that's where you're headed, pal."

"I can pass for normal if I have to."

"Yeah, and I'm Nancy Reagan's wrestling coach."

Julie puts her hand out and I shake it.

She shakes her head.

"No thanks. I have my car."

"Drive safe."

"Thanks."

"She seems nice," says Candy, biting into a jelly donut. "What else did she bring you?"

I pick up the note from Blackburn and drop it again.

"I have to go and see one of the few guys in town who can call in a hit on me. I saw a kid get crushed today. I got a phone call from Downtown. And now this."

I look at Candy. She's already headed for the stairs.

"These are really good donuts."

"Thank you for your concern."

"Don't whine to me. You forgot the coffee. Now I have to go make some. Forget those papers for tonight. Come upstairs and have something to eat, fatty."

I can tell by her tone she's going to be calling me that for a long time.

Before we fall asleep I almost ask her why she never told me about the Ommahs. Almost. Maybe I'll ask later when we're not so tired. Yeah, then.

I CAN'T SLEEP, so I get up at the crack of eleven. Candy is still asleep, so I pull on my clothes quietly and go into the bathroom to brush the taste of lard and sugar out of my mouth. We killed most of the bag watching *Barbarella* and *Danger: Diabolik* last night. I don't need to experience the wonders of fried dough again for a year.

I'm sick of hiding from the world, moving through the Room all the time. When I'm ready to leave I go around to the

Houston. Lies, all lies, and they know it, but do they understand it? It's animal stuff. Zebras don't hang around a watering hole when the lions show up.

Maybe this parade of chickenshit civilians knows more than the rest of us Vigil and Sub Rosa types determined to tough it out until the end. I mean, why should the Angra pick L.A. to be their launching pad? Then again, why not? Maybe Zhuyigdanatha wants to do an open-mic night at the Comedy Store. Maybe the Angra want to have a drink at the Rainbow Bar & Grill like real old-time rock-and-rollers. Maybe they want to stomp us into the dirt because L.A. defines reality for three-quarters of the world. Or maybe because Mr. Muninn used to live here and they fucking hate him and the rest of the God brothers.

The brothers make up what's left of God. See, he had a little nervous breakdown a few millennia back and split into five pieces. He's weak, and one part of him, the brother called Neshemah, is dead. Murdered by Aelita and cheered on by big brother Ruach. Like the Ramones said, we're a happy family.

Maybe I'm making too much of it all. L.A. is turning into Atlantis, slowly sinking beneath the waves. If the rain keeps up, those Brentwood blue bloods will be chain-sawing their mansions into arks, loading up the kids, the Pekingese, their favorite Bentleys, and heading for warmer climes. Trust-fund pirates and showbiz buccaneers, sailing the briny to Palm Springs and Vegas, where it never rains and Armageddon can't get through the guards at the gated communities without an engraved invitation.

Ishii says, "Stark. Don't you even know enough to get out of the rain?"

"I like it. Makes this neighborhood smell less like a piss factory."

"Well, you'd know all about living like a pig, would you?"

"Are you trying to insult me? 'Cause I can't hear you over the sound of your garbage-bag tuxedo."

One or two of his crew smile, but sober up when he throws them a look.

"What do you want here?"

"Don't fuck around, man. You know I'm here to see Blackburn."

He looks me and the bike over.

"I couldn't help noticing you weren't wearing a helmet when you drove up. You're aware that the state of California has clearly spelled out helmet laws, aren't you?"

He takes a couple of steps back and spreads his arms wide.

"And there's no way this, whatever the hell this thing is, is street legal. It doesn't even have a license plate."

"So, write me a ticket, Eliot Ness. Just get out of my way."

Ishii holds up a finger.

"Before I maybe let you in, I'm going to have to search you for weapons."

"Try it and the last thing you'll see is me pulling your skull out by the eye sockets."

That does it. Ishii's goons go on high alert, guns, hexes, and potions at the ready. It's kind of fun really. Like a scene from some kind of hobo Power Rangers movie.

"Not smart," says Ishii. "You know I can have you arrested this fast for making a terrorist threat."

He abruptly stops talking.

"Yes, sir. No, sir. I understand."

He purses his lips as he fumbles the phone back into his coat. Waves his arm in my direction.

"Let him through, boys."

His crew gets out of the way so I can roll the bike to the curb and heel down the kickstand.

Getting off, I say, "Your problem, Ishii, is that you like playing protector of the realm for the Augur because it gives you a power hard-on. But you really don't respect the man. I mean, he peeks into the future. He probably knew exactly what you were going to do before you did. The only reason he waited this long to do anything about it is he wanted to give you a chance to pull your head out of your ass."

Ishii looks at his watch, waves his people back to their posts. He doesn't want to look at me.

"Stop talking, Stark. And go inside before my gun goes off by accident."

"Have fun with the fishes, Noah."

The door is open for me when I reach the hotel.

The outside of Blackburn's house might be a wreck, but the inside is something else. The inner sanctum is a Victorian fever dream of potted palms, gaslights, silk settees, and arsenic-green walls. You half expect to see Dickens and Queen Victoria sipping laudanum in the living room. I know the layout, so I stroll through the place to the parlor, where Blackburn has his office.

The Augur is a scryer. A seer. All Augurs are scryers and Blackburn is supposed to be a good one. He's an okay guy in an executive kind of way. His suit looks like it was cut by

barrels and has about twelve different tastes going down. It's not Aqua Regia, but it will do.

I say, "Nasrudin Hodja sent a car full of punks after me a while back. They shot up the street and nearly killed a friend of mine. Were you in on that?"

He sets down his drink.

"No. I give you my word."

His heartbeat doesn't change. He's not sweating. He's telling the truth.

Tuatha Fortune, his wife, comes in. Perches on the edge of Blackburn's desk. She's in a white silk blouse and black pants. Old-money modest.

"He's not lying," she says. "I was there during the discussion."

"He didn't try to have me killed. He just talked about it. I'm all relieved now."

"Nasrudin came to me and asked permission to right the insult after you tortured his nephews in that bar."

A few weeks back, while looking for the Qomrama, I hassled some Cold Case soul merchants at Bamboo House of Dolls. Stripped them and made them think I was skinning one of them. It was just a spell, a Hellion hoodoo trick. Nothing bad happened except to their egos. Some people can't take a joke.

"I didn't torture anyone. They were as safe as baby chickens under mom's wings. I scared them a little and sent them to bed without their supper. That's it."

Blackburn pours his wife a drink. It's a little early in the day for whiskey, even for me. They really don't like having me in their house.

I hardly know Tuatha at all. When I first met her she

good when you dispatched Norris Quay. I can tell you truthfully, he won't be missed."

Old, decrepit Norris Quay was the richest man in California, but not anymore. He's severely dead.

"I bet. But I didn't dispatch him. He was killed by crazies in the basement of Kill City."

"Naturally," says Blackburn, humoring me but not believing a word of it. He opens a desk drawer and pulls out an old book. It's battered, like one of the heretical books in Father Traven's library.

"However it happened, it's given us access to his considerable collection of occult objects and texts. My great-grandfather wrote this one. One of the first set of bylaws and family trees for the American Sub Rosa. Would you like to see it?"

"Thanks. But I'm afraid I'll spill my drink on it."

"Of course," he says, disappointed I didn't want to be dazzled by his family roots.

"In any case," he says, "I've sent a particularly interesting book to the Golden Vigil. I understand they have an actual Buddhist priest helping with them with research."

"They do."

"You could have knocked me over with a feather when I heard that those old fundamentalists were consorting with Eastern heathens," says Tuatha. When she smiles there are lines at the corners of her eyes. I like that unlike a lot of Sub Rosa elite, she's not trying to glamour away her age. "Have you met him? What's he like? I've heard those old monks can be quite the pranksters. Fun workmates."

"'Fun' isn't the word I'd use. And I haven't worked with

going to argue about it. A politician like you, you'll have me convinced I wanted the job, that it was my idea, and that I wanted to be paid in candy corn."

"There's nothing I can offer you to change your mind?"

"It's nothing personal. I have a job to do, even if I have to do it with the Vigil. A friend died looking for the Qomrama. I'm not going to let that happen again."

Tuatha stands up and goes around to the back of the desk.

"My husband is afraid, Mr. Stark. He won't say it. He's seen dark days ahead, for the Sub Rosa and for us personally. Please reconsider."

"You have a whole army outside and you can get a bigger one. Talk to Wells. He doesn't like us pixies, but I bet he'd send people to protect the Augur."

Tuatha looks at Blackburn.

"That might not be a bad idea. And it will give Mr. Stark—excuse me, Stark, a chance to think things over."

To Tuatha I say, "Can I ask you something?"

"Of course."

"All this rain. Do you have something to do with it?"

She cocks her head to the side like she's telling a kid there are no monsters under the bed.

"That's a common misconception about the art of brontomancy. I'm a thunder worker," she says, and looks up as a monstrous clap of thunder rattles the windows. "I use thunder and even lightning for purposes of divination and spell casting. Brontomancers don't have anything to do with rain."

Her heart and breathing are steady. She's telling the truth too. These people are no fun.

"Do you know any rain workers who might be doing this?"

His crew stays put, trying to keep out of the rain, but ready to move when the ringmaster says "jump."

Ishii's phone doesn't ring. He looks more disappointed than a tiger at a vegan luau.

He hooks a thumb over his shoulder.

"You know, one of these times you're going to show up and there's going to be an accident," he says. "It won't be anyone's fault. Shit just happens sometimes, right?"

I get on the Hellion hog and kick it into life. It roars and the water around us steams.

"You're right," I say. "Here's some shit that just happened. Your boss offered me your job."

I pop the clutch and haul out of there before Ishii can say or, more importantly, do, anything.

It's nice to be wanted, but it's unsettling to see the boss of bosses rattled. As much as the mansion-on-the-hill crowd bugs me, it's weird seeing them actually scared. You want them dumb and arrogant. When they're scared it means that however bad you thought things were, they're worse.

I TAKE BACK streets all the way home. A lot of street- and stoplights are out, drowned in the endless rain. Whole neighborhoods—almost the entire length of Franklin Street—are dark. No lights on in the houses. No cars on the street or in driveways. The city really is emptying its guts onto the freeways. I wonder how many of us there will be left in the end. And who's going to be top of the food chain? Civilians, Sub Rosas, or Lurkers? I can deal with any kind of supernatural asshole playing King of the Hill, but civilians make me nervous. In times of stress they tend to grab pitchforks and

"I'm glad you're feeling better," I say.

She unplugs her guitar and amp. Picks up both.

"You're off the guest list for our first show."

"Then it won't be the first show I've crashed. I know all the back exits and kitchen doors on the Strip."

She comes over and stands on her toes.

"Kiss me and I won't hate you forever for being such a noise wimp."

I lean down and we kiss. She head-butts me lightly when we stop.

"Nope. I still hate you. You'll have to make it up to me later."

"How?"

"Be sure to lock the door tonight. We're going to play the Cowboy and the Duchess."

"I don't even know what that is."

"You will," she says. "And I make no promises that you'll be the cowboy."

"I wouldn't expect you to."

I get out of my wet clothes and leave them to dry in the bathtub. Pull on some dry jeans and a moth-eaten Max Overdrive T-shirt and go downstairs.

"Thank you," says Kasabian.

"If I'm the Duchess later, you're going to owe me."

"What?"

"Nothing. What's that you've got?"

He holds up a disc and wiggles it.

"Your witch stopped by with a new movie. The full eight-hour version of von Stroheim's *Greed*. Before us, only twelve people ever saw the uncut film. We can be the thirteenth and fourteenth."

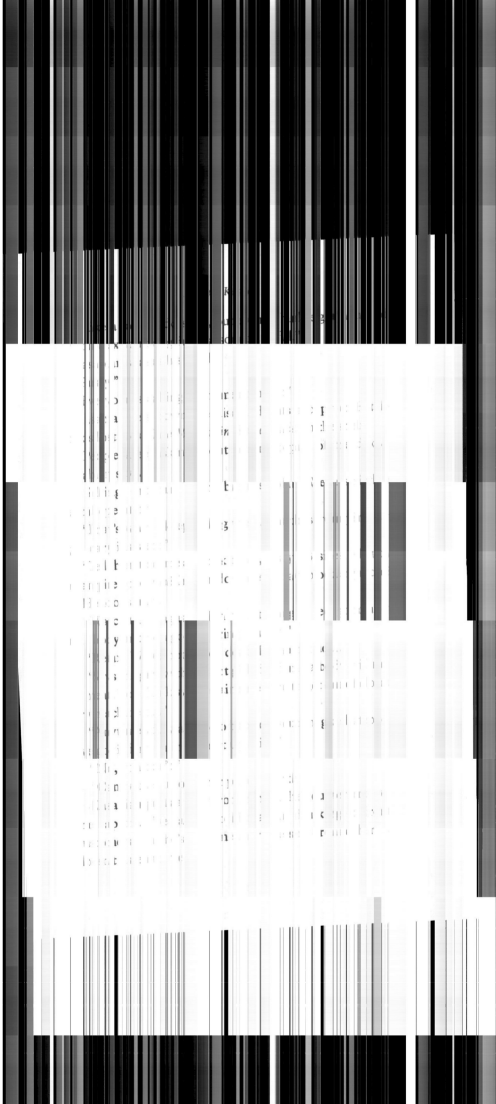

"You two are so domestic these days it's sickening."

"You should get out more, or at all," I say. "You'll meet someone nice and we'll have little puppy hellhounds running around the place."

"Speaking of shit that's never going to happen, guess who just showed up in Hell?"

"Who?"

"Chaya, the long lost God brother. He doesn't look too good. Like he booked a long weekend in an ass-kicking machine. You should go down and check it out."

"You just want me to do your swami work for you."

"We need the money, genius."

"I'm sick of talking about money."

"That's what people with no money say."

I want to say something. About an incident that's bothered me for almost a year. Even thinking about it makes me angry and ashamed. Angry she got killed and ashamed I couldn't do anything about it.

"I'll make you a deal," I say. "There's a green-haired girl in Hell somewhere. Find her for me."

"A green-haired girl? Sure. There can't be more than a million of those."

"She used to work at Donut Universe. I never told anyone, but I found her name in an online obit. Cindil Ashley. Find her and I'll do your job."

Kasabian waggles an eyebrow at me.

"An old love? You sly thing."

"You do not even want to begin joking about this," I say. "She was murdered by the Kissi right in front of me. If they weren't dead, I'd kill them all over again for it."

to be seen, a good screen and sound," he says. Then stops. When he starts up again he speaks in a rush. "I have a real good setup in my place. If you ever, you know."

She hesitates.

"I like to eat Chinese food when I watch movies. Do you, I don't mean this in a bad way, eat?"

"Sure. All the time. Ask him," he says.

I nod.

"He's a great white shark. Nature's perfect eating machine."

Fairuza shrugs.

"Sure. Why not? Find me something good and it's a date."

"Okay. Great," he says.

Candy starts torturing "Ace of Spades" again in the practice room. Fairuza points.

"That's my cue," she says.

"I'll have something for you when you're done," says Kasabian.

She smiles.

"Impress me."

He nods and she goes into the room.

I say, "I believe you have a date."

"Now all I have to do is find something dazzling."

"I don't think you know her well enough for *2001* or *Zardoz*. One's too weird and one's too slow."

"Yeah. Those are second-date movies."

"Third."

"You think?"

"At least."

"She means it, right? Like, you don't think she just said that to make fun of me?"

Inside Vigil headquarters is like the outside. Busy. Busy. Busy. Feds in suits and others in their golf togs disguises hustle from meetings with tablets under their arms. Others unpack and test angelic Vigil tech freshly shipped in from Washington. Maintenance crews swab the walls and floors. In the constant damp, mildew turns up here like anywhere else and the wet fouls some of the gear.

A group of Dreamers sits around a long plastic table in a break room. There's a crèche and a little aluminum Christmas tree by the microwave. The Dreamers seem tired and a little hung over themselves. Looks like holding reality together is a bad career choice these days. Keitu Brown is there with her parents. Ten years old, she's the leader of the bunch. Kids are always the strongest Dreamers. I met her once through Patty Templeton, a dead Dreamer I didn't do a very good job of protecting. Keitu gives me a little wave. I wave back. Dad gives me a look and puts his arm around his daughter's shoulder. I keep moving.

The door to the Shonin's magic room is locked and there's something new on the wall. A key pad and a box the size of an old PC, with a glass plate on the front.

There's a shade over the door to the Shonin's room, so I can't see if anyone is in there. I bang on the glass. A few seconds later an intercom crackles.

"Put your hand on the scanner, fatso."

I push the key on the intercom.

"The glass plate on the front?"

"No. The one sticking out of my ass, stupid."

I touch the plate and the panel lights up. I feel a gentle vibration as a light inside runs across my hand. A second later, a panel above the scanner lights up.

"I already have an iPhone. And this piece of shit is cracked," he says.

"Fuck you. I got this off a dead kid. He was possessed and I got a call from some really annoying people in Hell on it. I thought maybe you could do some hoodoo on it and learn something."

He looks at the phone. Presses it to his chest like he's listening for something.

"I hate this kind of technology. Old stuff. Wood. Fabric. Stone. Metal. It holds pieces of the spirits that move through it. This stuff," he says, tossing the phone onto the table with his books. "This stuff is empty. It beeps. It plays music. But it has no life."

"Can you do anything with it?"

"Me? No. But maybe one of Wells's machine fuckers. Boys and girls love staring at the screens. They think I don't see them jerking around, playing World of Warcraft. Planning attacks when they should be saving the world."

"Everyone needs to blow off steam."

I can't believe I have to defend federal geeks to a dead man.

"Tell it to Lamia or Zhuyigdanatha. Think they're blowing off steam?"

The Shonin stops for a second. Stares off into space, then grabs a pen and scribbles something on a yellow legal pad.

"That reminds me. The kid said something about the 'Hand.' He said something like he's many-handed. A hand for every soul on Earth."

The Shonin nods and goes to a whiteboard. The names of the thirteen Angra are written there. He puts a check mark next to a name I've never seen before.

"Funny you should use the word 'useless.' I'm starting to think of it when I think of you. You talk big about magic and studying the 8 Ball, but what have you got to show for it? Can you use the thing yet?"

"You think I'd be standing here talking to you if I could?" he says.

The Shonin stumbles and sits on a wooden stool next to the table with his books.

"It's not so simple, understanding the Qomrama. Remember, it's two things."

"It's a weapon. The Godeater."

"Yes, but it's also a summoning object. The Angra can pound on the door to our universe. They can stick a finger or toe in, but they can't enter without being summoned with it."

"I guess that helps us a little. But even a little piece of an Angra is trouble. Have you ever fought a demon? They're just tiny brainless fragments of the Angra. The dandruff of the old Gods that fell off when they were kicked out of here. But they can kill you as dead as a bullet."

"Seen a few. Never fought one," says the Shonin. "Of course, you have. You'd fight your own shadow if you got the chance."

"So, what does knowing it's a killer and a dinner bell get us?"

The Shonin shrugs.

"I don't know yet. That's why I have my books. And this new one your friend Blackburn gave us."

I go over to his desk.

"He told me he sent something over. Which book is it?"

The Shonin puts his hand on the box of glass vials.

will be, and all these poor fools will rely on someone who'd rather be eating pork chops."

"And all you do is make fat jokes when you should be teaching me about these things. Like, if the Angra can't get through to us, what about Lamia? I talked to her. She appeared as a demented little kid, but she still managed to murder a lot of people."

The Shonin nods impatiently.

"Her real name is Aswangana. What you saw was like a demon version of the goddess. Not all of her broke through to this dimension, but enough so she was smarter and more powerful than ordinary Qliphoth. What you defeated was a fragment of her essence. Do you believe you could do that to a full Angra?"

"I'm not stupid enough to think that."

"Good. You know something after all."

"The Angra sound a little like Hellions. They can't break out of Hell into this world, but they can influence the world through their worshipers and using the possession key. But they're no closer to bringing the Angra back than anyone on Earth."

"I'm trying to learn how to destroy the Qomrama. If it can be destroyed," says the Shonin. "I don't have much more faith in the Vigil than I have in you. If things go badly, destroying it might be the only way to save the universe."

"Have you found anything?"

He gets up and goes to the magnetic chamber holding the 8 Ball.

"No. I don't think it can be destroyed. Gods made it. Only a God can unmake it."

The Shonin stands and pulls his robes around him in mock outrage.

"Ooo, psychology," he says. "You took me down a peg, didn't you, you sly dog? Here's the truth. I didn't want to talk about it because I think all you want to do is compare it to your time in Hell and see who suffered the most. Think about it. What if I suffered more? Then you're the one who won't be so special anymore."

"I'm willing to take that chance."

The Shonin looks at me with his empty eye sockets. The bone around the edges is the color of dirty tea. He opens and closes his mouth. Thin lips stretched across rotten teeth.

"It begins with a thousand days," he says. "Fat rots the body, so you have to get rid of it. Even rice can make you fat. I ate only nuts and seeds, with a little tea, but mostly just water. I worked hard. Manual labor. It burns the body down to its essence. Want to hear more?"

"Right now it doesn't sound much worse than what an Olympic runner goes through."

The Shonin shakes his head.

"In the next thousand days there's nothing but bark and pine roots to eat. You'll find this part funny. To prepare my body I had to drink a kind of poison mixed with tea. Not strong, but it will ruin you if you drink enough. You puke your guts out. Maggots hate it. I drank plenty. I loved it more than you love tacos.

"When there is so little of us left in this world we're barely ghosts, monks like me, we enter our tombs. There's a tiny breathing hole and a bell. We sit and meditate. Clear our minds and let eternity enter us. Once a day I rang the bell to

opened up and swallowed me. Eleven years of torture, rape, slavery, and fighting monsters, that's not the nothing you want to make it out to be."

"I never said it was nothing. I'm saying you don't carry your suffering with grace."

"And you get to decide what grace is?"

"I've been dead, remember?"

"So have I. Think about this. Maybe what you're claiming is grace is you just wanting me to be more like you. You never knew me before and you don't know me now. Maybe I'm what grace looks like when God forgot you and you crawled out of Hell on your own."

"See? You're still complaining."

"And you're still bragging. You had four hundred years to sit around and think about how you were going to save the human race, and you fucking loved it. Every minute of suffering. You're no better than Lucifer at his worst. You're up to your eyeballs in the sin of pride."

"You're going to talk to me about sin, Abomination?"

"I'm talking to you about ego. You poisoned yourself once and now you're doing it again, you show-off. In L.A., you're what we call a one-hit wonder."

"And you have the grace of a three-legged elephant."

"That's the best you can come up with? My mom used to call me that."

The Shonin's kettle boils.

"Your mother sounds smart."

"She had her moments."

He nods and stirs his tea.

"Are you ladies done?"

He shrugs.

"We've had reality rips here before, but it sounds like the next one could be like a dam bursting."

"Why L.A.?" I say. "I mean, why is the shit coming down here?"

"We're sitting on a major power spot," says the Shonin. "A great part of the imagination of the world is attached to this city. Also, the Qomrama Om Ya is here. And you."

"Me?"

"You do seem to attract these things," says Wells.

I've wondered about that myself a few times. Do I have the bad luck to show up at the right time and place for Armageddons or am I a shit magnet that brings the monsters down on anyone in my general vicinity?

"And you love it," I say. "You secretly want it all to end 'cause you think you're going to get Raptured and that idea gives you a salvation hard-on."

"Language," Wells says.

But he doesn't deny it.

"I have something for both of you to do besides standing around catfighting and playing Marian the Librarian. There's been another Saint Nick killing. At least it looks like Saint Nick. You two are coming with me to check it out."

"Shouldn't we stay here and study the Qomrama?" says the Shonin.

"That would be nice, if you have time between rounds. But this isn't an ordinary killing. From the first reports, the scene sounds something like what Stark found in the meat locker. I want Stark there to see how well it matches and I want you there," he says, looking at the Shonin, "to keep an eye on him."

midnight all the time, even though I know it's the middle of the afternoon. I've heard that it's becoming a problem for some people, the ones susceptible to light. Seasonal affective disorder. Without sunlight, some people go into hibernation mode. Depression is up. The Vigil has its own stockpiles of drugs because L.A. is running out of every upper, mood stabilizer, and antidepressant known to man. Smack chic is a thing of the past. Who need drugs to stare at your shoe all day? Living half asleep all the time, it's easy. Meth is the new drug of choice, or coke for those with money to burn. And prices are going up, up, up. I should have invested that money the Dark Eternal gave me in coca-leaf futures and the plastic surgeons who are going to have to repair all the septums movie stars are burning out trying to stay awake.

We head north on the 110 toward Pasadena. Pull off on a side road and head onto a winding private road not far from Huntington Hospital. It's one of those funny places you find in even the poshest towns. Sort of a secret street backstage behind the world. Not quite an industrial district, but where deliveries and the help arrive for all the shiny places you see on the street.

We pull into a parking lot beside what looks like a two-story office building. Poured concrete exterior. Big mirrored windows. There's no name on the front. Not even an address. It looks like just the kind of discreet place you'd want to store crazy Aunt Sadie when the attic got full.

Our three vans pull up in a line. Wells gets out first in a clear plastic raincoat.

"You too," he says to me. "But keep your mouth shut. You're here to observe."

"Ample. I thought. Not many people in the city know it, but years ago this was a holding facility for prisoners on their way to or from county jail. We kept some of the old gates and cells in place."

"Sounds homey."

Wells steps in front of me.

"Do you know how many people are inside?"

"It was a holiday weekend, so, thankfully, the number of staff was low. Some patients who could went home with their families for Christmas. The last count I'm aware of was sixty-six patients plus twenty-four staff."

Wells nods, keeping up the good-cop routine.

"Right. Any unusual incidents lately? Hirings? Firings?"

"Magic?" I say. "Evidence of a haunting?"

"What?" says Aldridge.

Wells says, "What my associate means is did anyone, patients or staff, see anything unusual, anything they couldn't explain?"

"Nothing that I know about. It's usually quiet this time of year. Visits are down. People have other things on their mind."

"Do we need keys to get around inside?"

Aldridge shakes his head.

"What's the point? Everything is wide open."

"Thank you, sir. We'll be in touch," says Wells.

Aldridge says, "How did they do it?"

"They?"

"Of course. No one person could have done what's inside. It would take a large surgical team. More than one, probably. A dozen people working at once."

"If I implicated him."

"Right."

"Then I'm on your list of suspects."

"Not necessarily," says Wells. "Though you do have a history of decapitation."

"Meaning I'd be in the clear if I shot more people. I'll have to remember that."

"I'm not accusing you of anything."

"You're just open to possibilities."

"I want this chaos ended," he says. Without turning around, he waves his arm and the side doors on all three vans slide open. Vigil agents in transparent raincoats pile out and start unpacking gear. Two other agents wheel a crate on a dolly.

I open the front doors and let them in. Wells follows us. Once we're inside, one of the agents takes a crowbar from the side of the dolly and pries open the crate. Surrounded by a plush interior, like a piece of prized family porcelain, is the Shonin. He puts out a bony hand to me.

"Help me out of here, fatty. I'm an old man."

I want to yank the prick to his feet, but I'm afraid of pulling off his arm. I give him a hand and let him pull himself upright. He adjusts his conical headdress and looks around the lobby.

"Not bad," he says. "In my day, some families took their unstable relatives deep into the woods and left them there to die. Some became *tengu*. Most were just fox food."

"Can you smell?" I say.

He nods.

"I can smell this place."

through the second into the prison area. Once you're past that first gate, if the guard on the second gate doesn't like your look, he can lock down his side and you'll be trapped in a steel cage.

There's a long hall beyond reception that leads past the old prison cafeteria. They've transformed it into a homey dayroom with better furniture than any agent in this building has. Past that is a lockdown ward where the old prison doors have been left in place.

All the other doors have ten-key pads and card readers, including the employee restrooms. The real giveaway that the place used to be a prison is the other restrooms. Pure jailbird stuff. Clear plastic doors with a clear view of the toilet so the orderlies can make sure the patients aren't using drugs or each other. Maybe this place helped its patients, but I bet it made its staff a little crazy.

Wells comes up behind us with a piece of paper he must have picked up in reception. It's a sketchy map of the hospital layout. So far, nothing looks out of place.

"The initial report was that all the rodeo was down in the chapel," he says, and consults the map. "This way."

We find it around another corner. Like a lot of hospitals, it's a quiet nondenominational place. Back before the fun and games it might have been pretty. It's big enough to hold a congregation of maybe a hundred people. Not anymore. Someone pulled all the pews out of the floor and tossed them into the hall. All that's left of the original chapel are the stained glass windows and the altar. The rest is slaughterhouse chic by way of the Sistine Chapel.

Half finished, maybe rejected chop-shop bodies lie in piles

But it's not the corpses Saint Nick dragged here from his playpen that get to me. I keep wondering about the staff and patients. What would it be like to be the last person to go under the knife? To see almost ninety other people killed, gutted, and sewn back together again. I saw a few things during my years in Hell, but nothing like that. Maybe they party like that in one of the really shitty regions where guys like Stalin end up. The House of Knives, maybe.

In a weird way, I guess I was kind of lucky when torture time rolled around. I was never the last to get beaten or cut or spun around a Catherine wheel. The Hellions wanted to make an example of me, so I always went first. I never thought about that before. I didn't have to wait and piss myself watching everyone else get hammered. I guess if you can get lucky being tortured, I was lucky.

The Shonin and I walk around the room, checking out the piles, trying to make sense of things. Wells stands in the doorway, arms crossed. The poor sap can't come in. He's a God-fearing guy, and if there's any place I've seen in this world that says God's away on business, this is it. At least when Aelita went batshit, she was just one angel and he could imagine a Heaven full of other good and true halo polishers. But this is a bad, bad place. Wells got the Vigil back together, circling the wagons of true believers, and this is what he finds. The wagons are burning. Everyone is wounded and the cavalry isn't coming. Maybe that's why he put on the surgical mask. He didn't want his people to see him reciting Hail Marys.

I go over to the Shonin.

"Old dead mixed with new," I say.

a long weekend or could have made the meat church. But not both. That means using a crew or hoodoo. I hope to hell that Saint Nick had a crew. Worst-case scenario is someone with powerful hoodoo but with a crew too. That would put a Hulk Hogan–powerful magician right in the middle of an Angra sect. Why can't nutcase killers get their orders from talking dogs anymore? Life was so much simpler when crazy meant crazy.

The Shonin says, "Why does Saint Nick cut up the bodies?"

"Because he's an asshole with a Jack the Ripper complex."

"Don't talk like that. You know better."

"I don't know. He's making offerings maybe. Killing people isn't enough, so he cuts them up and puts pieces together 'cause the Angra prefer turducken to steak."

The Shonin walks back to Wells, who's come into the room. He's walking from pile to gory pile, as stunned as Aldridge was.

"All you all right?" says the Shonin.

"Are you?" Wells says.

"This is a bad place. There's an aura of malevolence. You and your people shouldn't remain here long."

Wells nods.

"I'll pull them out after they sweep the building."

The Shonin looks at me.

"These aren't sacrifices," he says. He points at the naves with the thirteen inverted bodies. "Those are sacrifices. The rest of these bodies, they are machines. Parts of machines. Do you see?"

"Not even a little."

"Saint Nick is creating empty vessels. Inhabiting an intact human body would be difficult for a God. But by using spe-

The Shonin leans on one of the broken church pews in the hall.

"I doubt it. This is very powerful magic. Qliphoth wouldn't have the skill or knowledge for it."

"What about another Lamia? A smarter piece of the Gods?"

"We would have heard about something like that by now," says Wells. "The Vigil is always on the alert for reports of possible Angra infiltration."

The Shonin puts his hand on my arm, steadying himself on the pew. If a dead man can look unwell, that's how he looks.

"You got all this from that book you're drinking?"

"Most of it. Why?"

"Think there might be another copy lying around somewhere?"

"It's doubtful, but anything is possible. Do you know someone who might have one?"

There's blood on the bottom of my boots. I scrape the soles on the side of a pew.

"I don't know. You're the expert. I'm just trying to keep up."

Wells says, "If you know something, Stark, speak up."

"It's not anyone here. Some Hellions I know are awfully anxious for the Angra to come home. I was wondering if you could do something like what we saw in there to fallen angels."

Wells shakes his head and checks his own shoes for blood. He doesn't care about Hell's problems. I can't say I blame him.

"It's an interesting question," says the Shonin. "If you find the answer let me know."

you saw caves within the fire when you were in Hobaica's mind. Do you remember anything more about them?"

I shake my head.

"Nothing more than I already said. I didn't get a good look."

Wells says, "There are old mines around the city. Tunnels where oil pipelines run. We're thinking of doing a search of the whole shebang. What do you think of that?"

I nod, not happy with where this is going.

"Sounds good. Sounds smart."

The Shonin says, "What happened in the chapel, this isn't the first time there's been a killing on a large scale. It's just the first time Saint Nick has been bold enough to do it in public. In the past he would have hidden it as bodies mutilated in bus or train accidents. Saint Nick needs a place where he can do more of these experiments in private. What better than somewhere underground that no one even knows exists?"

"When do you want to start?"

"In a day or two," says Wells. "We'll need to bring in some equipment from back east."

That's it then. I have a day to do something about the cavern. Back when zombies were running wild, I found tunnels under L.A. full of the city's dead. What's worse, they opened onto Mr. Muninn's private hidey-hole from when he lived here. He'd been under the city collecting bits and pieces of every human civilization since probably the beginning of time. He had trinkets from the heyday of Hollywood all the way back to kingdoms as big as Rome that existed ice ages ago. And a lot of what's in the cavern is magic and I don't want anyone, especially not the Vigil, getting their hands on

"Yeah, I heard. Hell of a thing, isn't it?"

"Okay," she says. "Maybe I'll go back to the clinic and volunteer with Allegra for a few days. At least until this clears up. I have to see her for my Jade methadone anyway. Maybe that's smarter than playing Dante with you right now."

I slide down the sofa a little and rub her back. She leans over and lets me.

"Tell Allegra I want a fucking diagnosis when I get back. Not just more drugs that make you feel better for maybe a day."

Candy sits up and slides back so she's leaning against the sofa. But she doesn't get any closer to me.

"Fine, asshole. Go play Dirty Harry. Just don't die without me. Okay?"

"Deal."

She rubs her temples. Her face is red, but I think this time it's just her trying not to cry.

I FEEL LIKE a heel for leaving her alone, but I do it anyway. I make sure she heads out for Allegra's before I take off.

Kasabian is downstairs working on his swami site while *The Devil's Rain* plays on his big screen.

"You heading back down to Dixie?" he says.

"It looks that way."

"You going to help me out with a client?"

"I can't this trip. Maybe some other time."

"Too bad. I already did a favor for you, so you're going to owe me one."

I already owe Muninn a favor. I don't like carrying debt around.

"I don't think you can sell food on eBay."

"Then bring me back a baseball cap with a logo. Something."

"Sure."

I head for a shadow by the front door.

Kasabian says, "What's the magic word?"

"What?"

" 'Thank you.' That's what we say when someone does us a favor."

"Right. Thanks."

" 'Thank you' is the proper way to say it."

"I've still got pieces of people's guts on my boots. Thanks is as good as it gets."

"You're welcome."

He swings back around to watch his movie. Ernest Borgnine is turning into a goat.

I pull up the hoodie I put on under my coat and step into the shadow.

I SPENT ELEVEN years trapped Downtown and have been back plenty of times since, but it gets harder each time. I was only Lucifer for three months, but it left me wary of Hell in ways that even being a slave there didn't. I used to kill Hellions because I didn't have a choice. When I was Lucifer I killed them to stay alive and sometimes just to make a point. Part of the job description for Lucifer is "ruthless bastard," and even if I was a joke when it came to running Downtown, I was employee of the month when it came to saving my own skin. Sometimes in rotten ways. Like dragging a Hellion to death behind my motorcycle. I can't see Mr. Muninn playing

of the city when I go down. Big mistake this time.

Like Kasabian said, it's raining in Hell. Being Hell, it's raining blood. Good thing I put on the coat Candy Scotchgarded for me. Too bad I didn't put any of the stuff on my pants. The blood soaks into them, weighing down the leather. It drips through my hood too and runs into my eyes. I step into a doorway before I look like one of those poor slobs back at the chapel.

I'm on Hell's equivalent of Hollywood Boulevard. It looks about the same as the Hollywood back home. Pretty much deserted. But I can see lights on in some of the stores and bars, so someone is around. They're just smart enough to get in out of the blood. No way I'm walking to Beverly Hills from here. I find a shadow under the streetlight and step through. I do something I've never done before. I come out right in Mr. Muninn's—Lucifer's—penthouse at the hotel. He once said I could. Let's see if he's a devil of his word.

I come out by his private elevator. I lean into his living room, ready to duck out if he gets all wrathful.

"Mr. Muninn? Hello. It's Stark."

I take a tentative step into the room.

Muninn comes in from another room in a long crimson robe, a little shocked anyone would just walk into Lucifer's apartment. The room is dark. He squints until he can make me out.

"James. It's you," he says, and turns on a desk lamp. "And you've tracked blood all over my carpet."

I look down. He's exaggerating a little. I only have one foot on the carpet, but the blood dripping off my clothes has made a nice red stain there and on the tile floor by the elevator.

"I'm sure it's quite benign for you. It's just hell on my carpet."

"Sorry about that."

He looks back in the direction of the living room.

"The cleaners will be thrilled to have something to do. And in any case, it's good to see a friendly face."

He brings two cups of coffee to a marble-topped island in the middle of the kitchen. We sit down across from each other. He slides a cup to me. Hell might have the worst food in the universe, but the coffee, at least Lucifer's, isn't that bad. Still, I take a small first sip. Lucky me. I can still stomach the stuff.

"To what do I owe the honor of this very surprising visit? I have a feeling you didn't just appear here out of the blue to bring me good news from Earth."

"Not exactly. Angra sects are getting pretty hot and bothered back home. They're turning churches into meat markets and it looks like they might be storing their extra bodies in the underground tunnels where you used to look after the dead."

"And they open into my storeroom."

"Yeah."

Mr. Muninn nods and sips his coffee. He looks a lot older than when I saw him just a few weeks ago.

"If you don't mind my saying so, you look like shit, Mr. Muninn."

He smiles. No one down here normally talks to Lucifer like that.

"I suppose I don't. Things were going badly here, and with a new war in Heaven, we don't even need a threat from the Angra to feel a bit grim."

wasn't dead, maybe the four of us could combine our strength and fight Ruach, but with just the three of us, it's doubtful. I don't know if the others want to try again."

I've never seen Mr. Muninn so down. And I'm the bastard who guilted him into becoming Lucifer.

"I'm guessing you're not working on repairing the city anymore."

"No one is left to do the work. Every sensible Hellion is at home hiding."

"Same thing in L.A. Some are running for the hills."

"I'm afraid there isn't anywhere for us to run."

"There won't be anywhere to run on Earth if the Angra keep making new little baby Angras."

He frowns every time I say their name.

I say, "You don't like talking about them, do you?"

"There is nothing but bad memories there. We—that is, I, when I was a single entity—flung the Angra from here and claimed this universe for myself. Not a noble gesture. But I was young and the young do all sorts of foolish and cruel things."

"And you were left with a universe you didn't quite know how to run."

"I did my best."

"That's what I told Mrs. McCarthy in fifth-grade Spanish. She still flunked me."

He sips his coffee and smiles.

"Yes. This is exactly like elementary school Spanish."

"I guess the idea I tossed out there the last time you were in L.A. isn't going to work. Shutting down Hell and letting everyone leave?"

mostly blind and half deaf. Deumos and Merihim have disappeared. I'm sure they're hiding somewhere in Pandemonium. They won't want to be far from the seat of power. But they have powerful allies and remain invisible to me."

"I got a phone call from Deumos."

"Did you? What did she say?"

"Nothing surprising. She wanted the 8 Ball. The Qomrama."

"No, not surprising at all. You're not giving it to her, I assume."

"She can have it right after she kisses my ass."

"Always the poet," says Muninn.

I wonder if he'd let me smoke a Malediction in here. I pat my pockets, then remember I'm not wearing my regular clothes. My cigarettes are back by the elevator, and probably soaked through.

"Let me have the Qomrama," says Muninn. "Bring it back to Hell, where it belongs."

"So Deumos and Merihim can grab it? I don't think so? They might have minions on Earth, but they don't have shit power yet. No. It's staying where it is."

Muninn says, "You owe me a favor, if you recall."

I knew sooner or later he was going to try and fuck me up with fairness and logic. Good thing I'm pretty much immune to those things.

"Do you know how to use it?"

He shakes his head.

"No."

"Then leave it with me. Believe it or not, I'm working with the Golden Vigil again. They've got this old Buddhist monk working on it. He seems pretty smart."

[illegible] talked about [illegible] and [illegible]
[illegible] your time [illegible] But [illegible]
[illegible] than I [illegible]
[illegible] strange company."
[illegible]
[illegible] used [illegible]
[illegible] of [illegible]
[illegible] with this [illegible]," [illegible] says. [illegible]
[illegible] was coming [illegible] toward [illegible]
[illegible]
"Thank you," says [illegible]. "I appreciate [illegible]
[illegible] you weren't [illegible] at the [illegible]. I don't
[illegible] much better, but [illegible]
[illegible] together so far [illegible] of [illegible] way."
[illegible]
"[illegible] with [illegible]." He [illegible] up [illegible]
[illegible] the [illegible]. He comes back [illegible] minutes [illegible]
[illegible] stopped [illegible]
"Take this [illegible] with you," he says. "[illegible] point [illegible]
[illegible] and [illegible] personal [illegible]
[illegible] able to detect it."
[illegible] the [illegible] more [illegible]
[illegible] hundred years [illegible]
[illegible] single [illegible]
"[illegible] the right [illegible] won't [illegible] enough to
[illegible] It will be fine."
"Go[illegible]"
"Y[illegible] Singularity [illegible] Mi[illegible]"
"S[illegible] in the Room[illegible]"

"Good. Don't remove them under any circumstances. If worst comes to worst, they might be our only hope."

It must be getting to him down here. I've never heard that kind of kamikaze talk coming from him before.

"I've got them. Don't sweat it."

He nods.

"Would you like to say hello to Samael while you're here? I could wake him up."

"Don't bother. I should get going. I didn't see Wild Bill last time I was here and I'm feeling kind of guilty about it."

"It's good to be close to family in times like these. Well, I'll see you out now. Keep those clothes, if you like. It's good to see you in something that doesn't make you look like a motorcycle delinquent."

"Thanks, Dad."

He comes around the table, takes my arm, and walks with me to the living room. He feels cold. God shouldn't feel cold, should he?

"These are the worst times we've faced, James. I had no right to do what I did to the Angra, but if they're allowed to come back now, they'll destroy everything."

"I know."

"It's going to take something drastic to stop them. I don't know what yet, but I have a feeling I'll be calling in that favor you owe me before this is over. Are you prepared to repay it?"

"Sure. Yeah."

"I think you hesitated."

"No. It's fine."

"Good. I just needed to know how loyal you'd be when the time comes."

I look around the place. The donuts are dry and sunken. Dusty. The coffee looks like fried sludge. The linoleum counter is cracked and half the stools are missing their seats. Donut Inferno looks like a wino crash pad fifty years past its prime.

I say, "You like it here?"

She shakes her head.

"No."

"You want to get out?"

"With you?"

"Yes. Right now."

She twists the dirty dishrag in her hands. Her face and arms are bruised, but her hair is still the same shade of green it was when she was alive.

She whispers, "I'll get in trouble."

"You're in Hell. How much worse can it get?"

"Lots. You haven't seen what I've seen."

I walk over and take the rag from her hand. Set it on the counter.

"I've seen what you've seen and lived what you've lived and I got away. I'm here to help you do the same."

"The last time I saw you I died."

"And I feel bad about that and I'm here to fix it."

"Why? You don't even know me."

"So what? I should have been able to help you before, but I didn't. Now I can. Come with me."

"Where?"

"To a friend's place. He's a hard old son of a bitch, but he'll take care of you."

Her eyes dart around the shop. She's confused. In panic mode.

isn't there anymore. Just half-collapsed tents, overturned tables, and oil drums full of charred garbage. The sad red rain slicks over everything, turning the rows between the deserted stalls to mud.

Cindil drops my hand and takes a step back.

"What just happened?"

"We took a shortcut across town. It's just a trick I can do."

She looks at me, her hair matting down around her face.

"You're a weird guy, you know?"

"That's going to be my epitaph. You want to get out of this rain?"

I point to the bar. She heads over and we go inside.

I want to say that the place is usually crowded at this time of day, but I don't know what time it is in Hell or Earth. Still, there's usually some kind of crowd. Not tonight, today, whatever. A lone soldier from one of Hell's legions sits by himself nursing the Hellion equivalent of beer. He barely glances up as we come in.

Hank Williams is on the jukebox singing "The Devil's Train." The man smoking a cigar behind the counter is tall and lean, with shoulder-length hair and a serious mustache. His name is James Butler Hickok. Wild Bill Hickok to his friends and enemies. We're blood, separated by around seven generations. He looks up when he sees us. Puts out his hand when we get close to him. He and I shake. Bill isn't a hugging kind of guy. He takes a look at Cindil and gets a bottle from beneath a bar, sets down three glasses, and pours us all a drink of the good stuff. As good as it gets in Hell.

"I was beginning to think you'd forgotten about your grandpappy."

"What are you talking about, son?" he says.

I look back at the legionnaire. We could be playing badminton with a baked ham for all he cares. I keep my voice low anyway.

"This is just between the three of us. I'm hoping that Lucifer can square things away Hell-wise, but it's not looking good. If he can't, I'm taking you both out of here. Be ready to leave in a hot second if I give you the word."

"I'm ready right now," says Bill.

I shake my head.

"This isn't the right time. Be patient. And trust me."

Cindil finishes her drink and Bill pours her another.

"You can leave here?" she says.

"This one can go any damned place he likes. He just visits with us Hell-bound folks when he gets bored carousing with monsters and disreputable types back home."

"Back home on Earth," she says.

I toss back another drink. It tastes better as it numbs your taste buds.

"Yes. I can go back and forth."

"Why can't we come with you now?"

"It's like I said, it's not time. There are consequences for everyone when I steal a soul from Hell. I have to wait until the good outweighs the bad."

I stole Father Traven's soul from Hell a month before. Things haven't been the same between me and Mr. Muninn since.

"How will you know when it's the right time?"

"I'll know. Trust me. I have someone watching Hell. If things get bad, I'll be back for both of you," I say. Then to Bill, "Until then, meet your new barback."

"It's called a jukebox," I say.

"I know what it's called. It's a damned foolish word and I'm not about to use it, especially not in front of a lady who looks like she's endured enough foolishness."

Cindil looks around the bar. It's a ragged place, but back when I was Lucifer I had it built to look as much like Bamboo House of Dolls as possible.

"I can really stay here?" she says.

"Yes, you can," says Bill.

"What if someone comes to take me back to the donut shop?"

"The powers that be have a lot on their plate right now," I say. "I doubt anyone's going to notice you're gone. And if they do, they're going to have a hard time finding you. If anyone comes for you, don't worry. I'll know about it."

I look at Bill.

"You should have taken that gun I offered you back at the palace."

"That funny Glock thing where I couldn't even see the bullets? No thanks. Besides, with all the drunks and ne'er-do-wells that pass through here, I've got all the guns and ammunition I need. Under the floorboards back here."

He sets the cigar on the bar and picks up his drink.

"You think it's going to come to that?"

"No. But in strange times like this it's better having too many guns than too few."

"Amen to that," says Bill.

I cock my head at the legionnaire.

"Is he someone to worry about?"

"Him?" says Bill. He smiles.

fer. I hated him more than all the Hellions put together. He's the only soul in Tartarus these days.

"There's plenty of room in Tartarus for a dumb guy with a big mouth. Especially a deserter. No one would notice or care if you disappeared. So you didn't see anything today. And if anyone asks, that girl over there has been working here since the day the place opened. Got it?"

His eyes are wide. When he tries to nod he sticks himself on the tip of the knife.

"Ow."

"I'll take that for a yes."

I put the blade back under my coat and head for the nearest shadow.

"And you didn't see this either, fucker," I say, and step into the dark.

I COME OUT in Mr. Muninn's cavern under the Bradbury Building. The shelves are crammed with books, ancient weapons, and scientific instruments. Animal teeth and dinosaur bones. Paintings cover the walls and sculptures fill every empty corner. In the distance is a drive-in movie screen. Who knows what else? You could spend a couple of lifetimes down here trying to inventory the place.

I go to where Muninn's fortress of solitude opens onto the main tunnel that used to be home for L.A.'s dead. Kneeling, I pour the potion across the floor. A wall quietly assembles itself from the surrounding stones and fills the gap. It only takes a few seconds to form and it looks like it's been there since T. rexes used the Rockies as a skateboard ramp.

There's a new war in Heaven. Angels eating their own.

In the morning, way too early in the goddamn morning, I'm back in a Vigil van moving through Hollywood. The streets are empty except for a couple of homeless people huddled asleep in the doorway of the wax museum near Highland. The traffic lights have stopped working, which doesn't matter since there's no traffic. Most stores are deserted, though a few places forgot to lock the door. Water sloshes up over the curb to soak their carpets. But the merchandise stays where it is. There's no one left even to loot the place.

An LAPD cruiser riverboats past us, too smart to slow or do anything but stare at our blacked-out caravan.

We pull over at the Hollywood and Vine underground metro stop. The place is locked down tight. There's a big "Closed for Maintenance, Sorry for the Inconvenience" sign on the gate blocking the stairs. Julie Sola jumps out of the second van, unlocks the gate, and pushes it out of the way. Just like at the funny farm, Wells's crew starts unloading personnel and forensic gear for our trip down the rails. The Shonin is back at headquarters, warm and dry. Mummies don't much like wading through ankle-deep water, and when we're downstairs, let's face it . . . the jerky on the guy's bones is going to attract rats. Best for everyone if he stays at the HQ sipping his poison book.

"Stark, stay close to me," says Wells.

"I didn't know you cared."

"I don't. I just don't want you making up your own mission and wandering off."

Someone gets the lights turned on below and we head down.

The Hollywood and Vine subway is a themed stop, a mu-

"You know what they say. Only a man with a guilty conscience keeps reminding you of how innocent he is."

"Okay, you got me. I *am* Saint Nick. And Mr. Bubbles. And the Easter Bunny."

Wells ignores me. The Vigil crew stops chattering, their gear pretty much squared away.

"If the Vigil knew about the corpse tunnels, why didn't you do anything about them?"

Wells slaps the cover shut on the tablet and puts it in his pocket.

"What was there to do? Move hundreds of thousands of bodies? To where?"

For a second he sounds like Mr. Muninn.

"Besides," he says, "before Jan and Koralin Geistwald came to town and turned the horde into a bunch of kill-crazy zombies, they weren't a problem. The Vigil has learned to let many of these things be and not to tamper with the balance of supernatural forces in the city, no matter how revolting and profane they might be."

A couple of the Vigil crew unfold portable staircases that extend from the platform to the tracks. Wells is the first person down. I follow him.

"You're not saying there's access to those dead tunnels from the subway, are you?"

"Don't be an idiot," he says. "I said they run parallel. There were never any stops in zombie country."

"Then why are we here?"

"We're looking for breaches."

"What does that mean?"

"You'll know it if we find one."

"Great. If you spot any Angra roadside-attraction signs let me know. I'll pick up a pecan log and a belt buckle."

Wells ignores me.

Sola whispers, "Why do you do that?"

"What?"

"Go out of your way to aggravate Wells?"

"I have to do something. I can't bring my knitting along."

"No. Seriously."

"Wells agrees with Aelita a hundred percent about me. I'm an Abomination. A monster. So I give him what he wants."

"Why don't you try to show him you're more than that?"

"Try to convince him I'm a good guy? That would scare him more than if I showed up like Kali with ten arms and wearing a belt of severed heads."

Sola is quiet for a minute. Then she says, "I'm trying to see you as a serious person."

"What do you care? Are you spying for him?"

"No. I told you before. Maybe we can work together when this is over. I can restart my PI service. But I need to know you're someone I can depend on."

"When this is over." I never took Sola for that kind of optimist. But I guess anyone who goes out on her own and hangs out her detective shingle has to believe there'll be something down the road.

"How's this? I've saved this world more than once already. I have friends here and I'll kill anything that walks, crawls, flies, or oozes out of the ground if it hurts one of them. I know God and the Devil and their worst secrets. I know how to pull the plug on this whole rotten world and I don't do it. You know why?"

crew. Lots of grins and quiet chuckles back there. Law enforcement. It's like high school with better guns.

"You don't have to do that to her," I say.

"Don't tell me how to run my people," Wells says.

"Aren't I one of your people now?"

"I'm not a hundred percent sure you are a person. Lots of things can walk on two legs. Monkeys. Dogs. Bears."

"You should have said parrots. Those others can't talk."

"I know. Just wishful thinking on my part."

We're well down the spur line now, heading to a dead end. There's nothing and no one down here.

Wells turns to his team.

"Anything, anyone? Life readings? Heat signatures? Any signs of Angra ritual marks or bodies?"

A few "No sirs" come from the back. Then a high-pitched whoop from somewhere. Like a howler monkey, but quiet. Then comes chattering, like a hundred people caught in the snow, their teeth tapping together. A scrabbling at the edges of the room. People look at their feet, checking for rats. I can hear breathing all around us.

"Take off your goggles," I say to Wells. "And tell them to do the same."

"Something's coming. I'm going to light this place up."

"Don't you dare," he says.

That's when the first person screams.

I say, "Wells!"

"Goggles off," he yells.

I don't wait to see who obeys the order. My hoodoo isn't subtle, but I figure that the tunnel is big enough to try it. I bark some Hellion and fire explodes across the ceiling. A lucky shot, as it turns

and the place is growing dark again. I manifest my Gladius, my flaming angelic sword. Its bright white fire lights up the tunnel like a movie premiere downtown. Nothing on Earth can stand up to an angelic sword. I slice the nearest chop-shop killer nearly in half with one slash and wade into a crowd that's surrounded Sola and Wells. There's not a lot of strategy in this. No big battle plan. Just hunt and slash and keep the monsters off the nonmonsters for as long as I can.

Good thing these chop-shop types aren't big on brains. They're all either teeth or claws, which makes them pretty easy to take down. I put down a dozen fast and open a hole for Sola and Wells to run through. It doesn't smell good, all burned meat and fried hair.

One of the Broken Teeth lands on my back and sinks his choppers into my neck. It's not even like he's biting me. It's like he's trying to chew right through my spine. It reminds me of something, but that's not important right now because I can't reach the asshole with my sword and I can feel blood—my blood this time, not some Heavenly angel's from the sky—running down my back.

The biter twitches. Once. Twice and falls off. Wells and Sola keep firing into its body as it tries to get up. I wade into another crowd of them and slash away. It doesn't take long for whatever part of their brains still works to cop to the idea that fire is bad and running is good. The ones still alive and on their feet take off away from the spur track, down one of the other rail lines, and disappear, making those howler-monkey whoops, claws still out and teeth still grinding.

I keep the Gladius burning until I'm good and certain they're gone. Then let it go out. The night-vision gear is scat-

"A couple over here, sir."

"Right. Bag them and get them back to Vigil headquarters right now. I want the Shonin to have a look at them."

"Want to hear a theory? Two really," I say.

"Make them fast," says Wells.

"The Shonin said the chop-shop bodies might be something to house Qliphoth. The way the crazies were moving, remind you of anything?"

"It was a little strange. What are you getting at?"

"Eaters and Diggers. Two of the most dangerous Qliphoth. They'd be good guard dogs if you wanted to keep something safe."

Wells watches his team wrap up the prisoners. They use some kind of expansion foam instead of cuffs on the arms and legs. Slide a harness with a rubber bit over each of their heads so they can't bite. Then zipper them into body bags with ventilation holes.

"You could be right. We'll let the Shonin decide."

They set the prisoners on hoodoo platforms like floating stretchers and glide them down the way we came, four agents holding on to the body and two riding shotgun.

"Want to hear the second theory?"

"Go on."

"We were ratted out."

Wells sighs. A few of his people continue to steal looks at me as they work.

"This again. You just said these things were guard dogs. You don't warn guard dogs. You just leave them in the junkyard for kids climbing over the fence."

"But what if they're not here all the time? What if they were here just for us?"

"You're not going in there alone, are you? I just said there might be Diggers around."

"No," he says. "You're coming with me. If you're that het up about it, you can go first."

A marshal hands me a set of goggles.

"Thanks. But you can go in first. I have this thing about getting my head bitten off."

I reload the Colt and put on the goggles. The world goes green and flat and very bright.

"You ready?" says Wells.

"Hell no."

Wells gets down on his knees. The hole is only waist-high, like something crawled out of it. He goes through and I follow. The bite on my neck hurts like hell. The last time I got bit by a dead man bad things happened. Like I almost went zombie. This time I'm going to see Allegra before anything interesting happens.

The inside of the cave is extremely nondramatic in the sense that nothing comes out of the shadows to eat our faces. Wells finds the light switch and turns it on. The cave fills with light and we take our goggles off.

He was right. The subway line runs right next to one of the old walking-dead tunnels. The area where we're standing is about fifty feet across and stretches into darkness at both ends. The walls are hacked out of raw stone. The lighting fixtures are made of human bones. Skulls and other bones are cemented together on the walls, making elaborate shapes. Thirteen of them. Angra sigils, I'm guessing.

There are a couple of hospital gurneys on one side of the room along with the same kind of gory surgical scene like we

"Dammit," says Wells.

"Watch the language."

Inside is a skull on a deep blue velvet pillow. Its metal teeth glitter and it has lips and a nose made of hammered gold. Its eyes are like elaborate silver brooches, each set with a blue stone in the middle. Rubies flow down the top of the skull from an old head wound, each ruby smaller than the one before it, so they form a line of blood down to the eye sockets.

"Ever seen anything like it?" I say.

"No. And that's the last playing around you get to do today. Get out of the tunnel. Grown-ups have to work."

We crawl out of the hole and back into the subway. Wells stands and brushes dirt off his pants. The forensic team pushes past us, wrapped up in sterile white Tyvek suits. Julie Sola comes over to me.

"I guess no one's in there."

"No one's used that place in a while. Those chop-shop crazies sure weren't working in there. And they sure didn't make that skull."

"Whose skull?" says Sola.

"Good question."

"I'm disturbed," says Wells. "After the hospital, this isn't what I was expecting."

"This was probably their rehearsal space."

Wells shakes his head.

"No. It's more than that. Maybe forensics will tell us what. DNA. Dental records for the skull."

"Forget that. The teeth were gold too."

"That's disappointing."

"That's not what bugs me."

"Hey, Stark," she says. "Candy already went home."

"Good. I'm here to see Allegra."

I touch my neck and show her the blood. She just opens the door. Everyone here is pretty used to seeing me bleeding.

Allegra comes out of the examining room, wiping her hands on a towel. Her café au lait skin contrasts with the bright white medical lab coat.

She comes over and gives me a loose hug, trying to not get rain from my coat all over her.

"He's fucked up again," says Fairuza.

Allegra's brow furrows.

"What happened?"

"A dead man bit me. Sort of dead. Walking around dead, but not a zombie. I just figured I should get it cleaned out or something."

"Look at you being sensible for once. Come on in."

"Need any help?" says Fairuza.

"No. I've sewn this one back together more times than I can remember."

She has me take off my coat and shirt and sit on the exam table.

She cleans off my neck with Betadine. I hate the smell of hospitals and clinics. They make you feel like you should be sick just stepping inside.

"That hurts."

"Baby," says Allegra. "I'd ask how the new job was working out, but you walking in here voluntarily tells me everything I need to know."

"They make me get up early too," I say. "It's pure abuse."

"The good news is that there's a lot of blood, but the wound itself isn't bad. I have a salve that will help the healing."

"No, and that has me worried. I think people have been watching the clinic. There was a pickup truck in the parking lot across the street all day yesterday. A van the day before that."

"Who do you think it was?"

"I have no idea. It just makes me nervous."

"Are you sure it wasn't just people looking for a place to get out of the rain for a few hours?"

"Maybe. Maybe seeing the city like this is just making me skittish. I'm scared."

She puts some gauze on the wound and tapes it into place. I hate the feel of tape on my skin.

"If it happens again, call me. I'll check out whoever it is."

"Thanks. That makes me feel better. There. All done."

I put on my shirt and coat. Allegra sees the dirt on my pants and boots.

"Where the hell have you been?"

"Have you ever been in an ossuary?"

"I'm not sure I know what that is."

"They have one in Paris. Vidocq will tell you about it. It'll be great pillow talk."

"It's something gruesome, isn't it?"

"I'll let you be the judge."

"Go home," she says. "And stay in. Both of you."

"That's the plan."

I start out and stop.

"Candy is going to be okay, right?"

Allegra washes her hands.

"She'll be fine. I'm sure it's just a Jade-specific virus or something. I'm reading up on it now. Don't worry so much."

"Understood. I'll guard future lamps with my very life."

"Good boy," she says, then kisses me and lies down.

For a while, lying in the dark, it feels like nothing is wrong at all. Then I hear the rain battering the window and I remember that pretty much everything is wrong.

I don't remember falling asleep. I'm just lying beside Candy and then I'm somewhere else.

It's a strange mix of the Angra subway cavern and the scene at the hospital. The meat chapel is surrounded by rough, raw stone, the bone sigils bright red in the reflected blood light.

The thirteen crucified bodies writhe on their inverted crosses, crying and gasping for air like they aren't quite dead.

I look at the walls, but can't see the sigils. They jitter like liquid mercury, forming and re-forming themselves into new shapes. They don't hold any one long enough to make sense and then I understand that I'm not looking at their symbols, but at the Angra themselves.

From a spiral of skulls all shattered on one side steps a golden woman. Her skin is patterned like circuit boards and snake scales. On her head is a headdress with swept-back wings. Half of her face is missing. An empty eye socket above a nonexistent cheek and a jaw stripped of its golden flesh are all that's left on her right side. Though she's in pain, with half her skull revealed she's stuck in a perpetual half smile.

I say, "I remember you."

She nods.

"We met in the water, as the building fell into the ocean."

"Yeah. Kill City. You grabbed my leg. You tried to drown me," I say.

The other side of her face smiles. She folds her hands.

floor. She's beautiful. The half of her that's covered in skin. The rest looks like Thanksgiving leftovers a couple of days past their prime.

"Even if I wanted to help you, I don't know how to use the Qomrama."

She reaches out her almost meatless hand.

"Don't worry. We'll teach you."

"How?"

The golden woman fades away, replaced by the swirling skeleton-fungus-tree thing.

"We'll speak again."

"Goody."

She's gone.

I hear a sound and turn to the reliquary. The rubies on the skull are gone and blood pours from the hole in the forehead. It spills onto the floor and pools in the cracks. I turn to go down the tunnel, but there's no way out. Blood pours from the skull and the sigils on the wall, covering the floor. I climb onto the filthy gurney to get away from it. It dawns on me that this whole thing has been a trap. That the cavern is going to fill with blood and that I'm going to drown. I should have been nicer to Ten Thousand Shadows. Or maybe had less Aqua Regia with the movie last night. Either way, this is a hell of an end to a shitty day. I hold my breath and try to get as close to the ceiling as I can. In a few minutes it won't make any difference.

I come awake to Candy shaking me.

"Wake up, goddammit," she says.

I choke on my own spit and gasp for air.

"What's wrong with you? You're thrashing all over."

IN THE MORNING, the bite is just bruises and a scab. There's no fieldwork or car chases scheduled for the Vigil today, so Candy heads off to help out at the clinic.

At Vigil headquarters, instead of the sneers and behind-the-back comments I usually hear, there's dead silence when I walk through. Julie Sola and Vidocq are coming out of the break room. Vidocq has a cup of tea and Sola is carrying a container of yogurt.

I say, "What's with the silent treatment around here? Did I suddenly get boring?"

"Just the opposite," says Vidocq.

Sola peels back the lip from the top of the yogurt and sticks in a spoon.

"Everyone knows about what you did yesterday. The flaming sword."

"The Gladius."

"You have to understand, even with all the fundamentalists around here, angels are still mostly an abstraction. To see something like that right in front of their eyes, well, you blew a few people's minds."

Vidocq says, "That silence you hear isn't boredom. It's awe."

"I don't like it."

Sola eats a spoonful of her yogurt.

"It's too late now. Even the old-timers only ever saw Aelita produce the Gladius, so they know you're at least as powerful as her. The younger ones, the ones who grew up with slasher movies and Ozzy, some of them think you're the Angel of Death."

It's funny how you get used to things and then when you

people strapped to a gurney. They're both over by the 8 Ball. The Shonin glances up when I come in.

"How was hunting yesterday, fatty? There's a rumor you got some new scars."

He doesn't have much in the way of lips left, so it's hard to tell if he's smiling.

"I heard one about someone using your skull as a bedpan."

The Shonin turns away in disgust.

"You have a dirty mind."

"Then stay out of it."

"At least show me your new trick."

"The Gladius? It's not new and it's not a trick and I'm not your dancing monkey."

He turns back to examining the body on the gurney.

"Too bad. For a few second there, you sounded almost interesting."

I watch the Shonin perform some kind of ritual over the chop-shop guy. He has incense burning and there are a dozen potion bottles open on a nearby table. He moves his hands in a slow, twisting pattern over the dead man's body, muttering spells. The guy on the table has a nice gash along his cheek, exposing his teeth. It reminds me of Ten Thousand Shadows, but I push her out of my head. He snarls and snaps at the Shonin's hands. He looks like one of yesterday's Eaters. Whatever the Shonin is trying to do, I don't think it's going well.

I settle down in a chair across the room and light a Malediction. Yeah, they smell like burning tires, but this place is so full of incense, I can barely breathe. One more layer of stench isn't going to hurt.

"What have you learned about the 8 Ball from your killer book?"

He flips through a notebook covered with long scribbled lines of kanji.

"Lots and lots. But the book is philosophical and theoretical. Not geared toward practicality. I can tell you the Qomrama's history, but not how to use it to attack or summon."

"Your book doesn't sound like it's worth a damn."

"It hasn't all been bad."

He looks at the 8 Ball rotating in the magnetic field.

"I got it to reverse direction for a few seconds once."

"I for one feel better knowing that you might have the power to make the Angra dizzy."

He flips through pages of his notebook.

"What am I not seeing?"

"That poison book is probably fucking with your mind. If it hasn't told you anything useful by now, why don't you stop drinking it?"

"Because what if it reveals something tomorrow? The answers we need might be in the next bottle. Or the one after that."

I walk over to the 8 Ball. Mr. Chop Shop bares his teeth at me. I want to knock them out.

"You keep drinking that stuff and the gristle holding you together is going to fall off. You know the old joke, a guy goes into his doctor's office and says, 'Doc, it hurts when I do this,' and the doctor says, 'So don't do that.' That's you. Stop doing that."

The Shonin sits up.

"That's your way," he says. "You can't conquer it with

"What are you doing?" shouts the Shonin. "Stop that."

I reach inside and pull the 8 Ball out of the field. It takes a couple of tries. The field doesn't want to let go. But with a little twisting, I work it out. And that's why the Kissi hand is so useful. In all the twisting and turning from a sphere covered in diamond plate to an egg covered in an intersecting pattern of serrated blades the 8 Ball doesn't do any damage. The Kissi hand is just too tough to cut and there's nothing to bleed.

"Put it back," says the Shonin. He backs away across the room.

I bring the saw-toothed 8 Ball over to Mr. Chop Shop. Instead of snarling and biting, he calms right down. The only sounds he makes are the ragged breaths through his torn mouth.

The Shonin slowly comes over to us.

"You're not entirely stupid after all," he says. "I don't know if it's of much value, but it's a little impressive."

"What do you mean it's not valuable? I calmed this fucker right down. That's more than you've done."

"It's a nice trick," he says, "but I caused the Qomrama to change rotation once. Is that any more useful than this?"

"Of course this is more useful. I'm controlling a Qliphoth. How is that not helpful?"

The Shonin looks at the 8 Ball and then at Mr. Chop Shop.

"All that power to control one little demon. I would think that with your experience you'd see the absurdity."

"You're just pissed because your holy books and snake oil got you nothing with a capital zero. Look. I can even touch the thing."

beaklike mouth. Concentric circles of cutting fangs and grinding molars. It's an Eater, but without a body. Just spiritual essence.

I plant my feet on the ground and pull, dragging the demon from Chop Shop's body.

Bad idea. It makes sense that a Qliphoth with no body wouldn't have any power. It makes sense, but it turns out it's not true.

The Eater twists and snaps at my face. I try to hold on, but it wriggles out of my hand and goes straight for the wall, attacking it with its massive choppers. In just a few seconds, it's almost through the concrete. I grab it with my Kissi hand and pull it back. Toss it across the room. It hits one of the lab tables by the door and bites right through it. Ripping through high-impact plastic and steel like it was cotton candy. It scrambles to its feet, pulling equipment off tables and the wall, cutting deep grooves into the floor, where it tears at them with its teeth. I throw a chair at the thing and its beak snaps it in two.

The Eater charges me. I pull the na'at and snap it open. It goes right through the Eater's mist body without slowing it.

Fuck me.

I'm reaching for my gun when the Eater hits me, driving me into the wall like a bull in a jet pack. The beak dives for my face.

And my Kissi hand closes on it. Holds it in place. Jerks up and snaps the beak like a Popsicle stick. It slides into the Eater's body to where its heart should be and closes on it. There's nothing in my hand but mist, but the Eater thrashes like I'm pulling its guts out. One more jerk, and the mist ex-

"Wisdom comes from knowledge. Knowledge begins with theories."

"I don't want wisdom. I want a bazooka."

"We have other demon-possessed bodies. We can try more experiments."

I get up. My back aches where the demon drove me into the wall.

"How many experiments do we do? A hundred? A thousand? That means we have to catch more chop-shop assholes. Do we have that much time?"

The Shonin goes back to his table. Sets down the box and starts straightening things.

"Probably not. Do you have any ideas?"

I could use a drink about now. Getting monster-hugged by the 8 Ball and fighting a demon, it's more than I counted on. But I don't suppose the Shonin keeps Aqua Regia around here.

"You have any sake around here?"

"For rituals. Not for you to guzzle."

"Too bad. A drink would help me think better."

"Look what you did to my room. You think I want to see you drunk?"

He picks up and drops a shattered alembic.

"Some say I'm charming that way."

"Then you should go and work with them. I don't think I like your methods."

"I don't like anything about any of this," I say. "I don't know any more about the 8 Ball than when I came here. You people said you knew how it worked, but you were lying. As usual, the Vigil is full of shit."

"I don't know why I ever tried correcting your speech,"

lated, another good indicator that he's telling the truth. I slip the na'at back under my coat.

"You're going to watch that kind of behavior for the next few hours," Wells says. "I'm pulling you off the Angra case for a while. You need to come with me."

"Am I getting detention?"

"You're going to want to watch that kind of thing too. Saragossa Blackburn is dead and someone is making accusations."

"Against me?"

"Yes. We need to deal with this."

"What happened to him?"

"Later. Shonin, I'll have some people come by to help you put your lab back together. Between that and the breakthrough with the demon, it sounds like you have enough work to keep you busy for a while."

"More than enough. You really think he killed Blackburn? I studied people a long time. He's a fool, not a murderer."

"We'll see," says Wells. He goes to the door and holds it open for me.

I turn to the Shonin.

"See you around, dead man."

"Keep your nose clean, dumb-ass."

IT'S A LONG walk to Wells's office. The silence is different this time. It's not the general silence of people going quiet as I pass. Now it's Wells's silence as he walks slightly ahead of me so he doesn't have to speak or look at me. This is truly fucked and potentially dangerous. But I have my na'at, my gun, and my blade. If things go bad for me, I'll make them worse for everybody else.

Ishii takes a plastic evidence bag from his pocket and drops it on the desk.

"We found this."

Wells has a look and hands it to me. It's the torn edge of a receipt from Max Overdrive. There's a mark on it like it was stuck to the bottom of someone's shoe. Or marked to look that way.

I say, "Seriously? You think I wouldn't check myself over before running off to kill the king of the Sub Rosa?"

"Blackburn told me that he was afraid for his family's safety," says Ishii. "He invited you over and a couple of days later he's dead and this is at the scene. You can't dismiss that."

I look at Wells. He's the sphinx. I don't get anything from him at all.

"I was there for him to offer me your job, asshole," I say, and wait for Wells to reprimand me. He's doesn't, which can't mean anything good. "What does Tuatha think? Does she think I'm Saint Nick?"

Ishii takes back his evidence bag.

"She's distraught. She doesn't know what to think."

"Meaning she doesn't think it was me. You've always had it in for me and now's your chance to prove you're the investigator to the stars."

Wells looks at me, then at Ishii.

"Is it true that Blackburn offered Stark a job?"

"According to him."

"Ask Tuatha," I say. "She was there."

"Where did the murder take place?" says Wells.

"In his office at home," Ishii says.

"What time?"

Now Ishii shoots Wells a death-beam look.

"I have the entire Sub Rosa board on my side. If you don't arrest Stark right now, I can't guarantee his safety."

Wells stands up and comes around his desk.

"You let me worry about his safety. And his criminal tendencies. Now, if you'll excuse us, we have a lot of work to do."

He goes to the door and holds it open. Ishii doesn't move.

"The chief of police is with us, Stark. There's nowhere you can hide in L.A."

I look at him for a minute.

"What size uniform do you wear? After your bang-up job protecting Blackburn, I'm picturing your next gig as a rent-a-cop guarding a Denny's in Fresno."

"That's it," says Wells. "Stark, you shut up. Mr. Ishii, thank you for the sad news about the Augur's passing and your concerns about his death. The Vigil will do whatever it can to aid in the investigation."

I know Ishii wants to say something more, but Wells looks like he's one deep breath from pepper-spraying the guy. Ishii turns and leaves.

Wells goes back to his desk. Takes out a handkerchief and wipes off Ishii's prints.

I say, "You finally convinced I'm not Saint Nick?"

"Not by that scene," Wells says.

He takes a print out from a manila envelope on his desk. It's a drawing. A crude map.

"Washington convinced me you're innocent. Their psychics are sure they've tracked down Saint Nick and he's not where you're standing."

"Where is he?"

you think I wanted her back on the team? She was just a rookie in the service, but she was experienced in special operations for an agency you don't need to know about."

So that's why she was with Vidocq. Probably picking up a few last minutes of B&E tips.

"When do we leave?"

"Tonight. Marshal Sola has sketched out a good plan. She'll get you up to speed later."

"Shouldn't we go over things now?"

"She has work to do first. And nothing you're doing is complicated. You're just there to get her through any doors she can't breach herself."

"I can probably do this whole thing myself in ten minutes."

"Or blow it in one. The plan is already in motion. Be back here at midnight."

I leave Wells's office and walk around looking for Sola and Vidocq, but can't find them. Not a bad day all in all. I saw Ishii tossed out on his ass. I'm cleared of being Saint Nick. And I got to sucker-punch a demon.

Armed guards stand around the entrance to the Shonin's room as movers take out the wrecked furniture and bring in new. I've always been in such a hurry to get inside I never noticed that he's hung mistletoe over the door.

I RIDE THE Hellion hog home from the Vigil compound through wet, empty streets. The rain beats down hard today. Fat drops the size of quarters. I rev the engine and speed the hog down Hollywood Boulevard, sending mini-tidal waves onto the sidewalk.

The lights are off, but I can see someone on top of him. I grab whoever it is by the collar and throw them as hard as I can out the door. They slam into the floor, slide, and bang into the far wall hard enough to leave a dent.

It isn't until she gets to her knees that I recognize her. It's Candy. She's gone full Jade. I've never seen her so far gone before. Her skin has gone almost obsidian and her nails are curved back into claws. She growls, showing a mouthful of white shark teeth. Her eyes are red slits in black ice. She's sweating and blood drips from her mouth where she bit herself.

I shout, "Candy. It's me. Stop."

She charges and hits me square in the chest, knocking me onto my back. She's ridiculously strong in this form, and as vicious as an Eater. All teeth and madness. Candy's teeth are bad enough, but then she stretches her mouth open like a snake, exposing needle-thin fangs she uses to inject the Jades' necrotizing poison.

Candy's my girl, but I don't want to die and I don't want anyone drinking me when I do. But this isn't her fault. She's fucked up and I don't want to punch her out.

I bark some Hellion and she flies off me like ghosts playing horseshoes. She's up a second later and charging me again.

I grab her, wrapping my arms and legs around her. Still, it's all I can do to hold on. I bark a sleeping hex into her ear. She slows down. Her eyes close. Then I feel her body tense again as she fights her way through it, snarling and clawing at me again.

She braces her feet on the ground and pushes back against me, freeing one leg. It's enough to wriggle a leg, then a hand free. She drags her claws down my arm, shredding my coat and skin.

points for brave. She sticks her hand into Candy's mouth and pries her jaws open enough to pour the potion into. It's green and smells of licorice like it has an absinthe base.

When Candy starts to relax, I speak Hellion to clear the hex. Her muscles unknot and her jaw drops open. In less than a minute, she's back to being Candy.

Allegra looks at me.

"We're going to have to restrain her until we know what's happened."

"I know. Try not to hurt her."

"I'll try to keep her unconscious until we figure out what's wrong."

She looks at my bloody wrist.

"You're bleeding. It's like the old days. You in here all the time covered in blood. Sit down. I'll get some gauze."

I do what I'm told simply because I don't want to argue. Allegra comes back a minute later with gauze and tape.

"I could stitch this up to stop the bleeding, but I know you'll say no."

"That's right."

"Why?"

"Because it's mine and I keep my scars."

She pushes up my sleeve, bandages my hand, and wraps gauze around it.

"Because you never want to let go of anything."

I look at Candy on the table. Fairuza puts straps around her feet and across her chest.

"I swear, if someone did this to her . . ."

"I know. But you have to prepare yourself for something worse."

"Fuck you."

I pick up the DVDs and Blu-rays and stack them on the counter. They can fucking wait until tomorrow to go back on the shelves.

"She going to be all right?" says Kasabian.

"I don't know. I'm waiting to hear."

He doesn't say anything for a minute.

"Candy's all right," he says. "Recent events aside."

"Yeah. She is."

"Did you see Fairuza at the clinic?"

"Yeah."

"Did she say anything about me?"

I give him a look.

"Right. Wrong time."

He finishes up the floor and climbs creakily up on his mechanical legs.

"Thing is," he says. "Candy is a good influence on you. Around her you're almost like a person."

"I know."

He throws the bloody paper towels into the trash and puts the spray bottle back in the storeroom.

"You want a drink?" he says. "I've still got some Belgian beer Fairuza brought over."

I shake my head.

"Some other time."

I start upstairs.

"She'll be all right," says Kasabian. "Allegra knows what she's doing."

I don't say anything. I go upstairs and close the door. Find a bottle of Aqua Regia and don't bother with a glass. I fire up

"Nothing. Just practicing."

"Okay."

She smiles and hops down from the cab, slamming the door shut. We're both dressed in black coveralls, courtesy of the Vigil. Mine are too tight. Julie's are too loose. We look like a couple of idiot thrift-store ninjas. She slings a pack onto her shoulder and we cross the street, heading for our target.

Walking makes my head hurt, but sitting made it hurt too. The night rain is cool. It helps wake me up and get focused. No one at the Vigil knows anything about Candy. Rogue Lurkers are subject to immediate arrest, no questions asked. I'm not going to take a chance on that happening.

We walk to an empty store that used to sell high-end sound systems. We're near the corner and have a great view of the Pickman Building. Inside the store, power cords, stereo cables, and coax snake the floor and hang from the ceiling like jungle vines.

I say, "What were those three things again?"

Julie kneels and starts taking things out of the pack, laying them in a semicircle around her.

"Diversion, intrusion, and extraction."

"This is the first one."

"It will be in a minute."

She looks at me.

"You're not drunk, are you?"

"I toasted a friend's health tonight, yes. But I'm fine."

"Damn," she says. "I need you Johnny on the spot tonight. Can you handle that?"

"No problem."

"Screw this up and you can go back to calling me Sola. Marshal Sola."

"Yeah. Get in clean, then run away. Two of my favorite things, especially the last one."

She flips a switch on the box with the joystick. The camera jumps as the truck shifts into gear.

"You ready?"

I think about Candy strapped to the exam table in the clinic and I want someone to shoot at me just so I can strangle them.

"Ready."

She pushes the joystick forward and the truck moves out into the flooded street. Julie has the windshield wipers on full. The truck picks up speed and blasts through a red light at the corner. Then she floors it.

As the truck picks up speed, the wipers can't keep up with the rain, and the windshield shows nothing but splotches and colored lights. Without missing a beat, she thumbs a switch and the camera shifts to infrared. The scene is clear again, the building straight ahead.

Out the window, the truck barrels past us. Julie hits a button and the truck's air horn blows three times.

At the corner of Robertson, she hits the front brakes and the trailer starts to swing around, threatening to pull the cab over on its side. But she hits the accelerator and lets up on the brakes at just the right moment so that the truck slides across the intersection, up over the curb, and crashes into the front of the Pickman Building broadside.

Smashing through the glass and steel walls, the truck doesn't slow until most of it is resting comfortably in the lobby. Julie cuts the engine. This isn't the time for random fires. Just a distracting truck with a dead driver. How tragic.

"Definitely."

I pull her into the shadow and out onto the tenth floor of the Pickman Building.

JULIE WAS RIGHT. There aren't any guards on the tenth floor. All that's there is a small room, a plastic cube in the center of the empty floor. This would be a cakewalk except that the floor is covered in magic circles. It was dumb luck that we came out between two of them.

"Don't move," I say. "This is why I don't like going into places I don't know. Step in any one of these circles and you're dead. Probably we're both dead and I'm not in the mood for that tonight."

"Damn. What do we do to get around them?"

"It's too dark for me to see them clearly, so I can't draw a countersign."

"I have climbing gear. We can go across the ceiling."

"Easy, Catwoman. That will probably be hexed too."

"What do we do?"

"If I knew what kind of hoodoo these were, I could answer that."

"These might help," she says, and pulls two sets of goggles from her pack.

I put mine on and find a button on the side. The room blazes with the light, showing every nook and cranny protected by hoodoo power. The only thing glowing brighter than the circles is Saint Nick himself in the plastic cube. I guess that answers Wells's question. I get the feeling he's locked up tight. Nick is no guest.

"Well?" says Julie. "Can you get us through?"

pulses like broken neon and goes out. I pull the trigger again and the second circle flickers off.

"Is it safe now?" says Julie.

"Only one way to find out."

I jump the small circles and the place where the first big circle glowed just a few seconds earlier. Nothing happens.

"Don't touch anything," I say. "There might be hoodoo the goggles can't see."

"Thanks."

"You know I'm stealing them, right? I mean, when this is over, these goggles are coming home with me."

Julie shakes her head.

"Just come up with a good story for the report. I didn't see anything."

We make it to Saint Nick's door. He's sitting in a plastic kitchen chair staring at us. Not hostile, but not looking like he's thrilled about being rescued. They might keep him drugged. Or he might be so crazy he doesn't know what's happening. That's the Saint Nick I'm hoping we don't have to deal with.

Julie flicks on a small flashlight, holds it between her teeth, and examines the cube's lock. It looks like some combination of a keypad and a physical lock. She pulls a small silver box from her pack and fits it over the mechanism. It glows and something whirs inside. Julie looks at her watch.

"The building has shielded generators. The power will be back on in the next three minutes. We need to move."

Through the goggles I can see a sigil burning on Saint Nick's door. It's a circle with designs I don't know. Tentacles and tree trunks and human limbs. At the bottom of the outer circle in letters like something off a beer-hall menu it says

pocket. Saint Nick looks around. Points to the far side of the room.

Qliphoth claw their way out of an altar built into the wall. A Digger comes first. It gets out and slams into the far side of the cube, clearly not getting the difficult concept of transparency. More Qliphoth crawl out behind it.

"What do we do?" says Julie.

"It's too light. There are no shadows. How far to the roof?"

"It's right above us."

"Come on."

I get down on one knee, lay the Colt's barrel flat on the floor, and pull the trigger. The bullet cuts a groove in the plastic tiles all the way to the door at the end of the room.

"Come on."

"What about the circles?" says Julie.

"I hope the bullet broke them. Otherwise we're dead."

That makes Saint Nick giggle.

I grab Julie and she grabs Saint Nick. We run for the door. Nothing comes out of the floor to bite off our legs, but the Qliphoth across the room are finding their way around the cube.

The door is locked. I start to blast it open, but if I do that, the Qliphoth will be able to follow us through. Julie doesn't need me to tell her that. She has another lock-picking device out and attaches it to the door.

The Qliphoth are coming at us fast. I manifest the Gladius and slice it through the air. The front ones come up short and the rest bunch up behind them. They growl and grab at us, but none want to chance becoming Gladius meat. Then it hits

I can already hear it in the distance. As much as I hate the Vigil, I'm suddenly thrilled with them and Uncle Sam for blowing all that money on a helicopter and the fuel it's going to take to rescue my sorry ass from a bunch of demonic accountants.

We move to a clear area near the street where the chopper can get in close. Julie sets off a blinking light and drops it at our feet. The chopper circles around, finally coming back to the building and hovering over us.

The thing about helicopters is they're very loud. Loud enough for a metric ton of security guards in night camo to sneak up on the roof behind us and open fire.

Someone gets a lucky shot and hits the tail rotor. The chopper spins in a wild circle. It tilts away from the building like it's looking for somewhere to land, but it's way too out of control for that. It swings back around, the guards still firing, and crashes into the roof, punching through and into the floor below. There's a small explosion, smoke, and the stink of burning rubber and fuel.

Now that the chopper is down, some of the guards are looking lean and hungry in our direction. I seriously do not have time for more bullshit tonight. I bark some Hellion and use a version of the hex I used on Candy earlier tonight. The one that knocked her off me. Only I don't hold back and rip the hex as hard and long as I can.

It's like a giant bowling ball blown by a hurricane. It knocks over the twenty or so duckpin guards, tossing some off the roof and others into the hole where the chopper went down.

But we still need a shadow. There's only one good light source in the area and only one wall that's going to have shadows.

"Damn," he says. "That's the most fun I've had in a long time."

He rolls over and grins at me and Julie. His face is covered in scars and sutures.

"Look at you. The Lone Ranger and Tonto. Saviors of the little people."

I kick him in the ribs.

"Don't talk to me like you know me."

He rolls up into a ball, hurting and laughing.

"Don't be a killjoy, Jimmy. Come over here and give me a hug."

It's like someone opened me up and emptied me out. I'm cold and hot at the same time. I want to throw up. I look down at Saint Nick. His face is different, but I recognize the voice.

It's Mason Faim.

ONCE UPON A time I was a regular jackass living a regular jackass life. I was part of a Magic Circle. There were six other people in the circle. All of them are dead now because I killed most of them, including and especially Mason Faim. Why? Good question. Because he was the prick who sent me to Hell and the others were the assholes who stood by and watched.

But that wasn't enough. Mason had my girlfriend Alice killed. That was just one little thing too much. I escaped Hell and came back gunning for everyone in the circle, Mason most of all.

Like any Sir Galahad asshole, I went for the worst revenge I could think of—I sent him to Hell alive to live among the slickest, sickest Hellion torturers in the universe. Only fairy tales are full of lies and Mason is the best liar I know. He just wouldn't take

"Your presence here is no longer required. Get out of here until we sort this out. You can give me your report in the morning."

I stand there, just breathing. Mason lies on the floor looking around at the assembled Vigil morons who don't have a clue about what's happening but know that it's really, really bad. Worst of all, no matter what happens after this, Mason knows he's won the war we've been waging for eleven years. Just making it back to Earth and into a skin suit puts him one up on every civilian, Sub Rosa, and angel that's ever lived. Which doesn't mean I'm giving up. I sent him Downtown once before and I can do it again. And this time I won't get fancy with Tartarus or anything else. I'll kill his body and destroy his soul, wiping him out of existence.

"Stark," says Julie. "Did you hear Marshal Wells?"

I look at him. He's still in reach. I could toss him across the room and kill Mason before anyone could stop me and he knows it, but he stays put. Slowly, it sinks in that maybe there's more to all this than Mason and me. There's a dozen bodies in a meat locker and around ninety more in an asylum. And how many more that we don't know about yet? And it's all tied up with the Angra. Kill Mason so we can't get any answers and it might be the biggest favor I can do for the end of the world.

I put the Colt away.

Wells nods to his crew.

"Get this thing out of here. Max lockdown. No one talks to him but me."

They haul Mason to his feet and hustle him away to the cells at the far end of the clubhouse. He hums "Onward, Christian Soldiers" until I can't hear him anymore.

[illegible] see [illegible] out of here [illegible] you're [illegible] office."

[illegible] behind [illegible] storage [illegible] there are [illegible] down [illegible] through [illegible]

[illegible] going to [illegible] night [illegible]

[illegible] get [illegible] here [illegible]

[illegible] be [illegible] night, so I [illegible] any [illegible] ns to [illegible], Okay?"

[illegible] step [illegible] shadow [illegible] ring [illegible] ID [illegible]

[illegible]"

[illegible] anything [illegible] minute [illegible]

[illegible] know [illegible]

[illegible] know [illegible] way. I was [illegible] minute."

[illegible] happen [illegible]

[illegible] n't [illegible] hasn't [illegible] you left [illegible]

[illegible] set [illegible] supplies?"

[illegible]?"

[illegible] should [illegible] because [illegible] Julie.

[illegible] I'm [illegible]. I can't [illegible] was [illegible]

[illegible] when I [illegible] back. [illegible] door [illegible]

[illegible] broke [illegible] gone [illegible] She's [illegible]."

[illegible] wrong [illegible] Julie.

[illegible] is going [illegible] in hour [illegible]

[illegible] this."

[illegible] back? [illegible] do?"

[illegible] past her [illegible] in front of [illegible]

"Stop. Talk to me. What's happened?"

"Candy is missing, and I know that motherfucker had something to do with it."

"Then what good is it killing him? Think about it."

I do. I start for the cells again.

"Stop," says Julie. "What's your plan? Kill Saint Nick? Tear up the city looking for Candy so you'll feel in control? The Vigil has resources you wouldn't believe. We can find anyone. What do you have besides anger? Be smart for once. Let me handle this. You go home. I'll call you when we find her."

I look at her. Is this more Vigil bullshit? Is she on their side or mine?

"Please," she says. "If you kill him, there's no coming back. You'll have the Marshals Service, Homeland Security, and the Vigil after you."

In my mind I can see Mason's head exploding. It feels even better than the first time.

Julie says, "I promise you I'll find her. Give me twelve hours."

I get out my phone and set a timer.

"Twelve hours. After that, he's mine and I'll hurt anyone who gets in my way."

Julie nods.

"Okay. Let me go talk to Wells and tell him what's happened."

I nod and start for a shadow.

"Twelve hours."

"Don't come back unless I call you," she says.

through this—to ask more questions. Man, I hate the sound of that. I just want to go back to the Chateau Marmont, order room service, get drunk together, and break all the furniture in the master bedroom. Is that too much to ask?

After the bike finally stalls a couple of times and the rain is coming down so hard I can't see more than five feet ahead of me, I turn back for Max Overdrive.

I'm putting on dry clothes when the phone rings. It's Julie.

"Have you found Candy?"

"Not yet, but we're following up on leads."

"Why did you call?"

"Wells wants you to come in. It's about Saint Nick."

"Stop calling him that. His name is Mason Faim."

"How do you know?"

"Because back when he was a person I killed him."

"You know a lot of dead people."

"What does Wells want?"

"Saint Nick, Mason Faim, whoever, won't talk to him. He wants to talk to you."

"I'll be right there."

I get a dry coat and a gun. I step through a shadow.

THEY HAVE MASON in a cell with walls thick enough to stop a meteor. They're covered from end to end, top to bottom, in a hasty scrawl of protective wards and crosses. It's like they let a gang of junior high taggers go at the cell with a copy of *The Little Wizard's Handbook of Scary-Looking Shit.*

Inside, Mason is seated at a metal table bolted to the floor. The walls are covered in binding hexes. Mason is cuffed hand and foot with cold iron shackles and dressed in orange cov-

ger. No, killing me just made things worse for everybody. Besides, you think I can't find my way into a new body? You could fill a stadium with all the bodies my friends and I have created. And all I need is one. You can't win playing your old games, Jimmy."

"Where's Candy?"

"In the cut-glass bowl on Grandma's coffee table."

Before he or Julie can move, I lean across the table and punch him. He shakes it off and looks at me.

"In a caravan to Timbuktu."

I hit him again.

"On the Matterhorn ride at Disneyland."

I start to hit him again when I hear Julie.

"Stark! Stop it."

Mason spits blood on the floor.

"Tell you what, Jimbo. You like games. Play a game with me and I'll tell you everything I know about your squeeze."

"What kind of game?"

He turns to Julie.

"Do you have any playing cards around here?"

"We have a few games in the break room," she says. "I'll check."

"Hurry back, darling."

Mason turns back and raises an eyebrow at me. His chop-shop face is almost as scarred as mine.

"One of yours?" he says.

"You don't need to know anything about her. Or anyone else here. I'm the only one you need to worry about."

"How is it?"

"How's what?"

"Chaos. Entropy. Catastrophe. Infinity."

"I don't know how to play that."

He sits up straight, his eyes on the cards.

"It's your whole life, Jimmy. You're an expert. You just don't know it."

I look at the time on my phone and then at Julie.

"Shouldn't you be out looking for someone?"

"I have a team on it."

"Ready?" says Mason.

"What are we playing?"

"Simple draw poker. You can handle that, can't you?"

"You don't have anything to bet."

"We have the whole world to bet."

"If I win you'll tell me about Candy."

"Everything. Deal."

I deal out five cards, each facedown. I get two threes, a queen of diamonds, a ten of clubs, and an ace of hearts.

Mason nods at his cards to Julie.

"Would you hold my cards up for me, dear?"

"Don't call me that again. I'm Marshal Sola."

"Would you hold my cards for me, Marshal Sola?"

She does it.

"Higher, please."

She raises the cards a little.

"Thank you."

I set my cards down and pick up the deck.

"How many do you want?"

"Four," he says.

"What's wrong with you? That's how a six-year-old plays."

"I'd like four."

us right now—hello, Mr. Shonin—I know exactly how the Qomrama works and I'll teach you. But you have to play my games and, of course, you have to win."

"The Vigil has all kinds of funny technology. I bet they have some kind of brain sucker around here. What's to keep them from hooking you up and downloading you into a Tamagotchi?"

Mason's face brightens.

"You have one of those? Neat. I'd love to see it."

"You didn't answer the question."

He drums his fingers on the table a couple of times.

"If the machine exists it wouldn't work on me for the same reason it wouldn't work on you. We wouldn't let it. Do you really think these Keystone Cops have anything that could hurt people like us? You ruled the Underworld. I escaped Tartarus. Their magic can't touch ours."

"You didn't escape Tartarus. Someone broke you out. Merihim and Deumos or some of their people."

"They cracked open the door but I'm the one who did the heavy lifting, like when you first made it out of Hell."

"So this is how we figure out the fate of the universe? Poker?"

"Of course not. That was nothing. That wasn't even the appetizer before dinner. It was just to see if I should invite you for a full meal."

"Should you?"

"Do you want to know how the Qomrama works?"

"The Shonin will figure it out."

"Not in time."

"How do I know you know anything?"

"I can do anything I like."

"Don't take the bait," says Julie. "He's crazy and he'll never tell you the truth."

"She's right. I'll continue my work," says the Shonin.

Mason looks at him.

"Do you know the Epistle of Saint Paul to the Romans?"

"I know many spiritual books."

"Chapter four, verse seven. Recite it."

The Shonin thinks for a minute.

" 'Blessed are they whose iniquities are forgiven: and whose sins are covered.' "

"Very good. Now, recite that backward in Hellion and you can make the Qomrama do the little trick I did a moment ago. You can also use it to return it to its original resting spot."

"That can't be all," says the Shonin. "A spell of that power would require meditation on a sacred object. A mandala or angelic sigil."

Mason holds up his hands from the table. Using the sharp edge on one of his cuffs, he's cut an inverted cross in a hex circle into his right palm.

I put my hand in my pocket around the Colt. Then let go and take my hand out. I turn to Julie.

"You have two hours to find Candy or I'm killing this guy, 8 Ball or no 8 Ball."

She checks her phone.

"I have a message. I'll see how the search is going."

She leaves and the Shonin goes to Mason's side of the table.

"You're been a very bad boy from what I hear."

Mason gives him a bland, condescending smile.

They're both lucky we have a serum that reverses the effects of Jade venom. The man will live."

"I want to see her."

"She's being processed. You can see her when she's done."

"No. Now."

Julie gets right in my face.

"Shut up and listen to me. I just did you a favor. Washington has classified Saint Nick's revived bodies as Lurkers, and under a new statute, any dangerous Lurker can be killed or detained indefinitely. My team had every legal right to kill a Jade attacking a civilian, but I gave them orders to bring her in. So you can fucking back off and wait until things cool down. And stop barking orders at me."

Julie turns and goes out, slamming the door behind her.

I want to follow her and make her take me to Candy, but if what she said about the new law is true? Then she really did do me and Candy a favor, and there aren't many people who would do that.

"You sure like the feisty ones, don't you," says Mason. "How's Alice these days? Heard from her recently? I hear that things aren't going too well in Heaven. I hope she's all right."

I knock on the door to be let out and head straight for an exit. Out in the parking lot I put my fist through the window on the side of a Vigil van.

Ow.

I forgot they use bulletproof glass. When I pull my hand back, I've peeled all the skin off my knuckles. I lean against the van, pull out a Malediction, and light it up. Out in the gloom across the drowning grass, a couple of Vigil cops play golf under a big umbrella.

turns to face me one of her cheeks is swollen, like she took a rifle butt to the face. She's mostly out of Jade mode. Mostly human-looking, but her eyes are still black, her pupils red pinpoints. I go up and grab a fistful of the net.

"You all right?"

She comes closer, but stops a few feet from the bars.

"I'm fine. Never better."

"You look like hell."

"Go peek in a mirror and then tell me how bad I look."

She starts to pace again.

"They say you tried to kill a civilian."

She puts a hand on her chest and opens her eyes all wide and innocent.

"I wasn't trying to kill anybody. I was just hungry."

I glance over to Julie. She has one hand resting gently on her gun.

I say, "This isn't your fault. Something went wrong with the potion. Allegra will figure it out and you'll be all right again."

Candy stops pacing and comes right up to the bars.

"Fuck Allegra. Fuck the potion. And fuck you. You want me to feel all right? I feel great. Like I'm myself for the first time in years."

"Like hell you do. Doc Kinski took you out of the killing life so something just like this wouldn't happen."

"Fuck Doc too."

That's new. I've never heard her talk that way about Kinski.

"You can't run around taking down random people and you know it."

"Most of the time."

"I know."

Julie leads me to the break room. I spot Vidocq, nursing a cup of tea.

"What are you doing here?"

"Marshal Sola called me when Candy was arrested. She thought you might need someone to talk to."

"I need someone to punch."

His eyes go to my knuckles.

"It looks like you already found that."

I look at my hand. The bleeding has stopped and a scab is forming. Still, it's pretty ugly to look at. I pull a paper towel off the roll and wrap it around my hand.

"I've never seen her like this before, and I've seen her turn Jade plenty of times."

"You've never seen it because she's never been this way before. She's been poisoned."

I sit down across from him.

"Keep talking."

"I tested the rest of the Jade potion Allegra had on hand. Not only has it been watered down, but there's a toxin in it I can't identify. I'm sure it's responsible for her behavior."

"Now all we have to do is convince the Vigil and the entire federal government that a murderous Jade didn't mean it and is really sorry."

"It's a problem, I admit."

I go over to the counter and pour myself some coffee. I want Aqua Regia, but this isn't the time for a fuzzy head.

"If you make more of the real Jade potion, will the Vigil let you give it to her?"

"It's pointless to think like that. Right now she needs rest and medication more than she needs you."

"She said something like that too, only louder."

"Go home," says Vidocq. "You must be exhausted. Waiting here like this benefits no one."

I rub a knot of muscles at the base of my neck.

"Maybe you're right. I need to talk to Mason again later and I want a clear head for that."

"I'll stay here. If anything changes, I'll call you."

"Thanks," I say. Then, "How's Allegra doing with all this?"

"Not well. She feels responsible for both the poisoned potion and Candy's escape."

"I still think there's an Angra mole in the Vigil. Could there be one at the clinic?"

"The only people who work there regularly are Allegra, Fairuza, Rinko, and sometimes Candy. But patients go in and out all day. I suppose one of them could have done it."

"We're not going to figure anything out tonight. I'm getting out of here."

"Rest easy, my friend."

"Next lifetime."

Later, when I'm asleep, I don't dream about Candy. I dream about the Angra. I'm back in the cavern, but it's not like the last time. Ten Thousand Shadows doesn't talk to me. I just see the meat chapel and hear something faint and faraway, like noise from an old sitcom. The sound of someone laughing at me.

I'M TEMPTED [illegible] go [illegible] Mason [illegible] in the [illegible] [illegible] ed and [illegible] [illegible] the [illegible] him [illegible] opped [illegible] until nearly [illegible] as [illegible] the barricade [illegible] entrance [illegible] get [illegible] but with box [illegible] say [illegible] I guess it [illegible] in [illegible] step [illegible] ters and [illegible] right [illegible] d goes [illegible]

This [illegible] al V [illegible] cause a metal [illegible] I [illegible] spo [illegible] not only [illegible] ping, [illegible] blade. [illegible] Mason's [illegible] my weapons [illegible] hen with [illegible] hands, [illegible] understand [illegible] for going [illegible] a little [illegible] with inside [illegible] Mason, [illegible] cuffed, but his hands are [illegible]

He [illegible] games [illegible] bolted [illegible] Wells [illegible]

I [illegible] press [illegible] speak [illegible] chair

M [illegible] and [illegible] [illegible] id? [illegible] ts [illegible] you [illegible] [illegible] to lo [illegible] play [illegible] the [illegible] Game

[illegible] en [illegible] it happens [illegible]

"The Angra?"

"Yes."

"I don't believe you."

"Someone in Hell sent them to me because they knew I could help their cause."

"Stop. I can't deal with your bullshit without a drink. What's today's game?"

"Billy Flinch."

Billy Flinch is a favorite game among the highly intoxicated and the clinically insane. It's William Tell, only you play it by yourself. Take potshots at the far wall and try to ricochet a bullet so that it breaks the glass on your head. Most people only play Billy Flinch once. It doesn't have an Old-Timers League.

"They took away my gun, so forget it."

"That's disappointing," he says.

As hard as Mason is to read, this time his pupils constrict a millimeter or two, so I know he's lying. He wants to play something else.

Two upside-down plastic cups sit on his side of the table. He pushes them into the middle and lifts them. A couple of scorpions make a break for it, but he corrals them back under the cups, laughing as he does it.

I look at him.

"Where the hell did you get scorpions?"

"What's the scarier answer? That I had them all along or that someone snuck them in to me?"

Neither one's a comfort, but this is Mason. Nothing about him is comfortable.

"What are we playing?"

"Shouldn't you be asking about the Angra instead of trying to fix your love life?"

When I don't make to pick up the cup, Mason reaches across the table and raises it.

"You might want to concentrate on the game."

The scorpion sits there for a minute, looking as pissed as I feel.

"You made her crazy and almost got some poor street slob killed for nothing."

"I got a lot more than nothing out of it. I got you to play with me. Just like old times. Your little friend is moving. Play or forfeit."

Now that the scorpion has decided to move, it's all over the place. Darting in one direction, then another. I try to follow it, but it never goes in a straight line for very long. Finally, I catch the rhythm of its turns. Get my hand hovering right over its stinger. I'm fast when I want to be. I snap my hand down to the bug, then back again before it can sting me. But I miss the paper. I do it again. And miss again. The third time I come really close, but still miss.

I see the problem. While I'm fast enough to outrun the scorpion, if I go full speed I'm going too fast to grab the paper. The trick is to slow down. Feel the bug's rhythm and move in at just the right moment.

Which is exactly what I don't do. The fucker stings me on my first try. I always heard that scorpion stings feel like bee stings. Whoever said that never met this particular scorpion because this thing stings like a hornet with a blowtorch.

I pull back my hand and try to shake some of the pain out of my fingers.

"Will Candy [illegible]?"

"[illegible]," says Mason. "I'm sure she'll be fine."

I go for another [illegible] and get [illegible] ing. I'm [illegible] Mason didn't [illegible] anything [illegible] limit on [illegible]. I'm going [illegible] the [illegible] for just [illegible] moment.

"Still, [illegible] murder," he says. "That's the [illegible] of [illegible] a person. [illegible] which the [illegible] there [illegible] place [illegible] show [illegible] in L.A."

I get stung again.

"Maybe you [illegible] a little [illegible] a [illegible]. She [illegible] white."

Okay. [illegible] concentration [illegible] about Candy [illegible] fucking [illegible] to get [illegible] Mason's tongue [illegible] him.

I get stung [illegible] more times [illegible] getting [illegible] off the [illegible] and [illegible] finger. [illegible] but I [illegible] a feeling that [illegible] les, and I [illegible] to ask [illegible] fucker [illegible].

I think [illegible] off Mason's head. I put [illegible] in Ta[illegible] top of him [illegible] will ever find him. [illegible] posts [illegible] there.

"So, [illegible] her?"

"Now it's my turn," Mason says.

With his cuffed hands, he knocks over his cup and lets his scorpion loose. Like mine, it looks confused and after a few seconds starts running randomly across the table.

He waits, tracking the scorpion's moves, trying to figure out the best moment to strike. He takes his sweet fucking time about it.

"Before Christmas, please."

When he moves, it's fast. He pins the scorpion's tail with the cuffs, and before it can rear back and get him with its pincers, he grabs the paper. Then slams the cup down on top of it.

"What the fuck, man? You cheated."

He sets the paper down between us.

"What was it you said when I complained about you putting a bullet in my head? My game. My rules."

"We're even now, asshole."

"Not even close."

He reaches for his paper, but I put my hand over it.

"Before we count up the points, tell me this. Whose skull is that in the cavern?"

"Mine, of course."

"I burned your body after I chucked your soul into Tartarus, so unless there's a rewind button on your bones, that skull isn't yours."

I lift up my hand and he slides the paper back to his side of the table.

"It's metaphorically mine. Putting it there was just a bit of fun. Give you a clue as to who Saint Nick might be."

"It's fucking hysterical. Who did you shoot in the head to make your joke?"

I lean back and cross my arms.

"You mean that whatever Candy says through the poison is the truth. I don't believe you."

"I don't have to lie. You talked to her. Did she seem woozy or drugged? You know I'm not lying. Like your hand, it stings, doesn't it?"

"Let's play another game."

"When you win you can decide when we play, but you lost, so go away until tomorrow."

I slam my fist down on the table hard enough that I knock over the cups. They're empty. The scorpions are gone.

"There's no time to fuck around like this."

Mason stacks one cup inside the other and pushes them to the side of the table.

"Fucking around is part of the game, or haven't you figured that out by now?"

"Who poisoned Candy's medicine?"

"You're being boring, James. Keep it up and I'll hurt you again. Do it twice and there won't be any game at all tomorrow."

Were the scorpions phantoms? A hoodoo hallucination? I look at my hand. Whatever just happened in here, my fingers really are swollen and they really hurt. I go over and knock on the cell door. It opens and a guard lets me out.

"Where's my gear?" I say.

He hands me the Colt and my knife.

"I unloaded the pistol. It's an unauthorized weapon. Rules."

I put it in the waistband at my back and put the blade in my coat.

I TRY SOME healing hoodoo from the arena days, but I've always been better at breaking things than fixing them, so my improvised spells don't work. Between the swelling from the scorpion and the last ragged remains of the scab from where I punched out the van window, my hand looks like I stuck it in a wood chipper and set it on frappé. I go downstairs to see if Kasabian has any aspirin.

He and Fairuza are sitting on some of the boxes outside his room, sipping beers. She sets hers down when she sees me.

"How's Candy?"

I shake my head.

"Everything's fucked. Candy's crazy and I'm playing Chinese checkers with a psycho. Oh, Kas, you'll be amused to know. Mason Faim is back from Hell."

His beer goes down the wrong way. He coughs and it takes him a minute to catch his breath.

"Mason? I thought you buried him under the floorboards."

"He's a roach. He got out."

Kasabian gets up and starts for his room.

"Bye."

"Who's Mason Faim?" says Fairuza.

"I'll tell you about him from my fallout shelter."

"Calm down," I say.

Kasabian points his beer at me.

"I've got some good news for you too. Someone just took a potshot at one of the God brothers."

"Muninn?"

"No. One of the others. I can't remember which is which."

"Is he alive?"

"The rain's messed up all kinds of stuff down there. I can't see everything."

"I [illegible] ntow[illegible] Maybe Mur[illegible] some [illegible] Mason."

Kasa[illegible] his [illegible].

"Go[illegible] you [illegible] see me for [illegible] be in [illegible]."

"You [illegible] place [illegible] Fairuza.

I shak[illegible].

"No[illegible] let [illegible] know [illegible] around [illegible] over [illegible] If Mason [illegible] might [illegible] you."

"Wh[illegible] Mason Fa[illegible]?" says Fairuza.

"You [illegible] stuff [illegible] about [illegible] Kasabia[illegible] worse. [illegible] when he [illegible] school [illegible] blow [illegible] off a mountain [illegible] [illegible] magic [illegible] that did [illegible] killed a [illegible] the [illegible] women, and [illegible] didn't [illegible] what Mason is. An[illegible] Mason [illegible] who [illegible]."

"[illegible] your [illegible] off."

"[illegible] just my head. He didn't [illegible]. That was [illegible]."

Fairuza [illegible] bag [illegible] her rain co[illegible] by the [illegible].

"[illegible] I'm leaving."

"[illegible] abian[illegible]."

She [illegible] ng [illegible]?"

"[illegible] with the robot [illegible] crazy [illegible] forget [illegible]. Sorry, Kas. I'll see [illegible] around."

[illegible] in the rain." [illegible] and slam[illegible] the [illegible] behind her.

"You happy?" says Kasabian. "Fairuza was as close to a love life as I was ever going to have."

"Relax. She's just freaked out. Give her some time to calm down."

"You just told her not to have anything to do with me."

"Until things settle down. Then go and bring her flowers and chocolates or drumsticks and scorpions, whatever it is she'd like. It'll work itself out."

"Nothing's going to work itself out as long as Mason is back. And what the hell happened to your hand?"

"Nothing. It's just a paper cut."

"Mason did it. Oh shit. How fucked are we?"

"Get a grip. The Vigil has him. He can't pull any heavy hoodoo in a prison protected by angelic tech."

"I hope you're right."

I don't tell him about the scorpions disappearing. I don't want to think about it myself.

Kasabian says, "Not to sound selfish or anything, but do you think he's going to come after me?"

"Probably. But he has a pretty busy schedule fucking with me right now, so I wouldn't worry about it."

"Okay. Thanks. Sorry."

"Don't worry about it."

"I'm going to go inside and lie in a fetal position for a while. Call me if the world doesn't end."

"You're top of the list."

He goes into his room, pulling the boxes back into place, leaning the door against them. It's a sad, small gesture, but I understand it. I'd like to hibernate for a few years myself, but I'm stuck in the middle of this thing. I need to see Mr. Muninn, but Hell is the last place I want to go right now.

got that much in common. He thought he locked out the Angra and I thought I buried Mason. Maybe Muninn and I can go halfsies on a few sessions with a life coach. Learn to set goals. Visualize our success. Take over a Denny's franchise in Fresno. Cash in on the hungry truckers. Easy money and no one gets hurt.

Who am I kidding? A month of that and I'd burn down the place for the insurance money. Hit the road with Candy and not look back. Like Doc and Carol McCoy in a cartoon version of *The Getaway*.

Only that's not going to happen. And the Angra aren't coming back to fix things. And the God brothers aren't going to square anything with them or us. We'll be lucky if we get out of this with any skin left, because whether it's Muninn or Ruach or Zhuyigdanatha or Lamia, we don't count. No matter which God is in charge, we're bugs on his windshield. Always were. Always will be. Amen.

I step through a shadow and come out in Hell.

I don't want to come out in Mr. Muninn's room after tracking the place up last time, so I step out into the palace lobby. The blood rain pounds down on the windows, as heavy as ever.

The first thing I want to know is if he and his brothers are all right. The second thing I want to know is how to deal with Mason. I get part of the answer to my first question without moving an inch.

There's blood everywhere, and not the kind tracked in from outside.

The lobby is cordoned off with iron grates, like cop crime-scene tape.

"Mr. Muninn?"

When no one answers I say it again.

Footsteps click down the hall, coming my way. Then nothing. Silence for maybe thirty seconds.

"Are you going to hide in the elevator all night or are you going to come have a drink with me and Father?"

It's Samael. At least his voice. I step out of the elevator with the na'at held high. Move around the corner until I can see the whole living room.

Samael is there. His suit isn't quite as sharp as usual. His smile is faint and gone in a second, like he was as uncertain about me as I was about him. I put the na'at back in my coat. There are stains on his shirt and trouser cuffs. Black blood.

"Come to comfort the bereaved? What a softie you've become. Everyone is in the library."

Samael starts down the hall.

"Which brother was it?"

He doesn't turn around.

"Nefesh."

I follow him down the hall.

This stinks. I'm the one who wanted Nefesh to come down to Hell in the first place. I told him he'd be safe here with Muninn. We met when he was hiding in a Roman bath at the bottom of the Kill City mall. Who knows how long he'd been there, hiding in noncorporeal form? Pretending he was nothing more than a mad old ghost. Then I came along with some friends and got him to tell us where Aelita had hidden the 8 Ball. I told him to give up the ghost game. Grow a pair and head Downtown for some face time with his brother and, most of all, safety. Things were bad enough back then that

Chaya says, "He wanted to know if we're all right. What a sweet murderer you are."

"Truth is, I was really checking on these other two. You I don't know from a hellhound's asshole."

Chaya's face turns kind of a dark fucked-up purple, which I guess is him turning red.

"Listen to him, Muninn. You let a mortal speak to you like that?"

"In case you haven't noticed," I say, "I'm not exactly a mortal."

"No. You're Abomination. Why didn't we kill you as an infant?"

"Maybe because you spent a billion years trying to find your ass with two hands and a sextant? I mean, you can't even keep your own angels in line. What chance did you have of finding one little kid?"

Chaya doesn't say a word and I'm pretty sure he's working up to a good smiting when Samael tugs on my arm.

"Why don't you take James to the kitchen," says Muninn. "I'll be along in a few minutes."

Samael heads out of the library, dragging me by the arm like a dog that just shit on the *Pietà*.

I half expect him to chew me out, when he lets go of my arm and says, "Thank you. I couldn't take one more minute of that old maid's squawking. He hasn't shut up since he got here."

"Sure. It was all part of my plan."

"Of course it was."

In the kitchen, Samael finds an open bottle of wine and pours us both a drink. He raises his glass in a brief toast and

"I don't understand. Aelita needed the 8 Ball when she killed the first brother, Neshamah. How could a bunch of grunts kill Nefesh with a few knives?"

"Ah," says Samael, taking down a bottle from the top shelf of a cupboard. He brings it to the table and takes a corkscrew from a drawer. When he gets the cork out of the bottle and pours himself a glass, he looks at me.

"The longer my fathers are separate entities, the weaker they get. No one can know, but Nefesh's death proves that you don't need—what's the Angra name for the Qomrama?"

"Godeater."

"Yes. You don't need the Godeater to kill a God anymore."

"All the blood and body parts in the lobby. Was that you?"

He takes a sip of wine and shakes his head.

"That was all Muninn. The only other time I've seen him like that was when he knocked me out of Heaven with a thunderbolt. He blew those traitors to bits with a wave of his hand. Good for you, Father."

He clinks his glass against mine and I have to sip more of the Hellion swill.

"Good for which one of us and for what?" says Muninn, coming into the room. He sees the open bottle of wine and gets himself a glass. Samael fills it for him.

"Your righteous wrath," says Samael.

"Oh. You mean the lobby. It was certainly wrathful, and I don't apologize for it. But I'm not so sure about righteous."

"Righteous enough," says Samael. "Those pissants got exactly what they deserved."

"Perhaps. I don't really want to talk about it."

"I'm sorry about your brother," I say.

Muninn puts his hands flat on the counter.

"Mason Faim," he says. "I hoped I'd never hear that name again."

He takes a long breath.

"I'll tell you right now that you have no chance of winning that game against someone like Mason Faim."

"Can't you teach me?"

"The Infinite Game is like its name. Infinite. It has no boundaries. The rules are impossible to explain and harder to learn. It's life, with all its complexities and contradictions. It takes longer than a human life-span to become proficient at it. If Mason has become adept at it in the few months he was in Tartarus, he had help."

"Deumos or Merihim or one of their Angra toadies," says Samael.

"Where did they learn it?"

"If they're in contact with the Angra they could have learned from them."

"If I killed both of them, would this thing be over?"

Muninn shakes his head.

"I wish it were that simple. But I can't say I'd object to seeing them gone."

Chaya stops by the kitchen door and looks us over.

"What's this thing still doing here? I thought you were sending him back to wherever it is he wallows."

"I wallow in L.A. And yeah, it can smell funny on a hot day, but at least it's not raining fucking blood."

"This is what happens when you don't discipline earthly trash regularly. That was supposed to be your job. Wasn't it, Muninn? But you hid in your cave, playing with your toys while mortal vermin ran wild over the world."

Muninn looks at me like he doesn't know what I'm talking about. I can't tell if he's distracted by the fight or getting slow as he gets weak. Then his eyes focus and he nods.

"You can't beat Mason, but maybe you can play him to a draw. Win a few small victories here and there. With that, you might get enough information that you won't need it all. Bring me whatever you find and we'll see what we can do with it."

"And how am I supposed to win these small victories?"

"Don't fight him. Play with him, not at him. When you don't understand what's happening—"

"That's all the time."

"Mimic him. Move the way he does. Move for move, if you like. He'll catch on but he won't be able to stop you because to get you to play badly he'll have to play badly himself and risk losing."

"That's not exactly the plans for D-Day."

Muninn looks at the kitchen door like he's expecting Chaya to come back and apologize.

"I'm sorry," he says. "As you can see, there are a few things going on here too. I've given you all I can for now."

"Thanks. It's more than I had when I got here."

"Now I really think it would be a good idea if you left. I'm going to see if I can calm Chaya down."

"I'll see you around, Mr. Muninn. Sorry again about Nefesh."

He walks out like he didn't even hear me.

"Let him go," says Samael. "Neither one of us can help him fight himself. I hate all this talk about brothers. It just covers up the fact that Father is slowly killing himself."

my demise. The addled dogs imprinted on me and even those hard-core Hellion soldiers backed off when I strolled out of the palace surrounded by my mechanical hounds. It looks like the imprinting stayed strong. When the hounds smell me they move to the front of their cages and press their heads to the bars so I can pet them as we walk past.

Samael would never admit it, but I know he's eating his heart out seeing his hounds so loyal to me. It's his fault for leaving me in Hell on my own way back when. How long ago was it? Just a few months. This year, ever since I escaped from Hell, time has been like a carnival midway. Loud, twisting, and confusing. Full of dead ends and dark, empty places. I look at Samael for a second. Does he know what I'm thinking? Maybe. Not much I can do about it, off kilter like this. Anyway, pride isn't the issue here. But I don't think it's hounds either.

"What are we doing here? It's nice to see the pups, but I don't have time to skip down memory lane."

Samael says, "Of course you do. It just depends on what you're skipping to."

He leads me around a corner of the kennel to where a man is shackled to the floor. The slave collar around his neck is attached to chains with links as large as a man's arm. They're so heavy, the man is slumped on the floor. Samael walks over and kicks him in the ass. The man's head jerks up like maybe he was asleep.

"Up, pest. You have company."

The man slowly rises to his feet, the heavy chains clanging against each other. He staggers a bit when he's up, trying to get his balance. His clothes are shredded and he's filthy, but I'd never forget that face. It's Merihim.

Death is coming. We're all going to die at the hands of the old Gods. The only question is how your death will come. Those of us who brought them home will die quickly and easily. While those who fought on the side of the beast in Heaven will die over aeons in unimaginable pain."

"You watched *The Exorcist* a lot when you were a kid, didn't you? You've got the whole spooky 'hail, Satan' patter down cold."

"Don't talk like a fool," Merihim shouts, rattling his chains loud enough to get the hellhounds growling. "You sound like Samael, the spoiled son, when you do that. Listen to me, Stark. You don't have to play the brave soldier anymore. That time is over. You're more on my side than his. You always have been. I know you have the Mithras hidden away. You could have burned the universe on your own, and you came close a few times, didn't you? Admit it. You hate this place. This universe that calls you Abomination. But you're not the Abomination. It's God. All the pain there ever was he started by exiling the Angra. He invented our doom that day. And he compounded the torment for creatures like you and me and even Samael, the fool, by exiling us in Hell. You owe angels and mad Gods nothing. The Angra will embrace you as a brother."

"And then they'll kill me."

"Death is our only release."

"I was just thinking about that. You know the one good thing about Mason Faim being back on Earth?"

"What?"

"There's a vacancy in Tartarus."

I pull out the Colt and shoot Merihim right between his

[illegible]dshe[illegible] The [illegible] the
[illegible] Hell [illegible] he ha[illegible] how
[illegible] pa[illegible] with the[illegible], tea[illegible] stone
[illegible] mo[illegible]

Di[illegible] good[illegible] says Samuel.

"Yea[illegible] Why don't [illegible] k to [illegible]
[illegible]ere's [illegible] people [illegible] ouldn't [illegible] help."

Sam[illegible] and [illegible] e with [illegible] of his
[illegible] fec[illegible]

"Be[illegible] ght [illegible] s. B[illegible] efore
[illegible]rde[illegible] ays [illegible] own [illegible] to sta
[illegible] re a[illegible] Father."

"Yo[illegible] Mumm, [illegible] thin[illegible] ould ge
[illegible]ong [illegible] the other on[illegible]

Sam[illegible] out a long [illegible]

"Th[illegible] problem. [illegible] y fa[illegible] l peop[illegible]
[illegible]y s[illegible] s when they [illegible] But [illegible] Fa[illegible]
[illegible] A[illegible] win. [illegible] dvice [illegible] ng with
[illegible]as[illegible]

"[illegible] you've got."

"[illegible] see him, ju[illegible] al [illegible] self."

I[illegible] ing it over, [illegible] of [illegible] iction in
Meri[illegible] k blood.

"[illegible] ind if [illegible] h the [illegible]
"[illegible] make more [illegible] n i[illegible] ogether."

Sa[illegible] ocks [illegible] and [illegible] his body
thro[illegible] cernel and [illegible] rain [illegible] ell ou[illegible]ds
follo[illegible] ning [illegible] ng. [illegible] ns pu[illegible]d-
ing t[illegible] wa[illegible] e twe[illegible] ders hoist
Meri[illegible]'s carcass into [illegible] ck [illegible] ma[illegible] ves

it a push and the cage swings back and forth like the pendulum in a grandfather clock. And I think about time again. But not for very long.

I have to shout to be heard over the downpour.

"Anyone who touches this body gets to be his roommate in Tartarus."

Samael goes back into the palace with the hellhounds and I step through a shadow.

Right into Mason's cell, where's he's asleep. I bark some hoodoo that should blow out all the surveillance cameras in the Vigil compound. Grab a fistful of Mason's jailbird jumpsuit and toss him across the cell into the steel door. That wakes him up in time for me to grab him again and toss him into a wall. Not too hard, just hard enough to keep him interested in the situation. I pull the black blade and hold it to his scarred throat.

"Prove to me that you'll teach me about the 8 Ball."

Mason looks up at me. What else is he going to do? I'm kneeling on his chest.

"What is it you want?" he wheezes, trying to get a breath.

I pull a quarter from my pocket.

"Call it in the air."

I toss the coin.

"Tails," he says.

I catch it and check. Show him the coin. It's heads.

I get up off his chest. He takes in a big lungful of air and I grab his hand. Bend his pinkie back, holding the blade tight against the top knuckle.

"Tell me something right now. Every time you lie I get to hurt you."

Bloody Hellion rain drips off me and covers the floor of Mason's cell. With my finger, I make up a scary-looking nonsense hoodoo circle and shove Mason into it. He slips and falls in the center just as Wells and the guards burst into the room. I'm out through a shadow by then. They'll find the circle and blame Mason for screwing the door and the cameras. One small consolation at the end of a shitty night.

I CAN'T STAND the idea of going home and listening to Kasabian whimper downstairs, so I head to Bamboo House of Dolls. I stand outside for a minute, letting the L.A. monsoon wash the last of the bloody Hellion rain out of my clothes.

Nothing but a skeleton crew in the bar. Carlos and a dozen or so hard-core drinkers. All Lurkers and Sub Rosa. Except for one.

"Jimmy," she says. "I was wondering if I'd see you here."

Brigitte comes over and kisses me on the cheek. She feels warm after being out in the rain and smells good after being Downtown. For a second, it's like something normal. Two friends running into each other at a favorite bar. But nothing is normal now and we both know it, though neither of us says anything.

"Nice to see you too. Buy you another martini?"

She empties her glass and sets it down on the bar.

"You must. I am bereft of drink."

Carlos comes over and takes a couple of light-beer bottles off the bar.

"The evening rush," he says, raising a hand to the nearly empty room. "I'm grateful for the few brave souls, but all anyone wants is beer and shots. If this kind lady hadn't ordered an actual drink, I would have drowned myself in the maraschino cherries."

thing together. Brief because Traven died killing Medea Bava and basically saving a lot of people's lives, including mine and Brigitte's.

"No, I didn't."

Traven was handed a first-class ticket Downtown when the Church excommunicated him for translating a forbidden book about the Angra. As far as most people know, Hell is where he went and Hell is where he stayed. I never wanted to tell Brigitte anything different because even though I stole Traven's soul out of Hell, he's still dead and I thought it was best for her to let him go. But with everything hanging by a thread, I'm not so sure anymore.

"I didn't see Traven because he's not in Hell."

Brigitte gives me a look. It's not quite surprise. More like confusion with just a little bit of hope.

"What does that mean? Where is he?"

"He was in Hell and it wasn't fair, so I did something about it."

"What?"

"I can't tell you everything, but I can tell you this much. He isn't stuck in Hell."

Her hand closes on my arm.

"Where is he?"

I don't want to tell her about taking him to Blue Heaven, a strange place outside of normal time. She might want to go there. I'm not willing to take her to a dead man she can't be with anymore.

"Listen. I dealt with it. He's in a better place. That's all I can tell you."

Getting Traven out of Hell cost me. I don't think Muninn

"Am I an unforgivable asshole? Unfair? Do I use people? Did I ever use either of you?"

"Used for what?" says Carlos. "If this is about the drinks and food, don't sweat it. You'll always eat and drink free as long as I run the place."

Brigitte says, "I don't think he's talking about that. I think he's talking about love."

That fucking word.

"Never mind," I say.

"Oh, Jimmy, I was only teasing."

"I know, and it's not about that. It's that whether I'm fucked up or not is beside the point. What's important is that the other person thinks I'm maybe too fucked up."

Brigitte shakes her head.

"That's not it at all. If someone unfairly accuses you of bad behavior or neglect, you are entitled to be upset, even angry about it."

I hate this. I can't deal with this angst bullshit. This is when I dream of Hell. Of the arena, where everything was simple and the closest thing to a next day was a knife in the belly or a club in the eye. Give me blood all the livelong day. What I can't take is all this being-human-and-being-responsible craziness. I want to tear my own head off. I want to go and snap Mason's neck. Chaya was right. I hate this place. Let the world burn and me with it.

"Never mind. Stupid question. Let's drop it."

Carlos picks up our glasses.

"For what it's worth, you're all right by me. I'll get us all another round."

He moves off to get our drinks, but I think what he's really doing is leaving me alone with Brigitte.

"Don't worry. I've got plenty on my plate. Till then, Ishii can piss his sorrows in a teapot and brew himself a hot cup of fuck off."

Carlos comes back with our drinks.

"What should we drink to?"

"To love," says Brigitte.

"To the few loyal customers I have left," says Carlos.

I have to think for a minute.

"To the dead. Let's think of them always, but not join them too soon."

Everyone in the bar drinks to that.

JULIE CALLS EARLY the next morning.

"Wells and the other bigwigs are at a meeting downtown. If you get over here right now, I can get you in to see Candy."

Lucky for me, I fell asleep in my clothes last night. I run a comb through my hair so I don't look like I escaped from Greendale House and go out through a shadow.

Julie is waiting for me when I come in and pulls me into an empty office.

She says, "As far as anyone knows, you're here to talk to her about Saint Nick. Got it?"

"Got it."

"Good. Now give me all your weapons."

"You too?"

She puts out her hand impatiently.

"It's procedure. And if any of the higher-ups come back early, it has to look like everything is by the book."

I hand her the Colt, the black blade, and my na'at. She puts them in an attaché case sitting on the desk.

"That's what they say."

"Is it true?"

She nervously twines her fingers in the netting threaded around the cell bars.

"I don't know. I didn't see the guy or anything, but Julie Sola told me about it and I trust her."

Candy looks at the cellblock door.

"They're never going to let me out of here, are they?"

"Why do you say that?"

"I hear the guards talking. They're not big fans of Jades. Or any Lurkers."

"Point them out and I'll have a word with them."

She shakes her head. Her shaggy hair is a mess, tangled and pressed down on one side.

"Don't do that. I don't want any more trouble. I just want to know what happened."

"You were poisoned. Someone spiked your Jade potion. You had a relapse and it affected your mind."

She looks at her twining fingers.

"Relapse. That's a funny word."

"What do you mean?"

"Relapse for me means going back to my true nature. Like you think who I am is a disease."

"Yeah. You said something like that when they brought you in, only louder."

"Did I? It's all such a blur."

She lets go of the net and takes a small step backward. Looks up at me.

"Is that what you think?" she says quietly. "That I'm just some kind of disease?"

"Well, he doesn't look so good right now. He tripped and fell into a wall a couple of times."

She smiles and wraps her arms around herself.

"Did I say something wrong the other night? I can't remember and you're acting funny. What happened?"

I shake my head.

"You didn't say anything. I'm just worried is all."

"If I said anything to hurt you, I didn't mean it."

"I know."

"You forgive me?"

"There's nothing to forgive."

"You're lying, but that's okay. Us jailbirds need the occasional hopeful lie."

She puts her hand up against the net and holds it there. I reach out for her.

The cellblock door slides open and I pull my hand back.

"Stark," says Julie. "It's time to go."

"Thanks for coming to see me," says Candy.

"I'll be back soon."

"If I'm not out by Christmas, bake me a gingerbread man with a file in it."

"Baby, I'll bake you a neutron bomb."

She stands at the bars watching until the door closes.

I walk with Julie back to the empty office.

"Thanks for letting me see her."

"Just remember. If anyone asks, you were talking to her about Mason."

"They really think she's working with Mason?"

"All Lurkers are suspect right now. If you're not human, you might as well be an Angra."

"That naughty boy."

"That he is. There's just one thing."

"What's that?"

"He wrote a spell in blood, but the only cut we could find on him was a scratch on his little finger. And he had a black eye and some bruised ribs. You wouldn't know anything about that, would you?"

"Maybe he fell off his bunk."

Wells purses his lips like he's thinking.

"That's what he said. I guess accidents happen. We just need to make sure they never happen again or we'll have to transfer all the other prisoners out of this facility. You understand?"

"Yeah. I get it."

"Are we done here?"

"I was done five minutes ago."

Wells takes my arm and leads me aside.

"Go in there and win today. The Shonin isn't looking so good. He's drinking that lousy poison book because you're not coming up with the goods. Get something useful today."

"I'm working on it."

"Don't work on it. Do it."

He lets go and moves off with his suits. I'll give him one thing. He's got quite a grip.

EVERY TIME I walk into Mason's cell I half expect to see one of the meat cathedrals. Pink light glowing off his smug face. Flayed guards hung upside down in narrow naves. It's almost disappointing when the door opens and it's the same flat fluorescent light as always. I think I'd prefer an Angra butcher

"Aristocrats played it, but you killed off most of the people who might've taught it to you."

"How does it work?"

Mason cuts the cards, breaks the deck, and slides half the cards to me.

"I take something from you and then I give you something. A card in this case. Hellion cards are more interesting, but we'll just have to make do. You take something from me and give me something. The one with the most at the end wins."

"What am I giving and taking?"

"Anything."

"That doesn't make sense."

"You'll get the hang of it. I'll go first so you'll see how it works."

He lays his hand on his cards.

"I take your heart and give you . . ."

He draws a card.

"A three of spades. Your turn."

"That's it? That doesn't tell me anything."

"Just try it."

I keep waiting for him to laugh in my face and explain the real game, but he just sits there. I draw a card.

"I take your lace doily and give you . . ."

I throw down the card.

"A two of diamonds."

"See? It's easy. I take your eyes and . . ."

He draws a card.

"Give you an ace of clubs."

I take a card.

"I take your bullshit and give you a nine of hearts."

Alice? Thinking about her let me beat you once before. All these little people you think you care about now are ruining your concentration. Don't make the same mistake you made eleven years ago."

We run through a few more nonsense hands. I'm not going to win. I have to salvage something from this.

"Tell me about Blackburn."

"The late great. What about him?"

"Why did you kill him?"

"Did I?"

He takes my soul and throws a five.

"Saint Nick sure did. And I know there's not another Saint Nick because you have too big an ego for that."

"The reason for killing Blackburn should be obvious. Without the Augur, the Sub Rosas will panic and split into factions, attacking each other. Of course, I've been busy. How do you know it wasn't my friends who killed Blackburn?"

"*Der Zorn Götter?* Forget it. I've seen their hoodoo and it would take more than that to get to the Augur."

"If anyone needed to get to him."

"An inside job? Ishii is an asshole, but he's better at his job than that."

"Play," he says.

"I take your sense of satisfaction and give you a queen of spades."

"Now you're talking," says Mason. "Of course, what if Ishii was Saint Nick? For a few minutes, I mean."

"Possession? I don't buy it. One of his people would have noticed if he showed up for lunch with a chain saw and twenty feet of intestines."

"Who knows? Besides, now that I think about it, it was probably me. I've killed so many they tend to blur together."

"You're really having fun, aren't you?"

"The time of my life. You know, in Tartarus I was adrift. Truly going mad. All I wanted was some sense of control. And now I have it and it feels great."

He draws a card.

"Now that I think about it, yes, I did kill Blackburn. I'm sure of it. Still, you might want to ask Tuatha about the clogged kitchen plumbing. Terrible timing too. While she's planning her husband's funeral and all."

"All these lies. They're obvious and boring."

"Is our biblical flood boring?"

"You're not claiming credit for the rain, are you?"

"No. That's the Angra. Just their approach brings calamity. Can you imagine what it will be like when they arrive?"

"It's like you've got Tourette's. All the shit that comes out of your mouth."

"I take your fear and give you the king of spades."

"I take your never seeing daylight again and give you a deuce of clubs."

"Tell the lovely Ms. Fortune to count her nightgowns. I bet she'll find one missing. Covered in blood and down the drain with her hubby's guts. Your turn."

I don't want to believe him, but he seems to be telling the truth. Maybe he meant what he said. Tartarus made him even crazier than when I put him in. He talks like a suicidal Hellion. Does he want me to kill him or does he want to kill himself? I'll tell Wells to put more guards on him.

"I mean, if you're incapacitated. Besides, the game is almost over. There's just a few more hands."

"Let me finish," says the Shonin.

He takes a step toward the table and his legs give out. I grab him by the shoulders and lift him up. He's just bones and robes. He weighs nothing. By the time I have him up, the cell door is open and guards are coming in, their guns drawn.

The Shonin punches me in the shoulder. It's so feeble I wouldn't have known it happened if I hadn't seen it.

"Put me down."

I set him on his feet.

"I'll finish with the book," he says. "I'm learning great things. But you must play the game. I can't do both."

"Go and lie down, old man. Let me handle this."

The guards help the Shonin out, locking the door behind him.

"That was dramatic," says Mason. "He's even more pathetic than you and Muninn. Always running to help the older gents. Those daddy issues run deep."

"You know if you call the Angra, they'll kill you too."

"All those L.A. good vibes you've picked up have made you afraid of death. But death is what you and I do."

There's only one thing I haven't tried.

"Forget it. I quit. You win."

Mason cocks his head like he's waiting for me to say something else. He sighs and pushes his cards away.

"I admit. That's the last thing I expected from you."

"Then I did win after all."

He smiles.

"No, but you fooled me. And you played horribly, even

side shitting fried green tomatoes, waiting for me to get more information, but I'm lucky Mason gave me this much.

"Thanks for the freebie."

Mason nods.

"Of course, I'm still going to hurt you."

I put my Kissi hand on the table and take off the glove.

"I owe you a finger. Take it."

He looks at it like a chef would look at rat shit in a Dumpster.

"I don't think I want it anymore. I'll have to hurt you some other way."

"I'm ready."

He shakes his head.

"Later. We're done for now. Come back around dinnertime for tomorrow's game. I have some preparations to make."

I put the glove back on, happy my hand was too ugly for even Mason to want it.

"Tomorrow then?" he says.

I think for a minute.

"Forget the Infinite Game. I'll play you Russian roulette again. This time by your rules."

He looks right through me.

"I'll watch, but that's your game. I want to play mine."

He gathers up the cards from the table.

"Send in the guards on the way out. I want to get started on the new game right away."

After checking on the Shonin and translating as much as I can remember of the conversation in Mason's cell into English, I head home. Vidocq calls about an hour later.

"I thought you'd want to know. They burned the clinic."

two pieces of divine light glass that heal most injuries. There are a couple of small vials on the end that I don't recognize.

"They're potions for Candy. Allegra made them fresh herself, so there's no chance of them being poisoned," says Vidocq.

I didn't hear him come in.

"How's Allegra doing?"

He shrugs.

"Badly. But it could be worse. Thank you for coming over."

"Anytime. What else can I do?"

He drops down onto the old couch. Rubs his eyes.

"Nothing. She's asleep now. I think when she wakes she'd like to be alone for a while to collect her thoughts."

"Sure. I'll take off."

"I don't mean to throw you out."

"Don't worry about it. But there's one thing," I say.

I set down a Desert Eagle .50 that some Satanists gave me a while back.

"That will shoot through a wall and still kill anything on the other side. Don't be shy about using it."

Vidocq picks up the gun and weighs it in his hand. Sights down the barrel. He nods.

"I don't like these things, but times like this force us to reconsider our prejudices."

"Call me if you need anything."

"Thank you."

"I know it will sound lame, but tell Allegra I'm sorry and I'll try to find out who did it."

"I'll tell her."

I ride the hog home. It's morning, but no brighter than it

I walk around the apartment. Look at Candy's things and wonder if I found something that might make her feel better, would Wells let me give it to her? I doubt it. He doesn't want to look like he's doing me any more favors than he's already done.

I keep hoping for a call that Mason wants me to come in early so we can get things over with. After yesterday's crash-and-burn, I don't want to lose my cool again. He's going to try another one of his nonsense games and I can't let it get to me. Follow Muninn's advice. Go with whatever Mason wants. Don't fight back. Watch him. Go total Zen on the little prick and see what happens.

Sometime in the night Kasabian stuffed towels around the bottom of the front door when water started leaking in. They're soaked through. I go down and replace them. There. That used up a whole two minutes. I keep checking the time.

Kasabian watches the news sometimes. I should ask him if things are this crazy in the rest of the world. But do I really want to know?

My phone rings. I grab it without bothering to check the number.

"You didn't think I was going to leave him to the vultures, did you?" says Deumos.

"Vultures. Worms. Hellhounds. It's all the same to me, as long as he's dead."

"You could've joined us, but that moment has passed."

"I guess so. Anything else on your mind?"

"Enjoy what's coming."

"Nothing is coming. I'm going to stop it and you're going to live a good long miserable life in Hell with all your idiot followers. Assuming they don't lynch you."

"Is Fairuza all right?"

"I don't know."

"What do you know?"

"Go downstairs and watch your movie. There's nothing you can do."

He comes over, looking like a tin toy John Wayne.

"Where is she?"

"LAPD and the feds are rounding up Lurkers."

"What's going to happen to her?"

"I don't know. They still have Candy at Vigil headquarters, so maybe they're just holding everyone until Washington decides what it wants."

"You're not going to let them hurt her, are you?"

"I don't even know where she is."

He takes a beer from the fridge, but he doesn't open it. Just stands there holding it.

"I have some of her stuff. We could do a locator spell."

I nod and smoke.

"Tell you what. You do it and tell me what you find. I'll see what I can do after that."

"Can't you help? You're the better magician."

"Am I? I'm not feeling so good hoodoo-wise right now."

"Mason's really getting to you, isn't he?"

"No. I just can't get these soup stains out of the drapes."

"You want some advice?"

"Not even a little."

"Kill him. He beat you once and sent you to Hell. He's going to beat you again and it'll be worse for everyone this time."

"I can't. He has information I need."

"He'll never give it to you."

"Is Brigitte in it?"

"No."

"Is there any nudity?"

"Not so far."

"Put it on and let's cross our fingers."

I WALK INTO Mason's cell a little after eight. He looks the same as usual. Sitting at his table in a prison jumpsuit, a cat-that-ate-the-canary grin on his face, and his handcuffs secured to the table. There's a little more slack in the cuffs today. The reason why is spread out in front of me, so big that the sides hang off the ends of the table.

It looks like Mason raided the Vigil's break room and didn't leave anything behind. Six or eight game boards—right off, I recognize Monopoly, Go, Risk, and backgammon—are duct-taped together to form a stripped-down version of Metatron's Cube, the mystical symbol that's part of the ritual I used to track down the meat-locker asshole, Joseph Hobaica, on his way to Hell. The Cube is a power symbol I used a lot back when Mason and I were in the same Magic Circle. Points to you, Mason, for remembering that.

The game boards are in the shape of a six-pointed star with a circle in the middle containing playing pieces. At the point of each star is another circle. Straight lines cut from a chessboard connect each of these outer circles. I don't bother asking how he got the boards apart or how he put them back together again because he'll lie and I don't need to start off aggravated.

"Did the trash fairy shit on your table for Christmas?"

Mason taps his fingers on the collection of game boards.

"Don't tell me you don't appreciate my work. It took me all night and all day to put this together."

The longer I look at the board, the less sense it makes. It's hypnotic. Like heat dancing off the asphalt in the desert. I get woozy staring at the twisted thing and soon I don't care about saving the world. I want to leave. I don't want to be in this room with this lunatic. I can't breathe. I can't think straight. The harder I try to understand the board, the dizzier I feel. Finally, I have to look away. And Mason sees all of it. All my weakness and doubt. Nothing I can do about it now. Hell, maybe feeling sick is part of the Infinite Game too. Maybe if I throw up on the board I'll get a free turn.

We start with thirteen pieces in the middle. Mason tosses a coin and I call it.

"Heads."

It's tails.

"You lose," he says. "You have to move seven pieces around the board to win. I only have to move six."

Naturally. I was losing before I walked in the room.

"One more thing. After each move we say . . ." He pronounces a Hellion word. It literally means "power to you," but is really a sarcastic version of "good luck." Something you say when you want to see someone face-plant.

Head games within head games.

Mason makes the first move. He closes his eyes and picks up a few Go stones.

Three black and two white.

"Three times two," he says. "I move six."

There's a three-inch-tall metal Empire State Building with the game pieces. He moves it six spaces along a piece of a Candy Land board. Then he growls, "Power to you."

It's my turn. I reach for the Go stones. He shakes his head.

The game goes on for another two hours. I know that somewhere Wells and the Shonin are watching us. I'd love to know what they're thinking right now. Especially the Shonin. Does he have any more of a clue about the game than I do?

Mason says, "Feel free to keep imitating my moves if it makes you feel better. With the rules changing, the move that hurts me might bring you luck."

He deserves a "fuck you," but I give him a "power to you" instead and he gives it right back to me.

The things we do to stay alive for another year. Another day. Another hour. The deals we make with the universe and ourselves. You start to feel dirty. I made plenty of deals Downtown. Found tricks to kill my way out of most of them. Why not? What's a deal with a Hellion worth? It's like a joke the Irish used to tell.

"What do you call a dead Englishman?"

"What?"

"A good start."

Where has all the killing and all the deals left me? Worse off than ever. I stopped Mason's Hellion war with Heaven, but looking back, maybe I should have let them go ahead with their attack. Let Ruach and his angels slaughter the legions from their golden fortress. The Hellions would have satisfied their suicide fetish and maybe that would have been enough to stop this apocalyptic freak show before it got rolling.

But I also stopped the war for my own selfish reasons. I wanted to get hold of Mason and kill him myself. Then I abandoned Hell to come home when I could have stayed and maybe stopped Merihim and Deumos and their Angra games before they came to Earth. When I left, I made a deal with myself. I [illegible] want [illegible] went [illegible] and se[illegible] [illegible] my [illegible] go back to [illegible] lost so[illegible] [illegible] more [illegible] bad [illegible]. Only [illegible] gave [illegible] L.A. [illegible] never g[illegible] Saint[illegible] Deumos [illegible] time they n[illegible]. That [illegible] dead-as [illegible] nail [illegible] so [illegible] he c[illegible] [illegible] respo[illegible] for Mason [illegible] his [illegible] to repla[illegible] Russ[illegible] pat[illegible] would [illegible] laugh if [illegible] I was [illegible] this [illegible]. I even s[illegible] save [illegible] good guy[illegible] Seven [illegible]s. I sh[illegible] [illegible] rice far[illegible] the ma[illegible] Doc [illegible] [illegible] in H[illegible] one [illegible] jo[illegible] a ra[illegible] out for [illegible] right, s[illegible]one [illegible] that [illegible] and [illegible] more. I'd [illegible] n't [illegible] [illegible] killing [illegible] Angr[illegible] on c[illegible] the [illegible] I won't [illegible] that m[illegible] him [illegible] [illegible]rmation [illegible] the di[illegible] pers[illegible] [illegible] visit him [illegible] entrance t[illegible] May[illegible] see i[illegible] he ne[illegible] out [illegible] Styx. [illegible] [illegible]ndy wa[illegible] summer [illegible] she [illegible] [illegible] any [illegible] than L.A., the[illegible] [illegible] work [illegible] Hell's [illegible] [illegible] way [illegible]

But fi[illegible] the game [illegible] before [illegible] in.

"Earth[illegible] [illegible] re?" [illegible]

Beauti[illegible] lost [illegible] saw [illegible] good start to [illegible] matic conclu[illegible]

"Is it [illegible]"

"There's [illegible] of [illegible]

"I don't know what to do."

"It's an easy round. Draw a card. Move that many spaces. Eleven for a face card. Twelve for an ace."

I draw a five. I move a white checker across five countries on a Risk board. I don't know if the move is legit, but Mason doesn't say anything.

"Don't forget," he says.

I growl, "Power to you."

"Good boy," he says, eyeing his next move.

He spins the number wheel and moves a Go stone.

"Now that we've been playing for a while, are you figuring out the game?"

"I've got it down. I'm going to write a goddamn book about it."

"I'm not sure I entirely believe you."

"Why's that?"

"Because I just won."

I look over the board. He's moved each of his six pieces into one of the six circles on the tips of the star.

"But you didn't touch all the spaces on the board."

He gives an exaggerated sigh.

"You didn't really think I'd play something that tedious, did you? I told you I might lie as part of the game. I'm just sad you weren't paying more attention."

"I'll fucking kill you."

"Too late, Sandman Slim."

He slams his right hand down on the metal Empire State Building. It goes all the way through. Blood splatters the board, pooling under his palm.

He shouts, "Power to you!"

I shout, "Stop it. Or I'll make you stop."

"I told you I'd rather die than go back to Tartarus. You let these people and their rules muddle your head. You could have killed me when you found me, but you didn't. More fool you."

Gunshots crack against the cell door. More shots as the guards return fire. Then it stops. The door opens. Wells comes in.

"Wells. He started the ritual. We have to stop it."

"You can't stop it," says Mason. "I'm the only one who knows how. That's why I'm the end of the ritual."

Mason closes his eyes.

Wells brings up his Glock and empties the clip into Mason's head. Keeps pulling the trigger even after the last bullet is gone.

I knock the gun out of his hand and shoulder-butt him. He hits the steel wall, but he doesn't go down.

This isn't over. I still have time to use the Metatron's Cube ritual to find Mason before he goes to Hell. I'll crack his arms and legs until he tells me how to stop the summoning.

Like everything else today, that plan doesn't work out so well.

I grab the 8 Ball, hoping that will slow down the summoning. It responds like it did when the Shonin and I used it on the chop-shop body. First, it wraps itself lovingly around my Kissi hand. Then it draws Mason's soul out of his goddamn corpse. I swear the fucker is smiling as it happens. And just like it did with the Qliphoth, it eats Mason's soul.

The last of the ritual. The Angra's stooge sets off the summoning, then sacrifices himself so that no one can stop it. A hell of a fail-safe. And Mason's last laugh at me.

The building lurches again, harder this time. A steady

self again. I don't think he's noticed the blood on his nice suit where he shot the Vigil agents as he broke into Mason's cell.

"Stark," he says. "What happened to the Shonin? Did you move the Qomrama? Why?"

"I was trying to save the world again. More than you've been doing."

"Mason is dead in there. Did you kill him?"

"Guess again. You did it."

Wells loses his balance on the wreckage. Takes a couple of steps back.

"That's ridiculous. You smuggled in a gun."

He turns to the door.

"Guards. Get in here. Arrest this man."

"They have you on surveillance putting a bullet into Mason's skull. You're fucked. Welcome to my world."

"Quiet," he says. "You're unstable. It was a mistake to ever try to work with you."

"You might want to start running, Richard Kimble."

A group of agents comes in, led by Julie Sola.

"Marshal Sola, arrest this man for the murder of Mason Faim."

"I can't do that, sir."

"Why not?"

She takes out her handcuffs.

"Because you shot him. Along with four other agents standing guard. Chief Deputy Marshal Larson Wells, I'm placing you under arrest for murder."

He looks at them, then at me.

"It's true, Wells. But it wasn't your fault."

I turn to Julie.

[illegible] possessed [illegible] testify [illegible]

[illegible] up. Tries [illegible] standing [illegible]

has [illegible] right now. I'll tell [illegible] that it [illegible]

[illegible] going [illegible] weigh [illegible]

Was [illegible] suits who [illegible] is Gr[illegible] telling [illegible]

[illegible] finger.

"[illegible] happened [illegible]," he says.

"[illegible] started the [illegible] ritual, [illegible] Ba[illegible]

[illegible] stopped i[illegible]ed. B[illegible] was open

for [illegible] seconds."

"[illegible] said W[illegible]

"[illegible] something," he [illegible] "Fix the [illegible] your

job [illegible] your respons[illegible]

[illegible] but [illegible] don't [illegible] ready [illegible] t[illegible]

pa[illegible] compoun[illegible]

I'[illegible] to Candy [illegible] is jam[illegible] ha[illegible]

[illegible] times before [illegible] creaks

[illegible] pressed again [illegible] trying [illegible] who's [illegible]

[illegible] and blown [illegible] own.

"[illegible]?"

"[illegible]," I say, and [illegible] her cell.

She grabs me wh[illegible] and [illegible] through [illegible]

[illegible]

"[illegible] going on [illegible]?"

"[illegible] a party. Th[illegible] twenty [illegible] a Chr[illegible]

[illegible]

[illegible] perhaps her [illegible] mine.

"They're putting [illegible] in my [illegible]

[illegible] can't think [illegible] stay a[illegible]

[illegible] case?"

"There's no going back if I do this."

"The world is ending. Who's going to come after us?"

"The Vigil will. And it won't be an arrest. They'll shoot you like Old Yeller."

"I don't care."

I slip into her cell through a shadow and she throws her arms around me. Not like it's great to see me. More like she wants to make sure I'm not a drug illusion. She feels weak and drunk in my arms. She is definitely on something. I bring her to a shadow.

"Last chance to not be a fugitive forever."

"Take me home."

"I have to come back and talk to the Shonin."

"I'll bake an apple pie to pass the time."

I kiss her and we step through the Room and out again into Max Overdrive.

Kasabian is eating microwave chow mein when he sees us. He blinks at Candy.

"I thought you were under arrest."

"It wasn't any fun. And I missed you," she says.

I have to hold up her upright.

"Get over here," I say.

"Is she safe?" he says.

"She's fine. Don't be such a jellyfish and get over here."

He puts down the chow mein and comes over. I put her arm around his shoulders. Candy smiles at us.

"Do-si-do, boys."

I aim them at the stairs.

"Take her to our room. She'll show you where my guns are. If anyone but me tries to get in, shoot them."

"He's got his own problems."

"Like me," he says, waving around his crushed arm.

"A little while ago, you told me I was the 8 Ball's uncle. Is there some way we can use that?"

He picks up the teacup and studies it.

"You have something that the Angra need. And I don't mean the Qomrama."

"I have a gun, a knife, and a video store. What the hell do they want with me?"

He sips the tea.

"Tell me about your old Hellion master, Azazel."

"He bought and paid for me when I was still in the arena. I still had to fight sometimes, but from then on I also had to play slave boy to one of the most powerful Hellions Downtown."

"You were his assassin."

"Yeah. Mainly other upper-crust Hellions. Anyone with pull. Anyone who pissed him off or got in his way."

"His political enemies."

"Right."

"He told you this?"

"No. But it was obvious. I was only killing off other generals and blue bloods. Hellions that had Lucifer's ear. Hellions are like Sub Rosas. Heavy into social status. Azazel wanted to be number one. Right behind the boss himself."

"And all the years you were killing for him you had the key to the Room of Thirteen Doors inside you. You could have escaped Hell at any time."

"He told me that my old girlfriend Alice was safe as long as I stayed. Then she was dead and I knew he'd been lying. So

The Shonin looks at me with his big empty eye sockets.

"He invented you. He invented Sandman Slim to destroy the universe."

I feel a little queasy inside, like when I was looking at Mason's game board.

"It would probably have worked if Mason hadn't killed Alice."

"Now Mason has brought down the Angra to destroy us all. And he used you to do it. Quite a revenge."

"Mason was right all along. He was the better magician."

"That's all you have to say, fatty? No bluster? Nothing clever?"

"How do I stop it?"

He sets the teacup on the desk. There's a fine crack running from the lip to the base.

"Lock yourself in the Room and blow your brains out so no one else can use it. You can't stop the Angra from coming, but you can stop them from spreading across the universe."

"As long as I can burn all of creation with the Mithras, I'm not offing myself."

I look up at the rain coming down through the ceiling. The clouds open to reveal the stars beyond. The twinkly bastards look kind of ominous to me right now.

"On the other hand, your stupid idea gives me a good one."

"Tell me," says the Shonin.

"Later. If you eat all your vegetables. Right now I need all the protective wards and sealing charms you have."

The Shonin waves a bony hand at me.

"Idiot. You can't seal the Room. You need it to fight the

The lights come back on.

"You're with me on this?"

"Go. Do what you need to do," says the Shonin.

With all the rubble around, there are plenty of nice shadows. I step through one and head Downtown.

I COME OUT by the elevators in Mr. Muninn's penthouse. Lucifer's penthouse. I'll always have a hard time thinking of him as the Devil. I should never have guilted him into taking the job. He's not cut out for it and now I might have to ask him to do something worse.

Chaya is by the big picture window watching the red rain fall. I clear my throat and he turns my way.

"How dare you break in here?"

"I didn't break in. Mr. Muninn said I could come in whenever I wanted."

"Muninn. You don't even know his real name."

"He goes by Muninn and that's good enough for me."

"Not for me."

Chaya sweeps his hand across the room and I'm Peter Pan doing a clumsy air pirouette, before slamming into the far wall and hanging there like a mounted moose head.

"I'd say this is what all you ungrateful mortals deserve, but you're not a mortal, are you? Still, you're good practice."

My throat closes up. I try to get some air. Can't. The world shrinks to a very small dot and I can't believe that after all I've been through I'm going to die because some metaphysical buzzkill is having a tantrum.

I hear Muninn's voice.

"W[illegible] the con[illegible]en, "[illegible]ut hi[illegible] own [illegible]

"I'v[illegible] with thi[illegible] Do[illegible]u see? [illegible] or la[illegible]r he'll [illegible] Godeater [illegible]s."

"L[illegible]."

I [illegible]t's going [illegible] I'm [illegible] on the [illegible] of fainting, but Ch[illegible]nts me to [illegible] eve[illegible]nute [illegible] game, so he won't [illegible] Even whe[illegible] wi[illegible] all he air go[illegible] still awake [illegible] the [illegible] a gre[illegible] garag[illegible]

M[illegible]eps in fro[illegible] his [illegible]er and [illegible]n. Ch[illegible] is s[illegible] enough to [illegible] bo[illegible] car[illegible] Mu[illegible]es a smal[illegible] and [illegible] into m[illegible] lung[illegible] a long, co[illegible] Even [illegible]g Heli[illegible] air [illegible]d right [illegible]

C[illegible]ubs his ch[illegible] Mu[illegible]oks [illegible] kill, [illegible]gra would [illegible]s pie[illegible]d to [illegible] with[illegible]

M[illegible]says, "St[illegible] h[illegible]ore tha[illegible] opp[illegible] nity [illegible] on us an[illegible] hasn['t] done so."

"[illegible]iller."

"[illegible] friend."

"[illegible]lk like t[illegible]ng an[illegible]ns us [illegible]

[illegible] comes o[illegible] he[illegible]e get[illegible]et.

"[illegible] all right?"

[illegible] use a dri[illegible]

[illegible] pours me [illegible]m a d[illegible]n the [illegible] tak[illegible]iff the st[illegible] good. [illegible]rus h[illegible] sm[illegible] to Earth [illegible] caver[illegible] his [illegible] t[illegible] I can't bl[illegible] him. [illegible]eing h[illegible] That [illegible] all over. I swallow the drink. It tastes like good whiskey and honey and burns like an August wildfire all the way down my mangled throat.

"Feeling better?"

"Yeah. Thanks."

Samael comes in wearing a silk bathrobe, like Cary Grant looking for Katharine Hepburn.

"I heard noise. Did I miss anything fun?"

I give him the finger. He looks at me slumped on the couch and Chaya's red face.

"I did. Damn."

"Shut your mouth, child," says Chaya to Samael. "You never did know your place."

"My place? I'm quite comfortable in Hell, Father. You're the one who looks like a peacock in the Sahara."

"Enough, you two," says Muninn.

He takes the empty glass from my hand and sits down across from me.

"Why are you here, James?"

I cough a couple of times, trying to get my voice back.

"The Angra are on their way. Mason did the summoning ritual. I stopped it before he was done, but something still got through."

Muninn turns and looks out the window.

"It had to happen. It was just a matter of time. Still, if we had a little longer maybe there's something else . . . I don't know. We'd be so much stronger if we could reunite with Ruach."

"He'd rather die and see us dead first," says Chaya.

I set down my glass.

"We'll still be incomplete. Nefesh and Neshamah are dead."

"The alternative is for one of us to die and we'd be weaker still."

"I don't trust the Abomination. He is made of lies."

"We should try."

"I won't do it."

"Yes. You will."

Muninn lunges at his brother. Grabs him by the shoulders and pushes him into the wall hard enough that they leave a dent. Chaya grabs Muninn's arms and spins him around. Now he's against the wall and Chaya tries to push him away, but only succeeds in driving him farther into the drywall. Muninn hugs his brother, pulling Chaya's body onto his. Their bodies blur, like a camera going out of focus, then sharpening again. They're drained of color. Just a couple of round gray men settling a family squabble that's been festering for aeons. Muninn lays his hands on Chaya's face, and when he pulls them back, Chaya's skin comes with him, stretching like warm taffy. Chaya pushes away, but Muninn leans in like he wants to head-butt his brother. Everywhere Muninn touches Chaya, they sink into each other. Chaya fights back, pulling away from Muninn so their half-melted flesh rips and snaps. But each time he does, Muninn moves in again, and they sink into each other. They fall on the floor, a writhing gray mass of furious protoplasm.

Then it stops. The mass breaks apart. The two brothers lie sprawled on the carpet, each regaining his color. Muninn sits up first. He tries to talk, but he's out of breath.

"It won't work. Chaya is too resistant and I'm too weak."

not to be a deity. And Chaya, dog shit in a tight suit, but one who'll never give up. He'll fight forever to stay alive.

Samael and I get in the elevator and go down to the basement and the kennels.

"Do me a favor and make sure the hounds are hungry and ready to go. I have a feeling we'll need them before the night is over."

He looks around at the beasts pawing at their cages.

"I'll make sure. And I'll join you in Los Angeles when Father settles on how he wants to handle things."

"We should talk about that."

"How so?"

"Later. When you come to town. For now work on the dogs. I need to make a stop before going home."

"I'd give you one of the cars, but you don't want to be seen in the streets. Neither do I. Not after what we did to Merihim."

"You sorry about that?"

"Not in the slightest."

"Good. See you Uptown."

"Don't destroy the world without me."

I step into a shadow and come out by the deserted market across from Wild Bill's bar.

PANDEMONIUM IS AS waterlogged as L.A. and just as deserted. Are all the little Hellions huddled in their grimy Hobbit holes or, like L.A.'s scaredy cats, on the run, hoping to find a haven less obviously doomed?

I walk through the bloody downpour and push open the door to the bar.

[illegible] coming h[illegible] [illegible] the [illegible] [illegible] teals and [illegible] a Texas [illegible] seated at a [illegible] front of them [illegible] don't even [illegible]

[illegible] mething [illegible] iff of the [illegible] bother w[illegible] One of the[illegible] ght. Four [illegible] le platoon [illegible] y hands up [illegible] of me gets [illegible] ry coat, fe[illegible] ing solid, [illegible] That he go[illegible] dy brawn [illegible] at and [illegible] under his [illegible] counted th[illegible] been crouch[illegible] goldcoats [illegible] e still hol[illegible] ing knocks [illegible] too far [illegible] Hellion a[illegible] than I real[illegible] gun, but I can't, so I pull the na'at. I feign a fall, and as the cold-cocker moves in to hit me again, I swing the na'at, extending it into a barbed spear. It goes deep into the soldier's gut, and when I pull it back, a fair amount of insides comes with it. The sight freezes his buddies long enough for me to get out the black blade and toss it through the eye of a soldier by the jukebox.

A legionnaire by the bar pops off a few shots. Seeing his friends go down so fast must have spooked him because he fires wildly, murdering furniture and the floor. I move in on him as he finally remembers he's a soldier and raises his gun. He hits me twice in the chest and I go down face-first.

I'm beginning to think no one in Hell likes me.

I try to sit up and meet a gun barrel halfway there. Mr. Sausage Fingers has his Glock pointed at my head. He squeezes the trigger and there isn't a goddamned thing I can do about it.

A gun goes off and the first thing I notice is how extremely not dead I am and how Mr. Sausage Fingers has a fist-size hole in his chest. I look over and there's Cindil, shaky-legged, her mouth open like she's either going to puke or sing "America the Beautiful," holding my Colt. She shoots again and Mr. Sausage Fingers hits the deck.

Cue all hell breaking loose. The three remaining legionnaires open up on the room, some shooting at me and some at the others. I roll behind Sausage Fingers' body, find his dropped Glock, and fire back. My hand is unsteady enough that I hit absolutely nothing of interest.

Cindil keeps firing my Colt, even while Bill drags her behind the bar. I don't know if she hits any of the soldiers, but she looks fierce enough to give them something to worry about.

"You can't stay here and you can't come back. More soldiers will come looking for their friends."

"You can't stay either. You're both coming with me."

"Where to?" says Cindil.

"To meet Lucifer. Well, retired Lucifer. He'll explain it."

By the time I finish the drink my head feels like it's back on straight again. I get up and head for a shadow.

"You two coming?"

They follow me over and I lead them through the Room and out again into the hellhound kennel.

Samael is still there, smoking a Malediction and drinking from a silver flask. He raises his eyebrows at us.

"That was quick," he says. Then eyes my shirt. "But you took the time to hurt yourself again. If only you were this productive when you ran Hell."

Cindil looks at me.

"You ran Hell?"

"I was more of a summer intern. Samael will explain everything."

I point to each of them in turn.

"This is Cindil and this is Wild Bill. Take care of them, will you?"

Samael graciously offers his flask to his guests. Both decline.

"Of course I will. And then I'll wash your car, shall I?"

"You know I ride a bike these days. But it could use some detailing."

I nod toward the cages.

"You three might want to get out of here. I'm letting the hounds out."

Samael leads Bill and Cindil to the elevator.

As the doors close Samael says, "Love you in red, James."

"It is good to finally meet, Sandman Slim. I heard so much about you from Aswangana."

"How is Lamia? She looked better in a party dress."

"You could have killed her when she was in such a vulnerable form. Why did you hesitate?"

"I guess I felt sorry for her. Fucked over once by God and again by the people controlling her earthly form."

The God cocks his head. It goes from the blond man to a bird's skull to something dark and gelatinous.

"Sympathy for a fallen God," he says. "That is why we respect you. You have a better sense of us than most. That is why I'm here. The nephilim and Angra are outcasts together. Join us and be an outcast no more."

"What's your name?"

He looks at me like it's a strange question.

"I do not have a name. My name is the sound of the trembling void between the stars."

"Listen, Shaky, some of your friends already tried the sales pitch. I told them no and I'll tell you no. I understand how pissed off you are. I've felt it too. It isn't easy being the only one of me in a universe where everyone hates you. But I can't let you destroy the place. All my friends are here, and so's my stuff. I mean, I just got *Bullet for the General* on Blu-ray."

"I know you cannot use the Qomrama Om Ya. Give it to me. Only a portion of me came through the rift. I will summon myself and then the other Angra. You will see. It will be glorious."

"It's not just me, you know. The Vigil will fight you. The Sub Rosa too."

the vertebrae and muscle at the back so his head pops off and slops onto the wet ground. Shaky kneels down and picks it up.

"Let's see if you can put yourself together before I figure out the 8 Ball."

Shaky sets his head onto his shoulders and walks away into the dark.

Rain begins to fall again.

So, to sum up. Tonight I had my throat crushed. I was tossed around like a beanbag. I was beaten with a gun butt. I was shot. And now another God hates me. I want a smoke, but when I cough I taste blood. Maybe some bullet fragments in a lung. I put the Maledictions back in my pocket.

It's nights like this that make me want to give up the glamorous work of world saving and take up woodworking or needlepoint. Something soothing and without quite so much ass kicking aimed in my direction.

I wipe the blood off my mouth and head inside.

THE PLACE IS still a mess. Marshals clear away wreckage and try to salvage equipment. They're dispatching patrols to make sure the rest of the city didn't fall down. Rain pours in through the roof, making the floor slick and dangerous. No one pays the slightest attention to me.

The Shonin's lab is still a wreck, but a pathway has been cleared from the door to his worktable. He's picking through the wreckage, looking for books and manuscripts he might be able to save. When he hears me he drops into his chair, cradling his broken arm in his good one.

"So, did you mess everything up, fatso?"

club. A funny end to a strange life. But he came through when he had to, and that's more than I can say for most people.

I straighten him upright in the chair and lay his hands in his lap in the Dhyana mudra, the only bit of dilettante L.A. Buddhism I can remember.

Someone is at the door. I look up and see Julie. She stops and grimaces.

"You're shot."

"Yeah. I'm hard on clothes."

"Where have you been?"

"I just got my ass kicked in Hell. How are you?"

She comes in and looks around the room.

"I never know what to believe when you open your mouth."

"Want to meet the Devil?" I put out my hand. "Just say the word."

"I'll pass."

I try to angle myself between her and the magnetic chamber, hoping she won't notice that it is gone. But she isn't looking at me. She's spotted the Shonin and goes over to him.

"My God. What happened?"

"I think the book finally finished him. Will you take care of his body?"

She shakes her head.

"I can't. We have a report of a mob of Saint Nick's corpses around Hollywood Forever Cemetery. They're starting to move into the streets, destroying everything in the way. Believe it or not, there are still civilians in the city."

Hollywood Forever. I can't get away from the place. When I die for the last time, dump me in the ocean or a landfill or

[illegible] and [illegible] the state [illegible]
[illegible] Forester.

"[illegible] hard [illegible]."

"By yourself?" [illegible]

"I'll have [illegible] don't want [illegible] anyone in."

[illegible] that happened, these [illegible]

"Listen. After [illegible] I don't know [illegible]
[illegible] to get out [illegible] meeting [illegible]
[illegible] the [illegible] for an hour [illegible]

"This [illegible]
[illegible] of our [illegible]

She [illegible]

"Hal [illegible]"

"Go [illegible]"

I start [illegible]

"You [illegible] somebody [illegible]?"

She looks [illegible]

"[illegible] I in."

"Yeah. [illegible]"

"[illegible] something?"

"[illegible] me a favor."

Harvey [illegible]

"Why [illegible]"

"Because [illegible] I'll [illegible]."

"[illegible]"

When I [illegible] I take a shower [illegible]
[illegible] and head D[illegible] Not
[illegible] else who c[illegible]
[illegible] a [illegible]

hounds wander restlessly. I'm in and out fast in case anyone wanders down here. I only have a half hour and I don't want to spend it explaining anything to anyone.

As soon as I corral the last hounds I lead them into a shadow at the far end of the place. Their growls and the grinding of their gears fill the air. Their claws tear up the concrete. It's beautiful.

We come out right in front of Hollywood Forever.

Julie said there were chop shops here and she wasn't exaggerating. Only they're not in the cemetery anymore.

It's like New Year's fucking Eve outside the gates. Wall-to-wall, shoulder-to-shoulder Qliphoth morons claw their way onto Santa Monica Boulevard. When the street opens up enough that they have room, they head off in different directions, splashing like happy monster pups off to gnaw on what's left of L.A.'s soggy carcass.

I don't have to tell the hellhounds what to do. They sense it the moment they get a look at Mason's berserkers and rip into the mob without a word from me. The chop shops fight back, but they're just stitched together meat salads and no match for a hyped-up mob of mechanical hellspawn. In just a minute, it's like a holiday sale at Ed Gein's butcher shop. Arms and legs in the half-price bin. Bones and livers on special, two for one.

I can't say the carnage is pretty, but it is satisfying. Mason got the better of me with the games, but I can take back a little from him by flattening his street muscle.

The hounds are well trained. They don't hang around playing with the dead chop shops. Groups of them peel off and follow the rest of the mob through the storm into town.

"Come on, guys. We're wasting time. Let me just show you my ID."

"If you do not comply we are authorized to use deadly force."

I should have seen that coming. Martial-law bullshit. Shoot looters on sight and harass stragglers while you're at it.

I walk backward to the men in blue. It's not as easy as it sounds in ankle-deep water with your hands over your head throwing off your balance. But I make it out of Dixie and into the promised land of the cops' headlights.

"The ID is in my back pocket if you want to get it out yourselves."

I hear someone splash up behind me.

"Don't even breathe," he says.

He sounds like the nervous type, so I keep my hands up and my mouth shut while he spelunks in my jeans.

"What's this?" he says, pulling the Colt from behind my back.

"That's my gun. Like I've been saying, I'm with the Golden Vigil."

He reaches into my back pocket and comes out with something. It's quiet behind me for a while. Maybe reading wasn't his strongest area back at the academy. I'm sure he has other redeeming qualities.

"Stark," he says. "James Stark."

"That's me."

"The Golden goddamn Vigil."

"Can I put my hands down now?"

"Hey, boys," he says, calling to the other cops. "Want to meet a real live Vigil agent?"

The sound of splashing coming up behind me. No one

back. I hear the rattle of cuffs and know that if the bastard ever gets them on me I'm dead.

I push back with one hand and buck the cop off. Then I have the other three on top of me and I can't move. Someone else gets their cuffs out. I feel one close on my wrist. Even though I know I'm going to lose, I'm not going to make killing me easy. I kick back and launch one of them off me and get a swift knee to the back of my head. It forces me all the way down under the filthy street water. I have to hold my breath to keep from drowning. I can't even fight anymore.

At first, the sound of screams is muffled by the water. It churns around me as one by one the cops disappear off my back. I sit up and gulp in a lungful of air.

Hellhounds are outlined in the squad-car headlights. One gnaws on a downed cop's leg and the others are off chasing the rest. I hear gunshots, but can't see out into the dark. I don't have to because I know what's happening. The cops are losing. Hellhounds are bad one-on-one. When they're in a pack, there isn't much that can stop them. Sure as hell not a few cop sidearms.

I crawl over to the downed cop and feel around his belt. Find his keys and unlock the handcuff snapped around my wrist. I get up and look around the scene for my gun and ID. I find both by one of the squad cars. The gun is all right, but the ID is a little waterlogged. I slip it into my pocket and put the Colt in the waistband behind my back. Candy has been on me to get a holster. She says my not using one is part of my just-passing-through mentality and that I should get over it. Maybe she's right. Not necessarily about the holster, but about the passing-through thing. Here I am half drowned and

"Just who the fuck do you think you are?"

"The wronged returned for retribution," he says.

The squad car fishtails to a stop fifty feet from us. The cops get out and hunker down behind the doors. They don't bother with pistols. One has a shotgun and the other an HK rifle.

"Put your hands on your head," shouts the woman cop.

Shaky looks at me. I shrug.

"I'm not doing it. But you can do what you want."

He looks at the cops and says, "Die, God's favorites."

The cops evaporate, like ice dropped into boiling water.

"I could have used that trick five minutes ago."

Shaky turns back to me.

"Give me the Qomrama. I won't ask again."

"No."

"Do you doubt who I am?"

"I know who you are, but it's in my best interest not to give a damn."

Shaky walks to the corner, by the old Hollywood First National Bank Building. Like a lot of L.A. buildings, it can't decide what it wants to be when it grows up. A weird mix of Gothic, Art Deco, with a little Spanish thrown in, it's the perfect place for Shaky to duck into—an empty eleven-story hulk, way past its sell-by date. Just like him.

Only he doesn't duck inside. Shaky strolls into a wall, softens, spreads out like mist, and merges with the concrete.

I hear his voice in my head.

"Perhaps my godly power will not hurt you as long as you possess the Qomrama, but that does not mean you cannot be hurt."

The building shakes like we're having another quake, but the street stays perfectly still. It's just the bank that's moving.

Ruach cocks his head this way and that. Blind, he's listening for Shaky, but Muninn said he's half deaf too, so his moves are slow and tentative. But that doesn't mean he's helpless.

Shaky reaches for him and the whole street rumbles and shakes. Ruach swings his arms in Shaky's direction and lets go with a thunderbolt that leaves me blind for a few seconds. When I can see again, Shaky is flat on his back. He slams his concrete-and-steel fists into the street, crushing cars and knocking over streetlights, hauling himself back onto his feet. He roars, blowing out windows up and down the boulevard. I put my hands over my ears and watch him lunge at the small figure of Ruach.

The God brother doesn't move as the bank lands on top of him, leaving a deep crater in the intersection. Shaky stands with Ruach in his giant mitt. He raises his arm and slams Ruach into the crater.

For a moment there's only the sound of the rain. Then another thunderbolt explodes from the crater, hitting Shaky full on, shattering the windows in his chest. Plate glass cascades like a shower of diamonds into the street.

This fight has been a long time coming. How long has it been since Ruach and Shaky have seen each other? A few billion years ago when God was still in one piece and he gave the Angras the bum rush out of town. That's a long time to nurse a grudge. It must be the way I feel about Sylvester Stallone after he remade *Get Carter.*

Shaky staggers as Ruach steps out of the crater. He makes a sweeping gesture and the crushed cars and trucks all along one side of Hollywood Boulevard rapid-fire launch themselves at the bank. Concrete shatters. Steel snaps. But Shaky

If I wasn't trying to dodge a couple of angry Gods, I might have looked her over before I got too close. The Eater in her chop-shop body doesn't appreciate my dime-store chivalry and lets me know by trying to gnaw my arm off.

I'm hurt and I don't have time for this noise. I shove the 8 Ball in her face. The moment it touches her she screams. I pull the Qomrama back, drawing the Eater out of her body. As it dies, the woman face-plants in the street.

I head back for the bike, but Ruach is headed there too. I'd bet that, even blind, he saw the 8 Ball light up like a flare and he knows exactly where to find me. He runs toward me, his scarred yellow body glowing into holy fire. I hold up the 8 Ball and it just seems to make him angrier. There's nowhere for me to run.

"Father."

Ruach slows and looks around.

"Father, what are you doing wasting time with this mortal? Your enemy is behind you."

Samael walks calmly across the shattered boulevard to stand beside me.

Ruach points.

"He used the Godeater."

"Not on you."

Ruach starts to say something else when a concrete hand the size of a truck grabs him and pulls him away.

"This might be a good moment to leave," says Samael.

"Hold on a second. I have an idea."

I grab the Hellion hog and roll it off the street, hiding it in a flooded restaurant, between the broken furniture and the islands of rotting arugula.

"That's sweet. Do you have my ice cream?"

"Not exactly. But I have a corpse and a few hundred hellhounds. And I stole a cop car."

"That's fun. Pick me up. We'll toss a coin to see who gets the handcuffs first. A car will be harder to break than furniture, but maybe more fun."

"Sounds great, but I'm sort of busy right now. I did mention the corpse and hellhounds, right?"

"Fine. Be a drag. But come home soon. I don't want to spend my last hours on Earth drinking peppermint tea with Kasabian."

"Peppermint tea?"

"I'm still a little dizzy. Peppermint helps."

"I'm living with a hippie."

"Shut up, thief. For once don't forget to wipe your prints off the car before you ditch it."

"Anything else, dear?"

"Seriously, if it looks like things aren't going to work out, come home."

"They're going to work out."

"But if they don't."

"I'll be there."

"What's the corpse for?"

"A long shot. Got to go."

"Don't forget the handcuffs."

"I know. And ice cream."

I hang up. I don't have the heart to tell her that the handcuffs disappeared with the cops.

need you to do the opposite here. Seal these doors. Use whatever powers you have to lock them tight so they can never be opened again."

He raps on the last door with his knuckles.

"This one is already sealed."

"That's the Door to Nothing. I sealed it, but I didn't know what I was doing. I need it done right."

"Why?"

"It's where the Kissi lived."

He makes a face.

"You did us all a favor locking them out. What's that door?"

"The Door to Fire. Listen, we don't have time for a full tour."

"This is probably the last chance I'll get to see the place."

"Me too, so stop whining."

I check the time on my phone. It's nine thirty.

"Make sure you bring Mr. Muninn and Chaya to Pershing Square by ten."

"Why there and why then?"

"It's a nice open space. I want to keep clear of big buildings. And I want to make this happen soon. The longer we fuck around, the more Shaky and Ruach are going to trash the city."

"And the world."

"That too."

"Ten o'clock then."

"When Shaky gets there be ready. Things are going to happen fast."

"Of course."

"And let me handle the big stuff. If I need help, you'll know it."

"Good to see you. Please come in," he says.

I go in and look around for Allegra, but I don't see her.

"How is she?"

He shrugs.

"Comme ci comme ça."

"I'm fine."

It's Allegra's voice, coming from the kitchen. She walks in with coffee for her and Vidocq. She offers me her cup. I shake my head.

"I'm okay," she says. "It's the clinic that's ruined."

"I'm really sorry."

She sits on the sofa, clutching the cup in her hands.

"I don't suppose it could have lasted forever. Sooner or later someone would find the place and shut it down. The cops. The Board of Health. Someone. I was just hoping it would last a little longer."

Vidocq sits down and puts his arm around her. She rests her head on his shoulder. Lifts it off a moment later and looks at me.

"Are you hurt again?"

I pull my coat closed.

"I tripped on a chocolate bunny."

"I have enough supplies to fix you, you know. And I could use the distraction," she says.

I shake my head.

"Thanks. Tomorrow."

"You look worried. Can we help with something?" says Vidocq.

I listen to the door for a minute in case someone walks down the hall. I don't hear anything.

"I know you lost a lot of gear in the clinic, but remember

THE SQUARE IS above street level, so it's fairly clear of the flooding. There are trees and benches and not much else around us for a giant to crush me with. The monsoons have backed off a little and the rain has gone from pounding to merely drenching.

After everything that's happened and everything the Shonin told me, I still don't feel like the thing that came along to destroy the universe. Not that I'd know what that felt like. But I have to believe it would feel like something. Not evil or anger or anything like that. Maybe hunger. A deep-down gnawing hunger that won't be filled until it swallows all of creation. What do you chase the universe with? Beer or a cold Coke?

I wonder what oblivion will be like? Let's face it. The chances of everything working out the way I want, the chances of anything I plan working out, are dim at best. Still. What else is there to do? I have a lot to make up for, I guess, even if I never intended to murder everything. Yeah. I thought about it, but I never did it and now I find out I was doing it all along. Funny, the things you find out about yourself. Maybe I should get my aura read or try going macrobiotic. That should take the edge off being a universe killer, right?

I don't know what to think anymore. If I can't trust my own past, what can I trust? And don't say the future because one, there might not be one, and two, how do I know I'm not something else nefarious? A jaywalker or a sleepwalking flimflam man?

I guess I'm supposed to be okay with everything dying. Marcus Aurelius, a guy I read when I was stuck in Hell and finished all the coloring books said, "Death, like birth, is a secret of nature." Only with birth you get a blanket and a bottle. You get a blanket with death too, but they call it a shroud and

middle. Her eyes and lips don't quite line up right. Her face is a mass of wrong angles.

"I won't engage with you, Stark. You're just stalling and you know it's futile. Just give us the Qomrama."

Shaky looks a little bruised after his fight with Ruach.

"Don't waste any more of my time or I'll kill all of your loved ones and make you watch," he says.

I toss the 8 Ball one more time.

"You know, I think I can pull Deumos out with this thing. I wonder if I can do any other tricks?"

I touch it to Deumos's body. The ball glows for a second and stops.

"You see?" she says. "Nothing."

"I'm not so sure. I think you're stuck in that body now."

"What difference does that make?"

"You won't die like an angel. You'll die like meat. Like a mortal."

I check my phone. It's ten o'clock.

Shaky puts out his hand.

"Now, Abomination. Give it to me or see the young Jade die."

"Okay."

I toss it to him. The 8 Ball bounces off his chest and he catches it. Stares at it for a second like he doesn't quite believe it's real. Then he smiles, a wild, ecstatic thing. A smile that's been coming for a billion years.

Shaky holds up the 8 Ball and it sort of unfolds, becomes a hundred different shapes at once. Some alive and some inert. It writhes, spins, flaps, swims, burns, melts. Grows wings, eyes, spines like icebergs, and limbs like dead trees. It does all this at once. I can't look. It hurts my eyes. It hurts my head, trying

Watching his brother being killed, Muninn walks forward so the Angra can see him. He's a brave son of a bitch. Samael keeps a hand on Muninn's shoulder and Muninn doesn't seem to mind. Chaya looks like he'd like a one-way ticket to Zanzibar or wherever the farthest place from Pershing Square is.

The Angra spread out across the sky.

Shaky looks down at us, his lunatic smile smeared with God blood. It's easy to tell when he spots Muninn because he lets out a shriek that deafens every bird and sets off every car alarm from L.A. to downtown Tokyo.

All thirteen of the Angra Om Ya, pissed, crazy, sporting vengeance hard-ons the size of Mount Rushmore, dive for Pershing Square.

Muninn moves closer to the door. He can't let them get him. He has to draw them inside for this to work.

It's hard to figure out the exact timing on everything. Staring up through the rain at flying elder Gods, it's not easy to get a sense of scale and distance. We're going to have to do this free jazz. Try to find a melody and a beat in the cacophony, and improvise our way to the end.

Samael walks Muninn closer to the door.

I go to Chaya.

"Aren't you going to say good-bye to your brother, you chickenshit?"

He looks like he wants to strangle me again, but he's too freaked out to do it. I shove him and he lets me. But he looks at me hard.

"Tread lightly, monster. I'll be the God of this universe soon."

I look over at Muninn, then up at the sky. The Angra are almost down on us.

I pull the Mithras out of my pocket and show it to him.

"Relax. Chaya bravely volunteered to swallow the Singularity. With all the doors locked, the Angra either died in the Big Bang when it went off or they have a whole new universe to play with. Whichever it was, they're stuck in the Room and they're not coming back."

Muninn looks at me.

"You killed my brother. You killed part of me."

"With all due respect, Mr. Muninn. You killed off all those other parts of yourself when you stole the universe and started this fight. I just made sure you were the last man standing."

Muninn puts his hands flat on his knees.

"You understand that you can never use the Room again."

"Maybe we can chip in and get him a bus pass," says Samael.

I look over at him.

"If your stupid brother hasn't killed my bike completely, I'll be fine."

Muninn stands up, looking into the sky, blinking against the rain.

"I have to go and think about things."

He vanishes.

Samael and I look at each other. He follows me under a tree and I light a Malediction.

"I'm kind of fucked, aren't I?"

He furrows his eyebrows.

"You he might just kill. I have to go home and live with the man. Which one of us is truly the fucked one?"

I puff the cigarette like it might be my last, because it might.

I COME AWAKE with someone shaking me. I expect Candy, but when I open my eyes I see Samael. He hands me my clothes and puts a finger to his mouth telling me to be quiet.

We go out into the living room and I close the bedroom door.

"What are you doing here?"

"I got you a black shirt to hide your wounds."

I take the shirt and start dressing.

"Did Mr. Muninn send you here to kill me?"

He looks out the widow and doesn't say anything for a minute.

"How does it feel to be stuck in one place at a time with no shadows to stroll through?"

"It's only been a night. Ask me in a week."

"You'll be begging Father for wings."

"Wings are for you angel types. Maybe I'll ask for a jet pack."

"I wouldn't ask for anything for a while."

He takes my arm, and in the time it takes to blink, we're in Muninn's penthouse in Hell.

Muninn is at his desk in the library signing and organizing papers.

"Hello, Mr. Muninn."

He doesn't say anything. He doesn't turn around. He just starts talking.

"However well intentioned your actions were last night, the fact remains that you broke our agreement. When I owed you a favor I complied. When you owed me a favor you couldn't fulfill the commitment."

"I'm sorry you feel that way, but I stand by what I said.

a gun to our heads and someday it'll go off. At least I know I'm not immortal. The laundry bills would have killed me."

Muninn goes out into the hall and we follow. He walks us down to the main room by the big picture windows.

"The real reason I wanted to bring you here was to remind you of the state Hell was in when you left."

I get a bad feeling in my gut.

"You're not going to make me Lucifer again, are you?"

"No. That would be cruel to the damned. But I wanted you to have a last look at the place. As I said before, everything is different now."

"Are you making Samael Lucifer again?"

Muninn seems lost in his thoughts again. Like he's still trying to find the words.

"There won't be any more Lucifers," he says. "And no more Hell. At least not in its present form."

"I'm not getting you."

"We talked once . . . well, you harangued and I politely listened, about opening the gates of Hell. Dismantling it in a sense. Opening Heaven to whoever among the fallen can make their way there and who choose to stay. Hell will remain as it is. With a few repairs to make it more hospitable. Any angel or soul that chooses to remain here can do so."

"That's great news. Really."

He nods, but doesn't look happy.

"Now that things have changed, we must change with them."

"You're going home now to run Heaven, I guess."

He shakes his head.

"No. I'm old and worn out and need a rest. Samael will rule in Heaven."

"You have some bad history with the key. I thought you might like to see that no one else had it. Even me."

"Is this another test? Like when you gave me the Mithras?"

He spoons leaves into a tea ball.

"I'm letting you test yourself."

I weigh the mangled key in my hand.

"I might actually have a use for this."

He looks up, surprised.

"You're going to use it, then?"

"Just once. And with her permission."

He puts a kettle on to boil.

"I'm too tired to care about your schemes. Do what you want as long as the other person agrees."

"Thanks."

He goes to the refrigerator and looks around for milk. Samael taps me on the shoulder.

"Time to go," he says.

"Bye, Mr. Muninn. I'll see you around. But not for a while."

"But not forever either."

"Don't say a word," says Samael. "For once, leave while you're still ahead."

We go down a few floors in the elevator.

"Your friends have adjoining rooms at the end of the hall on the right. I'm on the floor just below Father's. Take your time. Come get me when you're done and I'll take you home."

"Thanks."

He nods and goes back upstairs.

I walk down the hall and knock on a door. A man's voice says, "Come on in."

"What about you? Where are you headed?"

"When I came down here I thought maybe it was going to be permanent. But it doesn't look that way, so I'll be heading home to Earth."

He comes closer. Taps his finger on my chest. It hurts.

"Be good to your gal. I could've done a lot better in that department. Maybe I'll get a chance to make up for some things like that."

I nod so he'll stop poking me.

"Listen, Bill, something happened last night and I won't be able to come Downtown again or up to Heaven."

He puts his hands behind his back and looks at me.

"The old man finally clipped your wings?"

"Something like that."

"Well, it's been a hell of a time getting to know you. I owe you a lot, not a thing I say lightly."

"You don't owe me anything, Bill. Take care of yourself. We'll see each other again down the road."

"Make it a good long time."

"That's the plan."

He pours me a whiskey and we have a drink together.

"That little Cindil gal's been asking about you. You should go and see her."

"I will. Bye, Bill."

"Take care, son."

I go out into the hall and knock on the next door.

Cindil opens it.

"I thought I heard you in with Bill. I'm glad you're all right."

"I'm fine."

I go back upstairs and Samael takes me to where I left the Hellion hog in Hollywood. I just want to go home, but I have to go and see Julie. We have a lot to talk about.

I SLEEP THE whole next day with Candy curled beside me. When I dream it's about stars and churning clouds of gas and things moving through the void, shaping the new universe as they go. Sometimes I dream about the arena and how I'll never see it again, and in a strange way it makes me sad. But mostly, I don't dream at all and it feels good.

When I wake up, I open the curtains. The rain hasn't come back. The sky is still mostly clouds, but they're starting to break up. Patches of boring, flat blue L.A. sky flash by every now and then, looking great. The street in front of Max Overdrive is still wet, but the floodwaters are gone and it doesn't feel like we're riding steerage in Noah's ark anymore.

By the time I make it downstairs, Kasabian has cleared up his mountain of delivery- and frozen-food boxes and deposited them outside in the overflowing Dumpster. We don't talk to each other, just nod because it's too strange to talk and risk that this is a dream and that it's still pouring outside and talking will wake us. I take the wet towels away from the bottom of the door, bring them upstairs, and hang them over the shower rod. At some point, all this silence is going to get old, but for now it suits me just fine.

A half hour later, Candy comes sleepily out of the bedroom in one of the silk shirts left over from when I was Lucifer. I'm on the couch. She sits on my lap and wraps her arms around me like she's going to fall asleep again. We stay that way for a few minutes, but I have to break the clinch when the pressure of her on my chest grinds bullets against bone.

Vigil ID will be enough for a bank to believe I'm true blue or if I'll have to get one of Vidocq's crooked friends to set me up with a new identity. I should ask him anyway. Cindil will need one.

I check my watch. It's going to be a long day and I'm not looking forward to it.

There's a knock on the downstairs door around three. The sky is closing up again but it doesn't look like rain. I go downstairs and open the door. It's Julie and a whole football team of Vigil agents.

"Agent Sola. I thought it was a snow day and I could pick up my homework tomorrow."

She doesn't crack a smile.

"This isn't about you, Stark. It's about Candace Jade. Remember her? The prisoner you helped escape? Don't tell me she isn't here because I know she is. Go and get her or I'll have her extracted by force."

I look over her stone-faced Pinkertons.

"You're fucking kidding me. I do your job for you, clear out the chop shops myself and stop the goddamn Angra, and you pull this?"

"She's an escaped prisoner. There are rules."

"The Shonin wouldn't be happy with any of you right now. And he was a fucking monk. A holy man."

"Stop stalling."

"I asked him once if he worked for the Vigil or the world. He gave me the right answer. You loafer-wearing shitbirds don't have a clue what the right answer is."

Julie unbuttons her jacket. Puts a hand on her Glock.

"Now, Stark."

The video-shop door slams open. Candy comes running

[illegible] big [illegible] riding [illegible]

[illegible] Fu[illegible] sle[illegible] Jul[illegible]

[illegible] ut[illegible] she [illegible]

[illegible] drops [illegible] les [illegible] looks [illegible]

[illegible] It [illegible] cu[illegible] the street. [illegible]

[illegible] in [illegible] Julie t[illegible]

[illegible] body. [illegible] and [illegible]

[illegible] face [illegible]

[illegible] alive [illegible] "Don't [illegible] her. Somebody [illegible]"

[illegible] The [illegible]

[illegible] are [illegible] do[illegible] none [illegible]

[illegible] Julie pushes her [illegible] back [illegible]

[illegible] "You [illegible]"

[illegible]," says the [illegible]

[illegible] to [illegible] pose [illegible]

[illegible] t[illegible] w[illegible] doesn't [illegible]

[illegible] the facilities [illegible]

[illegible] gers [illegible] ds. [illegible]

[illegible] animal. [illegible]

[illegible] Vi[illegible]

[illegible] r.

E[illegible] according [illegible]

A[illegible] Christmas [illegible] at B[illegible] of I[illegible]

and [illegible] The [illegible] to [illegible] been [illegible]

wee[illegible] the [illegible] par[illegible]

town [illegible] so Christmas [illegible] Ante[illegible]

How many days has it been since the scene outside the store? I'm a little blurry on the matter. Anyway, it's the jolly time of year, right? And in a couple of days it will be exactly a year since I escaped from Hell, a place that, by now, might not exist anymore.

I'm back drinking Jack Daniel's. It's not bad, but it's not Aqua Regia and I can't go Downtown to get more. I'm down to my last carton of Maledictions. The world is closing in fast and I don't like it one bit.

People tried talking to me earlier, but I'm not in the mood, so now they're mostly leaving me alone. Except for Carlos. For once he's not tending bar. He hired Fairuza for the holidays. Turns out she can pour beer and whiskey in glasses as well as anyone, and she even knows how to make a couple of cocktails. Kasabian hangs around the end of the bar chatting her up at every opportunity. She even smiles back at him. I guess she's gotten over the Mason-is-coming-to-swallow-our-souls thing. Carlos is still pouring drinks, but I'm his only customer at the moment. I'm happy that the Sub Rosa stepped in and got the Lurkers released, but I don't want drinks from Fairuza because it makes me think about Candy's band and I don't want to go there right now.

Carlos and I are hunkered down at a table in the back corner of the bar, a bottle of Jack between us and two shot glasses. On the jukebox, Martin Denny is playing a tiki version of "White Christmas."

"You are one morose fuck, you know that?" says Carlos. "You're literally sucking the entire concept of happiness from my body."

"I've got a lot on my mind."

I wonder if I should get rid of all the sheets and pillowcases too. Candy brought them with her when she moved in.

Word is that the Vigil is cleaning up the last *Der Zorn Götter* cells around L.A. What do you charge people with for trying to murder the world? I'm sure the Vigil will come up with something suitably creative and vindictive. I hope so.

I'm learning to use the coffeemaker. Turns out there are manuals for that kind of thing. I hope the wash-and-fold place opens again soon. I need to clean the blood out of a few delicates.

The Sub Rosa is doing double shifts this holiday season, springing Lurkers like Fairuza from federal pens and covering up for dying Gods, walking buildings, and all the other catastrophic hoodoo that's been going down in L.A. The Augur might be gone, but the Sub Rosa still have friends in high-and-mighty places. Tuatha is running things temporarily while the board of directors searches for a new scryer. Lots of luck. If any Sub Rosas come around looking for trouble, I won't hit them. I'll tell them the one thing that they won't want to hear. That they're Qliphoth. Just Eaters, Diggers, and Gluttons in designer shoes.

Brigitte comes in with a blonde. She waves to me. The blonde raises her hand to wave, but Brigitte gets between us and steers her to the bar.

On the plus side of things, Audsley Ishii has disappeared. I'll probably have to kill him sometime, but not tonight. Tonight is eggnog and reindeer games. Ho ho ho.

I pour another shot.

When I look up, Julie is standing by the table.

"Can I sit down?"

"You own me. Why not?"

"Don't complain to me. You're the one who wanted a favor."

Julie squints at me.

"I hope you aren't going to write your reports in riddles like that."

Samael reaches our table.

"Too late now," I say.

"Too late for what?" says Samael.

"For her to avoid you. Now that you're here, please be nice."

He beams down at Julie and puts out his hand.

"Hello. I'm Samael."

"Another one-name guy. Like Stark."

He pulls up a chair and sits down.

"We do share that affectation, I'm afraid."

I point at him.

"For me it's an affectation. For him it's just his name. He doesn't have a last name."

"Everyone has a last name," says Julie.

"Not angels."

She looks at me, then Samael.

"Is this another one of your tall tales? Going to Hell? Hanging around with God?"

"This is your new employer?" says Samael. "She doesn't seems to have a lot of faith in you."

"What we are and what we do is hard for sane people to accept."

"You're serious," says Julie. "This man is an angel."

"Why is that so surprising?" he says. "It's Christmas. L.A. must be full of angels."

Samael reaches into his coat and pulls out a bottle of Aqua Regia and sets it on the table.

"[illegible] and [illegible]od," [illegible] say[illegible]

"[illegible] Bu[illegible] [illegible] [illegible]e[illegible]."

Ju[illegible] [illegible] loo[illegible] [illegible] us.

"[illegible] w[illegible] [illegible] so[illegible] [illegible]l[illegible] [illegible]."

Sa[illegible] [illegible] says "Th[illegible] [illegible] fi[illegible] [illegible] for you. He fought a serial killer [illegible] [illegible] [illegible] [illegible] be a more human. [illegible] killed [illegible] [illegible] with bullets in [illegible] and [illegible] for that I'm [illegible]."

Ju[illegible] [illegible]in[illegible].

"[illegible] [illegible]e's [illegible] [illegible] [illegible] a qu[illegible] [illegible] like that before."

Sa[illegible] [illegible] g[illegible] [illegible] [illegible] [illegible] [illegible] e.

"C[illegible] [illegible] [illegible] n[illegible] [illegible] There's no such thing [illegible] angels. They'[illegible] [illegible] [illegible] [illegible] [illegible] and virgin."

He [illegible] up [illegible] on [illegible] table [illegible] finger on top of the [illegible] bottle.

"I'[illegible] [illegible] lft [illegible] [illegible] his [illegible] [illegible] [illegible]ions at home [illegible]."

"N[illegible] Ch[illegible]mas Samuel."

"An[illegible] yo[illegible] [illegible]ice meeting [illegible] Ju[illegible]."

"H[illegible] do you know my name?"

"It's [illegible] a [illegible] [illegible] [illegible]."

"Sa[illegible] [illegible] aid [illegible] to me [illegible] [illegible] [illegible]."

"[illegible] all [illegible] [illegible] friend [illegible] [illegible] oke."

He [illegible] his way through the crowd, and [illegible] [illegible] g for [illegible] [illegible] de [illegible] Br[illegible]

"Wil[illegible] [illegible]ma[illegible] [illegible] a [illegible] when we're [illegible]ether [illegible] say [illegible] in [illegible] [illegible] [illegible]."

"And [illegible] 's [illegible] typ[illegible]."

She looks at me.

"Unfortunately, it is."

I start to get up and walk to the bathroom when I notice Brigitte heading our way. She comes over and hugs me.

"Merry Christmas, James."

"Merry Christmas to you."

She points to the blonde. She's Japanese. Young, in a shaggy pink fake-fur coat.

"Have you two met?"

"Hi," she says. "I'm Chihiro."

She puts out her hand and I shake it.

"Like the girl in *Spirited Away*."

"What's that?" she says.

"It's a movie."

She smiles crookedly.

"I'll have to watch it sometime."

"I think you'd like it."

"May we join you?" says Brigitte.

"Of course."

Brigitte brings over a chair. She sits next to Julie and Chihiro sits where Samael was, next to me.

Julie does a small wave.

"Hi. I'm Julie."

I can't take my eyes off Chihiro.

"Sorry. This is Julie. My new boss."

"New boss? What kind of work do you do?" says Chihiro.

"I used to work for the government. But now I run a detective agency."

Chihiro nods.

"This is a good town for it. Things go missing all the time."

Chihiro looks at me.

"Aren't you going to say good luck?"

"I don't think I have to. By the way, I have a guitar at home that no one is using. It's red . . ."

"Sold," she says. "When can I come by and see it?"

"Tomorrow. Around one?"

"A late riser? Me too. I'll be there on the dot."

Brigitte comes back with glasses and a bottle of vodka.

"I know the whiskey and I've heard of the vodka," says Julie.

She picks up the Aqua Regia.

"But what's this?"

"It's not from around here. And it's kind of strong. You wouldn't like it."

She sits back in her chair.

"That sounds like a challenge."

"It isn't. Trust me. Only very bad people drink this swill."

"You talked me into it."

Julie downs her Jack Daniel's and points to the empty glass.

"Hit me."

"Okay. But first I have to piss. Don't touch the stuff until I get back."

I give the bottle to Chihiro.

"You're in charge. Keep this away from her. If she's going to taste it, I want to be here to see."

She salutes me.

"I'm on it, sir," she says. "None shall pass."

I head to the bathroom in the back of the bar.

Okay. We met. But that's it for now. It will take awhile

I light a Malediction and draw the smoke slowly into my lungs. It hurts so good.

There's a light knock on the stall door. Great. The place wasn't clear after all.

"Go away. Sorry I blocked the door. Just move the can."

He knocks again, so light it's almost inaudible.

"Please go away."

No one says anything. I wait to hear the sounds of the trash can being moved.

"Mr. Stark?"

"Yeah?"

"May I speak to you for a moment?"

"No. It's Christmas. Go away."

"I can't."

"Sure you can. Aim your feet. First right, then left. Try it."

He knocks again.

"What?"

"Mr. Stark. I understand you do investigations."

"No. That's my boss. She's outside. In the back with a drunk Czech and a hot blonde. You can't miss them."

He knocks.

"Please, Mr. Stark. I'd rather deal with you. My case is unique."

"How unique?"

The guy who pushes the stall door open looks like yesterday's lunch, eaten and thrown back up again. A gray, patchy beard. Hair a terminal thicket of cowlicks. A trench coat that might have been tan once, but is now the color of cold grease and rhino shit.

"Please, Mr. Stark," he says. "It has to be you."

"Why?"

[illegible] pers[illegible]'t wea[illegible] shirt. His [illegible] [illegible] tor[illegible] [illegible]ked b[illegible] There's a ga[illegible] [illegible] is heart [illegible]

"Mr Stark[illegible] help [illegible] investigation. [illegible] Death [illegible] to ha[illegible] murdered?"

[illegible] at this jo[illegible] a f[illegible]

ABOUT THE AUTHOR

New York Times bestselling author Richard Kadrey has published nine novels, including *Sandman Slim, Kill the Dead, Aloha from Hell, Devil Said Bang, Kill City Blues, Butcher Bird,* and *Metrophage,* and more than fifty stories. He has been immortalized as an action figure, his short story "Goodbye Houston Street, Goodbye" was nominated for a British Science Fiction Association Award, and his novel *Butcher Bird* was nominated for the Prix Elbakin in France. The bestselling and acclaimed writer and photographer lives in San Francisco, California.

I BREAK HIS wrists so I don't have to break his neck.

He falls to his knees, but I don't think it's the pain, though I make sure there's plenty of that. It's the sound. The crack of bones as they shatter. A sound that lets you know they're never going to heal quite right and you're going to spend the rest of eternity drinking your ambrosia slushies with two hands.

I'm surprised to see an angel down here right now, considering all the cleanup going on in Heaven after the recent unpleasantness. Still, there are sore losers and bad winners in every bunch. I don't know which one this guy is, but I caught him spray-painting GODKILLER on the front of Maximum Overdrive, the video store where I live. I might have let him off easy if all he wanted to do was kill me. I'm used to that by now. But this fucker was ruining my windows. Do these winged pricks think I'm made of money? I'm about broke, and here's this high-and-mighty halo polisher setting me up for a trip to the hardware store to buy paint remover. I give his wrists an extra twist for that. He gulps in air and makes a gagging sound like he might throw up. I take a couple of

"You must pay for what you've done, unclean thing."

"Go home, angel. My store is a mess, and looking at the big picture, I'm more afraid of Netflix than I am of you."

To my surprise, the crippled creep is able to manifest his Gladius, an angelic sword of fire. He has to hold it with both hands, but he can move it around by swinging his shoulders back and forth. Maybe this guy is more trouble than I gave him credit for. A badass will try to break your bones, but someone crazy, who knows what they'll do? Mostly, though, I'm glad the neighbors aren't around so I have to explain the gimp with the lightsaber in my driveway.

The angel comes at me hard and fast, all *Seven Samurai,* ready to send me to asshole Heaven. In his present condition, he's still quick, but far off his game. I sidestep the Gladius and punch him in the throat. He falls. The Gladius turns the pavement molten where it touches. As the angel goes down, I snap up a knee and break his nose. He falls over backward and the Gladius goes out.

I walk around behind him and push him upright. His eyes have rolled back in his head. He's completely out. I take out a flask full of Aqua Regia, everyone's favorite drink in Hell, and pour some down his throat. The angel gasps and his eyes snap open. He looks up at me and sputters.

"You're trying to poison me."

"You were unconscious. If I wanted you dead, I could have drilled a hole in your skull and tea-bagged your brain. Now shut up and go home."

The angel crawls away and lurches to his feet. He's covered in blood and booze and his hands are sticking out at funny

the tank so the universe can go on dumbly spinning. The only angels anyone is happy to see take a powder are Death and the Devil, one of whom is currently asleep in the storage room at Max Overdrive.

But I'll get to that later.

So, the angels are fucking off and God's away on business. What do the mice do when the cat's not looking? They drink. And if they're smart they do it at Bamboo House of Dolls. Candy and me, we're mice with PhDs. I'll meet up with her at the bar.

Chihiro, I mean. Not Candy. I have to remember that. *Chihiro.* Candy is dead. So to speak. Dead enough that the feds and the cops aren't looking for her, and that's all that counts. Now she's Chihiro, with a different face and name and, well, everything. Everything we can think of. I just hope it's enough. I'm sure we've missed a few things. I hope not so many that anyone is going to notice. I might have to kill them.

I change and go back downstairs, my na'at, knife, and Colt under my coat.

"I'm going to Bamboo House. Want to get a drink?"

Kasabian shakes his head, carefully putting discs in clear plastic cases with the tips of his mechanical fingers.

"Nah. I'm waiting for Maria. She's coming by with a new delivery."

"Anything good?"

He looks up and shakes his head.

"Don't know. She said it's a western."

"Fingers crossed it brings some goddamn customers into this tomb."